EVERYMAN, I will go with thee,

and be thy guide,

In thy most need to go by thy side

GUY DE MAUPASSANT

Born in 1850. Obtained a post in the Ministry
of Marine in Paris, but was encouraged by
Flaubert to write. General paralysis set in,
1890, and he died in 1893.

GUY DE MAUPASSANT

Short Stories

TRANSLATED BY
MARJORIE LAURIE

INTRODUCTION BY
GERALD GOULD

DENT: LONDON AND TORONTO
EVERYMAN'S LIBRARY
DUTTON: NEW YORK

All rights reserved
Made in Great Britain
at the
Aldine Press · Letchworth · Herts
for
J. M. DENT & SONS LTD
Aldine House · Albemarle Street · London
This edition was first published in
Everyman's Library in 1934
Reprinted 1977

Published in the U.S.A. by arrangement
with J. M. Dent & Sons Ltd

No. 907   Hardback ISBN 0 460 00907 9
No. 1907   Paperback ISBN 0 460 01907 4

INTRODUCTION

Guy de Maupassant died in 1893. It is more usual to begin
the description of an author with the date of his birth than
with the date of his death, but it happens that the middle
nineties were of extreme significance in the development of
a particular theory of art. On the other hand, it is doubtful
whether this particular theory, or indeed any theory, makes
itself manifest in the actual masterpieces which Maupassant
left behind him. Anybody presented with a collection or
selection of his works, without any previous information about
his dates, friends or theories, would easily form certain conclusions: as, for instance, that he wrote when the bitterness
of defeat in the war of 1870 still lay heavy upon France;
that he was a man whose means and manners had enabled
him to mix in a fairly exclusive society, but that his most
instinctive sympathy went out to the peasantry and the
poor; that he was abnormally preoccupied with the problem
of prostitution, and, for all his greatness as an artist, not
unwilling to exploit that problem for obvious effects of sentimentality, achieving sometimes bathos rather than pathos.
So much the reader would gather at the first perusal, almost
at the first glance; but would he learn that Maupassant held
strict theories about literary composition, and imagined
himself to be one of a group entitled to lay down the laws of
art? It is scarcely probable. The general effect of Maupassant's writing is one of such ease and clarity that it seems as
if he wrote almost by a natural process, without having to
trouble to pause and think. Moreover, it is an historical fact
that his output in a comparatively short literary life was
enormous, so that he must have written with speed. Of
course, one result of his having written so much in so short
a time is that his work is unequal. Many of his short stories
have little significance or permanence, and perhaps none of
his novels reaches the standard of an absolute masterpiece.
However, his eminence—one might indeed say his pre-
eminence—in the short story, the *conte*, is pretty well

established. It is idle to discuss what is the greatest short story in the world, but, if we take into consideration bulk as well as beauty—if we ask ourselves: Who has written, not the best of short stories, but the largest number of short stories any one of which could reasonably be regarded as the best?—there seems practically no competitor. Tolstoy may have surpassed him in this form once or twice, Kuprin again once or twice, Turgenev, Flaubert, Anatole France; but not one of these could claim to have produced anything like such a body of *contes* of the highest class. Of Guy de Maupassant's standing, then, there is no question: the doubt remains whether his achievement was in any great degree due to his theories.

He was a friend and pupil of Flaubert's. The pupil accepted his master's views on many subjects, and even, as we shall see, believed himself to have resembled Flaubert in the relentless labour of composition. But this last conception, as we have seen already, is a little difficult to reconcile with Maupassant's apparent facility of output, whereas it is an indisputable fact that, for Flaubert, literary composition was a prolonged agony. Because Maupassant died so young (it is relevant at this stage to mention that he was born in 1850: there are few outstanding facts to record about his life, beyond his early athletic vigour, his consistent literary success, beginning in 1880 with *Boule de Suif,* and his sufferings from a disease which undoubtedly embittered his attitude to the whole relation of the sexes, and went far to explain his preoccupation, already noted, with one particular and deplorable element in that relation)—because he died so young, we are sometimes apt to forget that he was the junior, not only of Flaubert himself, but of the Goncourt brothers, of Daudet, of Zola, and of Anatole France. He may be said, in fact, to have served his literary apprenticeship to a school which had a certain point of view and certain watchwords, which, as is the habit of watchwords, soon degenerated into catchwords. It would be ridiculous, of course, even remotely to suggest that all the great writers just mentioned had one common technique, either in theory or in practice; but, speaking very broadly and loosely, they may be said to have represented the movement towards precision and realism. The search for the exact word, the injunction that the artist should keep his eye on the object. the refusal to accept abstract standards by which to arrange individual appreciations: these were the tendencies of the school and the times.

It is generally the fate of literary precept to be contradicted in practice, often by the preceptors themselves, almost always by disciples who carry the injunctions to excess. It would not be fantastic, for instance, to discover in these rules of realism the foundation of the James Joyce school, which is so pertinacious in its pursuit of exact reproduction that it has actually discarded the conventions of ordinary language and, instead of becoming completely and impossibly exact in the reproduction of truth and experience, has in fact degenerated into a jargon which makes its own unintelligibility. To go back to the masters themselves, there is no doubt that the beautiful precision of Flaubert's work owed a great deal to his creed and his method; but the boasted realism of Zola was, as has often been pointed out, really a selection of those parts of reality which happened to interest him most; and, indeed, is it not the essence and function of the artist, try as he may to define his processes, that, in the result, he is found, not to have reproduced reality, but to have transformed it? When he has transformed it into beauty, he has succeeded: when he has transformed it into banality, he has failed. Maupassant was too good an artist ever to be wholly banal: the lightest and cheapest of his anecdotes has the ring of originality; but we shall see reason to think that he has, in some respects, been over-praised. That is why a selection from his works is so admirable and necessary an undertaking. High as his average is, to read every story he ever wrote is something of a waste of time. Naturalistic as he tried to be, we find him sometimes descending to formal tricks, and not infrequently allowing the intrusion of false sentiment. But to miss his greatest works would be to miss some of the greatest works, in their kind, that the literature of the world has known. The excitement of discovering Maupassant for oneself when young is similar in kind, though of course not equal in degree, to the excitement of discovering Shakespeare. It is an actual physical exaltation, coupled with a wondering inability to believe that anything can be quite as good as what one is reading.

This applies, primarily, to the discovery of the stories in their original tongue. It has been said by a rather acid French critic that one reason why English people think so highly of

Maupassant as a writer is because his French is so easy. The gibe fails of its point, since Maupassant's worth was first recognized by his own compatriots, and precisely by those of his compatriots who had most highly specialized in the delicacies of language. Nevertheless, there is some truth in the contention. Maupassant's French *is* easy. It has a quite extraordinary straightforwardness, sweetness and simplicity, difficult to analyse or explain, but immediately comprehensible. It does not follow, unfortunately, because his works are easy for the foreigner to understand, that they are easy for the foreigner to translate. On the contrary, in each language it is found that the simplest is the hardest to transpose. It is infinitely easier to read Homer than it is to read the Attic tragedies, but nobody has even begun to succeed in rendering Homer's peculiar poetical magic. A schoolboy could be taught, in a very few weeks, sufficient Latin to read the simplest and most famous of the lyrics of Catullus, but there again translation has been found entirely hopeless. So, once more, the simplest lyrics of Heine can be comprehended by an Englishman with practically no knowledge of German, but they have been found far more baffling to the translator than more elaborate works. The difficulty does not hold, luckily, in prose to quite the same extent as in verse, and it is hoped that the present volume will prove that a very great deal, at any rate, of Maupassant's magic can be preserved in translation; but it would be idle to pretend that there is not an inevitable loss of an undeniable something.

Allowing for this, one may find relevant a few general observations on the nature of his achievement. An author is known by the company he *makes*. The test of his vitality is the meaning he imparts to the business of living. Maupassant kept his eye on the object; but he could see only one object at a time. The single scene, the sudden atmosphere, the overwhelming motive, are his material. That is why he is less at his ease with the novel than with the *conte*. Indeed, *Pierre et Jean*, sometimes considered his best novel, is only a *conte* slightly expanded. It has one situation— Pierre's jealousy of Jean and suspicion of his mother. *Une Vie*, longer, more varied, contains nothing but disillusionment; *Bel-Ami*, nothing but the hero's greedy and heartless exploitation of women. By contrast, how wide is the range, in subject, manner, colour, sympathy, of the short stories!

'*L'artiste*,' says Maupassant himself, '*essaie, réussit ou échoue. Le critique ne doit apprécier le résultat que suivant la nature de l'effort ; et il n'a pas le droit de se préoccuper des tendances.*' Yet, in fact, as a critic, Maupassant praised one tendency above another. It is what critics must do, even when their theory tells them that they must not. Maupassant, again, distinguishing between the poetic and the realistic, soon found himself insisting that the realist must give us something '*plus complète, plus saisissante, plus probante que la réalité même.*' Yet what is that but the poetic?

He recognized the common rights of different types of fiction; he should have gone further, and recognized the common laws. His example was better than his precept. He described himself (it suited his theory) as being among the writers without genius, '*nous autres qui sommes simplement des travailleurs conscients et tenaces,*' who contended against '*l'invincible découragement par la continuité de l'effort.*' But the genius which lights up his phrases, as it were from within, could never have come by taking thought. He is, like all great writers, neither poetic nor realistic alone, but both; his gift was to see the romance in the fact. What, in abstract, could be barer or uglier than the story of *La Maison Tellier*? There is a provincial brothel; the brothel-keeper closes her establishment for a day and a night to go across country to the confirmation of her brother's little girl, her own god-daughter; she takes the inmates of the establishment with her; they attend the ceremony, and return. What an opportunity for crude contrast between sin and innocence!—what scope for cheap sentiment and cheaper irony! Yet somehow the elements of farce and tragedy are mingled, are subdued to a deep and moving beauty; somehow, by art's most mysterious alchemy, an eternal law asserts itself in and through the grossest details.

Maupassant, of course, overwrote. And he used too freely one unpleasant theme. Even *Boule de Suif*, which made his fame, though it is marvellous and unforgettable, gives us too easy and formal a comparison between the journey on which all the respectables, fleeing from the Prussian wrath, are glad to eat the poor girl's food, and that other journey on which, having coerced the girl into degradation for their own profit, they refuse to share *their* food with *her*. Nor do the many facetious stories avoid a similar aesthetic weakness;

they are satirical, they are witty, they frequently have that unexpected turn—that 'sting-in-the-tail'—upon which short story writers, both bad and good, too much depend. But even in *Ce Cochon de Morin*, perhaps the subtlest and most famous of its kind, there is a cheapness of satire. Indeed, acute critics have been found to say that Maupassant's method was 'standardized,' and that, though it suited his own genius, it is entirely deceptive in its appearance of being a good model for others.

On the other hand, despite the fact that he combined his devotion to the thing seen with a habit of seeing things that were gross, Maupassant knew well the tenderness of pure and passionate love. Consider the tale of the priest who hates women, and goes out to find, to punish, his niece and her lover; he goes out to moonlight, and mist, and the nightingales; and, seeing the lovers walking in that paradise, says to himself: 'It may be that God has created nights like this in order to cast His divine veil over human loves.'

GERALD GOULD.

SELECT BIBLIOGRAPHY

Maupassant's first short story that appeared in print was *La Main de l'Ecorché*, written under the name of *Joseph Prunier*, and published in an obscure provincial almanac—*L'Almanach Lorrain de Pont-à-Mousson*, in 1875. It may be read in the *Misti* collection, but was later transformed into *La Main*. In 1880 there appeared almost simultaneously Maupassant's book of verse, *Des Vers*, and *Les Soirées de Médan*. The latter was a collection of short stories written by some young writers who frequented Zola's house at Médan, headed by Zola's own short story, *L'Attaque du Moulin*, and including the short story that was to make Maupassant famous, *Boule de Suif*. Then followed *La Maison Tellier*, 1881 (*Les Tombales* was added in 1891); *Mademoiselle Fifi*, 1882; *Contes de la Bécasse*, 1883; *Une Vie*, 1883; *Émile Zola* (a short study), 1883; *Clair de Lune*, 1884; *Les Sœurs Rondoli*, 1884; *Miss Harriet*, 1884; *Au Soleil* (travel descriptions), 1884; *Yvette*, 1885; *Contes du Jour et de la Nuit*, 1885; *Bel-Ami*, 1885; *Contes et Nouvelles*, 1885; *La Petite Roque*, 1886; *Monsieur Parent*, 1886; *Toine*, 1887; *Le Horla*, 1887; *Mont-Oriol*, 1887; *Le Rosier de Madame Husson*, 1888; *Sur l'Eau* (travel), 1888; *Pierre et Jean*, 1888; *La Main Gauche*, 1889; *Fort comme la Mort*, 1889; *L'Inutile Beauté*, 1890; *La Vie Errante* (travel), 1890; *Notre Cœur*, 1890. Maupassant left behind him unfinished portions of novels called *L'Angelus* and *L'Ame Etrangère*. Of his plays, *La Maison Turque à la Feuille de Rose* (written in collaboration with Robert Pinchon in 1873) was performed in 1875, *L'Histoire du Vieux Temps* (written about the same time) was performed in 1879, *Musotte* (written in collaboration with Jacques Normand) was performed in 1891, *La Paix du Ménage* in 1893, *La Répétition* in 1904. Practically all his work appeared in journals first, and those most favoured were *La Revue Bleue*, *Le Figaro*, *Le Gaulois*, *Revue des Deux Mondes*, *La*

Nouvelle Revue, Gil Blas, Revue de Paris. L'Echo de Paris. Posthumous collections are *Misti, Le Père Millon,* and *Les Dimanches d'un Bourgeois de Paris, Le Colporteur,* containing his early and immature writings. A complete edition was published in twenty-nine volumes in 1908–10, and the most extensive English translations are those by Marjorie Laurie (10 volumes, 1923–9) and by Ernest Boyd and Storm Jameson, 1928 (re-issued in England in 1930–2). A volume of stories translated by Lafcadio Hearn is deserving of mention—*Saint Anthony and other Stories,* 1925 (collected from the various American periodicals to which Hearn contributed as a young man).

The best biographical study of Maupassant in English is that by R. H. Sherard—*The Life, Work, and Evil Fate of Guy de Maupassant,* 1926. There is also a study by Ernest Boyd published in 1926. Works in French include *La Vie et l'Œuvre de Guy de Maupassant* by E. Maynial, 1906; *Souvenirs sur Maupassant,* by Baron Lombroso (containing a quantity of important correspondence), 1905; *Souvenirs sur Maupassant,* by François Tassart (a most valuable study by his valet), 1911; *La Jeunesse de Maupassant d'après des documents nouveaux,* by R. Dumesnil, 1933. Reference should also be made to *Journal des Goncourt,* 1887–96, and Marie Bashkirtseff's *Further Memoirs* (containing her correspondence with Maupassant, 1901. *See also* the *Life* by Paul Morand (1943), and Francis Steegmuller's biography (1950). Stanley Jackson wrote a critical study, *Guy de Maupassant,* in 1938, in 1941 appeared A. Artimian's *Maupassant Criticism in France, 1886–1940,* and in 1967 P. Ignotus's *The Paradox of Maupassant.* F. Steegmuller, *A Lion in the Path,* 1973. Michael Lerner, *Maupassant,* 1975.

The translations by Miss Marjorie Laurie are printed in this volume by arrangement with the publishers, T. Werner Laurie Ltd.

CONTENTS

BOULE DE SUIF

For several consecutive days, the remnants of a shattered army had been passing through the town. They were no longer a disciplined body, but a disorganized rabble. Their beards were unkempt and neglected, their uniforms ragged, and the men, separated from their colours and their regiments, marched listlessly. All of them seemed crushed and worn out, incapable of thought or initiative. They marched on from mere force of habit and, as soon as a man stopped moving, he collapsed. The bulk of them were civilians who had been called to the colours, easy-going citizens, who seemed bent down by the weight of their rifles, or undersized conscripts of the last line, quick of apprehension, as prone to panic as to enthusiasm, as ready for attack as for flight. Some regular soldiers in red breeches, sole survivors of a division ground to powder in a great battle, and some sombre gunners, mingled with these nondescript infantry men, and here and there appeared the flashing helmet of a booted dragoon, with difficulty keeping pace with the more lightly shod foot-soldier.

Detachments of *francs-tireurs*, who looked like bandits but bore grandiloquent names, such as 'Avengers of Defeat,' 'Citizens of the Grave,' 'The Brotherhood of Death,' passed through in their turn. Their leaders, all flannel and gold lace and armed to the teeth, were retired drapers, corn chandlers, dealers in soap and tallow, who had turned soldier by force of circumstance, and had been elected officers by virtue of their money or their moustaches. In loud, braggart tones, they discussed plans of campaign, as though they alone were sustaining France in her death agony upon their vainglorious shoulders. But they went in fear of their own men, who were a ruffianly gang and, though often desperately brave, could not be withheld from looting and debauchery.

There was a rumour that the Prussians were about to enter Rouen. The National Guard, who, for the last two months, had been engaged in reconnoitring cautiously the neighbouring woods, sometimes shooting their own sentries, and preparing for action every time a rabbit stirred in a bush, had returned to their firesides. Their arms, their uniforms, all the apparatus of slaughter, with which they had formerly terrorized every milestone within a radius of three leagues, had suddenly vanished.

The last of the French army had just crossed the Seine, making for Pont-Audemer by way of Saint-Sever and Bourg-Achard. The rear was brought up by the general marching on foot between two aides-de-camp. In despair, unable to attempt anything with this medley of broken units, he felt overwhelmed in the utter ruin of a people, hitherto accustomed to victory, but now, despite its heroic prestige, disastrously defeated.

And now, a deep calm, an atmosphere of shuddering, silent apprehension brooded over the city. Many a plump citizen, whose manhood had been sapped by commerce, anxiously awaited the conquerors, in dread lest his spits and his big kitchen knives should be regarded as weapons. Life seemed at a standstill. The shops were closed; the streets silent. Here and there a stray citizen, awed by the stillness, hurried along, keeping close to the wall. Such was the agony of suspense that the arrival of the enemy was looked forward to as a relief.

On the afternoon of the day following the departure of the French troops, some Uhlans, sprung no one knew whence, galloped through the town. A little later, dark masses of troops came pouring down the hill of St. Catherine, while two further torrents of invaders streamed along the roads from Darnetal and Boisguillaume. The advance guards of the three corps effected a well-timed junction in the square before the town hall, and down every street leading to the square the German army poured in, battalion after battalion, while the paved streets rang under their hard, measured tread.

Orders, shouted in strange guttural voices, resounded along the walls of houses, which seemed dead and deserted, though behind the closed shutters eyes were spying upon the victors, who by the rules of war were masters of the city, masters of the property and lives of all. In their darkened rooms, the inhabitants had succumbed to that dazed condition produced by natural cataclysms, devasting convulsions of the earth, against which neither strength nor wisdom avails. This sensation is experienced whenever the established order of things is overturned, when no feeling of security remains, and all that is usually protected by the laws of men or nature is at the mercy of blind and brutal force. The earthquake burying a whole nation beneath the ruins of their houses; the river bursting its banks, drowning peasants and their cattle, tearing rafters from roofs and sweeping all away; the triumphant army slaughtering all who resist, making prisoners of the rest, pillaging in the name of the sword and giving thanks to God amid the roar of cannon: all alike are terrifying visitations which shatter our belief in eternal justice and the confidence we have been taught to place in divine protection and human reason.

Small squads of men knocked at the door of every house and disappeared inside. This was the occupation, the sequel of the invasion. It was now the duty of the vanquished to show themselves courteous to the conquerors.

When the first panic had subsided, a new sort of calm succeeded. In many families, the Prussian officer sat at table with his hosts. If he happened to be a well-bred man, he politely deplored the woes of France and expressed his personal repugnance to the war. His hosts were grateful for these generous sentiments, and, besides, any day they might need his protection. If they humoured him, they might perhaps have fewer men billeted on them. Why should they hurt the man's feelings when they were entirely in his power? To do so would be an act of foolhardiness rather than courage, and foolhardiness is no longer a defect in the character of the burgesses of Rouen, however it might have been in the days of the heroic defences which made their city illustrious. Eventually, appealing to the traditions of French urbanity, they reasoned that it was quite permissible to treat the alien soldier with courtesy within doors, provided that there was no fraternization in public. Though they did not recognize him in the street, at home they were ready to talk to him, and the German soldier sat longer and longer every evening, warming himself at the domestic hearth.

Little by little, the town itself began to resume its normal appearance. For the present, the French population remained indoors, but the streets were swarming with Prussian soldiers. After all, the officers of the Blue Hussars, arrogantly trailing their great sabres along the pavement, did not treat the plain townsmen so very much more contemptuously than did their own light cavalry officers, who had sat drinking in the same cafés the year before.

Yet for all that there was something in the air, some

indefinable and subtle quality, a strange and intolerable atmosphere, a diffused exhalation—the effluvium of invasion. It penetrated into private houses and public places, tainting the food, producing an unhomelike feeling, as of exile in distant lands among tribes of hostile savages.

The victorious army demanded money, vast sums of money. The inhabitants went on paying up, and indeed they could afford to do so. But the wealthier he is, the more keenly the Norman trader feels the smallest sacrifice, the transfer of the least fraction of his property into the hands of another.

It was true that a few miles down the Seine, in the vicinity of Croisset, Dieppedalle or Biessart, bargemen and fishermen often brought up from the bottom the bloated corpse of a German soldier in uniform, who had been stabbed or kicked to death, or pushed into the water off a bridge, or had had his head battered in by a stone. The mud of the river engulfed the victims of these surreptitious acts of vengeance, savage yet justifiable, these deeds of obscure heroism, these secret assaults, more perilous than open battle and without the meed of fame. Hatred of the foreigner will always nerve some valiant soul to die for an idea.

At length, finding that the invaders, although subjecting the town to rigorous discipline, had not perpetrated any of the atrocities with which rumour had credited them throughout the whole course of their triumphant march, the population plucked up courage and the tradesmen's business instincts began to revive. Some of them had weighty interests at Havre, which was still held by the French, and were anxious to make an attempt to reach that port, travelling overland to Dieppe and embarking there. Through the influence of German officers, whose acquaintance they had made, a permit for leaving Rouen could be obtained from the general in command.

A large four-horse coach was accordingly engaged for the journey; ten persons had reserved seats in it, and it was agreed to set out one Tuesday morning, before daybreak, so as to avoid exciting attention. For some time there had been a hard frost; on the Monday afternoon great black clouds gathered from the north, and snow fell incessantly all that evening and the following night.

At half-past four in the morning, the travellers met in the yard of the Hôtel de Normandie, where they were to take the coach. They were still half asleep and shivered with cold under their wraps. It was too dark for them to see one another clearly. Under their accumulations of heavy winter clothes, they all resembled corpulent priests in long cassocks. Two men, however, recognized each other; a third joined them, and they entered into conversation.

'I have brought my wife,' said one.

'So have I.'

'And I, too.'

The first speaker added: 'We don't intend returning to Rouen. If the Prussians advance on Havre we shall make our way to England.'

All three were of the same pattern and had the same plans.

Meanwhile, there was no sign of the horses. An ostler carrying a little lantern emerged from time to time from one mysterious door only to disappear through another. Horses' hoofs could be heard stamping on the ground, the noise muffled by stable litter, and from the far end of the building came the voice of a man talking to the animals and swearing. The tinkling of little bells proclaimed that the harness was being got ready, and this sound soon developed into a clear, continuous jingling, in rhythm with the horses' movements, now and then ceasing, only to begin again with a sudden jerk, to the accompaniment of the dull clang of an iron-shod hoof on the stable floor. The door suddenly closed and everything was still. The half-frozen travellers stopped talking and stood there stiff and motionless. A curtain of glistening snow-flakes descended towards the earth, veiling every human form and covering inanimate objects with an icy fleece. In the intense stillness of the town, plunged in the deep repose of winter, no sound was audible save that vague, indefinable, fluttering whisper of the falling snow, felt rather than heard, the mingling of airy atoms, which seemed to fill all space and envelop the whole world.

The man with the lantern reappeared, dragging along by a rope a dejected and reluctant horse. He put the horse alongside the carriage-pole and spent a long time adjusting the harness, for he could only use one hand, as the other held the light. As he was going off to fetch the second horse, he noticed the travellers all standing there motionless and already white with snow.

'Why don't you get inside the coach?' he said. 'You would at least be under cover.'

Apparently this had not occurred to them, and they made a rush for the coach. The three husbands installed their wives at the far end and seated themselves beside them. The other veiled and vague forms took the remaining places without uttering a word.

Their feet sank into the straw which covered the floor. The ladies at the far end had brought little copper foot-warmers with a chemical preparation of charcoal which they lighted, and for some time, in subdued voices, they dwelt upon the advantages of these apparatuses, assuring one another of facts of which they had all long been aware.

At last the coach was ready. It had a team of six horses instead of four in consideration of the bad state of the roads. A voice from without asked: 'Is every one in?' A voice from within replied: 'Yes,' and they set off.

The progress of the coach was laborious and very slow. The wheels sank into the snow. Every joint in the whole structure creaked and moaned. The smoking horses slipped and panted, the driver's immense whip cracked incessantly, flickering in all directions, now tying itself into knots and uncoiling itself again like a slender snake, now stinging a bulging hind quarter and inciting its owner to more strenuous efforts. Imperceptibly, day began to dawn. The fall of ethereal snowflakes, which one of the travellers, a true-born native of Rouen, had compared to a shower of cotton, had ceased. A livid light filtered through the dense and lowering clouds, whose blackness set off the dazzling whiteness of the landscape. Here and there stood out a row of tall, frosted trees, or a cottage under a hood of snow.

Inside the carriage, the passengers scrutinized one another inquisitively by the melancholy light of dawn.

Dozing opposite each other in the best places at the end sat Monsieur and Madame Loiseau, wholesale wine merchants of the Rue Grand-pont. Originally a clerk in an office, after his employer's bankruptcy, Loiseau had bought the business and made a fortune. He sold very bad wine at very low prices to small retailers in country places. He was regarded by his friends and acquaintances as a knowing rascal and a true Norman, a jovial fellow, up to every dodge. His reputation for sharp practice was so notorious that one evening at a party at the Prefecture, Monsieur Tournel, a local celebrity, author of some songs and stories and a man of shrewd and caustic wit, proposed to the ladies, who seemed to him somewhat drowsy, a game of *Loiseau vole*, 'The bird steals away.' The jest flew through the Prefect's drawing-rooms and thence to all the other drawing-rooms in the town, and for a month it set the whole province laughing. Loiseau himself was famous for practical jokes of all kinds, good-natured and otherwise, so that no one mentioned his name without adding: 'That fellow Loiseau is really priceless.' He was short, his stomach bulged like a balloon and was surmounted by a red face fringed with grizzled whiskers. His wife, a tall, stout, determined woman, loud-voiced and positive, was the methodical and financial factor in the business, while he brought to it his own exuberant vitality.

Next to them, with the dignity of a higher class, sat Monsieur Carré-Lamadon, a man of good standing in the cotton business, owner of three spinning-mills, officer of the Legion of Honour and member of the Conseil Général. Under the Empire, he posed as leader of a benevolent opposition, solely in order to sell at a higher price his desertion to the side against which he had fought, though always, as he said, with weapons of courtesy. Madame Carré-Lamadon was much younger than her husband. She had been a great comfort to officers of good family, garrisoned at Rouen. A slight, dainty figure, muffled in furs, she sat opposite her husband, staring disconsolately at the deplorable interior of the coach.

Their neighbours were the Count and Countess Hubert de Bréville, who bore one of the oldest and most aristocratic names in Normandy. The count, an old nobleman of dignified demeanour, took pains to accentuate by tricks of the toilet his natural likeness to King Henry IV. According to a legend of which the family were very proud, that monarch had seduced a Madame de Bréville, and in return, had made her husband a count and governor of a province. He was associated with Monsieur Carré-Lamadon on the Conseil Général, and was the local representative of the Orléanist party. The story of his marriage with the daughter of a petty shipowner of Nantes had always been a mystery. But thanks to her stately air, her genius for entertaining, and the rumour that one of the sons of Louis Philippe had been her lover, all the local *noblesse* paid court to her. Her *salon* held its own as the first in the neighbourhood. Access to it was not easy, and it was the only drawing-room where old-world courtesy survived. The fortune of the Brévilles, all in landed estate, was said to yield an income of half a million francs.

These six were the backbone of the party. They represented the wealthy, placid, solid element of society, respectable, influential persons of religion and principle.

It so happened that all the women were seated on the same side. Next to the countess sat two nuns telling their long rosaries and muttering paternosters and aves. One of them was old; her skin was deeply pitted with smallpox as if she had received a charge of shot full in the face. Her companion was a puny creature with a pretty but sickly face and the narrow chest of a consumptive, a prey to that burning faith which creates visionaries and martyrs.

Opposite the two nuns sat a man and a woman who excited every one's interest. The man was Cornudet, a notorious democrat, the terror of all respectable people. For the last twenty years he had been dipping his long red beard in mugs of beer at every democratic pothouse. With the help of his boon companions, he had frittered away a respectable fortune which he had inherited from his father, a retired confectioner; and he looked forward eagerly to the coming of the Republic, when he would enter upon the office he had earned by all his libations to the Revolution. On the fourth of September, probably in consequence of a practical joke, he got the idea into his head that he had been elected prefect; but when he essayed to take up his duties, the clerks at the prefecture, who remained in sole possession, refused to recognize him and he was forced to beat a retreat. For all that, he was a very good fellow, harmless and obliging, and he had thrown himself heart and soul into organizing the defence of the town. He had had pits dug in the open country, had had all the young trees in the neighbouring forests cut down and traps set on all the roads, and, satisfied with his preparations, he had, at the approach of the enemy, scuttled back to the city. He felt now that he would be more useful at Havre, where fresh entrenchments would be needed.

The woman beside him was one of those who are technically called gay. She was famous for her premature portliness, which had earned for her the nickname of Boule de Suif, ball of lard, 'tallow-keech.' Short, perfectly spherical, fat as dripping, with puffy fingers, dented at the joints like strings of sausages, her skin shining and smooth, her enormous breasts swelling beneath her bodice, she had nevertheless remained so fresh and blooming that she continued to fascinate and allure. Her face was like a ruddy apple or a peony bud ready to burst into flower. Her magnificent black eyes were shaded and deepened by long, thick lashes. Her charming, pouting mouth, ripe for kisses, revealed two rows of tiny dazzling teeth. It was whispered that she had many other priceless qualities.

As soon as they recognized her, the respectable women began to murmur among themselves, and the words 'prostitute,' 'open shame' were whispered so audibly that she looked up. She bestowed upon her companions a glance so bold and challenging that a deep silence ensued and every one sat with downcast eyes, except Loiseau, who stole arch glances at her.

But very soon, the three ladies, united in a sudden friendship verging on intimacy by the intrusion of that brazen hussy, resumed their conversation. They felt that they must ensconce themselves behind the dignity of their wedded estate in face of this shameless hireling. For legalized love always assumes airs of superiority over its random brother.

The three husbands, on the other hand, were drawn together by a common defensive instinct at the sight of Cornudet. They discussed money matters in tones that implied their scorn of poorer folk. Count Hubert alluded to the losses in stolen cattle and ruined crops he had sustained at the hands of the Prussians in the negligent manner of a magnate worth ten millions, who is fully aware that the inconvenience will hardly be felt in a year's time.

Monsieur Carré-Lamadon, a cotton merchant of wide experience, had taken the precaution to send to England six hundred thousand francs as a provision for a rainy day. As for Loiseau, he had arranged to sell to the French Commissariat all the common wines still in his cellars, so that the State owed him a handsome sum which he counted on receiving at Havre.

The three men exchanged quick, friendly glances. Though of different standing, they were linked together by the common tie of money, members of that wide freemasonry of the well-to-do who can thrust their hands into their trouser pockets and jingle the gold there.

The coach moved so slowly that by ten o'clock they had not accomplished more than ten miles. On three occasions, the men got out and walked up the hills. They all began to feel uneasy. They had intended to lunch at Tôtes, but they had small hopes now of arriving there before nightfall. Every one was on the look out for a wayside inn, when the diligence plunged into a snowdrift from which they were not extricated for two hours. Their increasing hunger began to depress their spirits. There was no sign of the meanest tavern or wine shop; all the tradespeople had fled in terror before the advance of the Prussians and the retreat of the starving French troops. The men tried to get food from the farm-houses by the roadside, but could not obtain even plain bread, for the cautious peasants had hidden away their stores for fear of being plundered by the soldiers, desperate with hunger, who seized by force anything they could lay their hands on. Towards one o'clock, Loiseau announced that he was distinctly conscious of a painful vacuum in his interior. For some time every one had been suffering from the same complaint, and the steadily increasing pangs of hunger had put a stop to conversation. From time to time, one of the travellers yawned; and another would follow suit. One after the other, in accord with individual character, manners, and social position, they opened their mouths, some noisily, others quietly, hastily putting their hands up to hide the gaping chasm from which the breath issued in a cloud of steam.

Boule de Suif stooped down now and then as if looking for something under her petticoats. She would hesitate for a moment, glance at her neighbours, then quietly sit up again. The faces of all the travellers were pale and drawn. Loiseau vowed that he would give a thousand francs for a knuckle of ham. His wife made as if to protest but restrained herself. It was always painful to her to hear of money being squandered and she could not bear even a joke on that subject.

'I don't feel at all well,' said the count. 'Why didn't I think of bringing some provisions?'

Every one blamed himself for the same omission. Cornudet, however, had a flask of rum; he offered it to his companions, but they coldly declined. Loiseau alone took a couple of sips and thanked him as he returned the flask:

'That's some good, anyhow; it warms one up and cheats one's hunger.'

The spirits put him in a good humour, and he suggested that they should do as they did in the song about the little boat, eat the fattest of the company. This sly allusion to Boule de Suif shocked his more refined companions. They made no reply; only Cornudet smiled. The two nuns had left off telling their beads; they sat motionless, their hands thrust into their long sleeves; their eyes steadfastly downcast, doubtless offering as a sacrifice to Heaven the sufferings which it had imposed upon them.

At last, at three o'clock, when the coach was making its way across an interminable plain without a village in sight, Boule de Suif briskly bent down and drew from under the seat a large basket covered with a white napkin. First she took from it a little earthenware plate, next a dainty silver cup, and then a large dish containing two carved fowls embedded in their jelly. The basket revealed glimpses of other good things carefully packed—pies, fruit, dainties, sufficient provisions for a three days' journey without having to fall back on the cookery of the inns.

The necks of four bottles protruded from among the parcels of food. Taking the wing of a chicken, she began daintily to eat it, with one of those rolls of bread called *régence* in Normandy.

All eyes were fixed on her. The pleasant aroma of food was wafted abroad, and the result was seen in distended nostrils, watering mouths, and spasmodic contractions of the muscles of the jaw.

The ladies' contempt for the hussy rose to a fury; they were yearning to kill her or throw her out of the carriage into the snow, her, and her cup and her basket and her provisions.

Loiseau's eyes devoured the dish of fowls.

'Congratulations!' he said. 'Madame has been more foreseeing than the rest of us. Some people always think of everything.'

She turned towards him.

'Will you have some, sir?' she asked. 'It is hard to go fasting all day.'

He bowed.

'Frankly,' he replied, 'I cannot refuse; I am at my last gasp. Any port in a storm, as they say.' And casting a glance around him, he added: 'One is lucky to find a friend in need on an occasion like this.'

He spread a newspaper over his knees to save his trousers, and, with the point of a knife which he always carried in his pocket, he transfixed a leg of chicken thickly coated with jelly, tore at it with his teeth, and chewed it with such obvious enjoyment that his companions could not restrain a deep sigh of anguish.

In a low, gentle voice, Boule de Suif invited the two nuns to share her meal. They accepted with alacrity and, without raising their eyes, murmured their thanks and quickly set to work. Nor did Cornudet decline his neighbour's invitation, and between them they made a sort of table by spreading newspapers on their knees. Their jaws worked feverishly; they chewed and swallowed the food with ravenous haste.

Loiseau, busy in his corner, quietly pressed his wife to follow his example. She held out for a long time, but at last a piercing pang of hunger induced her to give way. Her husband with a well-turned phrase asked his 'charming companion' if he might offer Madame Loiseau a small portion.

'Why, certainly, sir,' she replied, with a pleasant smile, and handed him the dish.

A difficulty arose when the first bottle of Bordeaux was opened; there was only one cup. But they passed it round, each wiping it in turn. Cornudet alone, in a spirit of gallantry, set his lips to the rim still moist from the lips of his fair neighbour.

With people eating and drinking all around them, the Count and Countess de Bréville and Monsieur and Madame Carré-Lamadon, enveloped in the odour of food, endured the torments of Tantalus. Suddenly the manufacturer's wife gave a sigh which drew every one's attention. She was as white as the snow outside; her eyes closed, her head drooped, she had fainted. Her distracted husband uttered a general appeal for help. The other passengers were utterly at a loss, but the elder nun raised the patient's head, held Boule de Suif's cup to her lips, and induced her to swallow a few drops of wine. The pretty creature moved, opened her eyes, smiled, and in a faint voice declared that she felt perfectly well again. But, as a precaution, the nun made her drink a whole glass of Bordeaux, saying:

'It is nothing but sheer hunger.'

Blushing in confusion, Boule de Suif looked at the four travellers who were still fasting, and stammered out:

'Oh, dear, if only I might venture to offer these ladies and gentlemen . . .' She broke off, in dread of a snub.

Loiseau took the floor:

'Upon my soul, in cases like this, we are all brothers and should help one another. Come, ladies, the devil take ceremony; accept her offer. Why, we don't know whether we shall even find a night's lodging. At this rate, we shan't be at Tôtes before midday to-morrow.'

They all hesitated, no one caring to take the responsibility of saying 'Yes.'

It was the count who cut the knot. Turning to the embarrassed young women, and assuming his grandest air, he said:

'Madame, we gratefully accept your offer.'

The first step was the only difficulty. The Rubicon once crossed, they fell to with a will. The basket was emptied. It still contained a *pâté de foie gras*, a *pâté* of larks, smoked tongue, some Crassane pears, a Pont l'Évêque cheese, some little cakes, and a jar of pickled gherkins and onions. For, like all women, Boule de Suif had a taste for crude flavours.

It was impossible to eat the woman's food and not talk to her. They entered into conversation, at first with some reserve, but presently, in view of her admirable behaviour, with increasing freedom. Madame de Bréville and Madame Carré-Lamadon, who were women of the world, were tactful and courteous. The countess, in particular, treated Boule de Suif with the gracious condescension of very great ladies, whom no touch can soil, and was charming to her. Only stout Madame Loiseau, who had the soul of a gendarme, remained obdurate, saying little but eating all the more.

The conversation turned naturally upon the war, the horrors perpetrated by the Prussians, and the gallant deeds of the French. All these people, who were running away, paid tribute to the courage of those who remained behind. Presently they came to personal experiences, and Boule de Suif, with real feeling and that fervent eloquence that sometimes characterizes her class when carried away by emotion, gave her reasons for leaving Rouen:

'At first, I thought I could stay. My house was well stocked with food and I preferred to feed a few soldiers rather than go into exile, God knows where. But when I saw those Prussians, it was too much for me. They made my blood boil, and I cried

with shame all day long. Oh, if only I were a man! I watched
them out of my window, those fat swine with their spiked
helmets, and my maid had to hold my hands to stop me from
hurling chairs and tables on their heads. Then some of them
were billeted on me. I sprang at the throat of the first one;
they are no more difficult to strangle than any one else. I
should have done for him too if they had not dragged me off by
my hair. After that I had to hide. So when I saw a chance,
I came away, and here I am.'

They congratulated her warmly. She rose in the estimation
of her companions, who had not shown such pluck. Cornudet
listened to her with a benevolent and apostolic smile, like a
priest who hears one of his flock praising God, for these long-
bearded democrats think they have the monopoly of patriotism
just as the men in cassocks are monopolists in religion. Speaking in his turn, he laid down the law with a pomposity borrowed
from the proclamations posted up on the walls day after day;
and he wound up with a burst of eloquence, in which he inveighed
magisterially against that blackguard Badinguet, as he desig-
nated Napoleon III.

But Boule de Suif at once fired up, for she was a Bonapartist.
She flushed as red as a cherry and stammered with rage: 'I should
just like to see fellows like you in his position. A nice mess you
would have made of it. It's your sort who betrayed the man.
There would be nothing for it but to leave France if it were
governed by scoundrels like you.'

Cornudet was unmoved and continued to smile his disdainful
superior smile. But a violent outburst of abuse was only averted
by the count, who, not without difficulty, contrived to pacify
the angry young woman, authoritatively declaring that all
sincere opinions were entitled to respect. But the countess
and Madame Carré-Lamadon, who cherished the unreasonable
hatred felt by all respectable people for the Republic, and the
instinctive devotion with which every woman regards despotic
governments with their pomps and ceremonies, felt themselves
involuntarily drawn towards this prostitute of unbending
convictions and sentiments so closely allied to their own.

The basket was empty. Ten hungry people had made short
work of its contents. Their only regret was that it had not
been larger. Conversation continued for a while, but it grew
more constrained when the repast was over.

Night fell; the darkness gradually deepened, and the cold, always more keenly felt after a meal, made Boule de Suif shiver, well-covered though she was. At this, Madame de Bréville offered her her foot-warmer, in which the charcoal had been renewed several times since the morning. Boule de Suif accepted it with alacrity as her feet were like ice. Madame Carré-Lamadon and Madame Loiseau gave their foot-warmers to the two nuns.

The driver had lighted the lamps, which cast a vivid glare upon the cloud of steam rising from the reeking quarters of the wheelers, and upon the roadside snow which seemed to be unrolling itself under the shifting radiance. Within the carriage all was dark, but suddenly there was some by-play between Boule de Suif and Cornudet. Loiseau, straining his eyes through the gloom, thought he saw the man with the long beard start violently away, as if he had received a forcible but noiseless cuff.

On the road ahead, little points of light began to twinkle. It was Tôtes. They had been thirteen hours on the way, including four halts of half an hour each to rest and feed the horses. They entered the town and drew up at the Hôtel du Commerce.

The door of the carriage was flung open. A familiar sound made all the travellers shudder. It was the jingling of a scabbard on the ground. At the same time they heard an exclamation in a German voice.

Though the coach had stopped, no one got out. It was as if the travellers expected to be massacred as soon as they emerged. Then the driver came to the door, flashing his lamps into the farthest recesses of the coach and lighting up two rows of frightened faces with open mouths and eyes bulging with surprise and terror. Beside the driver, in the full glare of the lamp, stood a German officer, a tall, fair young man, extremely slender, squeezed into his uniform like a girl into her corset, wearing on one side his polished flat cap which gave him the appearance of a porter at an English hotel. His huge, long, straight moustache tapered on either side to a point consisting of a single yellow hair, so fine that the extremity was invisible. Its weight seemed to depress the corners of his mouth and by dragging down his cheeks to give to his lips the appearance of drooping. In the French of Alsace, he invited the travellers to alight, saying in a severe voice:

'Will you get out, ladies and gentlemen?'

The two nuns were the first to obey, with the docility of women habituated by their vows to implicit obedience. Next came the count and countess, followed by the manufacturer and his wife; then Loiseau, pushing his better half before him. When he set foot on the ground, Loiseau, from prudence rather than politeness, said to the officer: 'Good evening, sir.' The latter, with the insolence of authority, stared at him without reply. Boule de Suif and Cornudet, though nearest to the door, were the last to emerge, confronting the enemy with a grave and lofty air. The stout young woman endeavoured to control herself and to remain calm. The democrat twisted his long red beard with a histrionic gesture, defiant, yet timid. Conscious that in an encounter such as this, each individual is in some measure the representative of his country, they were anxious to preserve their dignity. Both alike were disgusted at their companions' servility. Boule de Suif desired to prove herself of loftier spirit than those honest women, her fellow-travellers, while Cornudet, realizing that it behoved him to set an example, continued by his attitude the task of resistance which he had begun when he dug up the roads. They went into the great kitchen of the inn, where the German officer, having demanded their permit for departure, signed by the general in command, in which were set forth the names, description, and profession of each of the travellers, minutely examined them all, comparing their appearance with the written record. Then he said abruptly: 'All right!' and disappeared.

They breathed once more. Being still hungry, they ordered supper. It was promised in half an hour; and while two maids were busy preparing it, they went to look at the bedrooms, all of which opened into a long passage, with a glazed door at the end.

Just as they were sitting down to supper, the host appeared. He was a retired horse-dealer, a stout man troubled with asthma, constantly wheezing, coughing and clearing his throat. His father had bequeathed to him the name of Follenvie.

'Mademoiselle Élisabeth Rousset?' he asked.

Boule de Suif turned to him in alarm.

'Yes?'

'Mademoiselle, the Prussian officer wishes to speak to you at once.'

'To me?'

'Yes, if you are really Mademoiselle Élisabeth Rousset?'

She hesitated for a moment in dismay, then she said roundly: 'He may want me, but I shan't go.'

This caused a sensation among the company. Every one gave his opinion, discussing the reason for the summons. The count went up to Boule de Suif:

'You are wrong, madam; for your refusal may have serious consequences, not only for yourself but all your companions. One should never resist those who have the upper hand. Compliance surely cannot involve you in any danger; no doubt it is on account of some formality which has been omitted.'

The others seconded him; they begged, urged, and lectured Boule de Suif till finally they persuaded her. For they dreaded the complications which might result from her rashness. At last she said:

'Well, remember it's for your sakes I do.'

The countess clasped her hand.

'You have our grateful thanks,' she said.

Boule de Suif left the room. The others awaited her return before sitting down to supper. Every one regretted not having been sent for instead of that headstrong, passionate girl, and each rehearsed in his mind suitable platitudes in case he should be summoned in his turn. In ten minutes' time, she returned, breathless, scarlet in the face, choking with rage and gasping out: 'The cad! The cad!'

They were eager to hear what had happened, but she would not say a word. And when the count insisted, she replied with much dignity:

'No, it doesn't concern you; I can't tell you.'

They gathered round a large soup-tureen which emitted a a smell of cabbage. In spite of the disturbing incident, it was a merry supper. The cider was good. Monsieur and Madame Loiseau and the nuns drank it from motives of economy. All the others sent for wine, except Cornudet, who demanded beer. He had his own way of opening the bottle, frothing up the liquor and contemplating it, first tilting his glass, then holding it up to the light to admire the colour. When he drank, his long beard, which was tinged with the colour of his favourite beverage, seemed to quiver with emotion; he squinted in his anxiety not to lose sight of his mug, and it seemed as if he were discharging the one function for which he had been created. One felt that he was effecting in his mind a junction; establishing an affinity between the two ruling passions of his life: Pale Ale and the Revolution. Clearly he could not taste the one without thinking of the other.

Monsieur and Madame Follenvie supped at the other end of the table. The innkeeper, wheezing like a broken-winded engine, suffered from a constriction of the chest, which prevented him from talking while he ate; but his wife's tongue clacked without ceasing. She gave a detailed account of all her feelings on the arrival of the Prussians, of everything they had done and said, abusing them first because they cost her money, next because she had two sons in the army. She addressed most of her remarks to the countess, flattered by the thought that she was speaking to a lady of quality. Presently she lowered her voice and entered upon such delicate topics, that her husband, every now and then, interrupted her with: 'You had much better keep quiet, Madame Follenvie!' But she paid no attention to him, and went on:

'Yes, madam, those fellows do nothing but eat potatoes and pork, and then more pork and potatoes. And they have filthy habits, and if you could only see them drilling in a field, hour after hour, day after day, marching and wheeling and turning in all directions. It isn't as if they worked on the land or mended the roads in their own country. No, madam, these soldiers are of no use to any one. And yet the poor have to support them, simply for them to learn how to slaughter people. It's true I'm only an ignorant old woman; but when I see these men wearing themselves out, tramping about from morning till night, I say to myself: "When there are people finding out so many useful things, why should others take all that trouble to destroy? Isn't it really abominable to kill people, whether they are Prussians or English or Poles or French? If you take revenge on someone who has wronged you, it's a crime, or you wouldn't be punished; but if you shoot down our lads like game, I suppose it's all right, as those who kill most are given decorations." I tell you, it's a thing I shall never understand.'

Cornudet raised his voice:

'War is barbarous when it's an attack on a peaceful neighbour. It is a sacred duty in the defence of one's country.'

The old woman nodded:

'Oh, yes, self-defence is quite another thing. But wouldn't it be better to kill all the kings, who make war for their own pleasure?'

Cornudet's eyes flashed.

'Bravo, citizeness,' he cried.

Monsieur Carré-Lamadon was plunged in deep thought. Though he had a passionate admiration for great soldiers, this peasant woman's common sense made him think of all the wealth that would accrue to a country, if all these idle hands, now a drain on its finances, all the sterile power it had to maintain, were employed on vast industrial enterprises, which in the present circumstances it would take centuries to achieve.

Loiseau, however, left his chair for a quiet talk with the fat innkeeper, who laughed and coughed and spat; his enormous paunch quivered with joy at his neighbour's jests, and he gave him an order for six half-hogsheads of Bordeaux to be delivered in the spring after the Prussians had gone.

Supper was hardly finished when the travellers, tired to death, went off to bed.

But Loiseau had been taking everything in. He sent his wife to bed and then applied ear and eye by turns to the keyhole with a view to discovering what he called 'the mysteries of the corridor.'

After about an hour, he heard a rustling sound, and hastily peeping out he saw Boule de Suif, looking fatter than ever in a blue cashmere dressing-gown, trimmed with white lace. She carried a candle and was making for the glazed door at the end of the corridor. Another door was cautiously opened, and when she presently returned, Cornudet came out in his shirtsleeves and followed her. There was a whispered conversation; then they came to a standstill. Boule de Suif seemed to be protesting energetically against Cornudet's entry into her bedroom. Loiseau was unfortunately unable to hear all that was said, but as they raised their voices, he at last caught a word here and there. Cornudet was insisting eagerly.

'Come now, don't be silly,' he said. 'What can it matter to you?'

She answered indignantly:

'No, my dear, there are times when these things are not done. Just now, it would be scandalous!'

Evidently he did not see her point, and pressed her for a reason. Roused to wrath, she exclaimed in still louder tones:

'You ask why? Don't you see why? When there are Prussians in the house, perhaps even in the next room!'

He was silenced. The patriotic delicacy of this poor outcast, who would not submit to an embrace while the enemy was within the gates, must have revived his waning sense of decency; for, after one kiss, he tiptoed back to his own room.

His senses stirred, Loiseau left the key-hole, cut a caper about the room, put on his night-cap, and turning back the sheet which covered the gaunt form of his spouse, woke her with a kiss, murmuring:

'Do you love me, darling?'

Silence then fell on the house. But soon there arose from some quarter difficult to define, which might have been the cellar or the garret, a powerful, monotonous, rhythmic snore, long drawn out, and vibrant as an engine boiler under pressure. Monsieur Follenvie slept.

As it had been arranged to start at eight o'clock the next morning, the party assembled in the kitchen at an early hour. But the coach, its top covered with snow, stood forlornly in the middle of the courtyard without horses or driver. They hunted vainly for the latter in stables, granary, and coach-house. The men then decided to go out and scour the country for him. They reached the market-place with the church at its far end, and on either side a row of low-roofed houses, where they caught sight of Prussian soldiers. The first one they saw was peeling potatoes. The next, a little farther on, was washing down the barber's shop. Another bearded warrior was petting a tiny child and endeavouring to check its tears by rocking it on his knees. The buxom peasant women, whose men had gone to the war, indicated by means of signs what tasks they desired their docile conquerors to undertake: wood to be split, or the coffee to be ground, or the soup to be poured on the bread. One soldier was actually doing the washing for his hostess, a helpless old grandam.

In surprise, the count questioned the beadle as he came out of the presbytery. The old church rat replied:

'Oh, this lot are not at all bad; they are not Prussians, I'm told, but come from farther off, I don't exactly know where. And every man of them has left a wife and children in his own country. The war is no joke to them, I'll be bound. Their women, too, are crying for their men-folk and are every bit as miserable as our own women here. However, just now we are not so badly off; the soldiers do no harm and are ready for any odd job just as if they were at home. You see, sir, poor folk must help one another. It is the great ones who make the wars.'

Cornudet felt indignant at the friendly feeling that united conquerors and conquered, and went off, preferring to shut himself up in the inn. Loiseau had his little joke:

'They are restocking the country.'

But Monsieur Carré-Lamadon solemnly said:

'They are making reparation.'

The driver was nowhere to be seen. At last they ran him to earth in the village café, fraternizing with the officer's orderly. The count addressed him:

'Weren't you ordered to have the carriage ready by eight o'clock?'

'Yes, to be sure, but I had another order afterwards.'

'What order?'

'Not to get ready at all.'

'Who gave you that order?'

'Why, the Prussian commandant.'

'For what reason?'

'I don't know. Go and ask him. I was told not to get it ready. So I didn't, and there you are.'

'Did he give you the order in person?'

'No, sir, it was through the innkeeper.'

'When was that?'

'Yesterday evening, as I was going to bed.'

The three men returned to the inn, feeling very uneasy. They asked for Monsieur Follenvie, but the maid answered that her master, on account of his asthma, never got up before ten o'clock. He had given strict orders that he was never to be called at an earlier hour, except in case of fire. They then desired to see the officer, but that was absolutely out of the question, although he was staying in the hotel. Monsieur Follenvie alone was authorized to speak to him on civil business. So they had to wait. The ladies went back to their rooms and passed the time in trifling occupations.

Cornudet installed himself in the kitchen chimney corner,

where a mighty fire was blazing. A pot of beer stood on a table in front of him; and he took out his pipe which, in democratic circles, was regarded with almost as much respect as its owner, as if in serving Cornudet it served the State. It was a fine meerschaum with a curved stem, beautifully coloured, as black as its master's teeth, redolent and shining, an old friend and a characteristic adjunct to his physiognomy. He sat perfectly still, his eyes now on the blazing hearth, now on the froth of his mug of beer, and whenever he had taken a pull he would pass his long, lean fingers through his greasy locks, while he sucked the froth from his moustache with an air of content.

Under pretext of stretching his legs, Loiseau went out to sell his wine to the local retailers. The count and the manufacturer talked politics and speculated as to the future of France. The one believed in the house of Orleans, the other looked for an unknown saviour, a hero who would come to the rescue when all seemed lost; a du Guesclin, perhaps, or a Joan of Arc, or a second Napoleon. Ah, if only the Prince Imperial were not so young! Cornudet listened with the smile of one who knows the secrets of destiny. The aroma of his pipe filled the kitchen.

On the stroke of ten, Monsieur Follenvie appeared. To their eager questions, he had only one reply, which he repeated two or three times.

'The officer said to me just like this: "Monsieur Follenvie, you will give orders not to have the carriage ready to-morrow for those travellers. I do not wish them to proceed without my consent. You understand? . . . Very good!"'

They then asked to see the officer. The count sent in his card, on which Monsieur Carré-Lamadon had written his name and all his distinctions. The Prussian sent word that he would receive them after luncheon, about one o'clock.

The ladies came down and, in spite of their uneasiness, they partook of a light meal. Boule de Suif seemed out of sorts and terribly worried. As they were finishing their coffee, the orderly came for the two gentlemen, and Loiseau joined the count and Monsieur Carré-Lamadon. They tried to enlist Cornudet to add weight to the deputation, but he declared haughtily that he was resolved never to hold any communication with Germans; and he sat down again in his chimney corner, and called for another pot of beer.

The three men went upstairs and were ushered into the best

room of the inn, where the officer received them. Lolling in an arm-chair, with both feet on the mantelpiece, he was smoking a long porcelain pipe and was wrapped in a gaudy dressing-gown, doubtless looted from the deserted house of some middle-class person of execrable taste. He neither rose nor saluted, nor even looked at them. He was a perfect specimen of the insolence which is natural to a victorious soldiery.

At last, after some moments had elapsed, he said:

'What do you want?'

The count was the spokesman:

'Sir, we wish to continue our journey.'

'You can't.'

'Might I venture to ask the reason of your refusal?'

'I don't wish you to go.'

'I would respectfully bring to your notice, sir, that the general in command has given us a permit to go to Dieppe; I am not aware that we have done anything to deserve this harsh treatment.'

'I don't wish it. That's all. You may go.'

The three delegates bowed and withdrew.

They spent a melancholy afternoon. Unable to interpret the capricious behaviour of the German officer, they were tormented by the most fantastic ideas. Gathered in the kitchen, they engaged in endless discussions and hazarded the wildest conjectures. Perhaps it was intended to keep them as hostages—but for what purpose?—or to take them away as prisoners, or, more likely still, to exact a substantial ransom? . . . At this suggestion they were panic-stricken. The wealthier they were the more they were horrified. They saw themselves forced to purchase their lives with bags of gold poured into the lap of that insolent soldier. They racked their brains to devise plausible falsehoods for disguising their wealth, and for passing themselves off for very poor people indeed. Loiseau took off his watch chain and hid it in his pocket. With nightfall, their fears increased. The lamp was lit, and as there were still two hours till dinner, Madame Loiseau proposed a game of *trente-et-un* to pass the time. Every one welcomed this suggestion, including Cornudet, who, out of politeness, extinguished his pipe.

The count shuffled the cards and dealt. Boule de Suif in the very first round held thirty-one. Very soon, in the excite-ment of the game, their haunting fears subsided. Cornudet, however, noticed that the two Loiseaus were helping each other to cheat.

Just as they were sitting down to dinner, Monsieur Follenvie came in. In his husky voice, he said:

'The Prussian officer wishes to know if Mademoiselle Élisabeth Rousset has changed her mind yet.'

Boule de Suif turned pale. She remained standing. But suddenly she flushed crimson, choking with rage, unable to utter a word. At last she broke out:

'You may tell that blackguard, that dirty scoundrel, that filthy Prussian, that I never will. Have you got it? Never, never, never.'

The fat innkeeper went off. The others gathered round Boule de Suif, teasing her with questions, imploring her to reveal the mystery of her interview with the Prussian. At first she stood out, but finally, carried away by her resentment, she cried:

'What does he want? . . . What does he want? . . . He wants to sleep with me!'

So keen was their indignation that no one was shocked at the phrase. Cornudet brought his mug so violently down on the table that he broke it. There was a general outcry against this ruffianly soldier. Swept by a common gust of anger, they resolved unanimously upon resistance, as if each of them had been called upon to contribute to the sacrifice.

With an air of disgust, the count declared that these fellows were behaving like the barbarians of old. The ladies, in particular, lavished upon Boule de Suif vehement demonstrations of sympathy. The nuns, who appeared only at meal times, bowed their heads and held their peace.

After the first burst of anger had subsided, they dined, but conversation languished; every one was pensive.

The ladies retired early; the men smoked and got up a game of écarté in which they invited Monsieur Follenvie to join, with the object of skilfully eliciting from him the best means of overcoming the officer's opposition. But he devoted his whole attention to the cards, listened to no questions, and made no reply; calling out continually: 'Play, gentlemen, play!' His attention was so closely fixed that he even forgot to spit, an omission which was liable to produce organ effects in his chest. His wheezing lungs ran through the whole asthmatical gamut, from deep bass notes to the shrill squawk of a cockerel trying to crow. He declined to go to bed when his wife, dropping with fatigue, came to look for him. So she went off alone, for she was an early bird, always up with the sun; while her husband preferred late hours and was always ready to make a night of it with his friends. He called out to her: 'Put my egg-flip before the fire,' and went on with the game.

When they saw that they could get nothing out of him, they declared that it was time for them to stop, and they all went off to bed.

They were up early again next morning, filled with a vague hope, an increasing desire to be gone, and a dread of another day in that horrible little inn.

Alas! the horses remained in the stable, and the driver was still invisible. For want of anything better to do, they hung about the coach.

Luncheon was a gloomy meal. A certain coldness began to manifest itself towards Boule de Suif. Taking counsel of their pillows had somewhat modified her companions' view of the case. By this time, they were almost ready to blame the girl for not having secretly sought out the Prussian officer, with a view to providing a pleasant surprise for her fellow-travellers the next morning. Could anything have been simpler? After all, who would have been the wiser? She could have saved her face by letting the officer know that she had taken pity on her fellow-travellers' distress. It would have been such a small matter for her. But as yet no one uttered these thoughts aloud.

In the afternoon, to relieve their devastating boredom, the count suggested a walk on the outskirts of the village. Carefully wrapped up, the little party set out, with the exception of Cornudet, who preferred to stay by the fire, and the nuns who were spending their days in church or at the parsonage The cold, which was daily increasing in intensity, sharply nipped their ears and noses; their feet ached so painfully that each step was torture. And the open country, under its pall of snow, stretching away beyond range of sight, produced upon them such a terrible impression of dreariness that they turned home, chilled and oppressed in heart and soul. The four women walked on ahead, while the three men followed at a little distance.

Loiseau, who had grasped the situation, suddenly asked if the 'wench' meant to keep them hanging on much longer like this. Chivalrous as ever, the count declared that they could not ask a woman to make so painful a sacrifice; it must be voluntary. Monsieur Carré-Lamadon observed that if the French, as was thought likely, turned and took the offensive by way of Dieppe, the engagement could only take place at Tôtes, a reflection which made the others uneasy.

'Suppose we escape on foot?' said Loiseau.

'Out of the question in all this snow, and with our wives too,' said the count shrugging his shoulders. 'Besides, they would be after us in no time; we should be caught within ten minutes and brought back as prisoners at the mercy of the soldiers.'

There was no answer to this, and they relapsed into silence.

The ladies discussed fashions, but a feeling of constraint seemed to disturb the harmony.

Suddenly, the Prussian officer appeared at the end of the street. His tall, wasp-waisted, uniformed figure stood out sharply against the snowy background. He walked with his knees well apart, with the gait characteristic of military men who are anxious not to splash their beautifully polished boots. He bowed as he passed the ladies, but glanced contemptuously at the men, who, for their part, did not lower themselves so far as to take off their hats, though Loiseau made as if to do so.

Boule de Suif blushed up to the eyes, and the three married women felt deeply mortified at having been seen by the officer in the company of the young woman whom he had treated so cavalierly.

Then they discussed him, criticizing his face and figure. Madame Carré-Lamadon, who had known a great many officers and spoke with the authority of an expert, declared that he was not at all unprepossessing. It was a pity, she actually said, that he was not a Frenchman; he would have made a very smart hussar, and all the women would have been crazy about him.

When they returned to the inn, they were at their wits' end for something to do. Sharp words were exchanged on the slightest provocation. Dinner was a short and silent meal, and every one went to bed, hoping to kill time by going to sleep. The next morning they came downstairs with jaded looks and nerves on edge. The women would hardly speak to Boule de Suif.

The church bell rang for a christening. Boule de Suif had a child of her own, who was being brought up in a peasant family at Yvetot. She saw it scarcely once a year and never troubled her head about it. But now the thought of the infant about to be christened awoke in her a sudden burst of tender feeling towards her own baby, and nothing would do but she must be present at the ceremony.

As soon as she had left the inn, the others exchanged glances and drew their chairs close together, for they felt that it was really time they came to some decision. Loiseau had an inspiration. His suggestion was to invite the officer to keep back Boule de Suif by herself and to let the others go. Monsieur Follenvie undertook to convey this message, but he came back almost at once. The German, who knew what men were, had turned him out of the room. He intended to keep the whole party till he had attained his desire.

At this, the innate vulgarity of Madame Loiseau broke out:

'Anyhow, we are not going to stay here till we die of old age. It's the wretched creature's trade. One man is as good as another from her point of view. What right has she to pick and choose? I ask you. She never refused any one who came along at Rouen, not even coachmen. Yes, indeed, madam, she carried on with the mayor's coachman. I know all about it because he buys his wine from us. And now, when it's a question of getting us out of a mess, she put on airs, the slut. Really, I think the officer is behaving very well. He has probably had no opportunities for a long time; and here are we three whom he would no doubt have preferred. But no, he is ready to content himself with a common woman. He has a proper respect for married women. Remember, he is master here. He has only to raise a finger, and his soldiers would seize us for him by force.'

The other women gave a little shudder. Pretty Madame Carré-Lamadon's eyes sparkled and she turned a little pale, as if she already felt herself forcibly seized by the officer.

The men, who had been privately conferring, now joined the ladies. Loiseau, in a fury, was for delivering the wretch, bound hand and foot, to the enemy. But the count, who was sprung from three generations of ambassadors and was himself a diplomat by instinct, counselled strategy.

'We must persuade her,' he said.

So they proceeded to concoct a plan.

The women put their heads together. Voices were lowered and the discussion became general, every one giving an opinion.

It was all conducted with the utmost propriety. The ladies displayed a special aptitude for expressing the most outrageous ideas by polite euphemisms and refined phrases. They were so careful of the conventions of speech that a stranger would have understood nothing. But since the veneer of modesty with which every woman is provided is purely superficial, they threw themselves heart and soul into this unsavoury affair, secretly revelling in it, perfectly in their element and dallying with the idea of the liaison with all the sensual emotion of a cook, himself a gourmand, preparing another person's supper.

Their spirits rose again at the humorous aspect of the adventure. The count ventured upon some rather risky jokes which were so neatly turned that no one could help smiling. Loiseau indulged in broader pleasantries, and even these were not resented. Every one was thinking of Madame Loiseau's brutally frank remark: 'It's her trade, so why should she pick and choose?' Indeed, charming Madame Carré-Lamadon seemed to think that if she were in her place she would rather have him than another.

A plan of blockade was carefully considered, as if for the investment of a fortress. To each conspirator a separate role was assigned, including appropriate arguments and manœuvres. A plan of attack, with strategic openings and surprise methods of assault, was agreed upon with a view to forcing this citadel of flesh and blood to admit the enemy.

They were so deeply engrossed that they did not hear Boule de Suif come in, till, at the count's whispered 'Hush!' every one looked up and saw her.

Conversation ceased abruptly and at first a feeling of embarrassment deterred them from addressing her. The countess, however, was more of an adept than her companions in social insincerity.

'Was it a pretty christening?' she asked.

Not without emotion, Boule de Suif described the whole proceedings, the congregation, the ceremony, and the church itself. She added:

'It does one good to say one's prayers now and then.'

Up to luncheon-time the ladies contented themselves with being pleasant to her, with the object of gaining her confidence and making her amenable to their advice. But as soon as they sat down to table the siege was opened. They began with a vague discussion of the virtue of self-sacrifice. Instances from antiquity were quoted: Judith and Holofernes, then, with utter inconsequence, Lucretia and Sextus, and Cleopatra, admitting to her bed all the enemy generals and making them her obedient slaves. Next was unfolded a fantastic story, hatched in the imagination of these ignorant plutocrats, of how the Roman women betook themselves to Capua and lulled to sleep in their arms Hannibal, his officers, and his phalanxes of mercenaries. They told of women who had stayed the tide of conquest, offering their persons as a battlefield and making of their own beauty an effective weapon; heroines whose caresses had compassed the overthrow of the vilest and most hateful of mankind, and who had sacrificed their chastity in a fervour of vengeance and self-immolation.

All these stories were told with due regard to propriety and good taste, with frequent outbursts of studied enthusiasm calculated to excite to emulation.

By the time they had finished, one would have supposed that the whole duty of woman here below was the repeated sacrifice of her person, a continual surrender of herself to a licentious soldiery.

Deep in their meditations, the two nuns did not seem to be listening, and Boule de Suif said not a word.

All that afternoon they left her to her own reflections. Only, instead of addressing her as 'Madame,' as they had hitherto done, they now said simply 'Mademoiselle,' no one quite knew why, unless it was to detract from the position of respect to which she had attained, and to bring home to her the shame of her calling.

While the soup was being served, Monsieur Follenvie appeared again, and repeated the question of the previous evening:

'The Prussian officer wishes to know if Mademoiselle Élisabeth Rousset has changed her mind yet.'

'No,' said Boule de Suif, curtly.

During dinner, the coalition showed signs of weakening. Loiseau made two or three unfortunate remarks. All the conspirators vainly racked their brains in search of fresh examples, when the countess, probably without design, and simply with a vague idea of showing respect to religion, questioned the elder nun about the main incidents in the lives of the saints. It appeared that many of the saints had been guilty of deeds which would be considered crimes in our eyes. But the Church makes no difficulty about granting absolution for heinous offences, provided that they are committed for the glory of God or the good of one's neighbour. Here was a powerful argument, and the countess jumped at it. It was either a case of that tacit understanding, that veiled connivance, for which all who wear the garb of the Church develop a special faculty, or simply the result of a fortunate lack of intelligence, an opportune stupidity. Whatever the cause, the old nun rendered yeoman's service to the intriguers. In spite of her apparent timidity, she showed herself bold, eloquent, forcible. She, for one, did not trouble to grope among the mazes of casuistry; her doctrine was as rigid as an iron bar; her faith was unswerving; her conscience knew no scruple. She regarded Abraham's sacrifice as perfectly natural, for she herself would have had no hesitation in slaying both father and mother at a command from on high. No act, she believed, could be displeasing to the Lord if the intention was praiseworthy. Taking advantage of the pious authority of this unexpected ally, the countess induced her to deliver an edifying exposition of the moral axiom: 'The end justifies the means.'

'Then, sister,' she said, 'you believe that all means are acceptable to God and that He will pardon any act if only the motive be pure?'

'Who can doubt it, madam? An act culpable in itself often becomes meritorious because of the idea which inspires it.'

And they continued in this strain, interpreting the will of God, anticipating His judgments, and involving Him in matters which were really no concern of His. And the whole drift of their discussion was veiled, insidious, discreet. Every word uttered by the holy woman in the nun's coif made a breach in the courtesan's fierce resistance. Presently the conversation took a somewhat different turn. She of the rosary spoke of the houses of her order, her superior, herself, her charming companion, dear Sister Saint - Nicéphore. They had been summoned to Havre to nurse in the hospitals hundreds of soldiers suffering from smallpox. She depicted these poor fellows, giving a detailed description of their disease. And while they were held up on their journey for a whim of this Prussian, scores of Frenchmen were perhaps dying, whom their ministrations might have saved. Nursing soldiers was her speciality. She had been in the Crimea, in Italy, in Austria. In relating her campaigns, she suddenly revealed herself as one of those nuns of fife and drum, whose destiny it is to follow the armies and bring in the wounded, cast up by the back-wash of battles, and whose word is more effective than a general's in subduing undisciplined soldiers. She was a real Sister Rub-a-dub, and her worn face, seamed with countless wrinkles, was like a symbol of the havoc of war.

The effect of her speech seemed so admirable that when she ceased no one said another word. As soon as dinner was over, the whole party retired at once to their rooms and did not come down till rather late the next morning. Luncheon passed quietly. The seed, which had been sown on the previous evening, was given time to germinate and bear fruit.

In the afternoon, the countess suggested a walk. The count, as had been arranged, gave his arm to Boule de Suif and lingered with her behind the others. He adopted towards her that familiar, paternal, somewhat supercilious manner, with which men of a certain position treat young women of her class, calling her 'my dear child' with the condescension arising from his social rank and his unquestioned respectability.

He went straight to the root of the matter:

'Then, you prefer to keep us here, exposed like yourself to all the outrages which would ensue if the Prussian troops suffered a reverse, rather than grant a favour which you have conceded so often as a matter of course?'

Boule de Suif made no reply.

He tried her with kindness, argument, appeals to sentiment, yet he never forgot his rank, even though obliged to pay court, to lavish compliments—in short, to make himself agreeable. He magnified the service she would render her companions and spoke of their gratitude; finally, with gay familiarity, he exclaimed:

'And you know, my dear, he will be able to boast of having enjoyed a prettier girl than he could often find in his own country.'

Boule de Suif still made no reply and caught up the others. As soon as she returned home she withdrew to her room and did not come down again. The rest of the party were greatly perturbed. What did she mean to do? If she still held out, it would be very awkward.

The dinner hour came, but they waited for her in vain. Then Monsieur Follenvie appeared and said that Mademoiselle Rousset was indisposed and that they might begin. They all pricked up their ears. The count went up to the innkeeper and asked in a whisper; 'Is it all right?' 'Yes,' he was told. From a sense of propriety, he said nothing to his companions, but he slightly nodded his head. Every one uttered a sigh of relief and every face lighted up. Loiseau exclaimed: 'Glory be! I'll stand champagne, if there is any in the house!' and Madame Loiseau writhed in agony when the host came back with four bottles. Every one at once became voluble and noisy. They were bubbling over with joy. The count appeared to awake to Madame Carré-Lamadon's charms; the manufacturer addressed compliments to the countess. The tone of the conversation grew lively, merry, and racy.

Suddenly, Loiseau raised his hands with an air of anxiety, and shouted: 'Silence!' Surprised, almost frightened, the whole party sat mute. He made a sign to them to keep still; stood in an attitude of attention, his eyes raised to the ceiling, and listened again. Then in his ordinary voice, he said: 'Be easy; all is well.' Slowly his meaning dawned upon them and they exchanged smiles.

A quarter of an hour later he went through the same performance, which he repeated at intervals throughout the evening. He pretended to be addressing questions to someone on the floor above, and proffering advice, which had a double meaning characteristic of his bagman's wit. With a sorrowful expression, he would sigh: 'Poor girl,' or he would murmur between his teeth as in a fury: 'Get out, you Prussian brute.' Sometimes, when the others were off their guard, he would cry repeatedly in a thrilling voice: 'Have done! Have done!' adding, as if to himself: 'I only hope we may see her again and that that scoundrel won't be the death of her.'

Though these jests were in deplorable taste, every one enjoyed them and no one was shocked. Like any other sentiment, virtuous indignation is the result of environment, and gradually an atmosphere had been created which was laden with obscene suggestion. At dessert, even the women, who had drunk a good deal and whose eyes were sparkling, made discreet but waggish allusions.

The count, who preserved, even when he fell from grace, his

grave and lofty bearing, drew a comparison, which was much relished, between their condition and that of ice-bound mariners at the Pole, rejoicing because winter is over and the way to the south open once more.

Loiseau jumped up, a glass of champagne in his hand: 'I drink to our deliverance!' Every one rose and drank the toast with acclamation. Even the two nuns yielded to the importunity of the other ladies and took a sip of the bubbling wine, which they had never tasted before. They said it was like effervescent lemonade, but admitted that it had a finer flavour.

Loiseau summed up the situation:

'What a pity we haven't a piano; we might have managed a quadrille.'

Cornudet had not uttered a word or made a sign. He seemed, indeed, as if plunged in serious thought, and now and then with a furious gesture he tugged at his great beard, as if he wished to make it longer still. At last, towards midnight, as the party was about to break up, Loiseau reeled up to him and poked him in the ribs.

'You 're not in good form this evening, old chap. Have you lost your tongue?'

Cornudet raised his head sharply and, glaring ferociously at the company, said:

'I tell you all that you have done an infamous thing.' He rose and made his way to the door.

'Infamous!' he repeated and disappeared.

The immediate effect of his words was to cast a blight on every one. Loiseau was utterly taken aback and stood there like a fool. But he quickly recovered himself. Convulsed with laughter, he exclaimed:

'The grapes are sour, old boy; the grapes are sour.'

As no one understood, he told his story of the mysteries of the corridor. There was a fresh outburst of gaiety. The ladies nearly died of laughing. The count and Monsieur Carré-Lamadon laughed till they cried. They could not believe their ears.

'What! are you sure? He really wanted to——?'

'I tell you I saw it!'

'And she refused?'

'Yes, because the Prussian was in the next room.'

'Is it possible?'

'I 'll take my oath.'

The count suffocated with laughter and the manufacturer held his sides. Loiseau resumed:

'And now you know why he didn't think it at all funny this evening!'

The three men exploded again, until they were out of breath and weak with laughing. Then they all went upstairs and the party dispersed.

Madame Loiseau, who was as spiteful as a stinging nettle, said to her husband as soon as they were in bed:

'That affected little minx, Madame Carré-Lamadon, was laughing on the wrong side of her mouth all the evening. When it comes to a uniform, you know, some women don't care whether it is French or Prussian; it's all one to them. Good Lord, isn't it revolting?'

All that night the darkened corridor was alive with rustling sounds, so light as to be almost inaudible, the pattering of bare feet, the faint creaking of boards. From the gleams of light that showed beneath the doors for a long time, it was obvious that no one went to sleep till a late hour. Champagne is said to make one restless.

Next morning, the snow glittered dazzlingly in the bright winter sun. The coach, ready at last, was standing at the door, while a flock of white pigeons, pink-eyed with black pupils, were preening their luxuriant plumage and stalking solemnly in and out between the legs of the six horses, picking up their sustenance.

Wrapped in his sheepskin, the driver was seated on the box, pulling at his pipe, and the delighted travellers were all of them busy packing up provisions for the rest of the journey. All they were now waiting for was Boule de Suif.

Presently she appeared. She seeemd somewhat ill at ease and ashamed, and as she moved timidly towards her fellow-travellers, they all unanimously turned away as if they had not seen her. The count, with a dignified air, took his wife's arm and drew her away from that contaminating contact.

Boule de Suif stood for a moment in amazement, then plucking up courage, she greeted the manufacturer's wife with a humble 'Good morning, madam.' The latter, however, merely returned an insolent little nod and a glance of virtuous indignation. Every one seemed to have a great deal to do and held aloof from her, as if she carried some infection in her petticoats. Then they made a rush for the coach. Boule de Suif was the last to reach it, and quietly slipped into the seat she had occupied during the first stage of her journey.

They pretended not to see or recognize her, but Madame Loiseau shot an indignant glance at her from a distance, and whispered audibly to her husband: 'I'm glad I'm not sitting next to her.'

The heavy coach lurched off and the journey was resumed. At first every one was silent. Boule de Suif did not venture to look up. She was disgusted with her companions and at the same time ashamed of having submitted to the defiling embraces of the Prussian officer, into whose arms she had been flung by these hypocrites.

Presently, turning to Madame Carré-Lamadon, the countess broke the painful silence:

'I think you know Madame d'Étrelles?'

'Yes, she is a friend of mine.'

'What a charming woman!'

'Perfectly delightful! Really distinguished, well-educated, and artistic to the finger-tips. She sings divinely and draws exquisitely.'

The manufacturer talked to the count; above the rattling of the windows, a word was now and then audible: 'dividend warrant—fall due—premium—mature.'

Loiseau, who had annexed from the inn its pack of old cards, greasy with five years' contact with dirty tables, played bezique with his wife.

The nuns, taking the long rosaries hanging at their waists, crossed themselves, and their lips began to move with ever-increasing speed, as though their muttered prayers were running a race. Every now and then they kissed a medallion, crossed themselves again, and resumed their rapid, continuous babbling.

Cornudet sat motionless, plunged in thought.

After they had been three hours or so on the way, Loiseau gathered up the cards, saying:

'I feel hungry!'

His wife produced a packet tied with string from which she took a piece of cold veal. She cut it into neat, thin slices and they both began to eat.

'Suppose we do the same,' said the countess. Her husband

agreed and she unpacked the provisions brought for themselves and the Carré-Lamadons. They consisted of an oblong dish with a hare in earthenware on the lid, which was an indication of the contents, a savoury hare-pie, in which the dark flesh, mixed with other finely chopped meat, was set off by streaks of white fat. There was also a fine piece of Gruyère, wrapped in a newspaper, with *Faits divers* impressed on its unctuous surface.

The two nuns took out a piece of sausage smelling of garlic; while Cornudet, thrusting both hands at once into the wide pockets of his loose greatcoat, extracted from one four hard-boiled eggs, from the other a crust of bread. Throwing the shells into the straw at his feet, he set to work on the eggs, scattering on his spreading beard yellow specks of yolk, which shone there like stars.

When she got up that morning Boule de Suif had been too much flustered and agitated to think of anything. Choking with rage and indignation, she watched all these people calmly eating away. Seething with fury, she opened her mouth to tell them what she thought of them, and a torrent of abuse rose to her lips; but her exasperation strangled her utterance. No one gave her a look or a thought. She felt overwhelmed by the contempt of these miserable churls, these respectable people, who had first sacrificed her and then flung her away like a thing useless and unclean. And then she remembered her big basket full of good things which they had greedily devoured, her two fowls in shining jelly, her *pâtés*, her pears, her four bottles of Bordeaux. Her rage suddenly gave way like a snapping cord and she felt on the verge of tears. She made a violent effort to brace herself and swallowed down her sobs as a child does; but tears rose to her eyes, glistened on her eyelashes, and soon two great drops rolled slowly down her cheeks. Then the tears came faster and faster, like drops of water trickling from a rock, and falling in regular succession on to her swelling bosom. She sat erect and looked straight before her, her face pale and set, in the hope that her distress would pass unnoticed. But the countess remarked it and with a gesture drew her husband's attention to it. He shrugged his shoulders as if to say: 'Well, what of it? It 's not my fault.'

Madame Loiseau, with a silent laugh of mockery, murmured: 'She is crying for shame.'

After wrapping up the remainder of their sausage, the two nuns returned to their prayers.

Cornudet, who was digesting his eggs, put up his long legs on the opposite seat, leant back with folded arms, and smiled like a man who has thought of a good joke. He began to whistle the *Marseillaise*.

Every face grew overcast. The song of the people certainly did not appeal to his companions in the least. They fidgeted nervously, and each looked ready to howl, like a dog at the sound of a barrel-organ. He realized this, and went on for all that. He even hummed a verse:

> Amour sacré de la patrie,
> Conduis, soutiens nos bras vengeurs,
> Liberté, liberté, chérie,
> Combats avec tes défenseurs!

As the snow hardened, their progress became more rapid. All the way to Dieppe, throughout the long weary hours of the journey; above the jolting of the coach, in the gathering gloom, in the subsequent deep darkness which filled the carriage, with savage resolution he kept up his monotonous, vindictive whistling. He forced their jaded, exasperated brains to follow the song from end to end, word by word, and note by note. All the time Boule de Suif never ceased to weep, and now and then, at a pause in the song, a sob that she could not repress was heard in the darkness.

THE NECKLACE

(*La Parure*)

SHE was one of those pretty and charming girls who, by some freak of destiny, are born into families that have always held subordinate appointments. Possessing neither dowry nor expectations, she had no hope of meeting some man of wealth and distinction, who would understand her, fall in love with her, and wed her. So she consented to marry a small clerk in the Ministry of Public Instruction.

She dressed plainly, because she could not afford to be elegant, but she felt as unhappy as if she had married beneath her. Women are dependent on neither caste nor ancestry. With them, beauty, grace, and charm take the place of birth and breeding. In their case, natural delicacy, instinctive refinement, and adaptability constitute their claims to aristocracy and raise girls of the lower classes to an equality with the greatest of great ladies. She was eternally restive under the conviction that she had been born to enjoy every refinement and luxury. Depressed by her humble surroundings, the sordid walls of her dwelling, its worn furniture and shabby fabrics were a torment to her. Details which another woman of her class would scarcely have noticed, tortured her and filled her with resentment. The sight of her little Breton maid-of-all-work roused in her forlorn repinings and frantic yearnings. She pictured to herself silent antechambers, upholstered with oriental tapestry, lighted by great bronze standard lamps, where two tall footmen in knee-breeches slumbered in huge arm-chairs, overcome by the oppressive heat from the stove. She dreamed of spacious drawing-rooms with hangings of antique silk, and beautiful tables laden with priceless ornaments: of fragrant and coquettish boudoirs, exquisitely adapted for afternoon chats with intimate friends, men of note and distinction, whose attentions are coveted by every woman.

She would sit down to dinner at the round table, its cloth already three days old, while her husband, seated opposite to her, removed the lid from the soup tureen and exclaimed, '*Pot-au-feu!* How splendid! My favourite soup!' But her own thoughts were dallying with the idea of exquisite dinners and shining silver, in rooms whose tapestried walls were gay with antique figures and grotesque birds in fairy forests. She would dream of delicious dishes served on wonderful plate, of soft, whispered nothings, which evoke a sphinx-like smile, while one trifles with the pink flesh of a trout or the wing of a plump pullet.

She had no pretty gowns, no jewels, nothing—and yet she cared for nothing else. She felt that it was for such things as these that she had been born. What joy it would have given her to attract, to charm, to be envied by women, courted by men! She had a wealthy friend, who had been at school at the same convent, but after a time she refused to go and see her, because she suffered so acutely after each visit. She spent whole days in tears of grief, regret, despair, and misery.

One evening her husband returned home in triumph with a large envelope in his hand.

'Here is something for you,' he cried.

Hastily she tore open the envelope and drew out a printed card with the following inscription:

'The Minister of Public Instruction and Madame Georges Ramponneau have the honour to request the company of Monsieur and Madame Loisel at an At Home at the Education Office on Monday, 18th January.'

Instead of being delighted as her husband had hoped, she flung the invitation irritably on the table, exclaiming:

'What good is that to me?'

'Why, my dear, I thought you would be pleased. You never go anywhere, and this is a really splendid chance for you. I had no end of trouble in getting it. Everybody is trying to get an invitation. It's very select, and only a few invitations are issued to the clerks. You will see all the officials there.'

She looked at him in exasperation, and exclaimed petulantly:

'What do you expect me to wear at a reception like that?'

He had not considered the matter, but he replied hesitatingly:

'Why, that dress you always wear to the theatre seems to me very nice indeed . . .'

He broke off. To his horror and consternation he saw that his wife was in tears. Two large drops were rolling slowly down her cheeks.

'What on earth is the matter?' he gasped.

With a violent effort she controlled her emotion, and drying her wet cheeks said in a calm voice:

'Nothing. Only I haven't a frock, and so I can't go to the reception. Give your invitation to some friend in your office, whose wife is better dressed than I am.'

He was greatly distressed.

'Let us talk it over, Mathilde. How much do you think a proper frock would cost, something quite simple that would come in useful for other occasions afterwards?'

She considered the matter for a few moments, busy with her calculations, and wondering how large a sum she might venture to name without shocking the little clerk's instincts of economy and provoking a prompt refusal.

'I hardly know,' she said at last, doubtfully, 'But I think I could manage with four hundred francs.'

He turned a little pale. She had named the exact sum that he had saved for buying a gun and treating himself to some Sunday shooting parties the following summer with some friends, who were going to shoot larks in the plain of Nanterre.

But he replied:

'Very well, I'll give you four hundred francs. But mind you buy a really handsome gown.'

.   .   .   .   .

The day of the party drew near. But although her gown was finished Madame Loisel seemed depressed and dissatisfied.

'What is the matter?' asked her husband one evening. 'You haven't been at all yourself the last three days.'

She answered: 'It vexes me to think that I haven't any jewellery to wear, not even a brooch. I shall feel like a perfect pauper. I would almost rather not go to the party.'

'You can wear some fresh flowers. They are very fashionable this year. For ten francs you can get two or three splendid roses.'

She was not convinced.

'No, there is nothing more humiliating than to have an air of poverty among a crowd of rich women.'

'How silly you are!' exclaimed her husband. 'Why don't you ask your friend, Madame Forestier, to lend you some jewellery. You know her quite well enough for that'

She uttered a cry of joy.

'Yes, of course, it never occurred to me.'

The next day she paid her friend a visit and explained her predicament.

Madame Forestier went to her wardrobe, took out a large jewel case and placed it open before her friend.

'Help yourself, my dear,' she said.

Madame Loisel saw some bracelets, a pearl necklace, a Venetian cross exquisitely worked in gold and jewels. She tried on these ornaments in front of the mirror and hesitated, reluctant to take them off and give them back.

'Have you nothing else?' she kept asking.

'Oh, yes, look for yourself. I don't know what you would prefer.'

At length, she discovered a black satin case containing a superb diamond necklace, and her heart began to beat with frantic desire. With trembling hands she took it out, fastened it over her high-necked gown, and stood gazing at herself in rapture.

Then, in an agony of doubt, she said:

'Will you lend me this? I shouldn't want anything else.'

'Yes, certainly.'

She threw her arms round her friend's neck, kissed her effusively, and then fled with her treasure.

. . . . .

It was the night of the reception. Madame Loisel's triumph was complete. All smiles and graciousness, in her exquisite gown, she was the prettiest woman in the room. Her head was in a whirl of joy. All the men stared at her and inquired her name and begged for an introduction; all the junior staff asked her for waltzes. She even attracted the attention of the minister himself.

Carried away by her enjoyment, glorying in her beauty and her success, she threw herself ecstatically into the dance. She moved as in a beatific dream, wherein were mingled all the homage and admiration she had evoked, all the desires she had kindled, all that complete and perfect triumph, so dear to a woman's heart.

It was close on four before she could tear herself away. Ever since midnight her husband had been dozing in a little, deserted drawing-room together with three other men whose wives were enjoying themselves immensely.

He threw her outdoor wraps round her shoulders, unpretentious, every-day garments, whose shabbiness contrasted strangely with the elegance of her ball dress. Conscious of the incongruity, she was eager to be gone, in order to escape the notice of the other women in their luxurious furs. Loisel tried to restrain her.

'Wait here while I fetch a cab. You will catch cold outside.'

But she would not listen to him and hurried down the staircase. They went out into the street, but there was no cab to be seen. They continued their search, vainly hailing drivers whom they caught sight of in the distance. Shivering with cold and in desperation they made their way towards the Seine. At last, on the quay, they found one of those old vehicles which are only seen in Paris after nightfall, as if ashamed to display their shabbiness by daylight.

The cab took them to their door in the Rue des Martyrs and they gloomily climbed the stairs to their dwelling. All was over for her. As for him, he was thinking that he would have to be in the office by ten o'clock.

She took off her wraps in front of the mirror, for the sake of one last glance at herself in all her glory. But suddenly she uttered a cry. The diamonds were no longer round her neck.

'What is the matter?' asked her husband, who was already half undressed.

She turned to him in horror. 'I . . . I've . . . lost Madame Forestier's necklace.'

He started in dismay. 'What? Lost the necklace? Impossible!'

They searched the pleats of the gown, the folds of the cloak, and all the pockets, but in vain.

'You are sure you had it on when you came away from the ball?'

'Yes, I remember feeling it in the lobby at the Education Office.'

'But if you had lost it in the street we should have heard it drop. It must be in the cab.'

'Yes. I expect it is. Did you take the number?'

'No. Did you?'

'No.'

They gazed at each other, utterly appalled. In the end Loisel put on his clothes again.

'I will go over the ground that we covered on foot and see if I cannot find it.'

He left the house. Lacking the strength to go to bed, unable to think, she collapsed into a chair and remained there in her evening gown, without a fire.

About seven o'clock her husband returned. He had not found the diamonds.

He applied to the police, advertised a reward in the newspapers, made inquiries of all the hackney cab offices; he visited every place that seemed to hold out a vestige of hope.

His wife waited all day long in the same distracted condition, overwhelmed by this appalling calamity.

Loisel returned home in the evening, pale and hollow-cheeked. His efforts had been in vain.

'You must write to your friend,' he said, 'and tell her that you have broken the catch of the necklace and that you are having it mended. That will give us time to think things over.'

She wrote a letter to his dictation.

.   .   .   .   .

After a week had elapsed, they gave up all hope. Loisel, who looked five years older, said:

'We must take steps to replace the diamonds.'

On the following day they took the empty case to the jeweller whose name was inside the lid. He consulted his books.

'The necklace was not bought here, madam; I can only have supplied the case.'

They went from jeweller to jeweller, in an endeavour to find a necklace exactly like the one they had lost, comparing their recollections. Both of them were ill with grief and despair.

At last in a shop in the Palais-Royal they found a diamond necklace, which seemed to them exactly like the other. Its price was forty thousand francs. The jeweller agreed to sell it to them for thirty-six. They begged him not to dispose of it for three days, and they stipulated for the right to sell it back for thirty-four thousand francs, if the original necklace was found before the end of February.

Loisel had eighteen thousand francs left to him by his father. The balance of the sum he proposed to borrow. He raised loans in all quarters, a thousand francs from one man, five hundred from another, five louis here, three louis there. He gave promissory notes, agreed to exorbitant terms, had dealings with usurers, and with all the money-lending hordes. He compromised his whole future, and had to risk his signature, hardly knowing if he would be able to honour it. Overwhelmed by the prospect of future suffering, the black misery which was about to come upon him, the physical privations and moral torments, he went to fetch the new necklace, and laid his thirty-six thousand francs down on the jeweller's counter.

When Madame Loisel brought back the necklace, Madame Forestier said reproachfully:

'You ought to have returned it sooner; I might have wanted to wear it.'

To Madame Loisel's relief she did not open the case. Supposing she had noticed the exchange, what would she have thought? What would she have said? Perhaps she would have taken her for a thief.

. . . . .

Madame Loisel now became acquainted with the horrors of extreme poverty. She made up her mind to it, and played her part heroically. This appalling debt had to be paid, and pay it she would. The maid was dismissed; the flat was given up, and they moved to a garret. She undertook all the rough household work and the odious duties of the kitchen. She washed up after meals and ruined her pink finger-nails scrubbing greasy dishes and saucepans. She washed the linen, the shirts, and the dusters, and hung them out on the line to dry. Every morning she carried down the sweepings to the street, and brought up the water, pausing for breath at each landing. Dressed like a working woman, she went with her basket on her arm to the greengrocer, the grocer, and the butcher, bargaining, wrangling, and fighting for every farthing.

Each month some of the promissory notes had to be redeemed, and others renewed, in order to gain time.

Her husband spent his evenings working at some tradesman's accounts, and at night he would often copy papers at five sous a page.

This existence went on for ten years.

At the end of that time they had paid off everything to the last penny, including the usurious rates and the accumulations of interest.

Madame Loisel now looked an old woman. She had become the typical poor man's wife, rough, coarse, hardbitten. Her hair was neglected, her skirts hung awry, and her hands were red. Her voice was no longer gentle, and she washed down the floors vigorously. But now and then, when her husband was at the office, she would sit by the window and her thoughts would wander back to that far-away evening, the evening of her beauty and her triumph.

What would have been the end of it if she had not lost the necklace? Who could say? Who could say? How strange, how variable are the chances of life! How small a thing can serve to save or ruin you!

One Sunday she went for a stroll in the Champs-Élysées, for the sake of relaxation after the week's work, and she caught sight of a lady with a child. She recognized Madame Forestier, who looked as young, as pretty, and as attractive as ever. Madame Loisel felt a thrill of emotion. Should she speak to her? Why not? Now that the debt was paid, why should she not tell her the whole story? She went up to her.

'Good morning, Jeanne.'

Her friend did not recognize her and was surprised at being addressed so familiarly by this homely person.

'I am afraid I do not know you—you must have made a mistake,' she said hesitatingly.

'No. I am Mathilde Loisel.'

Her friend uttered a cry.

'Oh, my poor, dear Mathilde, how you have changed!'

'Yes, I have been through a very hard time since I saw you last, no end of trouble, and all through you.'

'Through me? What do you mean?'

'You remember the diamond necklace you lent me to wear at the reception at the Education Office?'

'Yes. Well?'

'Well, I lost it.'

'I don't understand; you brought it back to me.'

'What I brought you back was another one, exactly like it. And for the last ten years we have been paying for it. You will understand that it was not an easy matter for people like us, who hadn't a penny. However, it's all over now. I can't tell you what a relief it is.'

Madame Forestier stopped dead.

'You mean to say that you bought a diamond necklace to replace mine?'

'Yes. And you never noticed it? They were certainly very much alike.'

She smiled with ingenuous pride and satisfaction.

Madame Forestier seized both her hands in great distress.

'Oh, my poor, dear Mathilde! Why, mine was only imitation. At the most it was worth five hundred francs!'

VENDETTA

Paolo Saverini's widow dwelt alone with her son in a small, mean house on the ramparts of Bonifacio. Built on a spur of the mountain and in places actually overhanging the sea, the town looks across the rockstrewn straits to the low-lying coast of Sardinia. On the other side, girdling it almost completely, there is a fissure in the cliff, like an immense corridor, which serves as a port, and down this long channel, as far as the first houses, sail the small Italian and Sardinian fishing boats, and once a fortnight the broken-winded old steamer from Ajaccio. Clustered together on the white hill-side, the houses form a patch of even more dazzling whiteness. Clinging to the rock, gazing down upon those deadly straits where scarcely a ship ventures, they look like the nests of birds of prey. The sea and the barren coast, stripped of all but a scanty covering of grass, are for ever harassed by a restless wind, which sweeps along the narrow funnel, ravaging the banks on either side. In all directions the black points of innumerable rocks jut out from the water, with trails of white foam streaming from them, like torn shreds of linen, floating and fluttering on the surface of the waves.

The widow Saverini's house was planted on the very edge of the cliff, and its three windows opened upon this wild and dreary prospect. She lived there with her son Antoine and their dog Sémillante, a great gaunt brute of the sheep-dog variety, with a long, rough coat, which the young man took with him when he went out shooting.

One evening, Antoine Saverini was treacherously stabbed in a quarrel by Nicolas Ravolati, who escaped that same night to Sardinia.

At the sight of the body, which was brought home by passers-by, the old mother shed no tears, but she gazed long and silently at her dead son. Then, laying her wrinkled hand upon the corpse, she promised him the vendetta. She would not allow any one to remain with her, and shut herself up with the dead body. The dog Sémillante, who remained with her, stood at the foot of the bed and howled, with her head stretched out towards

47

her master and her tail between her legs. Neither of them stirred, neither the dog nor the old mother, who was now leaning over the body, gazing at it fixedly, and silently shedding great tears. Still wearing his rough jacket, which was pierced and torn at the breast, the boy lay on his back as if asleep, but there was blood all about him, on his shirt, which had been stripped off in order to expose the wound, on his waistcoat and his trousers, face and hands. His beard and hair were matted with clots of blood.

The old mother began to talk to him, and at the sound of her voice the dog stopped howling.

'Never fear, never fear, you shall be avenged, my son, my little son, my poor child. You may sleep in peace. You shall be avenged, I tell you. You have your mother's word, and you know she never breaks it.'

Slowly she bent down and pressed her cold lips to the dead lips of her son.

Sémillante resumed her howling, uttering a monotonous, long-drawn wail, heart-rending and terrible. And thus the two remained, the woman and the dog, till morning.

The next day Antoine Saverini was buried, and soon his name ceased to be mentioned in Bonifacio.

.   .   .   .   .

He had no brother, nor any near male relation. There was no man in the family who could take up the vendetta. Only his mother, his old mother, brooded over it.

From morning till night she could see, just across the straits, a white speck upon the coast. This was the little Sardinian village of Longosardo, where the Corsican bandits took refuge whenever the hunt for them grew too hot. They formed almost the entire population of the hamlet. In full view of their native shores they waited for a chance to return home and take to the *maquis* again. She knew that Nicolas Ravolati had sought shelter in that village.

All day long she sat alone at her window gazing at the opposite coast and thinking of her revenge, but what was she to do with no one to help her, and she herself so feeble and near her end? But she had promised; she had sworn by the dead body of her son; she could not forget, and she dared not delay. What was she to do? She could not sleep at night, she knew not a moment of rest or peace, but racked her brains unceasingly. Sémillante, asleep at her feet, would now and then raise her head and emit a piercing howl. Since her master had disappeared, this had become a habit; it was as if she were calling him, as if she, too, were inconsolable and preserved in her canine soul an ineffaceable memory of the dead.

One night, when Sémillante began to whine, the old mother had an inspiration of savage, vindictive ferocity. She thought about it till morning. At daybreak she rose and betook herself to church. Prostrate on the stone floor, humbling herself before God, she besought Him to aid and support her, to lend to her poor, worn-out body the strength she needed to avenge her son.

Then she returned home. In the yard stood an old barrel with one end knocked in, which caught the rainwater from the eaves. She turned it over, emptied it, and fixed it to the ground with stakes and stones. Then she chained up Sémillante to this kennel and went into the house.

With her eyes fixed on the Sardinian coast, she walked restlessly up and down her room. He was over there, the murderer.

The dog howled all day and all night. The next morning the old woman brought her a bowl of water, but no food, neither soup nor bread. Another day passed. Sémillante was worn out and slept. The next morning her eyes were gleaming, and her coat staring, and she tugged frantically at her chain. And again the old woman gave her nothing to eat. Maddened with hunger Sémillante barked hoarsely. Another night went by.

At daybreak, the widow went to a neighbour and begged for two trusses of straw. She took some old clothes that had belonged to her husband, stuffed them with straw to represent a human figure, and made a head out of a bundle of old rags. Then, in front of Sémillante's kennel, she fixed a stake in the ground and fastened the dummy to it in an upright position.

The dog looked at the straw figure in surprise and, although she was famished, stopped howling.

The old woman went to the pork butcher and bought a long piece of black pudding. When she came home she lighted a wood fire in the yard, close to the kennel, and fried the black pudding. Sémillante bounded up and down in a frenzy, foaming at the mouth, her eyes fixed on the gridiron with its maddening smell of meat.

Her mistress took the steaming pudding and wound it like a

cravat round the dummy's neck. She fastened it on tightly with string as if to force it inwards. When she had finished, she unchained the dog.

With one ferocious leap, Sémillante flew at the dummy's throat and, with her paws on its shoulders, began to tear it. She fell back with a portion of her prey between her jaws, sprang at it again, slashing at the string with her fangs, tore away some scraps of food, dropped for a moment, and hurled herself at it in renewed fury. She tore away the whole face with savage rendings and reduced the neck to shreds.

Motionless and silent, with burning eyes, the old woman looked on. Presently she chained the dog up again. She starved her another two days, and then put her through the same strange performance. For three months she accustomed her to this method of attack, and to tear her meals away with her fangs. She was no longer kept on the chain. At a sign from her mistress, the dog would fly at the dummy's throat.

She learned to tear it to pieces even when no food was concealed about its throat. Afterwards as a reward she was always given the black pudding her mistress had cooked for her.

As soon as she caught sight of the dummy, Sémillante quivered with excitement and looked at her mistress, who would raise her finger and cry in a shrill voice, 'Tear him!'

.   .   .   .   .

One Sunday morning when she thought the time had come, the widow Saverini went to confession and communion, in an ecstasy of devotion. Then she disguised herself like a tattered old beggar man, and struck a bargain with a Sardinian fisherman, who took her and her dog across to the opposite shore.

She carried a large piece of black pudding wrapped in a cloth bag. Sémillante had been starved for two days, and her mistress kept exciting her by letting her smell the savoury food.

The pair entered the village of Longosardo. The old woman hobbled along to a baker and asked for the house of Nicolas Ravolati. He had resumed his former occupation, which was that of a joiner, and he was working alone in the back of his shop.

The old woman threw open the door and called:
'Nicolas! Nicolas!'
He turned round. Slipping the dog's lead, she cried:
'Tear him! Tear him!'

The maddened animal flew at his throat. The man flung out his arms and grappled with the brute, and they rolled on the ground together. For some moments he struggled, kicking the floor with his feet. Then he lay still, while Sémillante tore his throat to shreds.

Two neighbours, seated at their doors, remembered to have seen an old beggar man emerge from the house and, at his heels, a lean black dog, which was eating, as it went along, some brown substance that its master was giving it.

By the evening the old woman had reached home again.

That night she slept well.

FEAR

(*La Peur*)

AFTER dinner we gathered on deck. The Mediterranean lay without a ripple, its surface shot with the silver radiance of the full moon. The great ship glided along, sending up to the star-strewn sky a snaky column of black smoke. In our wake foamed and whirled a white streak of water, ploughed up by the swift passage of the vessel, churned by the screw, and emitting such brilliant flashes of brightness that it seemed like liquid moonlight, all bubbling and boiling.

Six or seven of us stood there in silent admiration, our eyes turned towards the distant shores of Africa, whither we were bound. The captain, who had joined us and was smoking a cigar, resumed a conversation begun at the dinner-table.

'Yes, I knew what fear was that day. My ship lay for six hours spiked on a rock with the seas breaking over her. Luckily towards evening we were sighted and picked up by an English collier.'

A man, who had not yet spoken, now broke silence. He was tall, of tanned complexion and grave aspect, the type of man whom one instinctively assumes to have travelled through vast tracts of unexplored countries amid ever-threatening dangers; whose steady eyes retain in their depths something of the strange lands through which he has wandered, and who is courageous through and through.

'You say, captain, that you knew what fear was. I don't believe it. You are mistaken both as to the term you used and the sensation you experienced. A brave man has never any fear in the presence of imminent danger. He may be excited, agitated, and anxious, but as for fear, that is quite another thing.'

The captain laughed.

'Stuff and nonsense! I tell you I was in a blue funk.'

The bronze-faced man replied in deliberate tones:

'Allow me to explain. Fear—and the bravest of men can experience fear—is a dreadful thing; it is an appalling sensation, as if one's soul were disintegrating; it is a torturing pang, convulsing mind and heart; a horror, of which the mere remembrance evokes a shudder of anguish. But a brave man is not subject to it at the prospect of a hostile attack, or when confronted with certain death or any familiar form of danger. It comes upon him in certain abnormal conditions, when certain mysterious influences are at work, in the face of perils which he does not understand. True fear has in it something of the memory of fantastic terrors of long ago. Now a man who believes in ghosts, and thinks he sees a spectre in the night, is bound to experience fear in all its devastating horror.

'About ten years ago I myself had this feeling in broad daylight, and last winter it came upon me again, one December night. Yet I have often run risks and had death hanging over me, and I have seen a lot of fighting. I have been left for dead by brigands. I have been sentenced to be hanged as a rebel in America, and flung into the sea from the deck of a ship off the coast of China. Each time I gave myself up for lost, and accepted the situation without emotion, even without regret.

'But fear is a very different thing. I felt a first hint of it in Africa. And yet the North is its real home; the sun disperses it like a fog. This is an interesting point. With Orientals, life is of no account; they are fatalists, one and all. The clear eastern nights foster none of those sinister forebodings which haunt the minds of those who dwell in cold countries. In the East there is such a thing as panic, but fear is unknown.

'Well, this is what happened to me over there in Africa. I was crossing the vast sandhills south of Ouargla, one of the strangest tracts of country in the world. You all know what the smooth level sands of a sea beach are like, running on and on interminably. Now picture in your minds the ocean itself turned to sand in the middle of a hurricane. Imagine a tempest without sound and with billows of yellow sand that never move. To the height of mountains they rise, these irregular waves of all shapes and sizes, surging like the ungovernable waters of ocean, but vaster, and streaked like watered silk. And the pitiless rays of the devastating southern sun beat straight down upon that raging sea, lying there without sound or motion. A journey across these billows of golden dust is one continual ascent and descent, without a moment of respite or a vestige of shade. The horses pant and sink in up to their knees, and flounder down the slopes of these extraordinary hills.

'Our party consisted of my friend and myself, with an escort of eight spahis, four camels and their drivers. Overcome with heat and fatigue, parched with thirst as the burning desert itself, we rode in silence. Suddenly one of our men uttered a cry; every one halted; and we remained rooted to the spot, surprised by a phenomenon which, though familiar to travellers in those God-forsaken parts, has never been explained. From somewhere near at hand, but in a direction difficult to determine, came the roll of a drum, the mysterious drum of the sandhills. Its beating was distinct, now loud, now soft, now dying away, now resuming its weird tattoo.

'The Arabs looked at one another in horror, and one of them said in his own tongue:

'"Death is upon us."

'And as he spoke, my comrade, my friend, who was almost like a brother to me, fell headlong from his horse, struck down by sunstroke.

'For two hours, while I laboured in vain to save his life, that phantom drum filled my ears with its monotonous, intermittent, and baffling throbbing. And I felt fear, real fear, ghastly fear, glide into my bones, as I gazed at the body of the man I loved, there in that sun-baked hollow, between four sandhills, six hundred miles from the nearest French settlement, with that rapid, mysterious drumming echoing in our ears.

'That day I knew what fear was. I realized it even more profoundly on another occasion.'

The captain interrupted him:

'Excuse me, sir, but what was that drum?'

'I don't know,' the traveller replied, 'nobody knows. Military officers, who have often been startled at this singular sound, are generally of opinion that it is caused by sand scudding before the wind and brushing against tufts of dry grass, the echo being intensified and multiplied to prodigious volume by the valley formation of that desert region. It has been observed that the phenomenon always occurs near small plants burnt up by the sun and as hard as parchment. According to this theory, the drum was simply a sort of sound mirage, nothing more. But I did not learn this till later.

'I come to my second experience.

'It was last winter in a forest in the north-east of France. The sky was so overcast that night fell two hours before its time. My guide was a peasant, who walked beside me along a narrow path beneath over-arching fir-trees, through which the wind howled. Through the tree-tops I saw the clouds scurrying past in wild confusion, as if fleeing in dismay and terror. Now and then, struck by a furious blast, the whole forest groaned as if in pain and swayed in one direction. In spite of my rapid pace and my thick clothes, I was perishing with cold. We were to sup and sleep at the house of a forest-guard, who lived not far away. I had come for some shooting.

'Now and then my guide looked up and muttered:

'"Miserable weather!"

'Then he talked about the people to whose house we were going. The master of the house had killed a poacher two years before, and ever since he had seemed depressed as if haunted by the memory. His two married sons lived with him.

'The darkness was intense. I could see nothing before me or around me, and the boughs of the trees, clashing together, filled the night with a ceaseless uproar. At last I saw a light, and my companion was soon knocking at a door. Shrill cries of women answered us. Then a man, speaking in a strangled voice, asked:

'"Who goes there?"

'My guide gave his name and we entered. It was a scene I shall never forget. A white-haired, wild-eyed old man stood waiting for us in the middle of the kitchen with a loaded gun in his hand, while two stout lads, armed with axes, guarded the door. I could make out two women kneeling in the dark corners of the room with their faces hidden against the wall.

'We explained our business. The old man replaced his weapon against the wall, and ordered my room to be made ready. As the women did not stir, he said to me abruptly:

'"You see, sir, two years ago to-night I killed a man. Last year he appeared and called me. I expect him again this evening.'

'And he added in a tone which made me smile:

'"So we are rather uneasy."

'I did what I could to soothe him and felt glad that I had come that evening, just in the nick of time to witness this exhibition of superstitious terror. I told stories and almost succeeded in calming them all down.

'By the fire lay an old dog, asleep with his head on his paws. He was nearly blind, and with his moustached muzzle he was the sort of dog that reminds one of some acquaintance.

'Outside the tempest beat fiercely on the little house, and through a small square opening, a sort of peep-hole near the door, I suddenly saw, by the glare of vivid lightning, a confused mass of trees, tossed about by the wind.

'I realized that, in spite of my efforts, these people were under the sway of some deep-seated terror. Whenever I stopped talking, every ear was straining into the distance. Tired of the spectacle of these foolish fears, I was about to retire to bed when the old forest-guard suddenly jumped up from his chair, seized his gun again, and gasped in frenzied tones:

'"There he is. There he is. I can hear him."

'The two women fell on their knees again and hid their faces; the sons picked up their axes. I was preparing to make another attempt to calm them when the sleeping dog suddenly raised his head and stretched his neck and, looking into the fire with his dim eyes, uttered one of those melancholy howls which startle the benighted traveller. All eyes turned towards him. He stood there perfectly rigid, as if he had seen a ghost. And again he howled at something invisible, something unknown, and, to judge from his bristling coat, something that frightened him.

'Livid with terror, the forest-guard cried out:

'"He scents him. He scents him. He was with me when I killed him."

'The two distracted women began to mingle their howls with those of the dog. In spite of myself, a cold shudder ran down my spine. The dog's clairvoyance, in that place, at that hour of the night, in the midst of those terror-stricken people, was an uncanny thing to see.

'For a whole hour that dog went on howling without stirring from the spot. He howled as if in the agony of a nightmare, and fear, appalling fear, came upon me. Fear of what? I have no idea. All I can say is that it was fear.

'We remained there pale and motionless, awaiting some dreadful sequel, with ears intent and beating hearts, convulsed by the slightest sound. Then the dog began to roam about the room, sniffing walls, and whining incessantly. The brute was driving us mad.   At last the peasant, my guide, seized him in a sort of paroxysm of angry terror and, throwing open a door, flung him out into a small courtyard.

'Immediately the dog was still, and we remained plunged in a silence, which was even more nerve-wracking.   Suddenly we all gave a simultaneous bound.   Something was gliding along the outer wall on the side nearest the forest.   It brushed against the door and seemed to fumble there with hesitating touch.   Then followed two minutes of a silence that maddened us.   Then the thing returned, brushing against the wall as before, and scratching on it lightly, like a child scratching with its finger-nail. Suddenly a head appeared at the peep-hole, a white face with gleaming eyes, like those of a wild beast.   And from its mouth came a vague sound like a plaintive moan.

'There was a noise of a tremendous explosion in the kitchen. The old forest-guard had fired his gun.   At the same time the two sons rushed to block up the peep-hole with the big table, which they reinforced with the dresser.

'And solemnly I assure you that at that unexpected report of the gun, such an agonizing pang shot through me, heart and soul and body, that I was ready to faint, ready to die of fear.

'We stayed there till dawn, unable to stir or utter a word in the grip of a horror I cannot describe.

'No one ventured to move the barricade till we saw, through a chink in the pent-roof, a slender ray of daylight.

'At the foot of the wall, close against the door, lay the old dog with a bullet in his throat.   He had got out of the court-yard by digging a hole under the fence.'

The man with the bronzed face ceased speaking.   Then he added:

'That night I was in no danger whatever.   But I would rather go through again all the worst perils I have encountered than that single moment when the gun was fired at that hairy face at the window.'

IN THE COUNTRY

(*Aux Champs*)

Two thatched cottages stood side by side at the foot of a hill, near a small watering-place. They were occupied by two peasants, who toiled hard to wrest from the barren soil a livelihood for their young families. In each household there were four children, ranging in age from six years to about fifteen months. Before the cottage doors all these youngsters swarmed about from morning till evening. Both couples had married, and had had children, at about the same time.

The two mothers could hardly distinguish their offspring when they were all together, and the two fathers mixed them up hopelessly. The eight names were for ever jumbled in their heads, and when they wanted one of the children, the men often called out two or three names before hitting on the right one.

In the first of the two dwellings, on the way from the little watering-place, lived the Tuvaches, who had three boys and a girl; in the other hut the Vallins, who had, at this time, three girls and a boy. Both families lived frugally on soup, potatoes, and fresh air. At seven in the morning, at midday, and at six in the evening, the mothers gathered their little ones in for their meal, like goose-girls herding their flocks. The children sat in order of age, at a wooden table polished by fifty years' use. The youngest baby's mouth was hardly on a level with the edge of the table. A deep dish full of bread, soaked in water in which the potatoes, half a cabbage, and two or three onions had been boiled, was set before them, and the whole crew ate till they were satisfied. The mother fed the smallest child herself. On Sundays, as a great treat, there was a scrap of meat cooked in the broth, and the father used to linger over his meal and say:

'I could do with this every day.'

One afternoon in August, a light trap drew up in front of the two cottages. The young lady who was driving exclaimed to the man at her side:

'Oh, Henri, look at that swarm of children. How pretty they look, tumbling about in the dust!'

Her companion made no reply. He was accustomed to these outbursts, which held for him a sting, almost a reproach. The young woman went on:

'I really must kiss them. How I should love to have one of them, that one there, the smallest!'

Jumping out of the trap, she ran to the children, caught up the youngest Tuvache, and lifting him in her arms, passionately kissed his dirty cheeks, his fair, curly hair all plastered with mud, his little hands, with which he struggled to free himself from these tiresome caresses. Then she went back to the trap and drove away at a fast trot. Next week she came again, seated herself on the ground, took the baby in her arms, stuffed it with cakes, distributed sweets among the rest, and played with them like a little street girl, while her husband waited patiently in the light trap.

She came again and again, with her pockets full of dainties and coppers, and she made friends with the parents. Her name was Madame Henri d'Hubières.

One morning her husband got down from the trap and accompanied her. Without lingering with the children, who by this time knew her well, she entered one of the cottages. The Tuvaches were within, chopping wood for the kitchen fire. They started up in surprise, offered the visitors chairs, and waited expectantly. The lady began in a hesitating, faltering voice:

'My good people, I have come to see you, because I should like . . . I should very much like . . . to carry off your little boy.'

The peasant and his wife were too utterly dumbfounded to reply. Madame d'Hubières took breath again and resumed:

'We have no children; we are all alone, my husband and I. . . . We should like to keep him. . . . Will you consent?'

The peasant woman began to understand.

'You want to take away our Charlot? Certainly not.'

Monsieur d'Hubières broke in:

'My wife has not explained herself clearly. We wish to adopt the child, but he shall come to see you. If he turns out well, as there is every reason to expect, he shall be our heir. If we should have children of our own, he would share equally with them. If he should not do justice to our bringing up, we would give him, when he came of age, twenty thousand francs; this sum will at once be placed in trust for him. We have thought of you, too, and will pay you an allowance of a hundred francs a month for the rest of your lives. Now do you understand?'

The woman started up in a fury.

'Do you want me to sell our Charlot? A nice thing to ask of a mother! No, no, it would be a horrible thing to do.'

Her husband looked serious and thoughtful and said nothing, but he kept nodding his head approvingly at his wife.

Madame d'Hubières was in despair, and began to cry. Turning to her husband, in a voice broken by sobs, the voice of a child used to having its own way in everything, she faltered:

'They won't, Henri, they won't.'

They made a final effort:

'But, my friends, think of your child's future, his happiness his . . .'

In a fury the woman cut them short:

'I know all about that; I've thought it all out. Be off and don't let me see you here again. The idea of carrying off a child like that!'

As she went out, Madame d'Hubières remembered that there were two tiny boys. With the insistence of a spoilt, self-willed woman, too impatient to wait, she asked through her tears:

'That other little fellow isn't yours, is he?'

Tuvache answered:

'No, he belongs next door. You can try there if you like.'

And he went back into the house, which still echoed with the angry voice of his wife.

The two Vallins were sitting at the table, slowly eating scantily buttered slices of bread, with one plate between them. Monsieur d'Hubières again made his proposal, but this time he went warily; he was more persuasive, more guarded in his arguments. At first the peasant and his wife shook their heads in refusal, but when they learnt that they would have a hundred francs a month, they glanced at each other questioningly, their resolution somewhat shaken.

For a long time, in a torment of indecision, they kept silence. At last the woman asked:

'What do you say to it, husband?'

He replied sententiously:

'I say it's not to be sneezed at.'

Then Madame d'Hubières, who was trembling with suspense,

spoke of the child's future, of his happiness, of all the money he would be able to give his parents later on.

The peasant asked:

'That annuity of twelve hundred francs, will it be promised in the presence of a lawyer?'

'Certainly. To-morrow,' replied Monsieur d'Hubières.

The wife, who had been thinking the matter over, said:

'A hundred francs a month isn't enough for taking away our child. In a few years he'll be able to work. We must have a hundred and twenty.'

Madame Hubières, who was stamping with impatience, agreed to this at once. And as she wanted to take the child then and there, she made the parents a present of a hundred francs, while her husband put the transaction in writing. The mayor and a neighbour were called in and obligingly witnessed the agreement.

The young woman went off in triumph with the screaming baby, as if carrying off from a shop some knick-knack on which she had set her heart. The Tuvaches stood in their doorway and watched the child's departure in stern silence; perhaps they were regretting their refusal.

.   .   .   .   .

Nothing more was heard of little Jean Vallin. His parents went every month to draw their hundred and twenty francs at the lawyer's office. They were on bad terms with their neighbours because Mother Tuvache made their lives a burden to them with her taunts. She went from house to house, saying how unnatural it was to sell one's own child, how horrible, disgusting, and abominable. And now and then she would ostentatiously clasp Charlot in her arms and exclaim, just as if he could understand:

'I didn't sell you, my pet, not I. I didn't sell you. I don't sell my children. I'm not rich, but I don't sell my children.'

Day after day, year after year, she stood on her doorstep making these insulting allusions in tones that could not fail to penetrate to the cottage next door. In the end Mother Tuvache came to fancy herself superior to the whole countryside, because she had not sold Charlot. And people said of her:

'I'm sure it must have been very tempting, but for all that she behaved like a good mother.'

She was held up as an example, and Charlot, now nearly eighteen, in whom this notion had been incessantly inculcated, regarded himself as superior to his companions, because he had not been sold.

Thanks to their annuity, the Vallins rubbed along very comfortably, while the Tuvaches had remained in squalid poverty. Their neighbours' prosperity was the real cause of the Tuvaches' inveterate animosity. The eldest Tuvache boy went away to do his military service. The second son died; Charlot alone remained to help his old father toil to support his mother and two younger sisters. He was getting on for twenty-one, when one morning a smart turnout drew up before the two cottages. A young gentleman, with a gold watch-chain, alighted, and shook hands with a white-haired old lady, who said:

'That 's it, my dear, the second house.'

And he entered the Vallins' hut as if it were his home. The old mother was washing aprons; the father, a feeble old man, was dozing by the hearth. Both of them looked up. The young man said:

'Good morning, father; good morning, mother.'

They started up in amazement. In her agitation, the old woman dropped her soap into the basin and faltered:

'Is that my son, my own son?'

He clasped her in his arms and kissed her, and said again:

'Good morning, mother.'

Although he was trembling with emotion, the old man merely remarked in his usual calm tones:

'Well, Jean, here you are again,' as if he had seen him not a month before.

As soon as they had recovered from their surprise, the parents insisted on showing him off to all the neighbourhood. They took him to see the mayor, the deputy mayor, the parish priest, and the schoolmaster.

Charlot stood on the threshold of the cottage and watched him go by. That evening at supper, he said to the old people:

'What fools you must have been to let them take the Vallins' brat!'

His mother answered sullenly:

'We weren't going to sell our child.'

His father said not a word.

The son continued:

'I call it hard luck to be sacrificed like that.'

Old Tuvache growled angrily:

'Do you mean to blame us for having kept you?'

'Yes, I do blame you for having been such fools. It 's parents like you who ruin their children's chances. It would serve you right if I left you.'

His mother wept into her plate. As she gulped down her soup, spilling half of it, she sobbed:

'That 's all one gets for working oneself to death for one's children.'

'I would sooner not have been born,' answered the young man roughly, 'than be as I am. When I saw that other fellow just now, my blood boiled, and I said to myself: "If I 'd had my rights, I should have been in his place."'

He rose from his chair.

'Look here, I see I had better get out of this. I should be casting it in your teeth from morning till night. I should make your life a burden. There it is. It 's a thing I 'll never forgive you, never.'

The old people sat and whimpered, speechless and overwhelmed.

He went on:

'The thought of it would be more than I could stand. I would rather go and earn my living somewhere else.'

He opened the door. A sound of voices entered. The Vallins, with the son who had come back to them, were holding festival. Charlot stamped his foot, and turning to his parents, shouted:

'You two old clod-hoppers!' and he disappeared into the night.

HIS SON

(*Un Fils*)

IN a garden full of flowers, where the spring was burgeoning gaily, two old friends were strolling together. One was a Senator, the other a member of the Academy. They were both men of standing and repute, of a sober and logical cast of mind. At first they chatted about politics, avoiding abstract ideas, and discussing instead their fellow-men, the topic of personalities being more entertaining than that of pure reason. Presently they revived memories of other days, and after a while they walked side by side in silence, relaxed by the warm, enervating air.

A great clump of wallflowers breathed forth a delicate sweet fragrance; a mass of blossoms of all kinds and colours wafted their scents abroad, while a laburnum scattered to the breeze, from its racemes of yellow flowers, pollen in a honey-scented cloud of gold-dust, fragrant as the clinging powder of perfume shops, diffusing its fertilizing sweetness through space. The Senator paused to inhale the cloud of vitalizing essences and looked at the tree, radiant as the sun, and shedding abroad with amorous lavishness its life-giving particles.

'Only to think,' he said, 'that these imperceptible atoms, which smell so sweet, will reproduce life hundreds of miles away, and are destined to thrill the fibres and sap of female trees and to create living organisms with roots of their own, sprung, like us, from a germ; mortal, like us; and, again like us, giving place to other generations of the same species.'

Then, standing before the glorious laburnum, whose stimulating odours were wafted on every breath of air, the Senator added:

'Ah, old boy, if you had to count up your progeny, you would have the devil of a job. Here's a fellow who begets his offspring without effort, abandons them without a pang, and thinks no more about them.'

The Academician replied:

'We do the same, my friend.'

'Yes,' replied the Senator, 'I don't deny it; we abandon them sometimes, but at least we do so consciously, and therein lies our superiority.'

His friend shook his head.

'No, that is not what I meant. What man is there, my dear fellow, who does not own children of whose existence he is unaware, children, registered with the remark "Father unknown," whom he has begotten almost as unconsciously as this tree begets? If we had to reckon up the women we have possessed, should we not be as much at a loss as this tree here, if it attempted to count its progeny? Between the ages of eighteen and forty, taking into account casual encounters, the transitory passions of an hour, one would have to confess to intimate relations with some two or three hundred women.

'Well, my friend, out of all that number, can you be sure that at least one of these liaisons has not borne fruit, and that you do not possess, in the streets or in prison, some rascal of a son, who robs and murders respectable people like us; or a daughter, either in some house of ill-fame, or, if she had the luck to be abandoned by her mother, cook in some family? Remember, too, nearly all public women, so called, have a child or two whose fathers are unknown to them, the haphazard offspring of promiscuous embraces at ten or twenty francs. Every trade has its profits and losses. These off-shoots are the losses of the profession. Who begot them? You and I and all of us, who call ourselves respectable. They are the outcome of festive dinners with our friends, of merry evenings, of hours when the body, in its exuberance, impels us to snatch a casual gratification. Thieves and vagabonds, all the scum of humanity, are our children. And yet we are better off than if the relationship were reversed; for they, too, these scoundrels, go on propagating.

'My own conscience is burdened with a very sordid story, which I will tell you. It tortures me with incessant remorse, and worse still, with constant doubt, an uncertainty that can never be resolved.

'At the age of twenty-five I went with one of my friends, now a State Councillor, on a walking tour in Brittany.

'After a fortnight or three weeks of vigorous tramping through the Côte du Nord and part of Finisterre, we came to Douarnenez;

thence, in one march, we reached the wild headland of the Raz, on the Baie des Trépassés, and slept in a village with a name ending in *of*. Next morning my friend was seized with a curious lassitude, and felt unable to leave his bed. I use the word "bed" from force of habit; in reality, our couch consisted of a couple of bundles of straw. It was out of the question to be laid up in a place like that. So I urged him to rise, and about four or five in the afternoon we arrived at Audierne. The following morning he was slightly better, and we set off again; but on the way he felt violently unwell, and it was with great difficulty that we got as far as Pont-Labbé.

'There we were lucky enough to find an inn. My friend went to bed and a doctor was summoned from Quimper. He diagnosed a high fever, but could not make out its nature.

'Do you know Pont-Labbé? No? Well, it is the most typically Breton town in all that intensely Breton part of Brittany, which extends from Cape du Raz to Morbihan; that district which preserves the very essence of Breton manners, customs, and legends. Even to this day, that little corner of the earth remains almost unchanged.

'I say *even to this day*, because, for my sins, I return there every year.

'There is an old castle, the base of whose towers is washed by a large lake of indescribable dreariness, frequented by wild fowl. A river flows out of the lake, and coasting vessels sail up this river as far as the town. In the narrow streets with their medieval houses the men still wear the enormous hat, the embroidered waistcoat, the four jackets, one on top of the other, the inside one a mere handbreadth, hardly reaching below the shoulder-blades, the top one stopping just short of the knees of the breeches. The girls are robust, pretty, and fresh-coloured. Their busts are squeezed into a cloth waistcoat like a cuirass, which compresses the figure so rigidly that even the contours of their swelling bosoms cannot be divined. They wear a curious head-dress. The face is framed by two brightly embroidered strips of cloth covering the temples; the hair is dragged back off the forehead, falls to the nape of the neck, and is then piled up on the crown of the head under a quaint bonnet which is often woven of gold or silver.

'The maid at the inn was not more than eighteen. She had eyes of pure blue, a light blue, in which the pupils showed like small black dots. Her small, even teeth, which she showed constantly as she laughed, looked strong enough to bite through granite. She did not know a word of French and spoke nothing but Breton, like most of her countrymen.

'My friend did not get much better, though no specific disease declared itself. The doctor refused to let him travel and prescribed complete rest. So I spent my days by his bedside, and the little maid kept coming in, now with dinner for me, now with a cooling drink for the patient.

'I teased her a little and she seemed amused, but naturally we did not converse as we did not know each other's language. Well, one night, as I went to my room after sitting up late with my sick friend, I met the maid going into hers. It was just opposite my open door. Abruptly, without thinking what I was doing, more for fun than anything else, I seized her round the waist, and before she recovered from her surprise, I pushed her into my room and locked the door. Startled, bewildered, and frightened, she stared at me, not daring to cry out for fear of a scandal and of being turned out of doors, certainly by her master and probably by her father into the bargain.

'I had begun in play, but as soon as she was in my room, passion overcame me. For a long time we struggled in silence, matched like wrestlers, twisting, straining, grappling each other, both of us breathless and wet with perspiration. Oh, she put up a good fight! Sometimes we collided with a table or chair or the wall, and at this, still gripping each other, we remained motionless for a few seconds, in dread lest the noise should have awakened someone in the house. Then we would continue our desperate struggle, in which I attacked while she defended herself. At length she was worn out and collapsed on the floor. She resisted no longer.

'As soon as she was free, she rushed to the door, drew the bolts, and fled.

'During the next few days I scarcely saw her. She would not let me come near her. But when my friend had recovered and we had decided to continue our journey next day, she followed me to my room at midnight, with bare feet and in her nightgown. She flung herself into my arms, strained me passionately to her heart, and till daybreak lay caressing me, sobbing and weeping, and giving me every proof of love and despair possible to a woman who did not know a word of my language.

'In a week's time I had forgotten this adventure, a common enough incident on a journey, the maidservants at an inn being generally expected to entertain travellers in that particular way.

'For thirty years I did not give the matter a thought and I went no more to Pont-Labbé. Then, in 1876, I happened to come there again in the course of a tour in Brittany, which I had undertaken for the purpose of steeping myself in local colour for a book I was writing. Nothing seemed changed. At the entrance of the town stood the same old castle, its grey walls washed by the lake; and the inn was just the same, though it had been done up and repainted and modernized. On entering I was met by two pleasant, fresh-faced Breton girls of eighteen, wearing the usual tight cloth waistcoats and silver head-dresses and the long strips of embroidery over their ears. It was about six in the evening. I sat down to dinner, and as the host made a point of waiting on me in person, some fatality prompted me to ask:

'"Did you know the former proprietors of this inn? I spent ten days here some thirty years back. I am speaking of long ago."

'"They were my parents, sir," he replied.

'I then told him the circumstances of my stay, how I had been kept there by a friend's illness. He broke in:

'"Oh, I remember perfectly! I was then fifteen or sixteen. You slept in the room at the end and your friend in the room looking over the street, which is now mine."

'Not till that moment did the vivid memory of the little maid flash upon me. I asked:

'"Do you remember a nice little maid your father had, with, if I remember rightly, pretty eyes and fine teeth?"

'"Yes, sir," he replied, "she died in child-bed some time after."

'And, pointing to the courtyard, where a lean, lame man was forking manure, he added:

'"There is her son."

'I burst out laughing.

'"He is not as handsome as his mother. I dare say he takes after his father."

'"That may be," replied the innkeeper, "but no one ever

knew who the father was. She died without revealing his name, and no one was aware that she had a lover. Everybody was much surprised when her condition was known. No one would believe it."

'I felt a shudder of dismay, one of those transitory but uncomfortable sensations that depress one like a premonition of grave trouble. I looked at the man in the courtyard. He had been drawing water for the horses and was limping along with his two buckets, painfully dragging his shorter leg. He was in rags and horribly dirty; his long, yellow hair was so matted that it hung like ends of string down his cheeks. The innkeeper added:

'"He isn't worth much; he has been kept in the house from charity. Perhaps he would have turned out better if he had been brought up like other people. But what would you have, sir? No father, no mother, no money. My parents took pity on the child, but after all he was not their own."

'I made no reply. But when I went to bed in my old room, all night long I thought with horror of that stable boy and kept saying to myself:

'"Suppose he is my son. Am I that creature's father? Am I the murderer of his mother?" After all, it was quite possible.

'I resolved to speak to the man and to find out the exact date of his birth. A difference of a couple of months would settle my doubts. Next day I sent for him. But, like his mother, he could not speak French. Indeed, he seemed incapable of understanding anything. He had no idea of his age when one of the maids questioned him on my behalf. He stood before me like an idiot, twisting his hat round and round in his knotted, repulsive hands, giggling inanely, though with a hint of his mother's smile in his eyes and the corners of his lips.

'The innkeeper, coming to the rescue, went to find the wretched creature's birth registration. He had come into the world eight months and twenty-six days after my stay at Pont-Labbé, for I remembered perfectly that I had arrived at Lorient on the 15th of August. The entry recorded "Father unknown" and the name of the mother, Jeanne Kerradec.

'At this my heart began to beat violently. I choked when I tried to speak, and I stared at this brute, whose long yellow hair looked fouler than the straw of a dung-heap, till the poor beggar grew uneasy under my gaze. He left off smiling, turned his head away, and tried to escape.

'I spent the day wandering along the banks of the little river, plunged in painful thoughts. But what was the use of reflection? I could reach no definite conclusion. For hours and hours I weighed every reason, good or bad, for and against the probability that I was the father, tormenting myself with hopelessly involved suppositions, only to return continually to the same horrible uncertainty, and finally to the still more frightful conviction that this man was indeed my son.

'I could eat no dinner, and I retired to my room. It was long before I could get to sleep. When slumber came it was haunted by appalling nightmares. I saw that low brute laughing in my face and calling me "Papa." Then he turned into a dog and bit my calves. Run as I might he followed me, but, instead of barking, he spoke and abused me. Then he appeared before a meeting of my colleagues of the Academy, who had been convened to decide whether I was really his father. One of them exclaimed:

'"There is no doubt about it. Look at the likeness."

'And I actually realized that the monster was like me. I woke with this idea fixed in my head, and with an insane desire to see the man again and determine whether we had features in common.

'It was Sunday, and I came upon him as he was going to church. I gave him five francs, while I scrutinized him anxiously. He began to laugh in his imbecile way and took the money; then growing restive again under my gaze, he ran off, stammering some half-articulate word, doubtless intended for thanks.

'I spent the day in the same agony as before. In the evening I sent for the innkeeper, and with infinite precaution and skilful diplomacy I told him that I was interested in this unfortunate creature, so friendless and destitute, and that I wished to do something for him.

'The host replied:

'"Don't worry about him, sir; he's not worth it. You will only be making trouble for yourself. I keep him to clean out the stables; that's all he is fit for. In return I give him his food and he sleeps with the horses. That's all he requires.

If you 've got an old pair of trousers, you might let him have them, though they 'll be in rags in a week."

'I did not press the matter, but promised myself to think it over. In the evening the poor beggar came home horribly drunk, nearly set fire to the house, laid out a horse with a pick-axe, and finally went to sleep in the mud with the rain beating down on him, and all this thanks to my bounty.

'Next day the innkeeper begged me not to give him money again. Brandy sent him raving mad, and if he had a couple of sous in his pocket he spent it on drink. The innkeeper added:

'"If you want to kill him, give him money."

'The fellow had never had any money in his life, except a few centimes tossed to him by travellers, and he knew no other destination for these coins but the public-house.

'I spent hours in my room with an open book in front of me which I pretended to read, doing nothing but stare at this brute, who was my son, my own son, trying to discover if he bore any resemblance to me. In the end I thought I recognized similar lines on the forehead and at the base of the nose, and soon convinced myself of a likeness which was obscured by difference of dress and by his hideous shock of hair.

'I could not prolong my stay without arousing suspicion, and I left with a heavy heart, after depositing with the innkeeper a sum of money for the benefit of his stable-boy. For the last six years I have been obsessed by this idea, this horrible uncertainty, this appalling problem. Every year an irresistible impulse drives me back to Pont-Labbé. Every year I subject myself to the penance of seeing that brute floundering about on his dunghill, of imagining that he is like me, of trying, but always in vain, to be of some use to him. And every year I return home more undecided, more anguished, more harassed.

'I have tried to have him taught. But he is a hopeless idiot. I have tried to make his life less rigorous. But he is an irreclaimable drunkard and spends on drink whatever money is given him, and he has discovered how to sell his new clothes to buy brandy with the proceeds. I have tried to soften his master towards him, and bribed him to treat him kindly. The innkeeper at last came to regard my efforts with surprise. He observed sensibly enough:

'"Anything you do for him, sir, will only help to ruin him. He must be kept as a prisoner. If he has nothing to do, or is in good spirits, he becomes mischievous. If you want to do some good, it's easy enough. There are plenty of other children who have been abandoned, but choose one who will reward your trouble."

'What answer could I make? If I allowed a suspicion of the doubts which torture me to penetrate to him, the idiot would have sufficient cunning to blackmail me, compromise and ruin me. He would shout "Papa" after me, just as he did in my dream. And I keep telling myself that I killed the mother and was the ruin of this stunted creature, this grub, hatched and reared on a dungheap, who, if he had been bred like other people, would have grown up like them.

'You cannot imagine the strange, complex, intolerable sensation that comes over me when I look at him and think that he owes his being to me, that he is linked to me by the close tie which binds father and son, that, by the dreadful laws of heredity, he is myself in a thousand ways, in flesh and blood, even with the seeds of my own diseases in him and the gusts of my own passions.

'I am obsessed by an insatiable and morbid craving to look upon him; yet the sight of him causes me horrible pain. Out of my window at Pont-Labbé I watch him for hours, forking and carting manure, and I say to myself:

'"There goes my son."

'Sometimes I feel an almost irresistible yearning to embrace him. But I have never even touched his filthy hand.'

The Academician ceased. His friend, the statesman, murmured:

'Yes, certainly we ought to do more for fatherless children.'

A breath of wind shook the yellow racemes of blossom on the tall laburnum and enveloped the two old men in a fragrant cloud of pollen, which they inhaled in deep breaths. And the Senator added:

'All the same, it is good to be five-and-twenty, and even to beget children like that.'

A DEAL

(*Une Vente*)

THE accused, Césaire Isidore Brument and Prosper Napoléon Cornu, came up for trial before the court of assize in the department of Seine-Inférieure, on a charge of attempted murder, by immersion, of the woman Brument, lawful wife of the accused Brument.

The two prisoners were seated side by side on the customary bench. They were both peasants. Brument was small and fat, with short arms and legs and a red, pimply face. His round head was set right down on his short, round body, without any sign of a neck. He lived at Cacheville-la-Goupil in the canton of Criquetot, and was a breeder of pigs. Cornu was lean, of middle height, with abnormally long arms. His face was distorted, his jaw crooked, and he had a squint. He wore a blue smock, as long as a shirt, which came down to his knees. His scanty, yellow hair was plastered close to his skull and gave his face a worn, soiled, damaged appearance, which was perfectly repulsive. He was nicknamed 'The Parson,' because he could imitate not only the singing in church but even the sound of the serpent. This accomplishment of his attracted to the public-house he kept at Criquetot many customers, who preferred Cornu's Mass to God's. The witnesses' bench was occupied by Madame Brument, a skinny peasant woman, who seemed to be always asleep. She sat motionless, her hands folded in her lap, her eyes staring blankly, and a vacant expression on her face. The judge proceeded with his examination.

'I understand, my good woman, that they entered your house and threw you into a barrel of water. Let us hear the facts in detail. Stand up, please.'

She rose to her feet, looking as tall as a maypole in her close-fitting white cap.

In a drawling voice she began her story.

'I was shelling haricot beans. They came in together. "They don't look natural," said I to myself. "They're up to some mischief, I'll be bound." They kept squinting at me sideways, especially Cornu, who squints anyhow. I never feel happy when I see them together, because neither of them is anything to boast of. I said to them: "What are you up to now?" But they didn't answer. I had a sort of suspicion . . .'

The accused, Brument, broke in abruptly:

'I was screwed.'

At this Cornu turned to his accomplice and remarked in a deep voice like an organ:

'If you say that we were both screwed, you won't be telling any lies.'

The Judge (severely) : 'You mean to say that you were intoxicated?'

Brument : 'There's nothing in that.'

Cornu : 'It might happen to anybody.'

The Judge (to the witness) : 'Pray continue your statement, my good woman.'

'Then Brument said to me, "Do you want to earn five francs?" I said yes, because you don't find five francs under every bush. Then he said to me, "Wake up, then, and I'll show you what to do." Then he went and fetched the big barrel with one end knocked out, which stands and catches the rainwater. And he tipped it over and brought it and stood it up in the middle of my kitchen, and then he said, "Go and fetch water and fill it up to the top." So I spent a whole hour going backwards and forwards to the pond with two buckets, bringing more and more water, for the barrel was as big as a vat, if you'll excuse me, your worship. And all the time Brument and Cornu kept on having glass after glass together, and filling themselves up, till I said to them: "You're full, you two, fuller than that barrel." So Brument said: "Don't you worry. You mind your own business. Your turn's coming, so look out." I took no notice, because I knew he was tipsy. When the barrel was brimful I said: "There you are. I've finished."

'Then Cornu gave me five francs—Cornu, not Brument, mind you; it was Cornu who gave them to me. Brument said: "Do you want to earn another five francs?" I said yes, because I don't often have windfalls like that. So he said to me: "Undress yourself." "Undress myself?" said I. "Yes," said he. "How far do you want me to undress?" said I. "If that's troubling you," said he, "you can keep your chemise on. We won't quarrel about that."

'Well, five francs are five francs. So I undressed, though I didn't like it with those two good-for-nothings looking on. I took off my cap and then my jacket, and then my skirt, and then my sabots. Brument said: "You can keep on your stockings. We're decent chaps," and Cornu said: "Yes, we're decent chaps." So there I was, almost like mother Eve. And then they got up, though they were so drunk they could hardly stand, saving your presence, your worship.

'"What next?" said I.

'So Brument said: "Are you ready?"

'"Ready," said Cornu.

'And then Brument took me by the head and Cornu by the feet, like a sheet that has been washed. And didn't I scream! Brument said: "Hold your tongue, you hussy." And then they lifted me right up in the air and stuck me into the barrel, and it gave me such a shock that all the blood in my body went the wrong way, and I was frozen to my vitals.

'And Brument said: "Is that all?" And Cornu said: "That's all." Brument said: "Her head isn't in, that ought to count." "Put her head in, then," said Cornu. So then he pushed my head down into the water, as if he meant to drown me, and the water went up my nose, and I thought I was going straight to heaven. And he kept on pushing till I went right under. Then he got a fright and pulled me out and said:

'"Hurry up and dry yourself, you old bag of bones."

'I took to my heels and ran to the parson, who lent me one of his maid's skirts, as I was in a state of nature. And he went and fetched Maître Chicot, the *garde*, and he went off to Criquetot and fetched the police, who came home with me. And there I found Brument and Cornu fighting like two rams. Brument roared:

'"It's a lie. I tell you there was at least a cubic metre. The method was all wrong."

'"Four bucketfuls," roared Cornu. "That's not even half a cubic metre. It's a fact and you can't deny it.'

'The police sergeant stopped them fighting. I couldn't do anything.'

She sat down.

There was an outburst of laughter in court, and the jury looked at one another in amazement. The judge addressed the accused, Cornu:

'You appear to have been the instigator of this disgraceful plot. Have you any explanation to offer?'

Cornu rose to his feet.

'Your worship, we were screwed.'

'I am aware of that,' replied the judge gravely. 'Proceed.'

'I am coming to it. Well, Brument came to my place about nine o'clock and called for a couple of brandies and said: "Have one, Cornu." I sat down opposite him and drank it and then stood him another out of politeness. Then he stood me one, in return, and I stood him another, and so on, glass after glass, until by twelve o'clock we were pretty well screwed.

'So then Brument began to cry, and I felt sorry for him, and asked him what was the matter. He said: "I must get a thousand francs by Thursday." I drew in my horns at that, of course. Then he said to me, as cool as you please: "I'll sell you my wife."

'Well, I was drunk, and, as I have lost my wife, it rather got me. I didn't know his wife, but a wife is always a wife. I said to him: "What will you sell her for?" He thought it over, or pretended to be thinking. When one's drunk, one isn't very clear-headed. And he said: "I'll sell her by the cubic metre."

'I wasn't surprised at this, because I was as drunk as he was, and I'm used to cubic metres in my trade. A cubic metre is a thousand litres. I agreed. The only thing to settle was the price, and that depends on quality.

'"What do you want for a cubic metre?" said I.

'"Two thousand francs," said he.

'I jumped like a rabbit, and then I thought to myself that a woman couldn't measure more than three hundred litres. All the same I said: "It's too dear." He replied: "I can't take less; I should lose by it."

'You see he wasn't a pig-dealer for nothing; he knew his trade. But though this bacon-seller is up to all the dodges, I've a spirit of my own, too, seeing as I sell spirits. Ha, ha, ha!

'I said to him: "If she were new, I wouldn't mind, but you've had her some time, so she's only second-hand. I'll give you fifteen hundred francs a cubic metre, and not a sou more. Will that suit you?"

'He said: "Done. Shake hands on it."

'I shook hands and we went off arm in arm. In this life we must help one another.

'Then something struck me. "How are you going to measure her by liquid measure, if she isn't a liquid?"

'So then he explained his idea, which wasn't an easy matter, considering how drunk he was. "I shall take a barrel," he said, "and fill it brimful with water and put her in. We'll measure all the water she upsets and reckon by that.'

'"That's a good idea," I said. "But the water that she upsets will run away. How will you catch it?'

'Then he called me a fathead and explained that all we had to do was to fill up the barrel again after his wife got out. We would reckon the amount of water that was put back. Say ten buckets: that would make a cubic metre. Oh, he's no fool even when he is drunk, the scoundrel.

'To cut it short, we went home and I had a look at the woman in question. Not what you would call a beauty. She's there, so you can all see for yourselves. I said to myself: "You've been had. But what does it matter? Pretty or plain, they all serve the same purpose." Don't they, your worship? And besides, I saw that she was as lean as a rake. I said to myself: "She doesn't amount to four hundred litres." I understand these things, being in the liquor trade.

'She has told you what happened; we let her keep on her chemise and stockings, though that was a loss to me. When it was over, she took to her heels. I said: "Look out, Brument, she's running away."

'"Don't worry," he replied, "we can easily catch her again. She'll come home to roost. Let's measure the deficit." So we measured it, and it wasn't even four bucketfuls. Ha, ha, ha!'

The prisoner burst into such uncontrollable laughter that a policeman had to pat him on the back.

When he had regained his composure, he resumed:

'To cut it short, Brument said: "Nothing doing. It isn't enough." Then I shouted and he shouted, and I shouted him down. I hit him; he thumped me back. It would have gone on till doomsday, as we were both drunk. Then along came the police. They cursed and swore and got hold of the wrong end of the stick and hauled us off to prison. I claim damages.'

He resumed his seat. Brument confirmed on all points the statement made by his accomplice. The bewildered jury withdrew to deliberate. In an hour's time they returned and acquitted both prisoners, but added a solemn rider concerning the sanctity of the marriage bond, and defining the limits within which commercial transactions should be restricted.

Brument set out for the conjugal roof, accompanied by his wife. Cornu returned to his tavern.

MADAME HUSSON'S ROSE-KING

(*Le Rosier de Mme Husson*)

WE had just passed Gisors, where I had roused myself on hearing the name of the station. As I was falling asleep again, a violent jolt shot me into the arms of the stout lady in the seat opposite. The engine, with one wheel broken, was lying across the track and beside it were the tender and luggage van, likewise derailed. Groaning, wheezing, gasping, sputtering in its death agony, the engine was like a fallen horse which, snorting, trembling in every limb, its flanks heaving, its chest labouring, seems incapable of making the smallest effort to struggle on to its legs again.

Apart from a few bruises, there were no casualties, for the train had not had time to get up speed. We gazed disconsolately at the huge, maimed iron monster, no longer able to draw us along, and blocking the line indefinitely until the breakdown train could be dispatched from Paris.

It was ten o'clock in the morning when this happened, and I at once made up my mind to return to Gisors and have luncheon there. As I was walking along the line I kept wondering: 'Gisors? Gisors? Surely I know someone there. Who can it be? Gisors? Let me think. I am certain that I have a friend there.'

And suddenly, a name flashed across my mind: 'Albert Marambot.' This was an old schoolfellow, whom I had not seen for at least twelve years. He was now a doctor, and in practice at Gisors. He had often invited me to pay him a visit, but hitherto, in spite of frequent promises, I had never done so. I now decided to seize the opportunity.

I asked the first man I met where Dr. Marambot lived.

'Rue Dauphine,' he replied at once, in the drawling Norman accent.

And to be sure, on the door of the house he had pointed out to me I saw a large brass plate with my old friend's name engraved upon it. I rang the bell, but the maid, a slow-moving girl with yellow hair, stolidly replied:

'He's not in, he's not in.'

I heard the rattle of cutlery and glasses.

'Marambot! Marambot!' I called.

A door was thrown open and a stout, whiskered man with a peevish expression came out, holding a table-napkin in his hand. I should certainly never have recognized him. He would have been taken for forty-five at least. In a single moment the whole effect of provincial life, with its deadening, coarsening, ageing influences, became plain to me. A flash of insight, swifter even than my proffered handshake, revealed to me his whole existence, his way of life, his type of mind, his theories of the universe. I divined the lengthy meals to which he owed the roundness of his belly; his post-prandial drowsiness; the lethargy induced by a sluggish digestion and nips of brandy; the absent-minded glances he would bestow upon his patients, while his thoughts were dallying with the roast chicken turning in front of his kitchen fire. The redness and puffiness of his cheeks, the grossness of his lips, the melancholy lustre of his eyes, sufficiently prepared me for his dissertations on cookery, cider, brandy, wine, the preparation of certain dishes, and the thickening appropriate to special sauces.

'You don't recognize me,' I said. 'I am Raoul Aubertin.'

He threw his arms round me and nearly smothered me, and this was his first remark:

'I hope you haven't had luncheon yet?'

'No.'

'What luck! I was just going to sit down. There's a splendid trout.'

Five minutes later I was seated opposite him at table.

'You're still a bachelor?' I asked him.

'Yes, rather.'

'And you enjoy life here?'

'I'm never bored. I've plenty to do. I have my patients and I have my friends. I live well, and I have my health. I enjoy a good laugh, and I'm fond of shooting. What more could you want?'

'Life isn't too dull in a little town like this?'

'No, my dear fellow, not if you know what to do with yourself. Essentially a small town is much the same as a large one. Its incidents and amusements haven't the same variety, but one magnifies their importance. Your friends are fewer, but you meet them oftener. If you know all the windows in a street, every one of them has more interest and piquancy than a whole street in Paris. A small town is very entertaining, very entertaining indeed. You see I have the story of this particular little town, Gisors, at my fingers' ends, from its earliest beginning down to the present day. You have no idea what a quaint history it has.'

'Are you a native of Gisors?'

'No. I come from Gournay, its neighbour and rival. Gournay is to Gisors what Lucullus was to Cicero. Here they are all out for glory, and people talk about the braggarts of Gisors. At Gournay their god is their belly and they are known as the gluttons of Gournay. Gisors looks down on Gournay, but Gournay laughs at Gisors. It's a very comical little corner of the world.'

I became aware that I was eating something particularly delicious, soft-boiled eggs embedded in a layer of meat jelly, seasoned with herbs, and discreetly iced. To please Marambot I smacked my lips.

'First-rate, this.'

He smiled, and said:

'The two essential ingredients are good jelly, which is not easily procured, and good eggs. How rare they are, really good eggs, with reddish yolks, and the proper flavour! I keep two poultry yards, one for eggs and one for fowls for the table. I have a special method of feeding my layers. I have my own ideas on the subject. In an egg, just as in chicken, beef, mutton, or milk, you recover, and you should be able to taste, the extract, the quintessence of all the food that the animal has consumed. How much better people would fare if they paid more attention to that point!'

'I see you are an epicure,' I laughed.

'I should think so. So is every one who isn't an idiot. Man is an epicure just as he is an artist, a scholar, a poet. The palate, my dear fellow, is as delicate and susceptible of training as the eye or ear, and equally deserving of respect. To be without a sense of taste is to be deficient in an exquisite faculty, that of appreciating the quality of comestibles, just as a person may lack the faculty of appreciating the quality of a book or a work of art. It is to want a vital sense, one of the elements of human superiority. It consigns a man to one of the innumerable categories of cripples, degenerates, and fools, of which our race is composed. In a word, it implies an alimentary stupidity, precisely on a footing with mental deficiency. A man who cannot tell a crayfish from a lobster, or a herring, that admirable fish which comprises in itself all the different flavours and essences of the sea, from a mackerel or a whiting, or a William pear from a Duchess, may be compared to a man who cannot distinguish Balzac from Eugène Sue, a Beethoven symphony from a military march by a regimental bandmaster, the Apollo Belvedere from the statue of General de Blanmont.'

'Who on earth is General de Blanmont?'

'Why, of course, you don't know. It is obvious that you are not a native of Gisors. As I remarked just now, my dear fellow, the inhabitants of this town bear the name of braggarts of Gisors, and never was an epithet better deserved. However, let us finish our luncheon first, and afterwards, when I show you round, I'll tell you all about the place.'

From time to time he ceased talking, in order to sip slowly half a glass of wine, which he eyed affectionately as he replaced it on the table. With his table-napkin round his neck, his flushed cheeks, his eyes bright with excitement, his whiskers fringing his never-resting jaws, he was a comical spectacle. He forced food upon me to the point of suffocation. Presently, as I wanted to get back to the station, he took my arm, and escorted me through the streets.

The town has a provincial prettiness of its own. Dominated by its fortress, the most remarkable specimen of twelfth-century military architecture in the whole of France, Gisors itself commands a long green valley in whose pastures the solid Norman cows browse and ruminate.

'Gisors,' said the doctor, 'is a town with a population of four thousand, and is situated on the borders of Eure. It is mentioned as early as the *Commentaries* of Caesar: Caesaris ostium, then Caesartium, Caesortium, Gisortium, Gisors. I won't insist upon you visiting the Roman encampment, traces of which are still plainly visible.'

'My dear fellow,' I replied laughingly, 'I'm afraid you are suffering from a disease which you, as a doctor, ought to study, the cult of the parish pump.'

He checked himself suddenly.

'The cult of the parish pump, my friend, is nothing but

instinctive patriotism. I have for my house an affection which extends to my town and my province, because in these I can still recognize the customs of my village. But if I have a feeling for the frontier, if I am ready to defend it, if I resent my neighbour's setting foot there, it is because I feel myself threatened in my house; it is because that unknown frontier is the gateway to my province. Now I am a Norman, a true Norman. Well, in spite of my bitterness towards the Germans and my longing for revenge, I do not detest them, I do not instinctively hate them, as I hate the English, who are the real, hereditary, natural enemies of the Normans. Over this country, the home of my ancestors, the English have swept a score of times, pillaging and ravaging, and hatred of that perfidious race was transmitted to me by my father with life itself. . . . Look, there 's the statue of the general.'

'Which general?'

'General de Blanmont. We had to have a statue. It isn't for nothing that we are the braggarts of Gisors. So we discovered General de Blanmont. Now look at the window of that bookshop.'

He drew me in front of a bookshop, where there was an attractive array of some fifteen volumes, in yellow, red, and blue bindings. I was seized with irrepressible laughter as I read the titles: *Gisors, its Origin and its Future*, by Monsieur X, member of several learned societies; *History of Gisors*, by Abbé A.; *Gisors, from the Time of Caesar to Our Own Days*, by Monsieur B., landowner; *Gisors and its Surroundings*, by Dr. C. D.; *Celebrities of Gisors*, by a Student.

'My dear fellow,' Marambot resumed, 'not a year elapses, not a single year, mind you, without the publication of a new history of Gisors; we have twenty-three already.'

'And the celebrities of Gisors?' I asked.

'Oh, I won't cite them all; I will merely mention the most important. First we have General de Blanmont; then Baron Davillier, the well-known ceramist, who explored Spain and the Balearic Islands, and brought to the notice of collectors the wonderful Spanish-Arabic faiences. In the realm of letters, we have Charles Brainne, a very able journalist, now dead; still living is Charles Lapierre, the distinguished manager of the *Nouvelliste de Rouen*, and there are many others, many others.'

We were strolling up a long street, built on a slight incline, and exposed from end to end to the glare of the June sun, which had driven all the residents within doors. At that moment we caught sight of a drunken man, reeling along at the far end of the street. With head thrust forward, arms dangling, and nerveless legs, he advanced towards us by short rushes of three, six, or ten rapid steps, followed by a pause. After a brief spasm of energy, he found himself in the middle of the street, where he stopped dead, swaying on his feet, hesitating between a fall and a fresh burst of activity. Suddenly he made off in a new direction. He ran up against a house, and clung to the wall as if to force his way through it. Then, with a start, he turned round, and gazed in front of him, open-mouthed, his eyes blinking in the sun. With a movement of the hips, he jerked his back away from the wall and continued on his way. A small yellow dog, a half-starved mongrel, followed him barking, halting when he halted, and moving when he moved.

'Look,' said Marambot, 'there 's one of Madame Husson's Rose-kings.'

I was puzzled by this remark. 'One of Madame Husson's Rose-kings? What do you mean by that?'

The doctor burst out laughing. 'Oh, it 's only a local name for drunkards. It 's derived from an old story which has now become legendary, although every detail of it is true.'

'Is it an amusing story?'

'Very amusing indeed.'

'Then let me hear it.'

'Delighted. Once there lived in this town an old lady called Madame Husson, very virtuous herself, and a patron of virtue in others. I must tell you that I am giving you the real names and not fictitious ones. Madame Husson devoted herself to good works, relieving the poor and encouraging the deserving. She was short, brisk of movement, and adorned with a black silk wig. Her manners were ceremoniously polite, and she was on excellent terms with God, as represented by Abbé Malou. She had a deep instinctive horror of vice and especially of that form of vice to which the Church refers as the lusts of the flesh. Irregularities before marriage put her beside herself, and exasperated her almost to fury. Now about this time, it was the custom round about Paris to award a chaplet of roses to girls distinguished for good behaviour, and Madame Husson took it into her head to have a Rose-queen at Gisors.

'So she laid the matter before Abbé Malou, who at once drew up a list of candidates. But Madame Husson had a maid, an old retainer called Françoise, who was as uncompromising as her mistress. As soon as the priest left the house, Madame Husson sent for her maid.

'"Look, Françoise," she said, "these are the girls whom the *curé* suggests for the prize of virtue. Try to find out what is said about them in the neighbourhood."

'Françoise set to work. She collected all the gossip, all the tales, all the tittle-tattle and scandal of the town. Lest the details should escape her memory, she wrote them down among her accounts in her marketing book, which she presented every morning to her mistress. After adjusting her spectacles on her narrow nose, Madame Husson would read as follows:

Bread	.	.	four sous
Milk	.	.	two sous
Butter	.	.	eight sous

Last year Malvina Levesque misconducted herself with Mathurin Poilu.

Leg of mutton	.	twenty-five sous
Salt	.	one sou

Madame Onésime, the laundress, met Rosalie Vatinel with Césaire Piénoir in the Riboudet wood at dusk on 20th July.

Radishes	.	one sou
Vinegar	.	two sous
Salts of sorrel	.	two sous

As far as one knows, Joséphine Durdent has never made a slip. At the same time, she corresponds with young Oportun, who is in service at Rouen, and who has sent her a present of a bonnet by diligence.

'Not one emerged spotless from this rigorous inquisition. Françoise questioned every one, the neighbours, the tradesmen, the schoolmaster, the school sisters, and accepted even the most insignificant rumours. No girl on earth entirely escapes the tattling tongues of gossips. In the whole neighbourhood not a single young woman could be found whom the breath of scandal had not touched. But Madame Husson insisted that, like Caesar's wife, the Rose-queen of Gisors should be above suspicion. Confronted with her maid's marketing book, she was plunged into the depths of dismay, disappointment, and despair.

'The adjacent villages were included in the quest, but the

result was the same. The mayor was consulted: his candidates
failed too. Nor, in spite of the definiteness of his professional
guarantees, were those of Dr. Barbesol more fortunate.

'At last one morning Françoise came home from some errand
and said to her mistress:

'"To tell the truth, ma'am, if you are determined to crown
someone, the only fit person in the district is Isidore."

'Madame Husson remained deep in thought. She knew all
about Isidore. He was the son of Virginie, who kept a greengrocer's shop. His chastity was proverbial, and had been for
several years a source of joy to Gisors. It was a topic of hilarious
conversation, and afforded endless amusement to the girls, who
delighted in teasing him. He was over twenty years of age, tall,
ungainly, slow and timid. He helped his mother in her shop,
and sat all day long in a chair before the door, sorting out fruit
or vegetables. He was possessed by a morbid terror of petticoats, which caused him to lower his eyes as soon as a customer
smiled at him, and this notorious bashfulness made him the butt
of every giddy girl in the town. He was so quick to blush at
loose words, ribald jests, and unseemly allusions, that Dr.
Barbesol nicknamed him the thermometer of modesty. Was
he ignorant, or was he not? some of the neighbours slyly
wondered. What was the cause of this emotion that so perturbed the son of Virginie, the greengrocer's widow? Was it a
mere conjecture concerning shameful and unknown mysteries,
or repugnance to the degrading embraces ordained by love?
The street boys would run past his shop, shouting frank ob-
scenities at him to make him lower his eyes. The girls would
amuse themselves by walking up and down in front of him,
indulging in indelicate jokes which drove him indoors. The
boldest of them were openly provocative, mockingly offering
him assignations, and making the most outrageous suggestions.

'No wonder Madame Husson was pensive. Undoubtedly,
Isidore was an instance of exceptional, conspicuous, impregnable
virtue. No one, not the most sceptical, the most incredulous of
mankind, could venture to suspect Isidore of the smallest in-
fringement of any moral law whatever. He had not so much
as been seen in a café, or in the streets of an evening. He always
went to bed at eight and rose at four. He was perfection; a
pearl of purity.

'And yet Madame Husson still wavered. The idea of

substituting a Rose-king for a Rose-queen perplexed and troubled her, and she made up her mind to consult Abbé Malou.

'"What do you wish to reward, Madame Husson? Virtue, I take it, virtue pure and simple. In that case, what does it matter to you whether its exponent be male of female? Virtue is eternal, and knows neither country nor sex. Virtue is simply virtue."

'Thus encouraged, Madame Husson paid a visit to the mayor, who entirely concurred.

'"We'll have an impressive ceremony," he said, "and another year, if we find a woman as deserving as Isidore, we will award the chaplet to a woman. We shall certainly be setting an admirable example to Nanterre. We mustn't be exclusive; let us welcome merit wherever we find it."

'When Isidore received the intimation, he blushed deeply, and seemed pleased.

'The coronation was fixed for 15th August, the fête of the Virgin Mary and of the Emperor Napoleon. The municipality were determined to invest the function with special brilliancy, and a platform had been erected on Les Couronneaux, a delightful extension of the ramparts of the old fortress, where I am just going to take you. As a result of a natural reaction in the popular mind, Isidore's virtue, hitherto held in derision, had suddenly become a respectable and enviable quality, since it was about to secure for him five hundred francs, a savings bank book, oceans of consideration, and of glory enough and to spare. The girls began to regret their levity, their laughter, their free behaviour, and Isidore, although he remained modest and timid, wore a little air of complacency, which revealed his secret gratification.

'By the evening of 14th August, the whole of the Rue Dauphine was beflagged. The route which the procession was to follow was strewn with flowers as for Corpus Christi Day, and the National Guard paraded under its commanding officer, Major Desbarres. This officer was an old stalwart of the Grand Army, and, side by side with the case that contained his Croix d'Honneur, bestowed by the emperor in person, he was wont proudly to exhibit a Cossack's beard, severed from its owner's chin by one stroke of the major's sabre, on the retreat from Russia. And, what is more, the corps he commanded was a crack corps, famous throughout the province. His company of

Gisors grenadiers used to be summoned to grace every function of note within a radius of fifteen or twenty miles. The story goes that when Louis-Philippe was reviewing the Eure militia, he halted in admiration before the Gisors company, and exclaimed:

'"Oh, who are these fine grenadiers?"

'"They are from Gisors," replied the general.

'"I ought to have guessed," murmured His Majesty.

'So Major Desbarres and his men, with a band at their head, marched to Virginie's shop to fetch Isidore. When a few bars of music had been played under his windows, the Rose-king himself appeared on the threshold. He was dressed from head to foot in white duck, and wore a straw hat, with a little bunch of orange blossom for a rosette. The question of his dress had greatly perplexed Madame Husson, who could not decide between the black coat worn by boys at their first communion and a complete suit of white. Françoise, her counsellor, however, had turned the balance in favour of the white suit, pointing out that the Rose-king would look like a swan. Behind him followed Madame Husson, his proud patroness and sponsor. As they emerged from the house, she took his arm, while the mayor placed himself on the Rose-king's left. The drums beat. Major Desbarres shouted: "Present arms!" The procession set out for the church through vast crowds, gathered together from all the neighbouring townships. After a short service and a touching address from Abbé Malou, the procession made its way to Les Couronneaux, where a banquet was served in a marquee.

'Before the guests seated themselves, the mayor made an oration. I can repeat it to you word for word. It was such a splendid speech that I learned it off by heart.

'"Young man, Madame Husson, a woman of substance, beloved by the poor, respected by the rich, to whom, on behalf of the whole neighbourhood, I tender thanks, has had the happy and beneficent thought of instituting in this town a prize for virtue, which will be of priceless encouragement to the population of this beautiful district. You, young man, are the first to wear the crown of this dynasty of virtue and chastity. Your name will head the list of those found worthy. I would impress upon you that all the rest of your life to your dying day must be in accordance with the promise of this auspicious beginning. To-day, in the presence of this noble woman who rewards your conduct, in the presence of these soldier citizens who have taken up their arms in your honour, in the presence of this deeply moved throng, gathered here to acclaim you, or rather, in your person to acclaim virtue, you enter into a solemn engagement with your town, with all of us, to maintain until the end of your days the admirable example of your youthful purity. Never forget, young man, that you are the first seed sown upon this field of our hopes. Bring forth the fruits we have a right to expect of you.'

'The mayor took three steps forward and clasped the sobbing Isidore to his bosom. The Rose-king wept, he hardly knew why. He was surging with confused emotions, in which joy and pride were mingled.

'Then the mayor placed in one of Isidore's hands a silken purse. There was gold in it, clinking gold, five hundred francs in gold. In his other hand he placed a savings bank book. And in a solemn voice he exclaimed:

'"All homage, glory, and wealth to virtue!"

'Major Desbarres roared: "Bravo!" The grenadiers shouted, the crowd clapped their hands. It was Madame Husson's turn to dry her eyes.

'After this, the guests seated themselves at the banqueting table.

'It was a magnificent affair of interminable length. Dish followed dish. Glasses of yellow cider and red wine stood fraternally side by side, to be presently mingled in the systems of the revellers. The clatter of plates, the sound of voices, the discreet music of the band, were all merged in a deep unceasing clamour, which lost itself in the blue sky where the swallows were circling. Now and then, as she chatted to Abbé Malou, Madame Husson would readjust her black silk wig, which kept slipping over one ear. The mayor was excitedly talking politics to Major Desbarres. As for Isidore, he was eating and he was drinking as he had never eaten and drunk in his life before. He had two helpings of everything. He was experiencing for the first time the delight of filling himself with good things, which were alike pleasant to the taste and comforting to the inner man. He had dexterously loosened his waistband, which was becoming too tight under the increasing expansion beneath it. He only stopped eating in order to raise his glass to his lips, and he kept it there as long as possible, enjoying the flavour at his leisure.

He sat in silence, feeling a little guilty because of a drop of wine that had fallen on his white coat.

'Later on, many toasts were proposed, and were enthusiastically honoured. Evening approached. The banquet had lasted ever since noon. Above the valley floated delicate wisps of milk-white mist, the filmy vesture in which night swathes brooks and meadows. The sun touched the horizon. From the misty pastures came the distant lowing of cows. It was all over. The party made their way back to Gisors. The procession, now disbanded, walked at its ease. Madame Husson, with her arm in Isidore's, was bestowing on her protégé much excellent and earnest advice. They halted at the greengrocer's door, and left the Rose-king at his mother's house.

'But his mother was still away. Her family had invited her to another function in honour of her son, and after following the procession to the marquee where the banquet was held she had gone to lunch with her sister. Isidore remained alone in the shop in the deepening dusk. His head was whirling with his triumph and with the wine he had drunk. He took a chair and looked about him. The close air of the room was heavy with the strong vegetable odours of carrots, cabbages, and onions, mingled with the sweet, penetrating smell of strawberries, and the delicate, elusive fragrance of a basket of peaches. The Rose-king seized a peach, and took a large bite out of it, although his skin was as tight as a drum. Then, utterly beside himself with joy, he suddenly broke into a dance. Something jingled inside his coat.

'In surprise he plunged his hands into his pockets, and drew out the five hundred francs, which, in his intoxication, he had forgotten. Five hundred francs! Why, it was a fortune! He poured the louis out on the counter, then, with a slow, caressing gesture of his big, flat palm, he spread them out so that he could see them all simultaneously. There were twenty-five of them, twenty-five round gold coins, every one of them gold! They shone out on the wooden counter through the deep gloom, and he counted them over and over again, touching each coin with his finger and muttering:

'"One, two, three, four, five—a hundred; six, seven, eight, nine, ten—two hundred." Then he returned them to the purse, which he stowed away again in his pocket.

'Who knows, who can tell, what grim struggle raged in the

Rose-king's soul between the powers of good and evil; with what headlong attacks, stratagems, and temptations Satan beset that timid and virgin heart; what suggestions, images, and desires the Evil One conjured up, to compass the ruin of that elect soul? Madame Husson's paragon seized his hat, the very hat that still bore the little sprig of orange blossom. Escaping from the house by the little lane at the back, he disappeared into the night.

'When Virginie heard that her son had returned, she went home without delay, only to find the house empty. At first she waited without anxiety. But when a quarter of an hour had elapsed she began to make inquiries.

'The neighbours in the Rue Dauphine had seen Isidore enter the house, but had not seen him emerge. A search was made for him; he was, however, nowhere to be found. In her distress, Virginie hurried to the town hall. The mayor could give her no information, except that he had himself accompanied the Rose-king to his door. When the news of her protégé's disappearance reached Madame Husson she was already in bed. Immediately she rose and resumed her wig, and went to see Virginie. Virginie, with the rapid emotion of an uncultured mind, was sitting among her cabbages, carrots, and onions, dissolved in tears.

'Some accident must have happened to him. But what could it be? Major Desbarres ordered the constabulary to patrol the town. On the road to Pontoise, the little bunch of orange blossom was picked up. It was placed upon the table around which the authorities were deliberating. The Rose-king must have fallen a victim of some plot, some jealous machinations. But how, by what means, and with what motives, had this innocent been spirited away?

'Weary with their search, the authorities went to bed. Virginie alone spent the night watching and weeping.

'The next morning, however, on the return of the stage coach from Paris, Gisors learnt to its amazement that its Rose-king had stopped the coach some two hundred yards from the town, had taken a seat, paid for it with a louis, for which he had received change, and eventually had calmly alighted in the heart of the great city.

'The consternation was general. Letters were exchanged between the mayor of Gisors and the head of the Paris police, but led to no discovery.

'Day followed day, until a whole week had elapsed. At last,

Dr. Barbesol, out early one morning, saw a man in a suit of grey material, sitting in a doorway, fast asleep, with his head against the wall. He went up to him, and recognized Isidore. His attempts to wake him were without success. The ex-Rose-king was plunged in a deep, impenetrable, disquieting slumber. The doctor, in alarm, went for help to carry the young man to Boncheval's dispensary. When he was lifted from the ground, an empty bottle was found concealed beneath him, and after he had sniffed it, the doctor announced that it had contained brandy. It was a useful indication of the remedies to be employed. They were successful. Isidore was drunk, dead drunk, and utterly degraded by a whole week of debauchery. He was not fit to be touched by a rag-picker. Nothing was left of his immaculate suit of white duck but a mass of rags, stained grey and yellow, greasy, muddy, tattered, and vile. He stank of the gutter and of every form of degradation.

'He was washed and lectured and locked up, and for four days he did not stir from the house. He seemed to be penitent and ashamed. There was no trace of the purse with the five hundred francs, nor of his savings bank book, nor of his silver watch, a sacred legacy from his father the greengrocer.

'On the fifth day he ventured into the Rue Dauphine. Pursued by inquisitive glances, he slunk along close to the houses, with hanging head and furtive eyes. He vanished on the outskirts of the town in the direction of the valley. Two hours later he reappeared, chuckling to himself, and reeling against the walls. He was drunk, hopelessly drunk.

'He was incorrigible. His mother turned him out of the house, and he became a carter and carted coal for the firm of Pougrisel, which is still in existence.

'He gained such a reputation for drunkenness that even at Évreux people talked of Madame Husson's Rose-king, and all the drunkards in this neighbourhood have that nickname given to them. A good deed is never wasted.'

·   ·   ·   ·   ·

Dr. Marambot rubbed his hands together as he ended his story.

'Did you know the Rose-king personally?' I asked.

'Yes, I had the honour of closing his eyes.'

'What did he die of?'

'Why, a fit of delirium tremens, to be sure.'

We were close to the old fortress, a heap of ruined walls, still dominated by the massive tower of St. Thomas of Canterbury and by the so-called Prisoner's Keep.

Marambot told the story of the prisoner who, with the help of a nail, covered the walls of his cell with sculpture, following the course of the sun, as it filtered through the narrow slit of a loophole.

Next I learned that Clotaire II had bestowed the patrimony of Gisors upon his cousin, St. Romain, Bishop of Rouen; that after the Treaty of St. Clair-sur-Epte, Gisors had ceased to be the capital of the whole of the Vexin; that the town, being the strategical key to the whole of this region of France, had, in consequence of this distinction, been captured and recaptured times without number. By order of William Rufus, the celebrated engineer, Robert de Bellesme, constructed a powerful fortress, which was attacked later by Louis the Fat, then by the Norman barons: defended by Robert de Candos, surrendered by Geoffrey Plantagenet to Louis the Fat, recaptured by the English through the treachery of the Knights Templars; its possession contested by Philip Augustus and Richard Cœur de Lion; burnt by Edward III of England, who failed to take the castle; seized anew by the English in 1419, surrendered later to Charles VII by Richard of Marbury, taken by the Duke of Calabria, held by the League, inhabited by Henry IV, and so forth and so forth.

Marambot grew almost eloquent. He remarked again with conviction:

'What scoundrels the English are! And what drunkards, my dear fellow, Rose-kings every one of them, the hypocrites!'

After a pause he pointed to the slender stream, gleaming among the meadows.

'Did you know that Henry Monnier was one of the most ardent fishermen on the banks of the Epte?'

'No, I didn't know.'

'And, Bouffé, my dear fellow, Bouffé made stained glass here.'

'You don't say so!'

'Why, to be sure! Your ignorance is simply incredible.'

THE HOUSE OF MADAME TELLIER
(*La Maison Tellier*)

IT was the custom to drop in at Madame Tellier's house every evening about eleven o'clock, just as if it were a café. Its seven or eight regular customers never varied. They were none of them of dissipated habits; they were just respectable tradesmen and young men from the town. They would sip their chartreuse and tease the girls a little or have a quiet chat with the proprietress, whom they always treated with respect. And they all went home before midnight, except the younger men, who sometimes stayed on. The house had a certain homeliness. It was quite a small building, painted yellow, and it stood at the corner of a street behind the church of Saint-Étienne. The windows looked out upon the dock, which was full of ships unloading, and on the great salt marsh with the hill of La Vierge and its old grey chapel in the background. The proprietress came of a respectable family of peasants in the department of Eure, and she had adopted her particular profession just as she would have adopted that of milliner or draper. In towns prostitution is regarded with violent and deep-rooted prejudice, but there is no such feeling against it in the country parts of Normandy.

'It 's a paying trade,' says the peasant, and he sends his daughter to run a harem, just as if he were sending her to conduct a boarding-school for young ladies.

This house of Madame Tellier's came to her as a legacy from an old uncle. Formerly innkeepers near Yvetot, Monsieur and Madame Tellier had sold out at once, expecting higher profits from the business at Fécamp, and one fine morning they had arrived there and had taken over the management of the concern, which had been languishing in the absence of its owners. They were a worthy couple and had speedily won the affections both of their employees and their neighbours. Two years later the husband died of apoplexy. His new profession had maintained him in such comfort and inactivity that he had grown extremely stout, and had fallen a victim to the exuberance of his health.

Since she had been a widow, Madame Tellier had been sighed for in vain by all her customers. She had a reputation for unassailable virtue, and even her young women had never succeeded in catching her out. She was tall and plump and prepossessing. In her dimly lighted, ill-ventilated house, her complexion had lost its freshness and glistened as if her face had a coating of oil varnish. She wore a scanty false front of fluffy curls, which gave her a juvenile look contrasting oddly with the maturity of her figure. She was invariably cheerful; the expression on her face was frank and open, and she enjoyed a joke, but always with the shade of reserve which she yet retained in spite of her new profession. Coarse language still had the effect of shocking her slightly, and once, when an ill-bred youth called her establishment by its proper name, she was both hurt and indignant. In short, she possessed natural delicacy, and although she treated her young women as friends, she was fond of remarking that they were not out of the same basket as herself. Sometimes on a week-day she would hire a carriage and take some of her flock for an airing, and they would frisk about on the grassy bank of the little river which flows through the Valmont grounds. They behaved like truant schoolgirls, rushing about and playing childish games with all the rapture of nuns released from the cloister, intoxicated with fresh air. Seated on the grass they ate delicacies from the pork butcher's and drank cider, and at nightfall they would return home deliciously weary and in a mood of tender sentimentality. In the carriage they threw their arms round Madame Tellier and hugged her, as if she were an indulgent mother overflowing with kindness and good will.

The house possessed two entrances. At the corner there was a gloomy kind of tavern, which was opened in the evening for the benefit of sailors and working men. Two of the young women engaged in the traffic peculiar to the establishment were told off to minister to the needs of this section of Madame Tellier's customers. Aided by Frédéric the waiter, a short, fair, beardless youth, as strong as an ox, they brought round half-pints of wine and pots of beer to all the rickety marble-topped tables, and perching themselves on their customers' knees with their arms round their necks, they encouraged them to drink.

The three other ladies (there were only five in all) formed a sort of aristocracy and were reserved for the quality on the first floor, except on occasions when the first floor happened to be deserted and there was a rush of work downstairs.   The drawing-room, reserved for the respectable townsmen, was known as the hall of Jupiter.   On its blue wallpaper hung a large picture representing Leda and the Swan.   From these precincts led a winding staircase with a narrow, inconspicuous door at the foot, opening on to the street.   All night long, behind a trellis above the lintel, burned a small lantern, such as one still sees, here and there, burning at the feet of an image of the Virgin in a niche in the wall.

The house was old and damp, and a slight smell of mould hung about it.   Now and then a whiff of eau-de-Cologne was wafted along the passages, and at times, when a door had been left ajar downstairs, the coarse shouts of the revellers on the ground floor would echo through the house like a clap of thunder, and at this the faces of the gentlemen on the first floor would exhibit an expression of uneasy disgust.

Madame Tellier, who was on friendly terms with all her customers, always presided in the drawing-room and took a lively interest in all the gossip of the town which they retailed to her.   Her sensible conversation was a pleasant change from the desultory chatter of the three young women, and a relief, too, from the suggestive witticisms of these portly citizens whose nightly dissipation took the mild and decorous form of having a liqueur in doubtful society.

The names of the three houris attending on the first floor were Fernande, Raphaële and Rackety Rosa.   As the staff was limited in numbers, each member had been carefully selected as a particular sample, a characteristic type of feminine beauty, so that, in a general way at least, every client might find here the realization of his ideal.

Fernande's type was that of the handsome, strapping, pink and white country lass.   She was buxom, ran somewhat to fat, and had permanent freckles; her head was scantily covered with short, bleached hair, that looked like combed-out tow.

Raphaële was a native of Marseilles, and had walked the streets of various seaport towns.   Thin, with high cheek-bones plastered with rouge, and black oily hair arranged in ringlets on her fore-head, she filled the indispensable role of the handsome Jewess. Her eyes would have been fine, had it not been for a film which disfigured the right one.   Her hooked nose drooped above a heavy jaw, and two new upper teeth contrasted strangely with those in the lower row, to which age had lent the dark hues of old wood.

Rackety Rosa was a small, round dumpling of a creature, all stomach, and with diminutive legs. From morning till evening, in a rasping voice, she sang songs that were alternately senti-mental and indelicate; she was always embarking upon inter-minable and pointless stories, and she never stopped talking except to eat, and never stopped eating except to talk. She was never still, and in spite of her bulk and her stumpy legs, she was as active as a squirrel. Her laughter, a cataract of piercing shrieks, rang through the house, issuing incessantly from bed-room, attic or café, with meaningless reiteration.

The two young women on duty downstairs were Louise, nicknamed Cocote, and Flora, known as the See-saw, because of a slight limp. The one was arrayed as Liberty with a tri-colour sash; the other was supposed to be a Spanish girl, with copper sequins dancing in her carroty hair at each uneven step. They looked like kitchen-maids rigged out for a masquerade. Typical barmaids, they were just like any other women of the working class, neither handsomer nor homelier. In the harbour they were known as the two Pumps.

Thanks to Madame Tellier's tact and good humour, the peace was seldom broken between these five young women, in spite of their mutual jealousy. Her establishment, being the only one of its kind in the little town, did a steady trade. Its mistress had succeeded in investing it with such an air of propriety, she herself was so agreeable and obliging and her kindness of heart so well known, that she enjoyed a certain esteem. Her regular customers went out of their way to please her and plumed them-selves on any special mark of her favour. If two of them happened to meet in the course of the day's work, they would say: 'See you this evening in the usual place,' as others might have said: 'I suppose you'll be at the café after dinner.'

In short, Madame Tellier's had become quite an institution and there was seldom a member missing from the evening gathering.

Now one evening, towards the end of May, the first arrival, Monsieur Poulin the wood-merchant, ex-mayor of Fécamp, found the door locked and the little lantern behind the trellis extinguished. No sound issued from the house, which was silent as the grave. He knocked at the door, tentatively at first, then more vigorously, but there was no reply. Slowly he retraced his steps, and as he reached the market square he met Monsieur Duvert, the shipowner, who was bound for the same place. They made their way together, but with the same result. Suddenly they were alarmed by a violent outburst of noise close at hand, and looking round the corner of the house they saw a crowd of English and French sailors battering with their fists on the closed shutters of the café. Afraid of being compromised, the two were beating a retreat, when they were stopped by a whispered 'Hist!' It was Monsieur Tournevau, the fish-curer, who had recognized them. They explained the situation, which was all the more distressing for Monsieur Tournevau, because, being a married man with a family and under strict supervision, he could only venture there on Saturday nights. And as this happened to be his one evening, he found himself doomed to another week of deprivation.

The three men turned in the direction of the quay. On the way they fell in with young Monsieur Philippe, the banker's son, and Monsieur Pimpesse, the tax-collector, both of them members of the fraternity. They strolled back together along the Rue aux Juifs, with the idea of making one last attempt. But the infuriated sailors were now laying siege to the house, shouting and flinging stones. The first-floor customers beat an expeditious retreat and began roaming about the streets. Presently they met Monsieur Dupuis, the insurance agent, and later on Monsieur Vasse, the arbitrator, and they all set off for a long walk. First they went down to the jetty. They sat down in a row on the granite parapet and watched the waves breaking. In the darkness the foam on the crests of the waves flashed white for a moment, then disappeared from sight. The monotonous roar of the sea dashing against the rocks reverberated through the night, echoing along the whole length of the cliff. The disappointed revellers remained there some little time. At last Monsieur Tournevau remarked:

'I don't call this very cheerful.'

'Nor do I,' replied Monsieur Pimpesse, and they slowly resumed their walk.

They went along the Rue Sous-le-bois, which skirts the hill; returning by the plank bridge over the salt marsh, they passed near the railway line and came out again on the market square. At this point a sudden difference of opinion arose between

Monsieur Pimpesse, the tax-collector, and Monsieur Tournevau, the fish-curer, about a certain edible fungus, which one of them claimed to have found in the neighbourhood. Their disappointment had ruffled their tempers so completely that they might have come to blows, had not the others intervened. Monsieur Pimpesse went off in a rage, and immediately a fresh dispute arose between Monsieur Poulin, the ex-mayor, and Monsieur Dupuis, the insurance agent, about the tax-collector's emoluments and his possible perquisites. Insults were flying on either side, when suddenly with a prodigious uproar, the mob of sailors, who were tired of waiting outside closed doors, burst into the square. Two and two, and arm in arm, in a long procession, they swept onwards, yelling and shouting. The little group of townsmen shrank into a doorway, while the howling rabble disappeared in the direction of the abbey. The noise continued long after they were out of sight, gradually dying away like a receding thunderstorm till peace was restored.

Still nursing their wrath, Monsieur Poulin and Monsieur Dupuis went off in different directions without bidding each other good night. The other four continued their walk, their steps turning instinctively in the direction of Madame Tellier's house. But it remained closed, silent and impenetrable. A single drunken man, with calm persistency, kept knocking gently on the front door of the café. Every now and then he desisted and called cautiously for Frédéric the waiter. Receiving no reply, he sat down on the doorstep to await events. The four friends were about to withdraw when the rowdy gang of seamen reappeared at the end of the street, the Frenchmen bawling the *Marseillaise*, the Englishmen *Rule Britannia*. The peaceful citizens flattened themselves against the walls, and the ruffianly crew swept on towards the quay, where a fray ensued between the sailors of the two nations, in which an Englishman had his arm broken and a Frenchman his nose slit.

By this time the drunkard on the doorstep was weeping tipsily like a peevish child. At last the little group of townsmen dispersed, and gradually peace descended again upon the distracted town. Now and then the sound of voices would break out anew, only to die away in the distance.

But one man still forlornly roamed the streets; it was Monsieur Tournevau the fish-curer, in despair at the prospect of having to wait another week. The situation baffled him, but he still continued to cherish vague hopes. He felt exasperated with the police for closing an establishment of public utility, which was under its own protection and supervision. He retraced his steps and as he scanned the walls of Madame Tellier's house, seeking some solution to the problem, his eyes fell on a placard posted up on the shutter. Hurriedly striking a wax vesta he read the following words, scrawled in a large irregular hand:

'Closed on account of a First Communion.'

Realizing that this was indeed final, he turned away.

The drunken man had fallen asleep and was lying at full length across the inhospitable threshold.

The next day all the members of the coterie found some pretext or other for passing down that particular street, each carrying documents under his arm as an excuse. With furtive glances they read the mysterious announcement:

'Closed on account of a First Communion.'

II

The explanation was as follows. Madame Tellier had a brother who was a carpenter in their native village, Virville-en-Eure. In the days when she still kept the inn at Yvetot, she had stood sponsor to her brother's daughter and had bestowed upon her godchild the name of Constance—Constance Rivet, she herself being a Rivet on the father's side. The carpenter, who was aware that his sister was doing well, never lost touch with her, although they seldom met, both being tied to their respective businesses and also living at some distance from each other. But the little girl was nearly twelve now, and was to make her First Communion that year, so he seized this opportunity for renewing relations and wrote to his sister that he was counting on her to be present at the celebration. The grandparents being dead, she felt that she could not fail her goddaughter. So she accepted the invitation. Madame Tellier was childless, and Joseph, her brother, hoped to induce her, by assiduous attentions, to make a will in his daughter's favour.

He had no delicate scruples with regard to his sister's profession. Besides, no one in the village knew anything about it. When she was mentioned, she was described as residing at Fécamp, and from this remark it was assumed that she possessed a sufficient income. The distance between Fécamp and Virville

is at least fifty miles, and to a peasant a land journey of fifty
miles is a far more serious proposition than an ocean voyage to
a civilized person. The inhabitants of Virville had never been
farther than Rouen, and there was nothing to attract the inhabitants of Fécamp in a little village of five hundred houses,
buried in the depths of the country and belonging to a different
department. In short, the secret was well kept.

But as the day of the ceremony drew near, Madame Tellier
was confronted with a serious difficulty. She had no one to act
as deputy and she did not care to leave her establishment to its
own devices even for a single day. The smouldering jealousies
that existed between the ladies of the first floor and those of the
café would undoubtedly burst into open flame. Frédéric would
certainly get drunk, and when he was drunk he would lay a man
out for a look or a word. In the end she decided to take her
entire household with her, with the exception of the waiter, to
whom she gave two days' leave.

She made this proposal to her brother, who, far from objecting,
offered to put up the whole party for a night. Accordingly
Saturday morning saw Madame Tellier and her young women
embark on their journey in a second-class carriage on the eight
o'clock express.

As far as Beuzeville they had the carriage to themselves, and
chattered like magpies. At Beuzeville, however, a peasant and
his wife joined them. The old husband wore a blue blouse with
pleated collar and wide sleeves drawn in at the wrists and
trimmed with narrow white embroidery. His antiquated tall
hat had a brownish nap, which looked as if it had been brushed
the wrong way. One hand clutched a huge green umbrella, the
other an enormous basket, from which three frightened ducks
poked out their heads. The wife, who sat bolt upright in her
rustic dress, had a face like a hen and a nose resembling a beak.
Petrified with embarrassment at finding herself in such fine
company, she sat opposite her good man and did not venture
to stir.

The carriage certainly boasted a dazzling array of brilliant
colours. Madame Tellier, all in blue silk from head to foot, had
draped over her shoulders a French shawl of imitation cashmere
of the most blinding and violent red. Fernande was panting
in a tartan bodice into which she had been laced by the united
efforts of her companions. Forced upwards into two round

bosses, her lax bosom kept surging and rippling as if it were fluid beneath the gown that covered it. Raphaële, in a be-feathered hat like a nest full of birds, wore a mauve creation spangled with gold. It had a suggestion of the East, which suited her Jewish cast of countenance. Rackety Rosa, in a pink shirt with deep flounces, reminded one of an unwholesomely fat child or a corpulent dwarf. The two Pumps looked as if their weird garments had been made out of old window curtains of Restoration days, with floral patterns all over them.

When the strangers got in, the ladies composed their faces and began to make polite conversation in order to produce a favourable impression. But at Bolbec, a gentleman with fair whiskers, rings, and a gold watch-chain, entered the carriage and placed in the rack overhead various parcels wrapped in American cloth. He had a facetious and jovial air. Bowing and smiling, he said airily:

'These ladies are changing their garrison, I presume?'

This question covered the whole party with confusion. Madame Tellier, however, recovered herself, and stood up for the honour of her flock.

'You might at least be civil,' she replied sharply.

He hastened to apologize.

'I beg your pardon; I meant to say their convent.'

Unable to think of a suitable retort, or mollified by this amendment, Madame Tellier pursed up her lips and made him a dignified bow. After this, the gentleman, who had seated himself between Rosa and the old peasant, began winking at the three ducks who were thrusting their heads out of the big basket. When he thought he had captured the attention of his audience, he began to tickle the ducks under the beak, and to address to them facetious remarks, which were intended to poke fun at his companions.

'And so we 've left our little pond, quack, quack, quack, for our little spit.'

The unhappy creatures twisted and turned in their efforts to avoid his teasing hands, and struggled frantically to escape from their wicker prison. Suddenly all three of them uttered a heart-rending cry of distress:

'Quack, quack, quack!'

At this all the women burst out laughing, and they suddenly began to take an extravagant interest in the ducks, elbowing one

another in their efforts to bend down and look at them, while
the gentleman surpassed himself in fascinations, witticisms, and
suggestive jokes.

Rosa was in her element.   Leaning across her neighbour's
legs, she kissed the three ducks on the beak.   Then all the other
women had to kiss them, too, and the gentleman took the ladies
on his knees, dandled them and pinched them, and all at once
began to address them with the utmost familiarity.

The peasant and his wife were even more horrified than their
birds.   They sat rolling their eyes wildly, not venturing to stir
and without so much as a smile or a quiver on their wrinkled
old faces.

The gentleman proved to be a commercial traveller.   Jestingly
he offered to sell the ladies braces, and seizing one of his parcels,
he undid it.   This, however, was merely a trick, for the parcel
contained garters.   There were garters in all shades of silk, blue,
pink, red, mauve, violet, and flame-coloured, with metal buckles
formed by two gilt Cupids interlaced.   The ladies shrieked
with joy.   Then, with the gravity natural to every woman
when considering an article of dress, they began to examine the
samples.   Exchanging glances and whispers, they took counsel
with one another, while Madame Tellier longingly handled a
pair of orange garters, broader and more impressive than the
others, and worthy of her responsible position.

The gentleman waited; an idea had occurred to him.

'Now, my pretty dears,' he said, 'you must try them on.'

This suggestion provoked a storm of protests.   The ladies
tucked their skirts round their legs, as if in fear of some im-
propriety.   But he quietly bided his time.

'I see you don't want them,' he remarked.   'I may as well
pack them up again.'   Then he added slyly:

'Any lady who tries them on shall have whichever pair she
likes.'

But they would not accept his offer, and sat bolt upright, very
much on their dignity.   The two Pumps, however, appeared so
deeply distressed that he repeated his proposal.   Flora especially,
who was in torments of desire, was evidently wavering.

'Come, my dear,' he urged her, 'pluck up your courage.
Doesn't this mauve pair go well with your dress?'

She could resist no longer.   Raising her skirt, she revealed a
leg, as stout as a milkmaid's, in a coarse, ill-fitting stocking.

The commercial gentleman stooped down and clasped the garter below the knee at first, and then above it. Then he tickled the young woman gently, making her jump and utter little shrieks. Finally he presented her with the lilac garters.

'Whose turn next?' he inquired.

'Mine! Mine!' they exclaimed with one accord.

He began with Rackety Rosa, who displayed a round, shapeless limb without even a hint of an ankle—'a leg like a sausage,' as Raphaële remarked. Fernande, on the other hand, was complimented by the commercial traveller on her stalwart pillars, which impressed him greatly. The fair Jewess's scraggy calves were less admired. Louise Cocote sportively threw her petticoats over the gentleman's head, and Madame Tellier had to intervene to put a stop to this unseemly buffoonery. Last of all Madame Tellier exhibited her own shapely Norman legs, firm and solid. With true French chivalry, he showed his surprise and admiration by taking off his hat to these superlative calves. Petrified with horror, the peasant and his wife watched the proceedings out of the corner of one eye. They looked so exactly like two hens that the whiskered gentleman jumped up from his seat and shouted 'Cock-a-doodle-doo!' in their faces, a sally which provoked a fresh outburst of hilarity.

At Motteville, the old couple got out with their basket, ducks, and umbrella. As they moved away, the woman was heard remarking to her husband:

'Another lot of hussies going off to that accursed Paris.'

At Rouen the facetious gentleman left them, after behaving so outrageously that Madame Tellier had to put him severely in his place. She pointed the moral:

'This will be a lesson to us not to talk to strangers.'

They changed at Oissel, and a station farther on they found Monsieur Joseph Rivet awaiting them with a large cart which was furnished with chairs and drawn by a white pony.

The carpenter politely kissed all the ladies and handed them into the vehicle. Three of the party sat on chairs at the back; Raphaële, Madame Tellier, and her brother occupied three chairs in front; while Rosa, for whom there was no seat, accommodated herself as best she could on the knees of the buxom Fernande. The cart set off. But it jolted so violently with the rough paces of the pony that the chairs began to dance about. With terrorstricken faces, their occupants were hurled into the air like Jackin-the-boxes and flung from side to side, while their cries of alarm were cut short every now and then by some unusually severe shock. The ladies clung to the sides of the cart, their hats dangling down their backs, or over their eyes, or on to their shoulders. The white pony trotted along, with his head poked forwards and his little hairless rat's tail straight out, except when he twitched it over his quarters. With one foot on the shaft and the other tucked under him and his elbows well up in the air, Joseph Rivet held the reins, and kept making guttural sounds to the pony, who pricked up his ears and stepped out faster.

On either side of the road the green landscape stretched away into the distance. Flowering rape, in sheets of undulating yellow, diffused far and wide its strong, wholesome odour, penetrating and sweet. In among the rye, which was already fairly tall, cornflowers raised their small deep-blue heads, tempting the women to pick them. Monsieur Rivet, however, refused to halt. Here and there were fields so thick with poppies that they looked as if soaked in blood. And through these plains, aglow with Nature's flowers, drove the cart with its bouquet of other flowers of still more garish hues. Drawn at a trot by the white pony, it vanished behind the tall trees sheltering some farm, to reappear beyond the screen of foliage, speeding through the sunshine and flaunting its dazzling bevy of women between the green and yellow crops, flecked with patches of red and blue.

One o'clock struck as they drew up at the door of the carpenter's house. The women, who had had nothing to eat since their departure, were faint with hunger and weariness. Madame Rivet hastened to help them out of the cart and kissed each of her guests as they alighted. As for her sister-in-law, whom she was anxious to monopolize, it seemed as if she would never stop embracing her.

Luncheon was served in the workshop, which had been cleared of its benches for the next day's banquet. An excellent omelette was followed by fried sausage, washed down with strong sparkling cider, and the meal restored every one's spirits. Rivet toasted his guests, while his wife dished up and waited on them, confidentially asking each of them if she had what she liked. The planks, which were stacked against the wall, and the heaps of shavings and chips in the corners of the room emitted that characteristic odour of planed wood, that resinous essence, which clings about a carpenter's shop and penetrates to the lungs.

The guests inquired for the little girl, but were told that she was at church and not expected home till the evening. The whole party then went for a walk in the village. Virville was a small hamlet, straddling the high road. On either side of its one street stood a row of a dozen houses, occupied by the local shop-keepers, the butcher, the grocer, the innkeeper, the carpenter, the cobbler, the baker. At one end of the street, in the middle of a small cemetery, stood the church, completely overshadowed by four great lime-trees that grew outside the porch. Built of dressed flint, it had no architectural merit, and was surmounted by a belfry built of slates. Beyond the church lay the open country, which was broken up by occasional clumps of trees, in which farms nestled.

Though still in his working clothes, Rivet had ceremoniously offered his sister his arm and escorted her majestically. Quite overcome by Raphaële's gold-spangled gown, Madame Rivet was walking between her and Fernande. Dumpy little Rosa brought up the rear with Louise Cocote and Flora, who was limping wearily.

All the villagers came to their doors, and the children stopped playing. Here and there a head in a muslin cap peeped out from behind a lifted curtain. One old woman, on crutches and almost blind, crossed herself, as at a religious procession, and every one cast long and lingering glances after all these fine ladies from the town, who had come such a distance for the First Communion of Joseph Rivet's little girl. A prodigious amount of glory was reflected upon the carpenter himself.

As they passed the church they heard the children singing, their shrill young voices raised in a canticle to heaven. Madame Tellier, however, dissuaded her companions from entering for fear of disturbing the little cherubs. After a stroll in the neighbourhood during which Joseph Rivet discoursed about the principal estates and their yield in crops and cattle, he escorted his flock home again and showed them their rooms.

The accommodation being strictly limited, the guests had been distributed in pairs in all the available rooms. Rivet him-self was to sleep on the shavings in the workshop, while his wife shared her bed with her sister-in-law. Fernande and Raphaële occupied the room next door, and Louise and Flora were quartered in the kitchen, where a mattress had been laid on the floor. Rosa was lodged by herself in a small dark cupboard over the stairs at the entrance to a narrow loft, where Constance was to sleep on the eve of her First Communion.

When the child came home, kisses were showered upon her. All the women were eager to fondle her, seeking an outlet for those affectionate demonstrations, that habit of caressing induced by their profession, which had impelled them to kiss the ducks in the railway carriage. Each in turn took her on her lap, played with her fair, silky hair, and hugged her in passionate transports of spontaneous affection. Steeped in pious emotion, absorbed in her own thoughts, with the seal of absolution upon her, the well-behaved child submitted patiently to their endearments.

It had been a trying day for the whole household, and they all went to bed directly after dinner. The infinite peace of the country, the pervasive and boundless silence reaching to the stars, enfolded the village in a hush that was almost religious. This calm that brooded over the landscape affected the nerves of these young women who were accustomed to noisy evenings in Madame Tellier's public rooms. They shuddered, not with cold, but with a sense of loneliness, which stole into their restless, troubled hearts. As soon as they had retired to bed, each clung to her companion, as if to protect herself from the influence of that profound repose that enveloped the earth. Rackety Rosa, all alone in her dark cupboard, and unaccustomed to sleeping with empty arms, was possessed by a vague and uncomfortable feeling of restlessness. As she tossed about, unable to get to sleep, she heard on the other side of the partition behind her head a low sound as of a child sobbing. She was frightened and called out softly, and a small tearful voice replied. It came from little Constance, who was used to sleeping in her mother's room and felt afraid all by herself in her narrow loft. Overjoyed, Rosa got up quietly to avoid disturbing any one, and took the child into her own warm bed. She hugged her in her arms, kissed her and fondled her, lavishing passionate endearments upon her, until her own agitation had subsided and she fell asleep. And the little communicant slept till morning, her head pillowed on the bare bosom of the prostitute.

As early as five o'clock, the ladies, who were accustomed to spend the whole morning in well-earned repose, were roused by the little church bell, vigorously ringing the Angelus. The villagers were already astir. Women were bustling from house to house, chattering volubly, some carrying, with the utmost care, short muslin frocks, starched as stiff as cardboard; others gigantic candles with gold-fringed, silk bows round the middle and hollowed-out places for the hands to grip. The sun was already high in a pure blue sky, with a tinge of pink still lingering on the horizon, the faint after-glow of dawn. Hens with their broods were already running about in front of the hen-houses, and here and there a black cock with a glossy neck raised his red comb, flapped his wings, and flung to the wind his clarion call, which was echoed by all the other cocks.

From the neighbouring villages carts were coming in, setting down at the different doors tall Norman peasant women in dark-coloured dresses with fichus crossed over the bosom and kept in place with old silver brooches. The men wore blue smocks over their new frock-coats or over their old coats of green cloth with the two long tails showing below.

After the horses had been put up in the stables, there was a double line of rustic vehicles of every description and every age drawn up along the whole length of the street: carts, chaises, gigs, wagonettes. Some were tilted forward; others had their tailboards resting on the ground and their shafts in the air.

The carpenter's house was humming like a beehive. The ladies in dressing-gowns and petticoats, their hair hanging down their backs in short, scanty locks that looked as if they had seen much service, were busy dressing little Constance. The child was standing perfectly still on the table, while Madame Tellier directed the operations of her flying squadron. They washed her, combed and dressed her hair, put on her frock, and, with the help of countless pins, arranged the pleats in the skirt, took in the bodice where it was too loose, and gave a dainty finish to the whole. When the last touches had been bestowed, they placed their victim in a chair, exhorting her not to move. Then, in great excitement, all the women ran off to attend to their own adornment.

The church bell began to ring again. Its plaintive tinkle rose in the air only to die away in the vaulted sky, like a feeble voice soon drowned in the infinite depths of ether.

The communicants emerged from their houses and made their way to the public building, containing the two schools and the municipal office, and standing at one end of the village, while the House of God occupied the other. Behind the children followed the parents in their Sunday best; they had the uncouth appearance and the clumsy movements of labourers bent with a lifetime of toil. The small girls were lost in clouds of tulle, as snowy as whipped cream, while the little boys looked like miniature waiters with their hair plastered down with pomade. They walked with their legs wide apart to avoid splashing their black trousers.

It was a great distinction to have one's child surrounded by a large gathering of relations who had come from a distance, and the carpenter's triumph was supreme. In the wake of Constance went the entire Tellier contingent, with its mistress at its head. Her father gave his arm to his sister; her mother paired off with Raphaële, Fernande with Rosa, and the two Pumps with each other. The party deployed majestically like a general staff in full uniform. The impression produced on the village was overwhelming. At the school, all the girls clustered about the good Sister's white coif, while the boys rallied round the schoolmaster's hat. He was a handsome man of imposing presence. Striking up a canticle, the procession began to move. First came the boys, moving in double file between the two rows of horseless carriages; then the girls in the same formation, while the ladies from the town, to whom the villagers had courteously given precedence, followed immediately after the little girls, like them in double file, three on the right, three on the left, looking like a display of fireworks in their dazzling raiment.

Their arrival in church caused intense excitement. The congregation turned round, jostling and elbowing one another in their eagerness to look. Some of the worshippers actually began to talk out loud, completely demoralized by these gorgeous ladies, who outdid even the choristers in their vestments. The mayor himself offered them his pew, the first one on the right next to the choir. This was occupied by Madame Tellier, her sister-in-law, Fernande, and Raphaële, while Rackety Rosa with the two Pumps and the carpenter seated themselves in the pew just behind. The chancel was crowded with kneeling children, the boys on one side, the girls on the other, all carrying in their hands long tapers, which looked like lances, pointing in all directions. At the lectern stood three members of the choir, singing lustily. They prolonged the sonorous Latin syllables, endlessly dragging out the A's of the Amens, their voices supported by the monotonous and interminable bray that issued from the serpent. A child's shrill treble sang the responses, and from time to time a priest in a square biretta rose from his stall, muttered a few words, and resumed his seat, whereupon the three precentors broke forth anew, their eyes intent on the huge book of plain-song that lay open before them on the outspread wings of a wooden eagle resting on a pivot. Then a silence ensued. With a unanimous movement the congregation fell on their knees, and the officiating priest, an old man, white-haired and venerable, entered the chancel, bending over the chalice which he bore in his left hand. Before him went two acolytes in red, and behind him, in heavy boots, followed the choristers, who ranged themselves on either side of the choir.

The tinkling of a little bell broke the deep silence, and the holy rite began. The priest moved slowly backwards and forwards in front of the gilded monstrance, genuflecting and chanting the preliminary prayers in a voice cracked and tremulous with age. When he paused, the whole choir, accompanied by the serpent, burst into song, and some of the worshippers in the body of the church joined in the singing, but in subdued and humble tones as became mere members of the congregation. Suddenly, issuing from the hearts and lungs of all those present, *Kyrie eleison* rose to heaven in so tremendous an outburst that it actually shook down from the old vaulted roof dust and particles of worm-eaten wood. The sun beating down on the slate roof made the little church like a furnace. Deep emotion, trembling anticipation at the approach of the ineffable Mystery, overpowered the hearts of the children and of their mothers.

The priest rose from his seat and returned to the altar. Baring his silvery hair, he began with tremulous movements the act of divine sacrifice. Turning to the worshippers, he stretched out his hands towards them, exclaiming: '*Orate, fratres,*' 'Pray, my brethren.' And the whole congregation obeyed. Then in a low voice he faltered the supreme and mystic words. The tinkling of the little bell was heard repeatedly; the kneeling throng invoked their God, and the children felt faint with unbearable suspense.

At that moment, Rosa, who was kneeling with her face buried in her hands, suddenly thought of her mother, of her own village church, and her own First Communion. It all came back to her.

She felt a little girl again, lost in white draperies, and she began to cry. At first she wept quietly; the tears formed slowly on her eyelashes; but with her reviving memories, her emotion increased, until, with swelling throat and heaving bosom, she began to sob aloud. She had taken out her pocket handkerchief and was mopping her eyes and pressing it to her mouth and nose, in a vain attempt to check her cries. A groan issued from her lips and was answered by two deep, heart-rending sighs from her two neighbours, Louise and Flora, who, likewise a prey to similar memories of the past, were completely overcome, dissolved in tears and moans.

Tears are infectious. Madame Tellier soon became conscious that her own lids were wet, and glancing at her sister-in-law, she found that every one in her pew was weeping.

The priest consummated the sacred mystery. No longer capable of thought, the children were prostrate on the stone pavement in an ecstasy of religious terror. Here and there, some woman, a sister or a mother, in the grip of that strange sympathy which is communicated by violent emotion, and overcome by the spectacle of all those fine ladies who were kneeling there, convulsed with sobs and shudders, began to cry into her check calico handkerchief, while she held her left hand pressed to her palpitating heart.

Like a spark which sets fire to a whole field of ripe corn, the tears of Rosa and her companions had instantly spread to the entire congregation. Soon every one was sobbing, men and women, even the old grandfathers and the lads in their new smocks. It was as if some supernatural essence were hovering above their heads, the emanation of a soul, the mighty breath of an invisible and omnipotent Being.

Then, in the chancel, a small sharp sound broke the silence. The good Sister was tapping on her book as a signal to the communicants to draw near to receive the Sacrament. Trembling with religious ecstasy, the children approached the sacred table. They all knelt down in a row. Holding in his hand the silver-gilt pyx, the aged priest passed along the line, presenting to them the Host, which the children received with closed eyes and pale faces, twitching with nervousness, and the long white linen cloth, draped over the railing, rippled like flowing water, as they held it up beneath their chins. A sudden frenzy spread like wild-fire through the church, the mutterings of a delirious

crowd, a paroxysm of sobs and cries.   It swept over the worship
pers like a gale that bends the trees of a forest.   Paralysed with
emotion, the priest stood rooted to the spot with the Host in his
hand, murmuring:

'It is God, God Himself, who has come among us, God, who is
manifesting Himself, who, at my voice, has descended upon
His kneeling people.'

And he faltered distracted prayers, the inarticulate prayers
of the soul, in a rapturous transport of adoration.   He adminis-
tered the Sacrament to all the children in such a fervour of
devotion that his limbs failed him, and when he himself had
drunk of the cup, he was overwhelmed by a veritable passion
of thanksgiving.

By degrees the congregation regained their composure, and
the precentors, in all the dignity of their white surplices, resumed
their singing, but in voices that still shook with tearful emotion.
Even the serpent sounded husky, as if it, too, had been weeping.
Then raising his hands the priest signed to all to be silent and he
moved forward between the two ranks of communicants, who
were still lost in ecstasies of bliss, until he reached the railing
of the chancel.   Vigorously wringing their handkerchiefs, the
congregation pushed back their chairs noisily and resumed their
seats.   As soon as they saw the priest, there was silence.   In a
muffled voice, in low, hesitating tones, he addressed his flock:

'My dear brethren, my beloved children, I thank you from
the bottom of my heart.   It is to you I owe the greatest joy of
my life.   I have felt the presence of God, who at my invocation
descended upon us.   He came; He was here present; He filled
your souls so that your eyes wept tears.   I am the oldest priest
in the diocese; I am also to-day the happiest.   A miracle has
been worked among us, a true, a great, a sublime miracle.   Even
as Christ entered for the first time into the bodies of these little
ones, the Holy Spirit, the Heavenly Dove, the breath of God,
descended upon you, mastered and possessed you, and bent you
like reeds shaken by the wind.'

Addressing himself to the two pews occupied by the carpenter's
guests, he raised his voice and added:

'More especially my thanks are due to you, my beloved sisters,
who have come from far away, and who by your presence among
us, by your manifest faith and ardent piety, have afforded us an
example of incalculable value.   You have been a source of

edification to my parish; your emotion has warmed our hearts. Had it not been for you, this memorable day might never have been crowned with so divine a manifestation. Often the presence of a single lamb from the true fold may move the Lord to descend upon His flock.'

His voice failed him.

'Grace be with you,' he added, 'Amen.'

He returned to the altar to bring the service to a close. By this time the congregation were eager to be gone. Even the children were fidgeting, over-taxed by the prolonged mental strain. They were hungry, too, and without waiting for the final gospel, the parents gradually slipped away to put the finishing touches to the dinner.

A crowd clustered around the church door, a vociferous crowd, raising a confused babel of sound, in which the Norman accent predominated. The congregation grouped themselves on either side of the porch, and as the children trooped out of church, each family swooped down upon its own offspring.

Constance found herself surrounded, hugged and kissed by all the women of her own household. Rosa seemed as if she would never weary of embracing her. At last, however, she took the child by one hand; Madame Tellier possessed herself of the other, while Raphaële and Fernande held up her long muslin skirts to keep them out of the dust. Louise and Flora, with Madame Rivet, brought up the rear. And thus the little girl went on her way with her guard of honour, her own thoughts uplifted and her whole being penetrated with the divine mystery of which she had partaken.

The banquet was served in the workshop on a long trestle table. Echoes of the village rejoicing drifted in through the door opening on the street. Every one was celebrating the occasion. Through every window people in their Sunday best could be seen seated at table, and sounds of revelry issued from every house. The peasants in their shirt sleeves were tossing off glass after glass of neat cider. Each party was centred around a pair of children, here two girls, there two boys, whose families had combined for the festive meal. Now and then, through the sultry heat of noon, a wagonette, drawn by an old jog-trotting pony, passed through the village, while the driver in his smock cast an envious glance at all this junketing.

At the carpenter's table, the merriment was somewhat sub-

THE HOUSE OF MADAME TELLIER

dued, as if still affected by the emotions of the morning. Rivet alone was in high spirits and was drinking to excess. Madame Tellier kept looking at the clock. Unless she was to lose two days' custom, she had to catch the three-fifty train, which reached Fécamp that evening.

The carpenter did his utmost to distract her attention in the hope of keeping his guests till the following day. But Madame Tellier was not to be put off. She never joked when it was a question of business. Directly after coffee she ordered her young women to get ready immediately, and turning to her brother she added:

'And you, Joseph, harness the pony at once.'

She herself went upstairs to finish her packing. When she came down again, she found her sister-in-law waiting to talk to her about her little girl. They had a long conversation, which had, however, no definite result. The mother beat about the bush and made a great show of sentiment, but Madame Tellier, who held the child on her knees, would commit herself to nothing more definite than a vague promise that the child should not be forgotten, and the remark that there was plenty of time and there would be other family gatherings in the future.

There was still no sign either of the cart or of the young women. The noise of a scuffle, mingled with shrieks and loud bursts of laughter and applause, drifted down from the upper floor. Madame Rivet went along to the stable to see about the cart, and at last Madame Tellier proceeded upstairs. Rivet, very drunk, was making advances to Rosa, who was in convulsions of laughter. Shocked at such behaviour after the solemn ceremony of the morning, the two Pumps were holding him back by the arms and endeavouring to calm him. But Raphaële and Fernande, doubled up and holding their sides with mirth, kept egging him on with shrill screams of encouragement. In-dignantly Madame Tellier seized her brother by the shoulders, and flung him out of the room with such violence that he fell against the wall.

A minute later he was heard pumping water over his head in the yard, and when he brought the cart round, he was quite sober again. They all got in, and the little white pony set off at its former brisk, dancing trot. In the bright sunshine they recovered their spirits, which had been depressed during the meal. This time the young women found the jolting of the cart so diverting that they kept jogging their neighbours' chairs and going off into shrieks of laughter. Rivet's amorous advances had put them all in high good humour. Over the landscape hovered a dazzling radiance, shimmering and dancing before the eyes. The wheels ploughed two furrows through the dust, which hung in clouds above the road long after the cart had passed by. Presently Fernande, who was fond of music, asked Rosa for a song, and Rosa gaily struck up *The Fat Priest of Meudon*. But Madame Tellier stopped her at once. She felt that the song was hardly becoming on such a day as this.

'Sing us something of Béranger's instead,' she added.

After a moment's pause, Rosa in her worn-out voice began to sing *Grandmother's Song*:

> 'Grandmamma sipping her wine,
>   Shaking her head white as snow:
> "Lovers, how many were mine
>   In the glad days long ago!
> Alas, my waist so slim,
>   And my dimpled arm,
> My leg and ankle trim,
>   And every vanished charm." '

And the young women, led by Madame Tellier herself, joined in the chorus:

> '"Alas, my waist so slim,
>   And my dimpled arm,
> My leg and ankle trim,
>   And every vanished charm."'

'That 's something like,' exclaimed Rivet, carried away by the tune. And Rosa continued:

> '"To the winds all discretion you threw?"
>   "Ah, those nights without sleep, how divine!
> For at blushing fifteen well I knew,
>   What subtle enchantments were mine."'

They all bawled the chorus. Rivet beat time with his foot on the shaft and with the reins on the back of the white pony. The pony itself seemed to be carried away by the rollicking rhythm; it broke into a gallop, a furious gallop, which precipitated all the ladies into a heap on the floor of the cart. Laughing like lunatics, they picked themselves up and went on yelling the song at the tops of their voices. Beneath the burning sky, over the ripening fields, while the song continued the pony raced on madly, bolting at each chorus, punctuating it with a gallop of a hundred yards, to the great delight of the travellers. Now and then a man who was breaking stones by the roadside would start up and stare through his wire spectacles at this wild cartload of shrieking females, borne along in a cloud of dust.

When they reached the station Rivet sighed regretfully.

'What a pity you are going away! We might have had such larks.'

'There is a time for everything,' Madame Tellier replied judiciously. 'One can't always be frivolling.'

A brilliant idea occurred to the carpenter.

'I tell you what,' he said. 'I'll come and see you at Fécamp,' and his shining eyes shot a sly and meaning glance at Rosa.

'You can come if you like,' remarked Madame Tellier, 'but you must behave yourself and not play the fool.'

He made no reply, and as the whistle of the train was heard, he began to kiss them all good-bye. When it came to Rosa's turn he made violent efforts to reach her mouth, but laughing with compressed lips, she avoided him, turning her head quickly from side to side, and although he held her in his arms, he could not attain his desire, being hindered by his big whip, which he still clutched in one hand and in his desperate struggles kept brandishing behind Rosa's back.

'Take your seats for Rouen,' said the guard, and the ladies obeyed. The guard blew his whistle and immediately the engine began hissing violently, noisily letting off its first puffs of steam, while slowly and with effort the wheels began to turn.

Rivet left the station and hurried to the barriers for one last glimpse of Rosa. When the carriage with its human freight rushed past him, he began cracking his whip and shouting at the top of his voice:

> '"Alas, my waist so slim,
>   And my dimpled arm,
> My leg and ankle trim,
>   And every vanished charm."'

Someone waved a white handkerchief, and he watched it till it vanished in the distance.

III

They slept the sleep of a conscience at peace until they reached their destination. Rested, revived, and ready for their evening duties, they entered the house, and Madame Tellier could not help exclaiming:

'I don't mind telling you, I was wearying for home already.'

Supper was soon over, and when they had put on their war paint, they waited for their usual customers to arrive. Once more the lantern, the little votive lantern, burned above the door and announced to all who passed the house the return of the flock to the fold. The news spread abroad like wildfire, no one knew how. Monsieur Philippe, the banker's son, was prompted by his kindness of heart to send an express messenger to Tournevau, captive in the bosom of his family. The fish-curer always had several of his cousins to dinner on Sunday, and just as they were having coffee a man came in with a note. In great agitation Monsieur Tournevau tore open the envelope and turned pale. It contained nothing but these words in pencil:

'Cargo of cod. Ship now in harbour. Excellent opportunity for doing business. Come at once.'

He fumbled in his pocket, gave the messenger a franc, and blushing up to the eyes he exclaimed:

'I 'm afraid I shall have to leave you.' He handed his wife the laconic and mysterious note, rang for the maid, and de-manded his overcoat and hat. Once in the street, he broke into a run, whistling as he went. He was in such a fever of impa-tience that the way seemed twice its usual length.

Madame Tellier's house wore a festive air. A deafening noise came from the sailors on the ground floor. Louise and Flora hardly knew which way to turn; they drank first with one, then another, and more than ever earned their nickname. And all the time they were shouted for on every side, so that they were already quite unable to cope with the work in hand, and there was every prospect of a busy night.

By nine o'clock the society on the first floor had mustered a full attendance. Monsieur Vasse, the arbitrator, Madame Tellier's acknowledged but platonic admirer, was quietly chat-ting with her in a corner, and they were smiling at each other, as if on the verge of an understanding. Monsieur Poulin, the ex-mayor, had planted Rosa astride his knee; her face was close to his and her dumpy hands were playing with the worthy man's white whiskers. Her yellow silk skirt was turned up and revealed a glimpse of bare thigh, its whiteness contrasting with Monsieur Poulin's black trousers. Her red stockings were secured with a pair of blue garters, the offering of the commercial traveller.

Buxom Fernande lay at full length on the sofa with both feet on the lap of Monsieur Pimpesse, the tax-collector, while her head rested against Monsieur Philippe's waistcoat. Her right arm was round his neck and her left hand held a cigarette.

Raphaële seemed to be parleying with Monsieur Dupuis, the insurance agent, and she concluded by saying:

'Very well, my dear. I have no objection this evening.'

Then waltzing all round the room by herself, she exclaimed:

'Anything anybody likes this evening.'

The door burst open and Monsieur Tournevau appeared on the threshold. He was welcomed with shouts of delight:

'Three cheers for Tournevau!'

Raphaële, who was still gyrating about the room, fell on his neck. Without a word he caught her in a violent embrace, picked her up as if she were a feather, crossed the drawing-room with his living burden, and vanished amidst loud applause through the end door that opened on to the bedroom staircase.

Rosa, who was inflaming the passions of the ex-mayor with her incessant kisses, pulling him by both whiskers to keep his head straight, profited by this example.

'Come along,' she said. 'He has given us a lead.'

The worthy man rose from his chair, pulled down his waistcoat, and, fumbling in the pocket where his money was reposing, followed the young woman from the room. Fernande and Madame Tellier remained alone with the four other men.

'I'll stand champagne,' cried Monsieur Philippe. 'Three bottles, please, Madame.'

Fernande hugged him and whispered in his ear:

'Do play for us to dance, won't you?'

He rose from his chair. Seating himself at the ancient spinet which stood in the corner, he wrung from its wheezy interior a husky and plaintive waltz. Fernande and the tax-collector took the floor together, while Madame Tellier surrendered herself into the arms of Monsieur Vasse. The two couples revolved round the room, exchanging kisses with their partners as they danced. Monsieur Vasse, who had moved in good society, danced with an air, and Madame Tellier regarded him with fascinated eyes, eyes that answered 'Yes,' their silent acquiescence more discreet, more exquisite than any spoken word.

Frédéric brought the champagne. As the first cork popped, Monsieur Philippe struck up the opening bars of a quadrille. Bowing and curtsying with all the propriety, grace, and dignity of high society, the two couples went through all the figures. When the quadrille was over, they began upon the champagne. Presently Monsieur Tournevau returned, solaced and radiant.

'I don't know what has come over Raphaële,' he cried. 'She 's simply perfection this evening.'

At one draught he drained the glass of champagne which was handed to him, exclaiming:

'This is real luxury, this is.'

Monsieur Philippe broke into a lively polka, and Monsieur Tournevau whirled the fair Jewess away with her feet off the ground. Monsieur Pimpesse and Monsieur Vasse set off again with renewed vigour. Now and then one or other of the couples halted by the mantelpiece to toss off a glass of the sparkling wine. It seemed as if the dance would never end, when suddenly, flushed and animated, in nightgown and slippers, with her hair down her back and a candle in her hand, Rosa appeared at the half-open door.

'I want to dance,' she cried.

'But where 's your old man?' asked Raphaële.

'He? Oh, he 's asleep. He always goes to sleep at once.'

She seized Monsieur Dupuis, who was sitting idle on the sofa, and the polka was resumed. By this time all the champagne bottles were empty.

'I 'll pay for another,' Monsieur Tournevau volunteered.

'So will I,' exclaimed Monsieur Vasse.

'And so will I,' echoed Monsieur Dupuis amid general applause.

The dance developed into a regular ball. Even Louise and Flora dashed upstairs now and then and snatched a hurried turn or two, leaving their clients fuming and fretting downstairs. Then reluctantly and sorrowfully they would tear themselves away and run back to the café.

Midnight came and they were still dancing. Now and then one of the young women would slip away, and when the others looked for her to make up a set, one of the men was invariably discovered to be missing, too.

'And where have you been?' asked Monsieur Philippe playfully, as Monsieur Pimpesse re-entered the room with Fernande.

'Watching over Monsieur Poulin's slumbers,' replied the tax-collector.

This witticism was highly successful. All of them in rotation went upstairs to watch Monsieur Poulin's slumbers; they were accompanied by one or other of the ladies, who on this occasion showed themselves singularly obliging. Madame Tellier shut her eyes to everything. She herself held long intimate conversations in corners with Monsieur Vasse, as if to discuss the details of an affair that was already concluded.

At last, at one o'clock, the two married men, Monsieur Tournevau and Monsieur Pimpesse, declared that it was time to go, and asked for the bill. Nothing was charged for except the champagne, and this was reckoned at six francs a bottle instead of ten, the usual price. And when her clients protested at such generosity, Madame Tellier replied with a radiant smile:

'It's a red-letter day and they don't come often.'

THE HAND

(*La Main*)

THE whole party had gathered in a circle round Monsieur Bermutier, the magistrate, who was giving his opinion on the mysterious Saint-Cloud affair, an inexplicable crime which had been distracting Paris for a month. No one could make anything of it. Standing with his back to the fireplace, Monsieur Bermutier was discussing it, marshalling proofs, analysing theories, but arriving at no conclusion. Some of the ladies had risen from their chairs and had come nearer him. Clustering round him, they kept their eyes on the clean-shaven lips which uttered such weighty words. They shuddered and trembled, thrilled by that strange awe, that eager and insatiable craving for horrors, which haunts the mind of women and tortures them like the pangs of hunger. One of them, paler than the others, ventured to break a sudden silence:

'How ghastly! It has a touch of the supernatural. No one will ever find out the truth about it.'

Monsieur Bermutier turned to her.

'That is likely enough,' he said. 'But as for your word, "supernatural," it has no place in this affair. We are confronted with a crime which was ably conceived and very ably executed. It is wrapped in such profound mystery that we cannot disengage it from the impenetrable circumstances surrounding it. Still, within my own experience, I had once to follow up a case that really appeared to have an element of the supernatural in it. We had eventually to give it up, for lack of means to elucidate it.'

Several ladies exclaimed as with one voice:

'Oh, do tell us about it.'

With a grave smile appropriate to an investigating magistrate, Monsieur Bermutier resumed:

'At all events pray do not imagine that I myself have for one instant attributed anything of the supernatural to this incident

I believe in normal causes only. It would be much better if we used the word "inexplicable" instead of "supernatural" to express things that we did not understand. In any case, what was striking in the affair I am going to tell you about was not so much the event itself as the circumstances that attended and led up to it. Now for the facts.

'At that time I was investigating magistrate at Ajaccio, a little town of white houses, situated on the edge of a wonderful bay surrounded on all sides by lofty mountains. My principal task there was the investigation of vendettas. Some of these vendettas are sublime, savage, heroic, inconceivably dramatic. In them, one comes across the finest themes of revenge imaginable; hatreds that have endured for centuries, lying for a time in abeyance, but never extinguished; detestable stratagems, assassinations that are mere butchery, others that are almost heroic deeds. For two years I had heard nothing discussed there but the price of blood; nothing but this terrible Corsican tradition, which obliges a man who has been wronged to wreak his revenge upon the man who has wronged him, or upon his descendants or his next-of-kin. Old men, children, distant cousins, I had seen them all slaughtered, and my head was full of tales of vengeance.

'One day I was informed that an Englishman had just taken a lease for several years of a little villa at the far end of the bay. He had brought with him a French manservant, whom he had picked up while passing through Marseilles. It was not long before universal curiosity was excited by this eccentric person, who lived alone and never left his house except to go shooting or fishing. He spoke to no one, never came to the town, and practised for an hour or two every morning with his pistol and carbine. All sorts of legends sprang up about him. He was said to be an exalted personage who had fled his country for political reasons; to this succeeded a theory that he was in hiding because he had committed a horrible crime of which the most shocking details were given. In my official capacity, I was anxious to learn something about this man, but my inquiries were fruitless. The name he went by was Sir John Rowell. I had to be satisfied with keeping a close watch upon him, but I never really discovered anything suspicious about him. None the less the rumours never ceased, and they became so widespread that I determined to make an effort to see this stranger with my own eyes. I therefore took to shooting regularly in the neighbourhood of his property.

'My opportunity was long in arriving, but at length it presented itself in the form of a partridge which I shot under the Englishman's very nose. My dog brought me the bird, but I took it immediately to Sir John Rowell, and begged him to accept it, at the same time making my apologies for my breach of good manners. He was a red-headed, red-bearded man, very tall and massive, a sort of easy-going, well-mannered Hercules. He had none of the so-called British stiffness, and, speaking with a strong English accent, he thanked me warmly for my considerate behaviour. Before a month had elapsed we had conversed five or six times. One evening as I was passing his gate, I caught sight of him smoking his pipe. I greeted him, and he invited me to come in and have a glass of beer. I accepted his invitation with alacrity. He received me with all the meticulous English courtesy; and although he made shocking mistakes in grammar, he was full of the praises of France and Corsica and professed his affection for these countries. Very cautiously, and under the pretext of a lively interest, I began to question him about his life and his plans for the future. His replies were perfectly frank, and he told me that he had travelled much in Africa, India, and America.

'"Oh, yes, I have had plenty of adventures," he added, laughing.

'Then I turned the conversation on sport, and he gave me the most curious details about shooting hippopotamus, tiger, elephant, and even gorilla.

'"Those are all formidable brutes," I said.

'"Why, no," he said smiling. "Man is the worst of all."

'He laughed heartily, this big, genial Englishman.

'"I have done lots of man-hunting, too," he added.

'Then he talked about guns and invited me into his house to look at various makes. His drawing-room was hung with black silk, embroidered with golden flowers that shone like fire on the sombre background. It was Japanese work, he said.

'In the middle of the largest panel, a strange object attracted my attention; it stood out clearly against a square of red velvet. I went up to examine it. It was a hand, the hand of a man. Not a clean, white skeleton hand, but a black, dried-up hand, with yellow nails, bared muscles, and showing old traces of blood, black blood, crusted round the bones, which had been cut clean through as with an axe, about the middle of the forearm. Round the wrist of this unclean object was riveted a powerful chain, which was attached to the wall by a ring strong enough to hold an elephant.

'"What is that?" I asked.

'"That is my worst enemy," replied the Englishman calmly. "He was an American. His hand was chopped off with a sabre. Then it was skinned with sharp flints, and after that it was dried in the sun for a week. It was a good job for me."

'I touched this human relic. The man must have been a colossus. The fingers were abnormally long and were attached by enormous tendons to which fragments of skin still adhered. It was a terrible sight, this hand, all flayed; it could not but suggest some savage act of vengeance.

'"He must have been a stout fellow," I remarked.

'"Oh, yes," replied the Englishman gently. "He was strong, but I was stronger. I fixed that chain on his hand to keep it from escaping."

'Thinking that he was joking, I replied:

'"The chain is hardly needed now; the hand can't run away."

'Sir John answered gravely:

'"That hand is always trying to get away. The chain is necessary."

'I cast a rapid, questioning glance at him, wondering whether he was mad or making an unpleasant joke. But his face retained its calm, impenetrable, benevolent expression. I changed the subject and began to admire his guns. I noticed, however, that there were three loaded revolvers lying about on the chairs and tables. Apparently this man lived in constant dread of an attack.

'I went to see him several times, and then my visits ceased. People had become accustomed to his presence and took no further interest in him.

.   .   .   .   .

'A whole year passed. One morning towards the end of November my servant woke me with the news that Sir John Rowell had been murdered during the night. Half an hour later I was in the Englishman's house. With me were the superintendent of police and the captain of gendarmes. Sir

John's manservant was weeping at the door of the house; he was distraught and desperate. At first I suspected him. He was, however, innocent. Nor was the murderer ever discovered.

'When I entered the drawing-room, the first thing to strike me was the sight of Sir John's corpse lying flat on its back in the middle of the floor. His waistcoat was torn; one sleeve of his coat was ripped off. There was every indication that a terrible struggle had taken place.

'Death had been caused by strangulation. Sir John's face was black, swollen, and terrifying. It bore an expression of hideous dread. His teeth were clenched on some object. In his neck, which was covered with blood, there were five holes, which might have been made by iron fingers. A doctor arrived. After a prolonged examination of the fingermarks in the flesh, he uttered these strange words:

'"It almost looks as if he had been strangled by a skeleton."

'A shudder passed down my spine, and I cast a glance at the wall, at the spot where I had been wont to see that horrible, flayed hand. The hand was no longer there. The chain had been broken and was hanging loose. I bent down close to the corpse, and between his clenched teeth I found one of the fingers of that vanished hand. At the second joint it had been cut, or rather bitten, off by the dead man's teeth. An investigation was held, but without result. No door or window had been forced that night, no cupboard or drawer had been broken into. The watchdogs had not been disturbed. The substance of the servant's evidence can be given briefly. For a month past his master had seemed to have something on his mind. He had received many letters, which he had promptly burnt. Often he would snatch up a horse-whip and in a passion of rage, which suggested insanity, lash furiously at that withered hand, which had been riveted to the wall, and had mysteriously vanished at the very hour at which the crime was committed.

'Sir John, said the servant, went late to bed and locked himself carefully in his room. He always had firearms within reach. Often during the night he could be heard speaking in loud tones, as if he were wrangling with someone. On the night in question, however, he had made no sound, and it was only on coming to open the windows the next morning that the servant had discovered the murder. The witness suspected no one.

'I told the magistrates and police officers everything I knew about the deceased, and inquiries were made with scrupulous care throughout the whole island, but nothing was ever discovered.

'Well, one night, three months after the murder, I had a frightful nightmare. I thought I saw that hand, that ghastly hand, running like a scorpion or a spider over my curtains and walls. Thrice I awoke, and thrice fell asleep again, and thrice did I see that hideous relic gallop around my room, with its fingers running along like the legs of an insect. The next day the hand itself was brought to me. It had been found in the cemetery on Sir John's tomb. He had been buried there, as no trace of his family was discoverable. The index finger of the hand was missing. Ladies, that is my story. That is all I know about it.'

The ladies were horrified, pale and trembling. One of them protested:

'But the mystery is not solved. There is no explanation. We shall never be able to sleep if you don't tell us what you make of it yourself.'

The magistrate smiled a little grimly:

'Well, ladies, I'm afraid I shall deprive you of your nightmares. My theory is the perfectly simple one that the rightful owner of that hand was not dead at all, and that he came looking for his severed member with the one that was left him. But as for explaining how he managed it, that is beyond me. It was a kind of vendetta.'

Another lady protested:

'No, that can't be the real explanation.'

Still smiling, the narrator rejoined:

'I told you it wouldn't satisfy you.'

MOONLIGHT

(*Clair de Lune*)

THE Abbé Marignan's demeanour was not unworthy of one who bore the name of a battle. He was tall, lean, and fanatical, with a fervour that never abated, a conscience that never relaxed, beliefs that never swerved a hairbreadth. It was his profound conviction that he understood the God whom he worshipped, and was able to fathom His designs, His wishes, His purposes.

As he vigorously paced the garden paths of his little country parsonage, a question would sometimes present itself to his mind:

'What were God's motives for such and such an act?'

He would put himself in God's place, reason the matter out pertinaciously, and, as a rule, successfully. Not for him were those transports of devout surrender, in which the faithful murmur: 'Lord, Thy ways are hid from me.' On the contrary, he argued that as God's servant he had a right to know his Master's reasons, and if he did not actually know them, he would do his best to guess them. In his eyes the whole scheme of creation seemed to have been devised with a logical symmetry, which was absolute and admirable. Question and answer were ever in perfect equipoise. The purpose of dawn was to provide a glad awakening; of broad daylight to ripen the crops; of evening to dispose one to slumber; and of darkness to make one sleep sound. The course of the seasons coincided perfectly with the requirements of agriculture. Never can a suspicion have crossed his priestly mind that purpose cannot be attributed to nature; that, on the contrary, it is life that has had to adapt itself to the despotism of epochs, temperature, and the laws of matter.

For woman he had an instinctive hatred and contempt.

'Woman,' he would say, in the words of Christ, 'what have I to do with thee?' And he would further reflect:

'Surely God Himself can hardly have been pleased with this work of his.'

Woman was indeed to him, as the poet has described her, 'a child without a child's innocence.' She was the temptress, who had lured astray the first man and had never ceased from her work of damnation. Disturbing and unfathomable, she was, though feeble in herself, pregnant with danger to others. More even than her accursed flesh, he detested her unquenchable love of love. He had often felt her affection hovering around him, and although he knew himself proof against her, it angered him to see her perpetually quivering with this passionate hunger for love. To his mind, God had created woman merely as a trial and temptation, to be approached with defensive precautions, and to be shunned as one would shun a decoy. In fact, a decoy was precisely what she was, luring a man with kisses and caresses.

The only women whom he regarded with tolerance were sisters of religion, who had been rendered innocuous by their vows, but he was hard with them none the less, because he was conscious that in the depths of their enslaved and humbled hearts still lurked inextinguishable that never-dying tenderness, reaching out even to him, a priest. He read it in their eyes, which brimmed with devotion as those of a monk never did; he saw their sex intrude into their ecstasies, into their transports of love towards Christ, and he was indignant because he knew that this love was womanly and of the flesh. In their very docility, in their downcast eyes, in the gentleness of their voices when they spoke to him, in their tears of resignation when he reproved them harshly, in all this he discerned that same accursed sentiment. When he passed out of the convent doors, he would shake his cassock, and his strides would lengthen, as if he were fleeing from some danger.

He had a niece, who lived with her mother in a small house in the neighbourhood, and he had set his heart on making her a sister of charity. She was pretty, feather-brained, and inclined to make fun of things. When the abbé lectured her, she laughed; and when he was annoyed, she threw her arms round him and hugged him. He would make instinctive efforts to free himself from her embrace, and yet it gave him a tender joy and aroused in the depths of his nature that sense of fatherhood which lies dormant in all men. As he walked by her side along the field paths he would frequently speak to her about God as he conceived Him. But she hardly listened; she would gaze at the sky, the grass, the flowers, with the joy of life shining in her eyes. Sometimes she would dart away in pursuit of a butterfly, and when she had caught it she would exclaim:

'Look, uncle, how pretty it is. I could kiss it!'

And the priest was vexed, disturbed and shocked by this craving of hers to kiss insects or lilac buds, discerning even here the ineradicable fondness that ever germinates in a woman's heart.

Then came a day when the sexton's wife, who kept house for the abbé, gave him cautiously to understand that his niece had a lover. This information was a terrible shock to him, and he stood there choking, with his face all covered with soap, for he had been interrupted while shaving. When his powers of thought and speech returned to him, he exclaimed:

'You must be mistaken, Mélanie.'

But the housekeeper laid her hand on her heart and said:

'May the good Lord judge me, if I'm not speaking the truth! As soon as your sister is in bed, off goes your niece every evening. They meet along the river bank. You have only to go there between ten o'clock and midnight.'

He stopped scraping his chin, and began to walk violently up and down, as was his custom when he had something serious to consider. When he resumed his interrupted shave, he gashed himself thrice from nose to ear. Bursting with rage and indignation, he did not say one word all day. He felt the natural fury of a priest who has been defied by love the invincible; and, more than this, the chagrin of the moral instructor, the guardian, the spiritual guide, who has been deceived, tricked, made game of, by a child; the apoplectic vanity of parents, whose daughter informs them that she has, without them and in spite of them, made her own choice of a husband.

After dinner he tried to read a book, but could make nothing of it. Every hour saw his fury increase. On the stroke of ten he seized his walking-stick, a formidable oaken staff, which he used when he went out at night to visit the sick. Smiling grimly, he grasped this stout cudgel in his strong peasant's hands, and twirled it in menacing circles. Then suddenly he raised it high in the air, and, gnashing his teeth, brought it down on a chair with such violence that the back of the chair broke off and fell on the floor.

Then he opened the front door to go out. But on the threshold he stopped, astounded by the lustrous moon which shone with a splendour such as is seldom witnessed. And inasmuch as he was endowed with the spirit of lofty imagination, such a spirit as must have possessed those poet-dreamers, the Fathers of the Church, he felt moved to the soul by the infinite, serene beauty of that radiant night. In this little garden, all flooded with soft moonlight, the slender budding branches of his fruit-trees cast their clear-cut shadows across the path, and the giant honeysuckle which clung to the wall of the house sent forth its balmy breath, pervading the mild, clear evening with a sweet-ness that seemed itself almost a soul.

He began to breathe deeply, drinking in the air as drunkards drink wine, and he set forth at a slow pace. He was ravished, awestruck. The thought of his niece had almost vanished from his mind. As soon as he was clear of the houses, he paused to gaze upon the great sweep of country, flooded by that caressing radiance, bathed in the tender, languishing charm of that serenely beautiful night. The frogs never ceased uttering their short metallic note. With the seduction of the moonlight, distant nightingales mingled strains of that linked sweetness which begets reverie rather than thought, that light, vibrant music, fit accompaniment for kisses.

Somehow, as he started on his walk again, the abbé found his resolution failing. He was conscious of a sudden debility and lack of energy; he wanted to sit down where he was and stay there and look about him and adore God and His works.

Down in the river valley a long line of poplars wound its way by the course of the meandering stream. Above its steep banks hovered a delicate, white vapour, which was transfused with silvery radiance by the moonbeams. It lay along the tortuous windings of the stream like a floating veil of filmy tissue. Again the priest came to a halt, moved to the depth of his soul by an increasing and irresistible emotion. He was attacked by a doubt, a vague disquietude; confronted by one of those questions which he sometimes put to himself. What was God's purpose in all this? Night is destined for sleep, unconsciousness, repose, oblivion. Why then had God made it more enchanting than day, fairer than dawn or sunset? How was it that that heavenly orb, moving so slowly, so seductively, more full of poetry than the sun itself, and destined, so discreet it seemed, to shed its radiance on things too delicate, too mysterious for common daylight, had such power to make the darkness luminous? How came it that the most brilliant singer of all the singing birds refused to seek repose like its mates, preferring to utter its music in a haunted shade? Why was this half-transparent veil cast across the earth? Whence these stirrings of the heart, this emotion of the soul, these languors of the body? All humanity was asleep. Why then this display of loveliness for men who were steeped in unconsciousness, for whom were intended this sublime spectacle, this wealth of poetry, scattered so lavishly by heaven upon the earth?

The abbé could find no answer to his problem. But suddenly he caught sight of two shadowy figures, a youth and a maid, walking side by side on the edge of the fields. Above them, steeped in misty radiance, arched the vault of the great trees. The youth was the taller of the two. He had his arm round his companion's shoulders, and every now and then he kissed her on the forehead. These two at once gave significance to the placid landscape that fitted them like a heavenly frame. They seemed, the two of them, like one being, the very being for whom this calm and silent night was intended, and as they came nearer to the priest they seemed in very truth the answer, the living answer, which his Master was giving to his questionings.

The abbé stood there with beating heart, his mind in a whirl. Surely what he gazed upon was some scene from Holy Writ, the love of Ruth and Boaz, the fulfilment of God's will in one of those great dramatic effects that one reads of in the sacred books. In his head began to ring the verses of the Song of Songs; the ardent outpourings, the call of heart to heart, all the fervent poetry of that lyric of fire and love.

'It may be,' he reflected, 'that God has created nights like this in order to cast His divine veil over human loves.'

Linked together, the youth and the maid came nearer, and the abbé drew back. He recognized his niece, but now he was wondering whether he was not in danger of disobeying God. If God enveloped human love in this visible splendour, how could it be argued that He forbade it?

Completely bewildered, almost ashamed, as though he had penetrated a shrine which he had no right to enter, the abbé fairly took to flight.

MOHAMMED-FRIPOUILLE

'SHALL we have coffee on the roof?' asked Captain Marret.

'By all means,' I replied, and he rose from his chair.

It was already dark in the hall, which derived its light solely from the inner courtyard, as is usual in Moorish houses. Over the lofty pointed windows creepers drooped down from the wide roof-terrace on which the warm summer evenings were spent. The table had been cleared, except for fruit of different kinds: enormous African varieties, grapes as big as plums, soft figs with purple pulp, yellow pears, long, plump bananas, and Tougourt dates in a basket of esparto grass. The mulatto who was waiting on us opened the door, and I went up the staircase, its azure walls bathed in the soft glow of sunset. I breathed a deep sigh of delight when I found myself on the terrace, which commanded a view of Algiers, the port, the roadstead, and the distant coasts.

Captain Marret's house, formerly an Arab dwelling, was situated in the centre of the old town, in the midst of those labyrinthine alleys which never cease to hum with the life and the strange population of the African coasts. Below us the flat rectangular roofs descended like giant steps, until they gave way to the sloping roofs of the European quarter. Beyond the latter appeared the masts of anchored ships, and beyond those again the sea, the open sea, reflecting the peaceful azure of the vault of heaven. We stretched ourselves on mats, with cushions behind our heads, and while I slowly sipped the fragrant coffee they make in those parts, I watched the stars as they came out one by one in the darkening sky. They were barely visible, so far and faint were they; they hardly seemed fully kindled. A mild warmth, delicate as the brushing of a bird's wing, caressed us, and sometimes, more ardent, less ethereal, from over the peaks of Atlas, came the breath of the desert, charged with the vague odour that speaks of Africa.

'What a country!' said Captain Marret, as he lay on his back.

'Life is sweet here. Repose has some special quality of exquisiteness. Such nights as this are made for dreaming.'

For my part, with lazy yet alert interest, drowsy, but happy, I continued to watch the stars flash out one by one.

'You might tell me something of your life in the south,' I suggested sleepily.

Marret was one of the oldest officers in our African army. He was a soldier of fortune, and it was to his trusty sword that he owed his rise from the ranks. Thanks to him and his friends and connections, I had been enabled to enjoy a splendid tour in the desert, and I had come that evening to express my gratitude to him before I returned to France.

'What sort of a story would you like?' he asked. 'I have had many adventures during my twelve years in the desert, so many indeed that I can't remember a single one.'

'Tell me about the Arab women,' I rejoined.

He made no reply. Stretched at full length with his arms thrown back and his hands behind his head, he was smoking a cigar of which every now and then I caught a fragrant whiff. Its smoke floated straight upwards in the still night air.

Marret suddenly broke into a laugh.

'Very well. I'll tell you a curious incident that occurred about the time I first came to this country. In those days we had in our African army some extraordinary types, such as one never sees nowadays. They don't breed them any more. They would have interested you so much that you would have wanted to spend your whole life here.

'I was just a spahi, a young spahi of twenty, fair-haired, active and strong, a bit of a swaggerer, a regular Algerian swashbuckler. I was attached to the Boghar command. You know Boghar; it is called the balcony-window of the south. From the highest point of the fort, you have seen the beginning of that burning land, wasted, barren, grim, covered with red rocks. It is in truth the antechamber of the desert, the superb and blazing frontier of those vast regions of sandy solitudes.

'Well, at that time there were at Boghar about forty of us spahis, a company of the Bataillon d'Afrique, and a squadron of African light-horse. News was brought to us that the tribe of Ouled-Berghi had murdered an English traveller, who had come from God knows where, for all these English are possessed of a devil.

'This crime perpetrated on a European had to be avenged. But the officer in command was reluctant to send out a whole column, being of opinion that one Englishman hardly justified such a demonstration. As he was discussing the matter with his captain and lieutenant, one of our sergeant-majors, who was present, suddenly volunteered to punish the tribe himself, if he were given a squad of six men. In the outposts, as you are aware, the men enjoy greater freedom than in headquarters garrisons, and officers and common soldiers fraternize in a way that you do not find elsewhere.

'"You, my man?" laughed the captain.

'"Yes, sir. I'll bring back the whole tribe as prisoners if you like."

'The major, however, who was no slave to tradition, took him at his word.

'"You will start to-morrow morning with six men selected by yourself, and if you don't keep your word, look out for trouble."

'The sergeant smiled beneath his moustache.

'"Don't you be afraid, sir. The prisoners will be here by Wednesday at the latest."

'This sergeant-major, whom we called Mohammed-Fripouille, or Scallywag Mohammed, was a most surprising character. A pure-blooded Turk, he had enlisted in the French army after a much chequered, and doubtless not very reputable, career. He had travelled in Greece, Asia Minor, Egypt, Palestine, and must have left a trail of misdeeds on his wanderings. He was a true bashi-bazouk, bold, fond of a spree, fierce, and at the same time merry, but with the placid mirth of the Oriental. He was enormously stout, but as active as a monkey and a superb horseman. He had the thickest and longest moustaches you ever saw; they suggested to my mind something between a crescent moon and a scimitar. His hatred of the Arabs was intense, and he treated them with cunning and frightful cruelty, continually thinking out for their benefit new stratagems and calculated acts of horrible treachery. To all this he added prodigious strength and courage.

'"Choose your men, my lad," said the major.

'I was one of those chosen. Mohammed believed in me, and by choosing me he bound me to him, body and soul. It gave me more pleasure than the *croix d'honneur*, which I won later.

'At dawn the next morning we set out, seven of us all told. My comrades were of the piratical, freebooter type, who plunder and roam in every land under the sun, and eventually enlist in some foreign legion or other. At that time our African army was full of these ruffians, first-rate soldiers, to be sure, but utterly unscrupulous. Mohammed had given each of us a dozen pieces of rope about a yard long to carry, and I, as the youngest and lightest, was entrusted besides with a single rope of a hundred yards. When he was asked what he meant to do with all this tackle, he replied in his sly, quiet way:

'"We 're going to fish for Arabs."

'And he gave a knowing wink, an accomplishment he had learnt from an old African trooper who hailed from Paris.

'With his head wrapped in the red turban which he always wore in the field, he rode at the head of our troop. Under his enormous moustaches lurked a smile of ecstatic enjoyment. And he looked really splendid, this burly Turk, with his powerful frame, colossal shoulders, and unruffled demeanour. He was riding a sturdy white charger of average height and seemed ten times too big for his mount.

'During our march along a rocky, treeless, and sandy defile, which unites later with the valley of the Chélif, we discussed our expedition in every accent under the sun, my comrades including a Spaniard, two Greeks, an American, and two Frenchmen. As for Mohammed, you never heard such a rolling of r's. The terrible southern sun, of which one has no conception north of the Mediterranean, beat down on our backs, and we advanced at a walk, as is the custom in that country. We marched all day without seeing either a tree or an Arab. About an hour after noon we halted by a little stream which trickled among the rocks. There we opened our haversacks and ate our bread and dried mutton. After twenty minutes' rest we set out on our march again. By our leader's orders we took a circuitous route which brought us, about six o'clock, within sight of an encampment which lay behind an eminence. The low brown tents stood out like dark splashes on the yellow sand, as though huge mushrooms had sprouted up at the foot of this sun-baked hill.

'They were the very tribe we were seeking. Their horses were tethered a little distance away and were browsing at the edge of a stretch of dark esparto grass.

'Mohammed gave the order to charge, and we swept like a

hurricane into the midst of the encampment. The terror-stricken women, their tattered white clothing fluttering around then, hurriedly crept and crawled into the shelter of the tents, and crouched there, uttering cries like hunted animals. The men, however, came running from all directions, eager to defend their camp. We rode straight for the principal tent, that of the aga. Following Mohammed's example, we kept our sabres in their scabbards. Our leader, as he galloped, was worthy of notice. He sat bolt upright in the saddle, as steady as a rock, while in spite of the weight it carried his little charger seemed as if possessed, its impetuosity contrasting curiously with the imperturbability of its rider.

'The Arab chief emerged from his tent as we arrived in front of it. He was tall, lean, and dark, with shining eyes beneath arched eyebrows and prominent forehead.

'"What is your business?" he cried in Arabic.

'Mohammed checked his horse, and replied in the same tongue:

'"It was you who killed the English traveller?"

'"I am not answerable to you," retorted the aga emphatically.

'All around us a sound arose like the muttering of a storm. The Arabs ran up from all directions, and pressed close about us, vociferating furiously. With their prominent, hooked noses, their lean faces, and their ample robes flapping about them like wings, they resembled a flock of ferocious birds of prey. Mohammed, his turban awry, his eyes flashing, smiled, and his plump, lined, rather pendulous cheeks quivered with delight. In a voice of thunder, which quelled the surrounding clamour, he shouted:

'"Death to him who has dealt death."

'He pointed his revolver at the dark face of the aga, a puff of smoke issued from the barrel, and a red froth of blood and brains spurted from the chief's forehead. He fell backwards as though struck by a thunderbolt, and as he fell he flung his arms abroad and his wide burnous opened out on either side of him, like the pinions of a bird.

'I thought that certainly my last hour had come, so shocking was the uproar that broke out around us. Mohammed had drawn his sabre, and we followed his example. He whirled his sabre round him, driving back those who pressed too near.

'"Those who submit will be spared. Death to all who resist."

'He seized the nearest Arab in his herculean grasp, lifted him on to the saddle, tied his hands together, and roared to us to do as he did and cut down every man who resisted. Within five minutes we had twenty Arabs bound firmly by the wrists. Then we pursued those who had run away. The crowd around us had fled headlong at the sight of our naked sabres. We brought in about thirty more of the men.

'The whole plain was covered with fleeing white figures. Dragging their children after them, the women scattered with shrill cries of terror. Yellow dogs, like jackals, circled around us, barking and showing their yellow fangs. Beside himself with glee, Mohammed leaped from his horse, and seizing the long rope which I had brought, he shouted:

' "Attention, my men! Two of you dismount."

'Then he did a thing which was both farcical and horrible. He made a string of prisoners, or rather a string of hanged men. Having fastened firmly the wrists of the first captive, he made a slip-knot round his neck with the same rope, which he then passed first round the wrists, and then round the neck of the next man. Very soon our fifty prisoners found themselves tied together in such a fashion that if one of them made the least movement to break away, he strangled not only himself, but his two neighbours. Their slightest motion tightened the slip-knot round their necks, and when they walked they had to keep the same step and the same distance from one another on pain of being brought down like noosed hares.

'When he had finished this extraordinary job, Mohammed began to laugh that silent laugh of his, which shook his whole body with noiseless mirth.

' "There's your Arab chain," said he.

'The rest of us were convulsed with amusement at the terrified and piteous faces of our prisoners.

' "And now," cried our leader, "fix a stake at each end, my lads."

'Accordingly a stake was fixed at each end of this string of captives, who looked like phantoms in their white robes. They stood as motionless as if they had been turned into stone.

' "Now to dinner,"' cried Mohammed.

'We lit a fire and roasted a sheep, which we tore to pieces with our fingers. Then we ate some dates and drank some milk, which we found in the tents, where we also picked up a few silver ornaments left behind by the fugitives.

'We were peacefully finishing our meal when I saw on the opposite slope a singular gathering consisting entirely of the women who had just escaped. They were coming towards us at a run. I pointed them out to Mahommed, who remarked with a smile:

'"That's our dessert."

'A queer sort of dessert it was.

'They charged madly down upon us, hurling volleys of stones at us without checking their advance, and we saw that they were armed with knives, tent stakes, and old cooking pots.

'"Mount," ordered Mohammed, and not a moment too soon. The attack was desperate. Their object was to sever the rope and free the prisoners. Realizing our danger, Mohammed furiously shouted to us to cut the women down. Not a man stirred. Seeing that we were taken aback by this new sort of warfare, and were hesitating to kill women, he charged our assailants single-handed.

'All alone he faced that tatterdemalion battalion of women, and the ruffian wielded his sabre with such insensate fury, with such mad rage, that at each stroke a white-robed figure sank to the earth. Such was the terror he inspired that the women fled in panic as swiftly as they had come, leaving behind them a dozen dead and wounded, whose blood stained their white garments red.

'Then, with face convulsed, Mohammed returned to us.

'"Let's be off, my lads, they are sure to come back."

'We beat a retreat at a slow walk, leading our captives, who were paralysed by the fear of strangulation. It was noon on the following day when we arrived at Boghar with our chain of half-hanged men. Only six of them had died on the way, but every jerk threatened to choke a dozen prisoners, and we had to keep loosening the knots all along the line.'

Captain Marret had finished his story. I made no remark. I thought what a strange country this was, in which such scenes could be witnessed, and I looked up into the dark sky and gazed upon the radiant phalanx of innumerable stars.

MISS HARRIET

THERE were seven of us in the brake, four ladies and three men, one of whom sat on the box beside the coachman. Our horses were slowly climbing the long, steep road that wound round the hill. We had left Étretat at dawn in order to visit the ruins of Tancarville. Drugged by the strong morning air, we were still half asleep, especially the ladies, who were not accustomed to keep sportsmen's hours. Their eyelids kept drooping, their heads nodded, and they even yawned, all unconscious of the charm of the dawning day.

It was autumn. The harvest was in, and on either side of the road lay fields yellow with the stubble of oats and wheat, bristly like a badly-shaven chin. A mist, like steam, rose from the ground. High in the air larks were singing, and other birds were twittering in the thickets. At last before our eyes rose the sun, fiery red on the edge of the horizon. As it climbed higher, gaining in brightness minute by minute, the whole countryside seemed to awaken with a smile, to shake itself, and like a girl rising from her bed, to doff its vesture of white mist.

'Look, there's a hare,' exclaimed Count d'Étraille, who was on the box, and pointed to a field of clover on the left. The hare was stealing away, invisible except for its long ears; it crossed a stretch of ploughed land, then stopped short, galloped frantically first in one direction then another, stopped again uneasily, on the alert for danger, and doubtful which way safety lay. At last it bounded off with all the impetus of its powerful hind quarters, until it disappeared in a big square patch of beetroot. All the men roused themselves to watch its movements.

'We are not doing our duty by the ladies this morning,' remarked René Lemanoir, glancing at this neighbour, the young Baroness de Sérennes, who was struggling to keep awake.

'You are thinking of your husband, baroness,' he said to her in an undertone. 'Don't worry. He won't be back till Saturday. You have four more days.'

'How silly you are,' she replied with a sleepy smile. Then shaking off her drowsiness she added: 'Tell us something amusing and make us laugh. Monsieur Chenal, you are supposed to have had more successes than the Duke of Richelieu himself. Give us the story of some love affair of yours, any one you please.'

Léon Chenal was an old painter, who in his youth had been very handsome, very strong, very proud of his physique, and beloved of many ladies. He passed his hand over his long white beard and smiled. After a few moments' thought, however, he suddenly became grave.

'My story is not a cheerful one, ladies. I am going to tell you the most melancholy love affair of my life. May none of my friends ever inspire a passion so tragic!'

I

'I was twenty-five, a strolling painter, exploring the coast of Normandy. By this I mean roaming, knapsack on back, from inn to inn, on the pretext of making sketches and studies from nature. I know nothing pleasanter than such random wanderings. You are free and unfettered, without a care in the world or a thought for the morrow. You choose what road you please, with no guide but your own fancy, and no counsellor but the pleasure of the eyes. When something attracts you, be it a brook or the pleasing smell of fried potatoes issuing from an inn, you halt. Sometimes it is the scent of clematis that determines your choice, sometimes an artless glance from the innkeeper's daughter. Such rustic flirtations are not to be despised. These girls, too, have souls and senses, smooth cheeks and rosy lips. Their rough kisses have the piquant savour of wild fruit, and love has always a value of its own, whatever its origin. A heart that beats at your coming, eyes that weep at your departure, these are things too dear, too rare, too precious, ever to be despised. I have kept tryst by ditches full of primroses, behind cowsheds, in hay-lofts that still retained the heat of the day. I can yet recall the feel of coarse grey calico, that covers robust and supple limbs. Still am I haunted by the memory of those frank, ingenuous kisses, more seductive in their brutal directness than all the subtle delights that are offered by gracious women of the world.

'But the chief charm of such rambles lies in the country itself, in its woods, its sunrises, its dusk, its moonlight. For a painter it is, as it were, a honeymoon with Nature. In this long and tranquil communion you are alone with her in the closest intimacy. You throw yourself down in a meadow full of marguerites and poppies, and with wide open eyes you gaze through the bright sunshine at the little village in the distance and its pointed belfry with the clock just striking noon. You sit on the edge of a spring that bubbles up from beneath the root of an oak-tree, amid tall, delicate grasses vividly alive. You kneel down to drink the cold, clear water, which wets your moustache and nose, and you are conscious of a thrill of pleasure, as if, lip to lip, you were kissing the spring itself. Sometimes you come upon a pool in one of these slender rivulets, and in you plunge, stark naked, tingling from head to foot with the chill, delicious caress of the swift, dancing current. Gay on the hill-top, melancholy by the side of the lake, you are enraptured by the sight of the sun as it sinks down into a sea of blood-red clouds and suffuses the waters of the river with crimson light. And at night, when the moon rides high in the heavens, you are haunted by a thousand mystical thoughts, which would never visit you in the broad light of day.

'I was exploring this very district in which we are staying at present, and I came one evening to the little village of Bénouville, situated on the cliff between Yport and Étretat. I had come from Fécamp, along the coast, keeping to the lofty cliffs which rise like a perpendicular wall, broken by jutting rocks of chalk that fall sheer down to the sea. All that day I had been walking over the short turf, soft and springy as a carpet, which grows on the edge of the precipice in the salt wind from the ocean. Singing at the top of my voice, striding along lustily, and watching now the leisurely, wheeling flight of a gull, the curve of its white wings silhouetted against the blue sky, now the brown sail of a fishing boat on the emerald sea, I had spent a glorious day of careless freedom.

'I was directed to a little farm where strangers could find a lodging. It was a sort of inn with the usual Norman courtyard and a double row of beech-trees all around it. It was kept by a peasant woman. Leaving the cliff I made my way to the hamlet, nestling among its lofty trees, and I presented myself at Mother Lecacheur's door. She was old, wrinkled, and grim, and seemed always to receive her customers with an air of reluctance and suspicion.

'It was the month of May. Flowering apple-trees spread a canopy of scented blossom above the courtyard and rained a continual shower of fluttering rosy petals upon the grass and the passers-by.

'"Well, Madame Lecacheur," I said, "can you let me have a room?"

'Surprised to find that I knew her name, she replied:

'"That's as may be. All my rooms are taken. But we'll see what we can do."

'Five minutes later we had come to terms, and I deposited my knapsack on the floor of a rustic room containing a bed, two chairs, a table, and a basin. It opened off a big, smoky kitchen, where the guests took their meals with the farm hands and the widowed landlady.

'After I had washed my hands I went into the kitchen. The old woman was fricasseeing a chicken for dinner in the wide fire-place where a smoke-blackened pot-hook was hanging.

'"Then you have people staying here at present?" I asked.

'"I have one lady," she answered sourly. "An elderly Englishwoman. She has the other room."

'By paying an additional five sous a day I arranged to have my meals alone in the courtyard whenever it was fine. My table was laid outside the door, and I began to tackle the stringy limbs of the Norman hen to the accompaniment of sparkling cider and coarse white bread which, though four days old, was excellent none the less.

'Suddenly the wooden gate leading to the road was thrown open, and a singular female figure advanced towards the house. She was very thin and tall and had wound a red plaid Scotch shawl so tightly round her that one would have supposed her without arms had not a long hand appeared at the height of her hips, holding one of those white umbrellas that tourists carry. She had a face like a mummy; it was framed in grey corkscrew curls which bobbed at each step she took, and she reminded me, I hardly know why, of a red herring with butterflies fluttering round it. She passed me swiftly with downcast eyes, and vanished into the house. I was amused at this odd-looking apparition. Doubtless she was my fellow-guest, the elderly Englishwoman of whom the landlady had spoken. I did not see her again that day. The following morning I settled down to paint at the end of that delightful valley which you know, leading down to Étretat. Suddenly raising my eyes I caught sight of a curious object standing bolt upright on the brow of the hill, and looking like a dressed mast. It was the Englishwoman. As soon as she caught sight of me she disappeared.

'I returned home for luncheon and took my place at the common table, in order to make the acquaintance of this eccentric old maid. But she did not reply to my civilities and took no notice of my little attentions. Zealously I filled her glass with water; assiduously I passed her dishes. A slight, almost imperceptible, movement of the head, an English word murmured too softly for me to catch, were all the thanks I received.

'In the end I ceased to bother about her, although the idea of her continued to haunt me. In three days I knew as much about her as Madame Lecacheur herself.

'She was called Miss Harriet. Searching for some quiet village in which to spend the summer, she had stopped at Bénouville six weeks before and seemed loath to leave it. She never spoke at table, and ate hurriedly, reading a little book of Protestant propaganda all the time. Those books she distributed to every one. Even the parish priest had received four copies, brought to him by a small boy for a bribe of two *sous*. Sometimes, without any preparation, she would suddenly say to the landlady in her atrocious French:

'"I love the Lord above everything; I worship Him in His creation; I adore Him in all His works of nature; I carry Him always in my heart."

'And with these words she would bestow upon the bewildered countrywoman one of those tracts of hers, which were intended to convert the universe. She was not at all popular in the village. The schoolmaster had said:

'"She is an atheist."

'And from this pronouncement a sort of stigma rested upon her. But when Madame Lecacheur consulted the parish priest he replied:

'"She is a heretic, but God desireth not the death of a sinner, and I believe her to be a person of blameless morality."

'These words, "atheist," "heretic," of which they scarcely knew the meaning, roused dark suspicions in the minds of the villagers. It was rumoured, moreover, that the Englishwoman was wealthy, and that she spent her life travelling all over the world because her family had turned her out. And for what reason had her family done so? Why, because of her impiety.

'She was, in truth, one of those bigoted fanatics, one of those stubborn Puritans, whom England breeds in such numbers, those pious and insupportable old maids, who haunt all the tables d'hôte in Europe, who ruin Italy, poison Switzerland, and render the charming towns on the Riviera uninhabitable, introducing everywhere their weird manias, their manners of petrified vestals, their indescribable wardrobes, and a peculiar odour of rubber, as if they were put away in a waterproof case every night. Whenever I saw one in an hotel I used to take to flight, like a bird that has seen a scarecrow in a field. But this particular specimen seemed to me so remarkable that I could not dislike her.

'Instinctively hostile to anything outside her peasant life, Madame Lecacheur's limited intelligence conceived a hatred for the old maid's transports. She had hit upon a phrase to describe her, a disparaging phrase to be sure, which had sprung to her lips I know not how, born of some confused and mysterious working of her mind.

'"She is a demoniac," she declared. And this epithet, applied to that austere yet sentimental creature, seemed to me irresistibly droll. I never referred to her by any other name, and experienced a curious pleasure in uttering the word aloud, whenever I caught sight of her.

'"Well," I would say to Madame Lecacheur, "and what is our demoniac doing to-day?"

'In scandalized tones, my hostess would reply:

'"You'll never believe it, sir. She brought home a toad with a crushed leg, and put it in her basin and bandaged it as if it were human. Blasphemous I call it."

'Another day, when she was walking on the beach, she had bought a big fish which had just been caught, simply for the sake of throwing it back into the sea. Although he had been well paid, the fisherman had abused her roundly, and felt more indignant than if she had taken his money out of his pocket. Even after a month had elapsed, he could not speak of the incident without flying into a rage and using insulting language about her. Yes, she was certainly a demoniac, Miss Harriet

Mother Lecacheur had had an inspiration of genius when she christened her thus.

'The stable-boy, who was called Sapper because he had served in Africa in his young days, held a different opinion. He used to say slyly:

'"She 's an old soldier; she served her time."

'What would she have said, poor soul, if she had known all this? Céleste, the little maid, disliked waiting on her, I could never discover why. Perhaps it was simply because she was a foreigner, alien in race, language, and religion—in short, a demoniac.

'She spent her time wandering all over the countryside, seeking and worshipping God in His creation. One evening, attracted by a patch of red gleaming through the trees, I pushed aside the branches and came upon Miss Harriet on her knees in a thicket. Confused at having been caught in that attitude, she started to her feet, and fixed upon me the startled eyes of an owl surprised in broad daylight. Sometimes, when I was at work among the rocks, I would suddenly catch sight of her on the edge of the cliff, looking like a signal post. She stood there, gazing rapturously at the mighty ocean suffused with golden light; at the wide sky bathed in purple glow. Sometimes I espied her at the end of a valley, walking with her swift, elastic, English steps, and I went towards her, attracted, I hardly knew why, by the mere sight of her transfigured face, that withered, indescribable face of hers, with its expression of inward joy. Often I would come upon her near some farm, seated on the grass in the shade of an apple-tree, with her little book of devotions open on her knees, and her gaze on the distant prospect.

'I could not tear myself away from Bénouville. I felt myself linked to this peaceful countryside by a thousand ties of love— love for its wide enchanting landscapes. I was happy staying in this out-of-the-world farm, remote from mankind, close to the earth, to the bountiful, health-giving, fair green earth, which we shall some day enrich with our own bodies. And, I must confess, a faint stirring of curiosity detained me. I wanted to make friends with this strange Miss Harriet and to discover what goes on in the lonely souls of these elderly, wandering English ladies.

II

'We made friends in rather a curious way. I had just finished a picture, which seemed to me a beauty, as indeed it was. Fifteen years later it was sold for ten thousand francs. It was as simple as two and two make four, and it disregarded every academic rule. The entire right half of my canvas represented a rock, a huge rock, covered with seaweed, brown and yellow and red, with the light pouring over it like oil. The sun was at my back, but its radiance fell upon the rock and gilded it with fire. That was all. It had a dazzling foreground of flaming, glorious brightness, and on the left the sea, no blue, slate-coloured sea, but a sea of jade, greenish, milky, and hard, under a dark sky. Such was my delight over my work, that I danced with joy, as I carried it back to the inn. I should have liked every one to see it immediately. I remember showing it to a cow by the roadside, and exclaiming:

'"Look at that, old girl. You won't often see one as good."

'When I reached home, I shouted for the landlady at the top of my voice.

'"Hi, Mother Lecacheur, hi! Come here and take a look at this."

'The old rustic came up and contemplated my work with dull, unseeing eyes, hardly knowing whether it represented a house or a cow.

'At that moment Miss Harriet entered, and passed behind me just as I was holding my picture at arm's length and exhibiting it to the landlady. I was careful to hold the canvas in such a way that the demoniac could not help seeing it. Petrified with amazement, she stopped short. This, it seemed, was her favourite rock, the one she always climbed in order to indulge in her daydreams.

'"Oh!" she murmured in her English accent.

'Such was the flattery in her voice, that I turned to her with a smile.

'"My latest picture, Miss Harriet."

'With an expression of rapture, half ludicrous, half touching, she replied:

'"Your understanding of nature is thrilling."

'I tell you I blushed at her praise as if it had been spoken by a queen. I was charmed; I was completely conquered. Upon my soul, I could have kissed her. At table I seated myself beside her as usual. For the first time, she spoke to me, still uttering her thoughts aloud:

'"Oh, I do love nature so !"

'I passed her bread, water, and wine; she now accepted my attentions with a faint and cadaverous smile. We rose from the meal together and walked across the yard. Then, attracted doubtless by the flaming splendour in which the setting sun had bathed the ocean, I opened the gate leading to the cliff, and we wandered off together, perfectly happy, like two people who have just discovered a common bond of sympathy.

'It was a soft, warm evening, one of those evenings when body and soul are content. All is rapture, all is charm. One breathes with delight the warm, balmy air, scented with seaweed and grass; the palate is stimulated by the savour of the sea, while the spirit is soothed by the penetrating sweetness of the hour. We were walking on the edge of the cliff, and looking down on the mighty ocean, which rippled three hundred feet below us. With parted lips we drew in deep breaths of the cool sea breeze, wafted gently from the ocean, and salt with the lingering kiss of the waves. Wrapped in her check shawl, my companion watched with open-mouthed ecstasy the huge disk of the sun as it sank down into the sea. Far away on the skyline, a three-master in full sail stood out against the flaming background, and a steamer passed across the foreground, leaving a trail of smoke like an endless wisp of cloud right across the sky.

'The red orb of day was sinking slowly to rest. Presently it touched the water, just behind the motionless ship, which seemed as if framed in fire, in the very middle of the glowing sphere. Lower and lower sank the sun, until it was gradually swallowed up by the ocean. It plunged into the water, and disappeared. It was all over. But the little ship still remained silhouetted against the far-away golden background of the sky.

'With passionate delight, Miss Harriet watched the sumptuous close of day. She had a positively violent yearning to embrace the sky, and the sea and the whole prospect.

'"Oh," she exclaimed, "I love it, I love it, I love it !"

'I saw a tear sparkle in her eyes.

'"I wish I were a little bird," she added, "to fly away into the sky."

'She stood there, as I had so often seen her, planted on the cliff, a patch of vivid colour in her scarlet shawl. I was longing to sketch her in my notebook. She would have passed for a caricature of ecstasy. I turned away to hide a smile.

'Then I began to talk about painting, as if to a brother artist, discussing tones and values and intensity, without avoiding technical terms. She listened attentively and intelligently, trying to divine the meaning of obscure phrases and to reach the thought that lay beneath.

'Every now and then she exclaimed:

'"Oh, I understand, I understand. It is very thrilling."

'We went in.

'The next morning, as soon as she saw me, she held out her hand, and we were suddenly friends. She was a good creature, with a soul always on springs, ready to go off into ecstasies of enthusiasm. Like all old maids of fifty, she lacked balance. She seemed to be preserved in a kind of acid innocence, but her heart still retained something very youthful and passionate. She loved nature and animals with that exaggerated tenderness which ferments like wine that is kept too long, with that sensual passion which had never been lavished upon a man. At the sight of a dog suckling her puppies, a mare with her colt, a nest full of cheeping, gaping baby birds with big heads and naked bodies, she quivered with excessive emotion.

'Poor solitary souls, wandering sadly from table d'hôte to table d'hôte, poor souls, absurd and pitiable, having known one of you, my heart goes out to you all!

'I soon guessed that she had something to say to me, but was too shy to speak, and I was amused at her timidity. When I left the inn in the morning with my paint-box on my back, she would accompany me to the end of the village, silent, obviously perplexed, and trying to make a beginning. Then she would suddenly leave me, and walk swiftly away with that elastic step of hers.

'At last one day she plucked up courage.

'"I should like to see how you do your painting. May I? I am very curious."

'And she blushed as if she had said something very daring.

'I took her with me to the end of the Petit-Val, where I was beginning a large picture. She stood behind me, watching every stroke with concentration. Presently, as if afraid of disturbing me, she thanked me and went away.

'After a while she gained confidence, and took an obvious pleasure in accompanying me every day. Under her arm she carried a folding stool, of which she would not allow me to relieve her, and she would seat herself beside me. She stayed there for hours, motionless and silent, her eyes watching every movement of my brush. When I slapped a great dab of paint on to the canvas with my palette knife, unexpectedly producing the right effect, she could not restrain a soft "Oh!" of astonishment and delight and admiration. She had a tender respect for my canvases, a respect that was almost religious for these human reproductions of divine creation. They seemed to her almost like sacred pictures. Often she spoke to me of God, and endeavoured to convert me.

'He was a curious sort of fellow, this God of hers, a kind of rustic philosopher, without great resources or great power, for she imagined Him always grieving over the wrongs committed before His eyes—just as if He could not have prevented them. She was, it seemed, on excellent terms with Him, the confidante of His secrets and of His disappointments. "God wills," or "God does not will," fell from her lips, as if she were a sergeant passing on the colonel's orders to a recruit. She deeply deplored my ignorance of the divine purpose, which she endeavoured to reveal to me, and every day I found in my pockets, in my hat, when I had left it on the ground, in my paint-box, in the shoes outside my door, some of those little pious tracts, which she doubtless received direct from Paradise.

'I treated her with frank cordiality, like an old friend. But presently I saw that her manner had changed, though it was some time before I noticed it. When I was working, deep in my valley or in some hollow lane, I would see her suddenly appear with her quick elastic step. Palpitating as if she had been running, or as if in the grip of some violent emotion, she would sit down abruptly, flushed with that curious tone of red which is peculiar to the English. Then, without any apparent reason, she would turn a muddy white, as if on the verge of fainting. Gradually, however, I saw her resume her normal appearance, and she would begin talking to me, only to break off in the middle of a sentence, leap to her feet and dart away with such strange haste that I wondered what I could have done to offend her. At last I came to the conclusion that this must be her usual behaviour, which she had, no doubt, slightly modified for my

benefit in the early days of our acquaintance. After walking for
hours on the wind-swept hill, she used to return to the farm with
her long corkscrew curls as lank and limp as if their springs were
broken. In the early days of our acquaintance she had paid no
heed to this, and had sat down to table without embarrassment,
with her hair thus dishevelled by her sister, the wind. But
now she always went to her room and rearranged what I called
her chandelier drops. I often said to her with a friendly
gallantry, which always shocked her: "You are radiant as a
star to-day, Miss Harriet," and at this a slight flush rose to her
cheeks, the flush of a girl of fifteen.

'Presently she grew so shy that she no longer came to watch
me paint. I thought to myself:

'"It is only a passing phase; she 'll get over it."

'But she did not get over it. Whenever I spoke to her now
she answered with affected indifference or with sulky petulance.
She had fits of brusque impatience and attacks of nerves. I
never saw her except at meals, and we no longer conversed. I
came to the conclusion that I must have hurt her feelings in some
way, and one evening I said to her:

'"Miss Harriet, why don't you treat me as you used to do?
What have I done to vex you? You make me very unhappy."

'With curious passion in her voice she replied:

'"It 's not true. It 's not true. I have always treated you
the same," and she escaped to her room.

'Sometimes I saw her watching me in a strange way. Since
then I have often thought that a condemned person must wear
just that same expression when informed of the day of his execution. There was a look in her eyes, a look of insanity, of
mysticism, of violence, and more than that, a fever, a frantic
yearning, as if she were chafing at some secret thing she had not
realized and could never realize. And it seemed to me that a
struggle was going on within her, her heart matching itself against
some unknown force, which she strove to vanquish, and perhaps
there was something else. . . . Who knows? Who knows?

III

'The explanation of it all was strange enough.

'For some time I had been working every morning, from
daybreak, at a picture, the subject of which was as follows:

'A deep, precipitous ravine, winding away into the distance

between steep banks mantled with trees and brambles, lay bathed and veiled in that milky mist, that fleecy whiteness which floats above valleys at dawn. And through the depths of this dense yet transparent cloud, half seen, half divined, came a pair of lovers, a man and a maid, with their arms around each other, she raising her head towards him, he bending down to her, till their lips met. In the background, the sun's first ray, gliding through the branches, pierced the morning mist and suffused it with a rosy glow, irradiating the shadowy forms of the rustic lovers with silvery light. Upon my soul it was good, very good indeed.

'I was working on the hill-side which slopes down to the little valley of Étretat. It so happened that morning, that the floating mist was just as I wanted it.

'Something rose before my sight like a phantom. It was Miss Harriet. As soon as she saw me, she tried to escape, but I called to her:

'"Come here, Miss Harriet, come here. I have a little picture for you."

'Reluctantly she drew near me, and I handed her my sketch. She made no comment, but stood quite still, gazing at it for a long time. Then suddenly she burst into tears. She wept convulsively as people do who have been suppressing their tears and have come to the end of their resistance, but still struggle against their emotion, even while they yield to it. Touched by this sorrow, which I did not understand, I sprang to my feet, and with an impulse of spontaneous affection, an impulse characteristic of a Frenchman, who acts before he thinks, I seized her hands. She left them in mine for a few moments, and I felt them tremble as if she were quivering in every nerve. Then she drew, or rather snatched them, abruptly away. But I had recognized that shudder of hers; it was not the first time I had felt it, and I could never mistake it. Ah, that shudder of a woman in love, be she fifteen or fifty, of humble or gentle birth, it goes so straight to my heart that I can never fail to understand it. Her whole unhappy person had trembled, quivered, and collapsed. I understood. Before I could utter a word she went from me, leaving me astonished as at a miracle, and as wretched as if I had committed a crime.

'I did not return home for luncheon. I went for a walk round the cliffs, feeling as much disposed to cry as to laugh. The situation seemed to me as tragic as it was ludicrous. I felt ridiculous, and at the same time I realized that she was nearly crazy with unhappiness. I wondered what I ought to do, and came to the conclusion that my only course was to go away. This I decided to do at once. Somewhat sad and thoughtful, I roamed about till dinner-time, and then returned home. We sat down to table as usual. Miss Harriet was present, solemnly eating her dinner, without talking to any one or raising her eyes. Her appearance and behaviour were perfectly normal. I waited till the end of the meal. Then I turned to the landlady:

'"Well, Madame Lecacheur, I am going to leave you soon."

'The good woman was surprised and distressed.

'"What do you say, my dear young gentleman?" she cried in her drawling voice. "You're going to leave us, just when I had got used to you?"

'I stole a glance at Miss Harriet. Her face showed no sign of emotion. But Céleste, the little maid, raised her eyes to mine. She was a plump, fresh-faced, rosy-cheeked girl of eighteen, as strong as a horse and unusually clean in her person. I sometimes stole a kiss when I caught her in a corner, as is the way with men of my roving habits. But that was all.

'After dinner I went into the yard and walked up and down under the apple-trees, smoking my pipe. My meditations during the day, the extraordinary discovery of that grotesque and ardent passion which I had inspired, the memories, disturbing and charming, which this revelation had conjured up, and perhaps the little maid's glance when I announced my departure, the accumulation of all these mingled emotions and ideas put the devil into my bones, made my lips tingle with kisses, and infused into my veins that mysterious something which drives us to make fools of ourselves.

'Night fell, deepening the shadows beneath the trees. I caught sight of Céleste on her way to lock up the henhouse, which was on the other side of the enclosure. Stepping so lightly that she did not hear me, I ran after her, and when she straightened herself after lowering the trapdoor of the henhouse, I caught her in my arms and covered her broad, plump face with kisses. She struggled, laughing all the time, well accustomed to such episodes. What made me suddenly release her? Why did I turn round with a start? How was it that I felt someone behind me?

'It was Miss Harriet. Just as she was going indoors she had seen us, and she stood there motionless, as if confronted by a ghost. Then she vanished into the night. Ashamed and troubled, I returned to the inn, more distressed at her having caught me playing the fool than if she had seen me committing a positive crime. I was overtired, haunted by gloomy thoughts, and I slept badly. I thought I heard a sound of weeping, but I may have been mistaken. Several times, too, I thought I heard someone moving about the house and opening the door leading into the yard. Towards daybreak I fell asleep, utterly worn out, and it was late when I awoke. I did not make my appearance until luncheon; I was still feeling ashamed of myself and hardly knew what face to put upon it.

'No one had seen Miss Harriet. We waited for her in vain. Mother Lecacheur looked into her room, but she had gone out. Doubtless she had left the house at dawn, as she often did, in order to see the sunrise. No concern was felt, and we sat silently down to our meal. It was very hot indeed, one of those heavy, sultry days when not a leaf stirs. The table had been set out of doors under an apple-tree, and we were so thirsty that Sapper was always running down to the cellar to replenish the cider jug. Céleste brought the dishes from the kitchen, mutton stew with potatoes and a hare *sauté* with salad. Then she placed on the table a dish of cherries, the first of the season. I wanted to wash them and freshen them up and asked the maid to draw me a bucket of cold well-water.

'In five minutes she returned and said that the well had dried up. She had let down the rope to its full length and the bucket had touched the bottom and come up empty. Mother Lecacheur went to see for herself and looked down the well. When she came back she declared that she could see something in the well, something that ought not to be there. Doubtless a neighbour had thrown in bundles of straw out of spite. Hoping to obtain a better view I leaned over the edge and had an indistinct glimpse of something white. What could it be? It occurred to me to lower a lantern by a rope. The yellow light flickered on the stone walls of the well, as the lantern sank gradually into the depths. All four of us, including Sapper and Céleste, were bending down over the opening. Suddenly the lantern stopped at a strange, indistinguishable, mysterious mass of white and black.

'"It's a horse," cried Sapper. "I can see its hoof. It must have strayed from the field last night and fallen in."

'Suddenly I shuddered to the marrow of my bones. I recognized a human foot and leg projecting upwards, while the body and the other leg were submerged in the water. Trembling so violently that the lantern danced distractedly up and down above the shoe, I gasped in a broken whisper:

'"It's a woman . . . a woman. . . . It's Miss Harriet."

'Sapper did not move an eyelid. He had seen worse things in Africa. Uttering piercing screams, Mother Lecacheur and Céleste took to their heels. The dead body had to be recovered. I fastened a rope securely round the stable-boy's waist, lowered him very slowly by means of the pulley, and watched him disappearing into the gloom with the lantern and a second rope in his hands. Presently, in a voice which seemed to come from the bowels of the earth, he cried: "Stop now," and I saw him fishing something out of the water. It was the corpse's other leg. Then he tied both its feet together and called out:

'"Haul away!"

'I drew him up to the surface, though my arms felt so nerveless, my muscles so slack, that I was afraid of letting the rope slip and dropping my man back into the depths.

'"Well?" I said as soon as his head appeared above the brink, just as if I had expected him to give me news of her who was down in that darkness. We both climbed on to the stone coping of the well, and bending down over the opening from opposite sides, we hoisted the body up.

'Hidden behind the wall of the house, Madame Lecacheur and Céleste were watching us. As soon as they saw the drowned woman's black shoes and white stockings emerge from the well they vanished.

'Sapper seized her by the ankles, and dragged her out. Her head was a terrible sight, all bruised and battered, and her long, grey hair hung loose and dishevelled, dripping with water and slime; the corkscrew curls were gone for ever.

'"Lord, isn't she skinny!" said Sapper contemptuously.

'We carried her into her room, and as the two women did not return, with the help of the stable boy I prepared the body for its final resting-place. I washed her poor distorted face. The touch of my finger caused one eye to open a little. It looked at me with that cold wan glance, that frightful glance, with which the dead regard us, as if from beyond the grave. I ordered her wild locks as best I could, my unskilled hands arranging them on her brow in a strange, new fashion. Then I stripped off her dripping clothes, revealing shamefacedly, as if committing an act of sacrilege, her shoulders and bosom and her long arms, as thin as sticks. Then I gathered poppies, marguerites and cornflowers and fragrant grasses, with which I decked her funeral couch.

'Being the only person acquainted with her, I had to see to the various formalities. I found a letter in her pocket expressing her wish to be buried in this village where she had spent the last days of her life. A terrible thought clutched at my heart. Was it not for my sake that she desired to remain in this spot?

'Towards evening all the women in the village came to look at the dead, but I barred the door. I wished to remain alone, and I watched by her all night. By the light of the candles I gazed at this unhappy woman, whom no one knew, and who had perished thus miserably and far from home. Had she somewhere friends and kindred? Where had she spent her childhood and her subsequent existence? Whence had she come, all alone, homeless, forlorn like a dog driven from its dwelling? What secret suffering and despair were concealed beneath that forbidding exterior, that form which she was doomed to carry with her all through life, that absurd mask which alienated all love, all affection?

'What unhappy beings there are in the world! I was conscious of the eternal injustice of inexorable nature, which had weighed so heavily upon this poor human soul. All was over for her. Perhaps she had never known even that one hope which sustains the most forlorn of mankind, the hope of being loved once at least in life. Why else should she have hidden herself away and avoided her fellows? Why else had she lavished such passionate fondness on all things living, save mankind alone? I realized that she had indeed believed in God, and that she hoped to receive in another world full recompense for her sufferings here. And now her body would crumble into dust, and plants would spring from it. It would blossom in the sunshine: the cows would browse upon it; its seeds would be borne afar by the birds; in the flesh of cattle it would become part of a human body again. But that which we call the soul had perished in the dark bottom of the well. Its sufferings were over. She had exchanged her own life for the lives of those that would spring from the dust of her body.

'The hours of this sinister and silent vigil passed away. A faint light heralded the dawn. Then a red ray glided across the bed, resting like a bar of fire on the sheets and the dead woman's hands. This was the hour that she had always loved. The awakening birds were singing in the trees. I threw open the window and drew the curtains, so that the whole sky beheld us. Bending above the ice-cold body I took her disfigured head in both hands, and slowly, without horror or disgust, I printed a kiss, a lingering kiss, upon those lips that had never yet received one.'

.   .   .   .   .

Léon Chenal fell silent. The ladies were all in tears, and Count d'Étraille on the box kept using his handkerchief. The coachman alone was dozing, and the horses, untouched by the whip, had slowed down and were pulling languidly. The brake hardly moved. It seemed suddenly as heavy as if it carried a load of sorrow.

IN THE SPRING

(*Au Printemps*)

On the first sunny days of the year, when earth stirs in her sleep and clothes herself with green, when the balmy air caresses our cheeks, fills our lungs, and seems to penetrate to the very heart, a vague yearning for unknown joys steals over us, an impulse to run and leap, to roam at random in pursuit of adventure, and to drink deep draughts of the spring weather. After the severe winter of last year, the month of May inspired me with such longing to be free of all restraint, that it was like a fever in the blood or the swift flow of sap in my veins. When I woke up one morning I saw through my window, above the roofs of the neighbouring houses, the great blue vault of the sky, brilliant with sunshine. The canaries in their cages by the window were trilling their loudest. On every floor the maids were singing at their work. Cheerful sounds from the streets greeted my ears, and in holiday mood I escaped from the house without caring whither I went.

There were smiles on every face; spring, warm and radiant, had come again, and happiness was in the air. It was as if the whole town felt the caress of an amorous breeze. The young women who passed by in their morning frocks had a veiled tenderness in their glances, and in all their movements a languid grace which set my heart in a flutter. Half unconsciously I made my way to the Seine. Steamers were leaving for Suresnes, and I was suddenly seized with an irresistible longing for the woods.

The deck of the little steamer was crowded, for, resist as you may, the first sunshine of the year lures you out of the house. Every one is astir, coming and going, chatting with his neighbour.

My own neighbour happened to be a lady; a little work-girl, I judged her, with all the natural grace of the true-bred Parisian. She had a charming little head, hair like spun sunshine, clustering in curls round her temples, and rippling down to her ears and the

156

nape of her neck, where it ended in golden down so soft and fine that you could hardly see it and yet you were burning to cover it with kisses. I stared at her so hard that she turned towards me; then she suddenly lowered her eyelids, while the corners of her mouth quivered with the merest suggestion of a smile, revealing on her upper lip the same soft silken down, glinting faintly in the sun.

The river flowed smoothly between ever-widening banks. A warm peacefulness brooded in the atmosphere, and all space seemed full of murmurous life. My neighbour raised her eyes. Again they met mine, and this time she smiled deliberately. She was charming when she smiled, and her swift glance revealed to me a thousand mysteries I had never before suspected. I discovered in her eyes unknown depths, all the joys of love, all the poetry that inspires our dreams, all the bliss we are eternally seeking. I was seized with a mad desire to clasp her in my arms and bear her away to some spot where I could murmur in her ears the tender music of loving words.

I was just going to speak to her when someone touched me on the shoulder. I turned round in surprise and saw an ordinary-looking man, neither young nor old, who was gazing at me with a melancholy expression on his face.

'I have something to say to you,' he began. He must have noticed my expression of disgust, for he added:

'Something important.'

I rose and followed him to the other end of the boat.

'My dear sir,' he continued, 'when winter comes, bringing with it cold and rain and snow, your doctor is always saying to you: "Keep your feet warm and beware of chills, colds, bronchitis, and pleurisy." And you take all sorts of precautions, wear flannel underclothing and thick overcoats and shoes. And for all that you sometimes find yourself laid up for a couple of months. But when spring comes with its leaves and flowers, its warm, enervating breezes, its scents of field and meadow, stirring in you a vague restlessness and inexplicable emotions, there is no one to say to you: "Beware of love! It is lurking everywhere, lying in wait for you at every corner. Its snares are set; its weapons sharpened; all its wiles are prepared for you. Beware of love, beware! It is more dangerous than colds, bronchitis, or pleurisy. It never forgives and it drives us all to irreparable acts of folly." Yes, sir, I tell you Government ought to post huge placards upon the walls every year: "Spring is here again. Citizens of France, beware of love," just as one writes on the door of a house: "Mind the paint." Well, as Government neglects this duty I take it upon myself to say to you: Beware of love. It is ready to pounce upon you, and I am bound to warn you, just as in Russia one warns a passing stranger that his nose is threatened with frost-bite.'

I was amazed at this extraordinary individual. Assuming an air of dignity I replied:

'It seems to me, sir, that you are interfering in a matter that does not concern you.'

He made a deprecating gesture and replied:

'Oh, my dear sir, my dear sir, if I see a man in danger of drowning am I to leave him to perish? Let me tell you my story, and you will understand why I have ventured to speak to you like this. It was only last year, at this very season. I must begin by informing you that I am a clerk in the Admiralty, where the commissioners, our superiors, though mere office men, use their gold lace as warrant for treating us like common sailors. Oh, if all superior officers were civil—but I digress. From my office window I caught a glimpse of bright blue sky, where swallows were circling, and it made me feel like dancing among my black filing-cases. My longing for liberty rose to such a pitch that I screwed up my courage and went to see my own special slave-driver. He was a peevish little devil, always in a vile temper. I said I was feeling ill. He stared me in the face and said:

'"I don't believe a word of it. However, you can go. How do you think a man can run an office with clerks like you?"

'So I took myself off and went down to the Seine. It was just such weather as to-day and I boarded the steamer for Saint-Cloud.

'My dear sir, if only my chief had refused me leave! My whole nature seemed to expand in the sunshine. I was in love with everything, the steamer, the river, the trees, the houses, my neighbours. I was yearning for something to embrace, no matter what. Love was laying its snares for me. At the Trocadéro a girl came on board carrying a small parcel, and sat down opposite me. She was undoubtedly pretty, but it is extraordinary how much more attractive women appear to one in fine weather in the early spring. There is about them a heady charm, a mysterious something peculiar to themselves. It is like the taste of wine after cheese.

'I looked at her, and she, too, looked at me—but only now and then, like that girl of yours just now. At last I thought that we had advanced far enough with this exchange of glances to enter into conversation, so I spoke to her, and she replied. She was as charming as you please, and she turned my head completely.

'She left the boat at Saint-Cloud, where she had a parcel to deliver—and I followed her. When she returned from her errand the boat had gone. I walked beside her, and we sighed, both of us, affected by the balmy sweetness of the air.

'"It would be lovely in the woods," I said.

'"Yes, wouldn't it?" she agreed.

'"Would you care to come for a stroll?" I ventured.

'She stole a swift glance at me from beneath her eyelids, as if taking stock of me, and she hesitated a moment before she consented. Presently we were wandering side by side through the trees. The tall, thick grass, vividly green beneath the transparent shelter of the young leaves, was flooded with sunshine and swarming with tiny creatures, and they, too, were busy making love. Birds were singing in every bush. My companion suddenly began to skip and run, intoxicated with fresh air and the scents that rose from the earth. And I ran after her, frisking in the same ridiculous way. What a fool one does make of oneself sometimes!

'Wild with delight, she burst into a thousand ditties, airs from the operas, and that song of Musette. Oh, that song of Musette! How exquisitely poetic it seemed to me then! It moved me almost to tears. That's the sort of rubbish that turns one's head. Never take a girl into the country who sings, especially one who sings that song of Musette.

'Presently she was tired and sat down to rest on a green bank. I threw myself at her feet, and seized her hands, her little hands all covered with needle pricks. The sight of them went to my heart.

'"These," I said to myself, "are the sacred marks of toil."

'My dear sir, do you know what they really mean, those sacred marks of toil? They stand for all the gossip of the work-room, for whispered vulgarity, for minds polluted with obscene stories, for foolish tittle-tattle, for all the squalid usages of

life, for all the narrow-mindedness inevitable to all women of
the lower classes, but supreme with those whose finger-tips
bear those sacred marks of toil.

'We gazed lingeringly into each other's eyes.

'Oh, those eyes of women! What power is theirs, to be-
wilder and obsess, to conquer and dominate! How infinite
seems the promise within their depths! This practice is known
as looking into each other's soul. Stuff and nonsense, my dear
fellow! If one could really see into the soul, one would be far
more discreet.

'To cut a long story short, a madness seized me, and losing
my head I tried to clasp her in my arms.

'"Hands off!" she cried.

'At that I flung myself at her feet and poured out all the
pent-up emotion of my heart. She seemed surprised at my
changed demeanour and shot a sidelong glance at me, as if to say:
'"So that's the sort of fool you are! Very well, my friend,
we shall see."

'In love, we men are the innocent customers, while women
are the wide-awake shopkeepers. I might have done as I
pleased with her. Later on I realized my stupidity. But what
I was striving after was something immaterial, an ethereal,
an idealized love. I sought the shadow when I might have
gained the substance.

'When she was tired of my protestations, she rose and we
returned to Saint-Cloud. We did not part until we reached Paris,
and then she seemed so sad that I asked her the reason.

'"I was thinking how few days like this there are in life,"
she answered.

'My heart almost burst with emotion.

'We met again the following Sunday, and every succeeding
Sunday. I took her to Bougival, Saint-Germain, Maisons-
Laffitte, Poissy, to every haunt sacred to the suburban lover.
The little minx led me on, pretending a passion for me. I lost
my head entirely, and three months later I married her.

'I ask you, sir, what can a lonely man do, a mere clerk, with
no family to advise him? One thinks to oneself how happy
life would be with one woman. And so one marries her. And
then she scolds you from morning till night; you discover that
she is stupid and ignorant. She keeps on bawling that song of
Musette, that intolerable song of Musette. She wrangles with

the coal man, relates to the porter's wife intimate domestic details, confides to the servant next door secrets of the most delicate nature, involves her husband in difficulties with the tradesmen, and her head is stuffed with such absurd stories, such idiotic superstitions, such grotesque notions, such outrageous prejudices, that one could weep with disgust whenever one talks to her.'

He was so deeply agitated that he had to pause for breath. I looked compassionately at this poor simple-minded devil, and was on the point of replying when the steamer stopped at Saint-Cloud. The girl who had attracted my attention rose from her seat to go ashore. She brushed past me, with a side-long glance at me and a smile, at once furtive and seductive. Then she alighted on the pontoon.

I sprang up to follow her, when my neighbour seized me by the sleeve. I jerked myself free, but he caught me by the tails of my frock-coat and pulled me back.

'You shan't go, you shan't go,' he cried in such loud tones that every one turned round.

I heard a ripple of laughter on all sides, and I stood there, petrified and furious, but lacking the courage to face further ridicule and scandal.

And the steamer moved on.

The girl remained standing on the pontoon and watched me disappear with an air of disappointment, while my tormentor rubbed his hands together and whispered in my ear:

'There, young man, I have done you a real service.'

MADAME PARISSE

I

I HAD seated myself on the breakwater which protects the little harbour of Obernon, near the village of La Salis, to watch the sun set over Antibes. Never had I seen anything so astonishingly beautiful. Girt by Vauban's massive fortifications, the little town jutted out into the sea, midway along the shores of the imposing Gulf of Nice. Great rollers from the open sea broke at its foot, encircling it with a fringe of foam. Rising above the ramparts, the houses climbed one above the other up to the twin towers that stood out against the sky like the two horns of an ancient helmet, silhouetted against the milky whiteness of the Alps, those vast distant bastions of snow that bounded the horizon. Between the white foam at its feet and the white snow on the skyline, the radiant little town, in relief against the violet background of the foremost mountains, fronted the rays of the sinking sun like a pyramid of houses, of which the roofs were red, while the façades, white as the snow and the foam, had yet an infinite variety of tones in the evening light. Even the sky above the Alps was of a blue which was almost white, as if the paleness of the snow had touched it. A few silvery clouds hovered above the ghostly peaks, and on the other side of the Gulf lay Nice, a white ribbon stretched out between the sea and the mountain. Two great lateen-sailed vessels, driven by a strong breeze, sped over the waves. I gazed on the scene with wonder and delight. It was one of those spectacles, so rare and so entrancing, that they penetrate to the heart, and linger there like happy memories. Through the medium of sight, one lives, thinks, suffers, feels, and loves. To one who has this faculty, the contemplation of objects and persons brings the same pure, subtle, deep joy as a man experiences whose sensitive ear opens his soul to the ecstasies of music.

Turning to my companion, Monsieur Martini, a pure-blooded southerner, I remarked:

'This is one of the finest spectacles I have ever been privileged to enjoy. I have seen Mont Saint-Michel, that immense jewel wrought out of granite, springing up from the sands at daybreak. In the Sahara I have seen Lake Raianechergui, thirty-two miles long, shining in the light of a moon as brilliant as our northern sun, and from its surface I have seen a white mist, like a milky vapour, rising towards the moon. In the Lipari islands I have seen that fantastic, sulphurous crater of Volcanello, like a giant flower emitting smoke and flame, an immense yellow blossom blooming in the sea with a volcano for its stem. But I have never beheld anything more ravishing than Antibes at sunset, nestling at the foot of the Alps. I am haunted, I know not why, by echoes from antiquity. Lines from Homer are ringing in my ears. Antibes is a city of the East, of the classic past, of the Odyssey. It is Troy itself, though Troy was not a seaport.'

Monsieur Martini drew a guide-book from his pocket, and read an extract:

'"This town was originally founded as a colony by Phocaeans from Marseilles about 340 B.C. It received the Greek name Antipolis, that is to say, 'Opposite City,' because it lay opposite Nice, which was also colonized from Marseilles. After the conquest of Gaul, the Romans made Antibes a municipality, conferring upon its inhabitants the rights of Roman citizenship. We learn from one of Martial's epigrams that in his time——"'

Here I interrupted him.

'I don't care what it was. I tell you I am looking at a town out of the Odyssey. Whether they were on the Asiatic or the European coast, these cities were very much alike, and there is not one of them on the other side of the Mediterranean which stirs in me the memory of the heroic age as this one does.'

A sound of footsteps made me turn my head. A tall, dark woman was moving along the road which skirts the sea and leads to the cape.

'That's Madame Parisse, you know,' whispered Monsieur Martini.

I was not aware of it, but this name that he uttered, the name of the Trojan shepherd, strengthened the illusion.

'Who is Madame Parisse?' I asked.

He seemed gratified that I did not know her history. I assured him of my complete ignorance, and my eyes followed the woman, who went her way as in a dream without seeing us, moving with slow, dignified tread, as doubtless moved the ladies of antiquity. She may have been thirty-five, but she retained her beauty, although she had lost the slimness of youth.

This was Monsieur Martini's story.

II

A year before the war of 1870 Madame Parisse, one of the Combelombes, had married Monsieur Parisse, a Government official. In those days she was a beautiful girl, as slender and sprightly as she is now melancholy and stout. She had reluctantly accepted Monsieur Parisse, who was a pot-bellied little man with short legs that tripped along in trousers too wide for them.

After the war, Antibes was occupied by a single line battalion, commanded by Monsieur Jean de Carmelin, a young officer who had been decorated for services in the field and had just received his fourth gold stripe. He was terribly bored in this fortress, this suffocating rat-trap with its double girdle of huge walls, and to relieve the monotony of his existence he used to go for walks on the promontory, which was a sort of park or wood of pine-trees, exposed to all the winds from the sea. There he met Madame Parisse, who also used to betake herself thither on summer evenings to enjoy the cool air under the trees. How did they come to fall in love with each other? Who can say? They met, they gazed, and when they were out of sight of each other, doubtless they were in each other's thoughts. The image of the brown-eyed girl with her black hair and ivory skin, her fresh southern beauty and flashing teeth, hovered before the young man's eyes, and he continued his walk, biting the end of his cigar instead of smoking it. And when Monsieur Parisse, unshaven, badly dressed, short-legged and pot-bellied, came home for supper, doubtless his wife conjured up the image of the young officer, with his fair, curling moustache, his close-fitting, gold-laced tunic and red trousers.

They met so often that in the end perhaps they could not help smiling at each other, and soon they felt like old acquaintances. Doubtless he saluted her, and she, a little taken aback, responded with the slightest, the very slightest, bow, just sufficient to avoid discourtesy. But by the end of a fortnight she was acknowledging his salute from a distance before they actually met. At last he spoke to her—doubtless of the sunset. They admired it together, but they looked for it in the depths of each other's eyes rather than on the horizon. And every evening for a fortnight they made this their usual and conventional pretext for a few minutes' conversation. Presently they ventured to take a turn together, and while they discussed indifferent subjects, their eyes were already exchanging a thousand intimate secrets, the delightful mysteries that are reflected in a tender, passionate glance and set the heart beating, because they express the soul more eloquently than a spoken declaration. Then doubtless he took her hand and faltered words, whose meaning a woman divines, even while she seems not to hear them. And in this ethereal fashion they came to love each other. For her part she would have been content to linger at this stage of their passion, but he, her lover, was impatient for more. Each day he besought her more ardently to yield to his burning desire. She withstood him, resisted, and seemed resolved never to surrender. One evening, however, she said with a casual air:

'My husband has gone to Marseilles and will be away four days.'

Jean de Carmelin threw himself at her feet, and implored her to open to him that night at eleven o'clock. But she turned a deaf ear to his entreaties and left him as if she were affronted.

The commandant was in a fury all that evening. The next morning he rose at dawn in a raging temper, and made his rounds, flinging punishments at officers and men, like a man flinging stones into a crowd. But when he returned home for luncheon he found a note under his table-napkin, containing these four words:

Ten o'clock this evening.

And for no reason at all he gave his orderly five francs. The day seemed to him interminable. He spent part of the time curling his hair and scenting himself. As he was sitting down to dinner another envelope was brought to him with a telegram enclosed, which ran:

My dear, business finished. Arrive this evening at nine.—
PARISSE.

The commandant swore so violently that the orderly dropped the soup tureen on the floor. What was to be done? At all costs, he wanted her that very evening, and have her he would by hook or by crook, even if he had to have her husband arrested and locked up.   Suddenly a mad idea occurred to him, and he wrote a note:

He shall not come home this evening, I swear it, and at ten o'clock I shall be you know where.   Fear nothing.   I will answer for everything, on my honour as an officer.

                                        JEAN DE CARMELIN.

About eight o'clock he sent for his second in command, Captain Gribois.   Twisting Monsieur Parisse's crumpled telegram in his fingers, he said:

'I have just received a curious telegram, which I am not at liberty to show you.   You will immediately close all the town gates and place sentries on them, so that no one, no person whatever, you understand, can come in or go out before six to-morrow morning.   You will have the streets patrolled, and all the inhabitants are to be within doors by nine o'clock.   Any one out of doors after that hour will be taken to his house by a guard.   If any of your men meet me to-night, they will keep away from me and pretend not to recognize me.   You understand?'

'Yes, sir.'

'I shall hold you responsible for carrying out these orders.'

'Very good, sir.'

'Will you have some chartreuse?'

'Yes, thank you.'

They clinked glasses, drank the yellow liqueur, and Captain Gribois went away.

III

The train from Marseilles entered the station punctually at nine o'clock.   Two travellers alighted and the train went on towards Nice.   One of the passengers, Monsieur Saribe, who was an oil merchant, was tall and lean, while the other, Monsieur Parisse, was short and fat.   Carrying their handbags, they set out together for the town, which was about a mile away.   When they arrived at the harbour gate they were confronted by sentries, who crossed bayonets and ordered them to go back. Startled, amazed, discomfited, they retreated a little way to discuss the situation, and then cautiously returned in order to make their names known and to come to terms. But the soldiers clearly had strict orders, for they threatened to shoot, and the two terrified travellers fled helter-skelter, abandoning their impedimenta. Then they circled the ramparts and presented themselves at the gate on the road to Cannes. This also they found closed and guarded by a sentry. Like prudent men, Monsieur Saribe and Monsieur Parisse did not press the point, but returned to the railway station to find shelter for the night. Loitering about the fortifications was unsafe after nightfall. Roused out of his bed, the station-master gave them permission to spend the night in the waiting-room. Side by side, they sat there in the dark, too frightened even to think of sleep. The night seemed endless. About half-past six the next morning they were informed that the gates had been opened, and that they were at liberty to enter the town. They set off again, but failed to recover their abandoned baggage anywhere on the road.

Still a little uneasy, they were met at the gate of the town by the commandant, with a roguish twinkle in his eyes and the ends of his moustache twisted upwards. He had come in person to question and identify them. He saluted them politely and apologized for having caused them an uncomfortable night. But he had had to carry out his orders.

All Antibes was in consternation. Some spoke of a surprise attack by the Italians; others of a landing by the Prince Imperial; others again of an Orleanist conspiracy. The truth was not suspected until later, when it was known that the battalion had been transferred to a remote garrison and de Carmelin severely punished.

IV

Monsieur Martini had finished his story when Madame Parisse came back from her walk. She passed us with a dignified air. Her eyes were fixed on the Alpine summits, now rosy with the last rays of the setting sun. I had a strong desire to take off my hat to this sorrowful lady, whose thoughts doubtless never ceased to dwell on that night of love, now so remote, and that bold lover who had dared, for the sake of one kiss from her, to put a town in a state of siege, and to compromise his whole future. By this time he had doubtless forgotten her, unless, perhaps, over the wine, he told the story of this mad prank, this amorous extravagance. Had she ever seen him again? Did she still love him?

'Here,' I reflected, 'is a typical instance of modern love, grotesque and yet romantic. The Homer who would celebrate this Helen and the exploit of her lover, should possess the soul of a Paul de Kock. And yet the hero of this forsaken lady was gallant, dashing, handsome, strong as Achilles, more subtle than Ulysses.'

PLAYING WITH FIRE

THE little Marquise de Rennedou was still asleep in her snug perfumed bedroom. In her great, soft, low bed, between sheets of finest lawn, delicate as lace, caressing as a kiss, alone and in perfect tranquillity, she was plunged in the deep, the blissful slumber of a divorcée.

She was aroused by sounds of altercation from the little blue drawing-room, and recognized the voice of her best friend, the young Baroness de Grangerie, raised in argument with the maid, who was defending her mistress's door. At this the marquise rose, drew back the bolts, unlocked the door, lifted the curtain, and put out her head, just her head with its cloud of fair hair.

'What has possessed you to come so early?' she asked. 'It isn't nine o'clock yet.'

The baroness, who was pale and seemed feverishly excited, replied:

'I must speak to you. A terrible thing has happened to me.'

'Come in, my dear.'

She entered the room and the ladies kissed each other. Then the marquise returned to bed, while her maid opened the windows and let in fresh air and daylight. When the maid had left the room, Madame de Rennedou said:

'Now tell me all about it.'

Madame de Grangerie burst into tears, those crystal drops which add to a woman's charm. For fear of making her eyes red she refrained from drying them.

'Oh, my dear,' she exclaimed, 'I am in the most awful trouble. I haven't had a wink of sleep all night, not a wink. Just feel how my heart is beating.'

Seizing her friend's hand she laid it on her bosom, that round, firm bosom which encloses the heart of woman, and often so charms a man as to prevent him from seeking anything within. Her heart was certainly beating violently.

'It was yesterday afternoon, about four or half-past four, I can't say exactly. You know my flat and my little drawing-

room on the first floor, where I always sit, overlooking the
Rue Saint-Lazare. As you know, I have a passion for looking
out of the window and watching people pass. It is so busy,
so cheerful, so full of life, near a railway station. I simply
adore it. Well, yesterday I was sitting in a low chair in the
alcove by the open window, thinking of nothing in particular
and enjoying the air. You remember what a lovely day it
was yesterday.

'All at once I noticed on the opposite side of the road another
woman at her window. She was in red and I was in mauve;
you know that pretty mauve frock of mine. I did not know
the woman; she was a new-comer and had not had the flat
more than a few weeks, and as it rained all last month I had
not seen her before. But I saw at once that she was a—you
know what. At first I was shocked and disgusted at seeing her
at the window just like myself. But presently, as I watched
her, she began to interest me. She had her elbows on the
window-sill and was looking out for men, and all the men, or
nearly all of them, glanced up at her. When they came near
the house, it was just as if they had received some intimation;
as if they winded her, like dogs winding game. Up went their
heads and their glances crossed in a sort of freemasonry. Her
eyes said: "Will you?" And theirs replied: "No time now,"
or "Another day," or "Dead broke," or "Go and hide yourself,
you hussy." It was the married men's eyes that made this
last remark. You can't conceive how amusing it was watching
her at her game, or, I should say, her business.

'Sometimes she shut the window sharply, and then I would
see a man turn in at the door, caught, poor fellow, like a gudgeon
by an angler. Then I looked at my watch. These men stayed
a quarter of an hour or twenty minutes, never longer. I assure
you that spider-woman ended by getting me wildly excited.
And she was by no means plain, the minx. I wondered what
she did to make herself understood so thoroughly and so
quickly. Besides looking, did she make any sign with her head
or her hand? I took my opera glasses to find out how the
thing was done. It was simple enough. First a look, then a
smile, then the tiniest little movement of the head, which
meant "Are you coming up?" But the gesture was so slight,
so subtle, so discreet, that the woman must have been a real
artist to succeed as she did.

'Could I do it as well myself, I wondered, that little toss of of the head, bold and yet charming? for charming it certainly was. I went and tried it in front of the glass. My dear, I did it better than she, much better. I was enchanted and I returned to the window.

'She wasn't catching anybody now, poor girl, not a soul. She wasn't having any luck. When you come to think of it, what a terrible thing it must be to have to earn your living that way. But amusing, too, sometimes; for some of the men you see in the streets are quite presentable. They were all passing along my pavement now, which was the sunny side, while hers was deserted. Along they came, one after the other, young, old, dark, fair, grey heads, white heads. And some of them were really charming, far more so than my husband, or yours either—your former husband, I should say, as you 're divorced. You can take your choice now.

'Suppose, I said to myself, I made them a sign, would they understand me, a respectable married woman? And suddenly I was seized with a crazy desire to make the sign . . . a morbid, overwhelming desire . . . an appalling desire . . . the sort of impulse you simply can't resist. I 'm sometimes taken that way. Silly, isn't it? I think we women have souls like monkeys; a doctor once told me that our brains are very like those of monkeys. We are always imitating someone. First it 's our husbands, while we 're still in love with them; and after that our lovers and friends and father confessors, if they are good-looking. We pick up their ways of speaking and thinking; we use their expressions and mannerisms and everything. It 's simply absurd.

'As for me, I never resist temptation when it 's too strong.

'So I said to myself that I would try it on one man, just to see. What harm could it do? We would exchange a smile, and that would be the end of it. I should never meet him. If I did, he wouldn't recognize me; if he did recognize me, I should deny it.

'So I began choosing. I wanted someone really superior. At last I saw a tall, fair, very handsome young man coming along. As you know, I have a weakness for fair men. I looked at him; he looked at me. And I made the movement, oh, the merest suggestion of it, but he nodded his head, and then, my dear, in he walked, straight into the house through the front door.

'You have no idea how I felt at that moment. I thought I

should go mad. How frightened I was! Only think! He would speak to the servants, to Joseph, who is devoted to my husband. Joseph would certainly suppose that I had known him a long time.

'What was I to do? I ask you, what was I to do? In another minute, another second, he would be ringing the bell. What was I to do? It seemed to me that the best thing would be to run and meet him, to tell him he had made a mistake and to beseech him to go away. He would have mercy on a woman, a poor woman. So I rushed to the door, and opened it just as he was putting his hand on the bell.

'Quite beside myself I stammered:

'"Go away. Go away. You have made a mistake. I am a respectable married woman. It is a ghastly misunderstanding; I took you for a friend of mine, who is very like you. Have pity on me."

'The wretch actually laughed, my dear.

'"Good afternoon, puss," he said. "I have heard that story before. As you are married, it will be two louis instead of one. You shall have them. Come along. Show me the way."

'He pushed me in, closed the outer door, and as I stood there petrified with horror, he kissed me, put his arm round my waist, drew me through the open door into the drawing-room. Then he looked all round him like an auctioneer, and said:

'"By Jove, your flat is charming, perfectly charming. You must be badly on the rocks to have to play the window game."

'At this I began to implore him again.

'"Oh, do go away, please go away. My husband will be here immediately. It is just his time. I swear to you it's all a mistake."

'"Now, my dear," he replied calmly, "you have made enough fuss. If your husband comes I'll give him five francs to go and have a drink."

'He caught sight of Raoul's photograph on the mantlepiece.

'"Is that your . . . husband?" he asked.

'"Yes."

'"He does look a duffer. And who is this lady? A friend of yours?"

'It was your photograph, my dear, the one in evening dress. I hardly knew what I was saying.

'"Yes, she's a friend of mine," I faltered.

'"She is charming. You must introduce me."'

'The clock struck five, and Raoul is always back by half-past. Suppose he came home before the other man had gone! Then . . . then . . . I lost my head completely. I thought . . . I thought . . . the best thing to do was to get rid of him . . . as soon as possible. The sooner it was over . . . you see . . . and as it had to be . . . and there was no way out of it . . . otherwise he would never have gone . . . well, I—I just locked the door. That's all.'

Madame de Rennedou burst out laughing. Burying her head in the pillow she laughed wildly, while the whole bed shook under her. When she had recovered her composure she said:

'And was he really good-looking?'

'Yes, very.'

'Then what are you complaining of?'

'Well, you see, my dear, the fact is . . . he said he would come back to-morrow . . . at the same time, and I am simply terrified. You have no idea how determined he is . . . and how wilful. Tell me, what am I to do?'

Sitting up in bed Madame de Rennedou thought for a minute.

'Have him arrested!' she suddenly broke out.

Her friend was thunderstruck.

'What?' she faltered. 'What did you say? What are you thinking of? Have him arrested? On what charge?'

'Oh, that's quite simple. All you have to do is to go to the Commissaire of police and tell him that a man has been following you for the last three months, that yesterday he had the insolence to come up to your flat, that he threatens to repeat his visit to-morrow, and that you demand the protection of the law. Then two policemen will be told off to arrest him.'

'But, my dear, suppose he tells.'

'No one will believe him, you silly, once you have put up a good story to the Commissaire. You are a society woman of blameless reputation. Of course you will be believed.'

'Oh, I should never dare.'

'If you don't dare, my dear, you are lost.'

'But just think . . . what things he will say about me when he is arrested.'

'Never mind that. You will have your witnesses and you will get him sentenced.'

'Sentenced to what?'

'To pay damages. In a case like this you must have no mercy.'

'Ah, damages! That reminds me. There is another thing that worries me . . . worries me very much. He left two louis on the mantelpiece.'

'Two louis?'

'Yes.'

'Is that all?'

'Yes.'

'That wasn't much. I should feel insulted if I were you. Well?'

'Well, what am I to do with the money?'

After a little hesitation the Marquise de Rennedou said solemnly:

'My dear, you must . . . you must give your husband a little present. That is only fair.'

LOVE

(*Amour*)

AMONGST the miscellaneous items in the newspapers, 1 have just read an account of a tragic love affair, in which a lover killed first his sweetheart and then himself. Their personalities did not concern me. What interested me was the intensity of their passion, not because I was touched, or surprised, or thrilled, or saddened, but because it recalled to me a memory of my youth, a curious shooting incident, which was to me a revelation of love, like those visions of the Cross in the sky, which were granted to the early Christians.

By nature I have all the instincts and feelings of primitive man, though modified by the logic and the sensibilities of civilization. I am passionately devoted to shooting and hunting, and when I bring down a bird the blood on its feathers and on my hands thrills my heart so that it almost stops beating.

One year, as autumn lingered towards its close, winter came suddenly upon us, and I was invited by my cousin, Karl de Rauville, to go duck shooting with him in the marshes at daybreak. My cousin was a jovial fellow of forty, ruddy, strong, full-bearded, a typical country gentleman, a genial and lively savage, with a share of that Gallic wit which lends a charm even to mediocrity. He lived in a house, half farm, half manor, situated in a wide river valley. The slopes on either side were mantled with noble forest, whose magnificent trees harboured the rarest birds to be found in that part of France. Even eagles were sometimes shot there, and migrants which seldom visit our over-peopled regions almost invariably broke their journey in these ancient coverts, as if they knew or recognized that this small remnant of primeval forest had been spared to shelter them during their brief nocturnal halt. In the valley bottom lay broad meadows, watered by ditches and divided by hedges, and farther down, the river, which was canalized up to this point, widened out into a vast marsh. This marsh was the finest shooting ground I have ever seen, and my cousin took the deepest interest in it, and tended it as if it were a park. Through the close ranks of the reeds—a multitudinous, shivering, whispering company—narrow channels had been cut, down which flat-bottomed punts were poled, stealing silently through the still water, brushing past the reeds, frightening the fish, which took refuge among the weeds, and the wild-fowl, which dived, their black, pointed heads suddenly disappearing from sight.

I have an immoderate passion for water; for the sea, though so vast, so restless, so beyond one's comprehension; for rivers, beautiful, yet fugitive and elusive; but especially for marshes, teeming with all that mysterious life of the creatures that haunt them. A marsh is a whole world within a world, a different world, with a life of its own, with its own permanent denizens, its passing visitors, its voices, its sounds, its own strange mystery. There are times when a marsh is the most haunting, disturbing, and terrifying of places. Whence this fear which broods above the water-covered flats? Is it the vague whisper of the reeds, the weird will-o'-the-wisps, the profound hush of the stilly night, or the fantastic mists that trail their ghostly robes across the reeds, or that almost inaudible lapping of the water, so low, so gentle, and yet at times more unnerving than the artillery of man or heaven, investing the marsh with the atmosphere of a dreamland, an awe-inspiring region hiding some nameless and dreadful secret? No. There is another reason. In these thick mists hovers a deeper, more solemn mystery, the mystery of creation itself. Was it not in the stagnant mire, in the heavy humidity of swampy lands, steeped in the heat of the sun, that the first germ of life stirred, quivered, and awoke?

It was night, and freezing hard, when I arrived at my cousin's house. We dined in the great hall. On its sideboards, walls, and ceilings, mounted with outspread wings, or perched on branches secured with nails, were displayed all kinds of stuffed birds: hawks, herons, owls, goat-suckers, buzzards, kestrels, vultures, falcons. My cousin, looking himself like a strange animal from the Arctic regions in his sealskin coat, told me what arrangements he had made for that very night. We were to leave the house at half-past three in the morning so as to reach about half-past four the spot where we were to take up our stand. At this place a hut had been built with blocks of ice to shelter us from the biting wind which blows before dawn, that freezing wind, which rips the flesh like a saw, cuts like a knife, pierces like a poisoned goad, pinches as with pliers, and burns as with fire.

My cousin rubbed his hands.

'I have never known such a frost. By six o'clock this evening we had twenty-one degrees.'

Directly after dinner I went to bed and fell asleep by the light of a huge wood fire. I was called on the stroke of three. I threw on a sheepskin coat; and my cousin was wearing a bearskin. Each of us swallowed two cups of scalding coffee, followed by two glasses of brandy, and we set out, accompanied by a keeper and our dogs, Plongeon and Pierrot.

A few steps in the open air sufficed to chill us to the bone. It was one of those nights when the earth seems to have died of cold. Not a breath stirs; the freezing air strikes the face like solid ice; it is congealed and motionless; it gnaws, penetrates, and parches; kills trees, plants, and insects; even the little birds drop from the branches on to the iron ground and are frozen as hard as the soil itself.

The moon was in her last quarter, lying over on her side, even as if fainting in the midst of space, too weak to travel farther, and gripped and paralysed by the icy rigour of the firmament. She shed upon the earth her lustreless, melancholy rays, that livid, sickly light of her decline.

With our hands in our pockets and our guns under our arms, Karl and I slouched along side by side. We had wrapped woollen coverings round our boots, so that we might be able to walk over the frozen stream without slipping, and we marched noiselessly. The breath of our dogs rose in a white steam. Soon we reached the edge of the marsh and plunged into one of the passages cut through that miniature forest of dry reeds. Our elbows, brushing against the long, ribbon-like leaves, left in our wake a faint rustling, and I was seized as never before by that strange and potent emotion which marshes have the power of arousing in me. The marsh, it seemed, lay dead, dead of cold, and we were tramping over its corpse, between the ranks of its multitude of withered reeds.

Suddenly, at a bend in one of the passages, I caught sight of the ice hut built for our shelter. Entering it, and finding that we had almost an hour to pass before the flighting birds awoke, I wrapped myself in my sheepskin and endeavoured to get warm again. Lying on my back, I looked up at the moon, which, distorted by the vague transparency of the walls of this Arctic cabin, seemed to have four horns. But so intense was the cold from the frozen marsh, the icy walls, and the sky itself, that I began to cough. At this my cousin became uneasy.

'It will be a pity if we spoil our bag,' he remarked, 'but I don't want you to catch cold. We had better have a fire.'

So he ordered the keeper to cut down some reeds. Our hut had a hole at the top to allow the smoke to escape; we piled up the reeds in the middle of the floor, and in the heat of the red flames the icy walls began to melt, but very gradually, as if breaking out into perspiration. Karl cried to me to come outside and look. I obeyed, and stood spell-bound. Our cone-shaped shelter looked like a gigantic diamond with a fiery heart, sprung up suddenly on the frozen waters of the marsh. Within were visible the fantastic forms of our two dogs, who were warming themselves by the fire.

A strange, forlorn, wandering cry passed through the air above our heads. The wild-fowl were being roused by the light of our fire. Nothing thrills me like this first clamour of living creatures, as yet invisible, flying swift and far through the darkness, before the first wintry ray of light has illumined the horizon. That cry, that fugitive cry, borne upon the wings of a bird in that icy hour of dawn, is to me a sigh from the soul of the universe.

'Put out the fire,' said Karl, 'it is daybreak.'

And to be sure, the sky was growing pale, and against it could be seen dark wedges of wild duck in flight, sweeping past us, and swiftly vanishing into the distance. A flash of light pierced the darkness. Karl had fired, and the two dogs set off to retrieve the game. Every minute now one or other of us was taking quick aim as soon as the shadow of a flight of birds appeared above the reeds. Panting and joyful, Pierrot and Plongeon brought in the blood-stained birds; some of them, not quite dead, looked at us.

It was now broad daylight, and a bright, clear morning. The sun was rising at the far end of the valley and we were thinking of going home, when two birds, with necks outstretched and spreading wings, flew over our heads. I fired; one of them dropped almost at my feet. It was a silver-breasted teal. In the air above my head, there was a cry, the cry of a bird, a sharp, heart-rending, oft-repeated note. The other, the little creature that had escaped, began to wheel round and round in the blue sky, gazing down on its dead mate, which I was holding in my hands.

Kneeling with his gun to his shoulder, Karl watched the bird, waiting for it to come within range.

'You have killed the female,' he said. 'The male bird won't desert her.'

And indeed it did not desert her. It wheeled above our heads, uttering its desolate cry. Never was my heart so wrung as by this despairing appeal; it was like the bitter reproach of this unhappy creature, left alone in the solitude of space. Sometimes, under the menace of my cousin's gun, it would fly a little distance away, as if making up its mind to continue all by itself its journey across the sky. But soon its resolution failed it, and it returned in search of its mate.

'Put the dead bird on the ground,' said Karl, 'and the other will soon come near it.'

Reckless of danger, distracted by the love for a creature of its own kind, which I had killed, the male bird presently drew nearer. Karl fired. It was as if the bird had been hanging on a string, which had been suddenly cut. I saw a dark object falling; I heard it drop in the reeds, and Pierrot retrieved it for me. I put the two birds, already cold, in the same game-bag, and I left that very day for Paris.

MADEMOISELLE FIFI

THE officer commanding the Prussian troops, Major Count von Falsberg, was finishing the perusal of his letters. He was lolling in the depths of a big, upholstered arm-chair with his boots on the fine marble mantelpiece, where, during his three months' occupation of the Château d'Uville, his spurs had worn two well-marked grooves, which grew a little deeper every day. Beside him on a marqueterie stand steamed a cup of coffee. The graceful little table was stained with liqueurs, burnt with cigar ends, and scored with the penknife of the conquering hero, who would pause now and then, as he sharpened a pencil, to scratch on its surface figures or drawings according to his idle fancy.

When he had read his letters, and had skimmed the pages of the German newspapers which the regimental postman had brought him, he rose from his chair, threw on to the fire three or four huge billets of green wood from the park, which these gentlemen were gradually denuding of trees to keep themselves warm, and went to the window. Rain was falling in torrents, the driving rain of Normandy, which seems as if hurled upon the earth by the hand of a madman, a dense curtain of water, a wall of slanting lines, rain that stings and splashes and drowns and is entirely characteristic of the surroundings of Rouen, that slop-pail of France.

The major stood gazing at the flooded lawns and the swollen Andelle, which was rising above its banks, and he drummed upon the window-panes a Rhineland waltz. A sound behind him made him turn his head, and he saw his second-in-command, Captain Baron von Kelweingstein.

The major was a broad-shouldered colossus with a long beard which spread out like a fan on his chest. His whole enormous person gave the idea of a peacock in uniform, a peacock which had its tail unfolded on its breast. He had mild, cold, blue eyes, and across one cheek ran a sabre cut, which he had received in the Austrian war. He had the reputation of being a good fellow and a gallant officer.

The captain was a short, red-faced man, with a large stomach, and was tightly laced. He had flaming red hair, and although he was closely shaven, the short shining bristles gave to his face in certain lights such a curious glitter that it looked as if his skin had been rubbed with phosphorus. A night of dissipation had, he could not remember precisely how, cost him two teeth, and this gap made him splutter when he spoke and rendered his utterance thick and difficult to understand. On the top of his head he had a bald patch like a tonsure, surrounded with a shining fleece of short curly golden hair.

The major shook hands with him, and then drank off his cup of coffee, the sixth since the morning, while his second-in-command made his daily report. Then they both turned to the window, and remarked that it was not very cheerful. The major was a quiet man with a wife at home, and adapted himself to circumstances. The captain, however, who was a man of pleasure, a frequenter of low haunts and an insatiable woman-hunter, chafed under the forced asceticism of a three months' confinement in this God-forsaken post.

There was a tap at the door.

'Come in,' cried the major, and an orderly, one of their military automata, appeared on the threshold, silently signifying by his presence that luncheon was ready.

In the dining-room three officers of lower rank were waiting for them. They were Lieutenant Otto von Grossling and two second lieutenants, Fritz Scheunauburg and the Marquis Wilhelm von Eyrik, a fair-haired arrogant little martinet, brutal to his men, harsh to the conquered, and as explosive as gun-powder.

Since his arrival in France his brother officers never called him anything but Mademoiselle Fifi. He owed this nickname to the studied elegance of his dress, his slim figure, which looked as if it were corseted, his pale face, which showed only a faint sign of a budding moustache, and his constant habit of expressing his sovereign contempt for people and things in general by the French expletive 'Fi, fi donc,' which he pronounced with a slight whistle.

The long dining-room of the Château d'Uville was an apartment of royal magnificence. But its crystal mirrors, starred with bullet marks, its long Flemish tapestries slashed with sabre cuts and hanging in tatters, bore witness to the diversions of

Mademoiselle Fifi's idle hours. Three family portraits on the wall, a warrior in armour, a cardinal, and a president, were smoking long porcelain pipes, while in a gilded frame, tarnished with age, a noble lady in a tightly-laced bodice was wearing with a haughty air a pair of enormous moustaches done in charcoal.

Luncheon was a silent meal in this wreck of a room, rendered gloomier than ever by the rain. There was about it a depressing atmosphere of defeat, and the old parquet floor was now dingy as the earthen floor of a pot-house. After luncheon, over their tobacco and wine, the officers began to grumble as usual about the monotony of their existence. Brandy and liqueurs were passed round, and lolling back in their chairs they sipped glass after glass, without removing from their mouths the long bent pipe-stems with their egg-shaped china bowls, daubed with bright colours as if to captivate the eyes of Hottentots.

As soon as their glasses were empty they replenished them with a gesture of weary resignation. But Mademoiselle Fifi kept breaking glass after glass, and a soldier immediately substituted a new one. They sat lost in a haze of pungent smoke, sinking into that cheerless, lethargic drunkenness of men who have nothing else to do.

Suddenly the baron started up, seized by a violent revulsion.

'Good God!' he shouted. 'We can't go on like this. We must think of something to do.'

'But what, sir?' asked Lieutenant Otto and Second-Lieutenant Fritz, both of whom had the heavy, solemn German cast of countenance.

The baron thought for a few moments.

'Why,' he presently replied, 'we will give a party, with the major's permission.'

The major removed his pipe from his mouth.

'What sort of a party?'

The baron drew his chair nearer.

'I 'll make all the arrangements, sir. I 'll send Old Faithful into Rouen to fetch some ladies. I know where to go for them. We will have a supper-party. We have all that 's necessary, and at least we shall spend one festive evening.'

Count von Falsberg smiled and shrugged his shoulders:

'You must be crazy, my dear fellow.'

But all the other officers sprang from their chairs and surrounded the major.

'Don't say no, sir,' they pleaded. 'It's so deadly dull here.'

At last the major gave in. The baron sent for Old Faithful, a non-commissioned officer of long service, who had never been known to smile and who carried out with fanatical devotion all his officer's orders, no matter what they were.

Impassive as ever, Old Faithful received the baron's instructions. He left the room, and five minutes later a huge commissariat cart with a hood over it set off through the driving rain, drawn by four horses at a gallop. Immediately an awakening thrill seemed to stir the pulses of all the officers. They roused themselves from their languid postures; their faces brightened and they began to talk. Although the rain was pouring down with all its former violence, the major observed that it was not so dark, and Lieutenant Otto declared with conviction that it was going to clear up. Mademoiselle Fifi seemed unable to keep still. He was for ever jumping up and sitting down again. His hard, keen eyes scanned the room, looking for something to destroy. Suddenly the young reprobate fixed his gaze on the lady with the moustaches and drew his revolver.

'At any rate you shan't see it,' he exclaimed, and without rising from his chair he took aim. With two successive shots he pierced both her eyes.

'And now we'll have a mine,' he cried.

At this conversation ceased at once, as if a new and absorbing interest had presented itself. Springing mines was Mademoiselle Fifi's own invention, his own patent method of destruction and his favourite pastime. The rightful owner, Count Fernand d'Anoys d'Uville, had had to abandon his château so hastily that he had had no time to remove or hide any of his treasures, with the exception of the silver, which he concealed in a hole in the wall. He was a man of great wealth and magnificent tastes. Before his headlong flight, his great drawing-room, which opened off the dining-hall, had presented the aspect of a gallery in a museum. The walls were hung with oil paintings, drawings, and valuable water-colours. Tables, stands, and elegant glass cases displayed a thousand ornaments, vases of Japanese porcelain, statuettes, Chinese grotesques, ivory antiques, Venetian glass, so that the spacious apartment seemed thronged by a multitude of fantastic and precious denizens. Scarce one had survived. It was not that there had been any looting; this the major would never have permitted. But now and then Mademoiselle Fifi would spring a mine, and on these occasions all the officers really enjoyed themselves for quite five minutes.

The young marquis strolled into the drawing-room to look for what he required. He returned with an exquisite little teapot of *famille rose*. This he filled with gunpowder, and through the spout he carefully inserted a long fuse, which he lighted. Then he ran back to the drawing-room to deposit his infernal machine. He returned hastily to the dining-room and closed the door behind him. The German officers stood waiting with a smile of childish expectation on their faces, and as soon as the explosion had reverberated through the château they made a rush for the drawing-room. Mademoiselle Fifi was the first to enter. He clapped his hands in wild delight over a Venus in terra-cotta with its head blown off at last. His companions picked up fragments of porcelain, admiring the curious denticulations produced by the explosion, examined the fresh damage and debated whether this wreckage and that had not been caused by a previous mine. The major cast a benevolent glance around the great drawing-room, ruined in this Nero-like fashion, and strewn with shattered treasures of art. As he led the way out he remarked genially:

'That was a very successful effort.'

The atmosphere in the dining-room was so thick with mingled fumes of gunpowder and tobacco that it was impossible to breathe. The major threw open the window, and all the officers, who had come back for a final glass of brandy, gathered around it. The damp air rushed into the room in a fine spray which clung to their beards and moustaches and diffused a smell of sodden earth. They looked out at the tall trees, bowed beneath the deluge; at the wide valley shrouded in mists emanating from the water that poured from the low black clouds; at the distant belfry of the church, rising through the driving rain like a grey spike.

The church bell had never been rung since the first day of their occupation. The silence of this belfry, however, was the only form of resistance that the invaders had encountered throughout the district. The parish priest had in no way declined to receive or entertain the Prussian soldiers. On several occasions he had even gone so far as to drink a bottle of beer or Bordeaux with the Prussian commandant, who often employed him as a benevolent intermediary. But it was useless to ask him for even a single tinkle of his bell. He would have been shot rather than yield. This was his own special form of protest against the invasion; a pacific, a silent protest, the only protest, the only protest proper for a priest, a man of peace and not a man of blood. For ten miles round every one praised the firmness and heroism of the Abbé Chantavoine, who dared to assert and proclaim the public mourning by the persistent silence of his belfry. Inspired by his example, the whole village was prepared to support its pastor to the utmost, and to dare the worst, deeming this tacit protest a safeguard of the national honour. It seemed to the peasants that they deserved better of their country than either Belfort or Strasbourg; that they had set as fine an example, and had won immortal honour for their hamlet. With this one reservation, they refused the Prussian conquerors nothing. The major and his officers laughed together over this exhibition of harmless bravado, and as the whole village showed itself deferential and obliging towards the conquerors, they willingly tolerated this mute display of patriotism.

Only the young Marquis Wilhelm wanted to insist upon the bell being rung. The diplomatic condescension with which his superior officer treated the priest infuriated him, and every day he besought the major to order a single ding-dong, just once, once only, for fun. He pleaded with the coaxing grace of a cat, the winning wiles of a woman, the wheedling tones of a mistress who has set her heart on something. But the major would not give in, and Mademoiselle Fifi had to console himself with springing mines in the Château d'Uville.

For several minutes the five men remained grouped at the window, breathing the damp air. At last Lieutenant Fritz said with a husky laugh:

'I'm afraid those ladies won't have good weather for their drive.'

Then they dispersed. Each man went off to his work; the captain, for his part, had a great many preparations to make for the supper-party.

Towards evening they met again, and they burst out laughing when they saw how spick and span they all were, each one of them as carefully perfumed and pomaded as if for a grand review. The major's hair looked a shade less grey than in the morning. The captain had shaved and had retained only his moustache, which lay like a line of flame on his upper lip. One or other of them kept going to the window, which had been left open in spite of the rain. At ten minutes past six the baron announced that he heard a rumble of wheels in the distance. They all rushed to the door, and soon the heavy vehicle arrived at the château at a gallop, its four horses steaming and panting and splashed with mud up to the withers.

Five young women alighted on the perron, five handsome girls, carefully selected by a brother officer, to whom Old Faithful had delivered a note from the captain. They had raised no objections. They were sure of being well paid, and thanks to their experiences of the last three months, they were used to Prussians. Philosophically they accepted men and things as they came.

'It 's all in the day's work,' they remarked during the drive, as if to quiet the secret qualms of such vestiges of conscience as still remained to them.

They were ushered at once into the dining-room. When it was lighted up it seemed drearier than ever in its pitiful condition of dilapidation. The table, laden with food, exquisite china, and the silver that had been unearthed from its hiding-place in the wall, gave it the appearance of a tavern full of bandits, supping after a successful raid. Wreathed in smiles, the captain took possession of the ladies, viewing them with the air of an expert, kissing them, breathing in their perfume and estimating them at their professional value. The junior officers were eager to appropriate a lady apiece, but he refused to allow this, authoritatively claiming the right to distribute the young women with due respect for rank and seniority. In order to avoid all arguments, disputes, and accusations of partiality he ranged the five girls in a row according to height. Addressing the tallest one, he said in a voice of command:

'Your name?'

'Paméla,' she replied in soldierly tones.

'Number one, name of Paméla, awarded to the major.'

Then the captain kissed Blondine, the next in height, in token of ownership. Buxom Amanda was assigned to Lieutenant Otto; Éva the Tomato to Second Lieutenant Fritz; and to slim Wilhelm von Eyrik, the most junior of the officers, Rachel, the smallest girl, a young brunette with eyes as black as ink, a Jewess, whose turned-up nose served to prove the rule which attributes hooked noses to all her race. They were all sufficiently pretty and plump, with nothing particularly distinctive in their faces. In figure and complexion all conformed more or less to the same type, by virtue of their daily traffic and their common existence in houses of resort.

The three junior officers were anxious to carry off their young women at once on the pretext of lending them hair-brushes and soap. But the captain very sensibly objected to this proposal. He declared that the ladies were quite tidy enough for dinner, and that if they took their partners to their rooms now they would only want to change them when they came down again, and would interfere with the other couples. They accepted the expert's advice and contented themselves with innumerable kisses by way of a preliminary. All at once Rachel began to choke; she coughed till the tears came into her eyes, while smoke issued from her nostrils. Pretending that he wanted to kiss her, the marquis had puffed tobacco smoke into her mouth. She did not fly into a rage, or utter a single reproach. She merely gazed fixedly at her owner with dawning anger in the depths of her dark eyes.

They sat down to dinner. Even the major appeared to be enjoying himself. He placed Paméla on his right and Blondine on his left, remarking as he unfolded his table-napkin:

'It was certainly an excellent idea of yours, captain.'

Lieutenant Otto and Lieutenant Fritz were as polite as if in the company of women of their own class, somewhat to the embarrassment of their neighbours. But Baron von Kelweingstein, radiant and revelling in his favourite vice, kept making unseemly jokes, while his halo of red hair appeared to blaze. He made love in his Rhenish French, expectorating his tap-room gallantries through the gap left by his two broken teeth. The women, however, could not understand him. They gave no sign of intelligence except when he spluttered out obscene words and gross expressions, which were mangled by his accent. At this they all went off into wild shrieks of laughter, falling on their neighbours' necks and mimicking the baron, who kept purposely mispronouncing his words for the pleasure of hearing them repeat his coarse phrases. The first few bottles of wine had gone to the young women's heads. They poured out a flow of vile language and, once more their natural selves, they resumed all their usual habits, lavishing kisses right and left, pinching their neighbours' arms, uttering shrill cries, and drinking out of anybody's glass. Now and then one of them would shout a verse or two of French, or a snatch of a German song picked up during her daily intercourse with the enemy.

Before very long, intoxicated with all this femininity within their reach, the men, too, lost their heads. They shouted and broke the plates, while behind their chairs the orderlies waited on them impassively. The major alone preserved some degree of self-control.

Mademoiselle Fifi had taken Rachel on his knees. Sometimes in a gust of frigid passion he frantically kissed the ebony ringlets on her neck, and breathed in the warmth and fragrance of her person. Sometimes with savage ferocity he pinched her so violently through her dress that he made her cry out. Again, crushing her in his arms, he pressed his lips lingeringly to the Jewish girl's red mouth, kissing the breath out of her body. Suddenly he bit her so viciously that a trickle of blood flowed down her chin and on to her bodice. Once again she looked him in the face and, as she bathed the wound, she muttered:

'You shall pay for this.'

'Oh, I'll pay for it,' he replied with a hard laugh.

Champagne was served at dessert. The major rose to his feet, and in the tones in which he would have proposed the health of the Empress Augusta, he exclaimed:

'The ladies!'

A series of toasts followed, toasts that smacked of their drunken gallantry, mingled with obscene jokes, rendered coarser than ever by their ignorance of the language. Each officer in turn sprang to his feet, and made a desperate attempt to be witty and amusing. Too drunk to stand, with vacant gaze and clammy lips, the women welcomed each sally with frantic applause.

Intending, doubtless, to lend to the orgy an atmosphere of gallantry, the captain raised his glass again:

'To our victories over hearts!'

At this Lieutenant Otto, a rough sort of bear from the Black Forest, saturated and inflamed with alcohol, started to his feet:

'To our victories over France!'

Drunk though they were, the women were struck silent, and with a shudder Rachel turned and looked at him:

'I know some Frenchmen before whom you wouldn't dare say a thing like that.'

The marquis, who still held her on his knee, had drunk himself into a state of great hilarity. He burst out laughing.

'Ha ha ha! Personally I have never seen any Frenchmen. As soon as we come on the scene they take to their heels.'

'Dirty liar!' the girl shouted furiously in his face.

For a moment he fixed her with his light eyes, just as he had done with the portrait of the lady before he had shot at it with his revolver.

'That's all very well, my beauty. But if they had had an ounce of pluck, should we be here? We are their masters,' he added with growing excitement. 'France is ours.'

She jerked herself off his knees and dropped into her chair. The marquis rose to his feet, and holding his glass half-way across the table he repeated:

'France is ours, and the French, and their woods, and their fields, and their houses.'

All the other men were suddenly inflamed with military ardour, with the enthusiasm of brutes. Seizing their glasses they shouted: 'Prussia for ever!' and emptied them at one draught.

The young women dared not protest. They sat cowed and silent. Even Rachel held her peace and did not venture to reply. Then the marquis balanced his newly-filled glass of champagne on Rachel's head, exclaiming:

'And the women of France are ours, too.'

At this Rachel sprang up so fiercely that she upset the glass, which emptied its yellow fluid as if in baptism all over her black hair. Then it fell to the ground and was shattered. Though her lips were trembling, her eyes braved the Prussian officer, who was still laughing. In a voice choking with passion she stammered:

'Oh, that's not true. At any rate that's not true. You will never have the women of France.'

The marquis sat down to give rein to his mirth, and, mimicking the accent of Paris, exclaimed:

'Isn't she funny? Isn't she funny? Then what are you doing here, my pretty dear?'

At first she was too much taken aback to reply. His meaning eluded her, but as soon as she grasped what he said, she burst out in vehement indignation:

'What am I doing here? I? I'm not a woman. I'm only a whore. And that's exactly what you Prussians deserve.'

The words were hardly out of her mouth when the marquis boxed her ears violently. He was raising his hand again in a fury, when she snatched up a small silver dessert knife from the table, and with a gesture so sudden that no one was aware of her intention, she drove it right into the hollow where the neck joins the chest. The word he was uttering was strangled in his throat, and he sat there with his mouth open and a terrible expression on his face.

A shout of horror burst from the whole party, and they all sprang to their feet in consternation. Rachel hurled her chair at the legs of Lieutenant Otto, who measured his length on the floor. Before any one could stop her, she rushed to the window, flung it open, and plunged into the night and the rain.

Two minutes later Mademoiselle Fifi was dead.

At this Fritz and Otto drew their swords to cut down the women, who had thrown themselves on their knees. The major had some difficulty in preventing this massacre. He shut up the four distracted girls in a room with two men to guard them. Then, as if he were disposing his soldiers for battle, he organized the pursuit, never doubting that the fugitive would be re-captured. Urged on by threats, fifty men were scattered all over the park. Two hundred more scoured the woods and searched every house in the valley.

In a moment the table was cleared. It served Mademoiselle Fifi for a bier. Suddenly sobered, the four remaining officers stood rigidly at the windows, peering into the night with the set faces of soldiers on duty. And still the rain poured in torrents. Out of the darkness came a pattering sound, a vague gurgling of water, falling, flowing, dripping, splashing.

All at once a shot rang out, followed by another in the far distance. And during the next four hours more shots were heard, remote or near, with rallying cries and unknown words shouted in guttural voices, as the men called to one another. In the morning the search parties returned to the château. Two soldiers had been killed and three others wounded by their comrades in the heat and confusion of this nocturnal hunt.

Rachel had not been found.

A reign of terror ensued for the inhabitants. Their houses were ransacked; the entire neighbourhood was scoured, searched, patrolled. But the young Jewess seemed to have vanished without leaving a single trace.

The affair was reported to the general, who ordered it to be hushed up, fearing the demoralizing effect of such an example on the army. He visited his displeasure on the major, who in turn punished his subordinates.

The general remarked:

'You do not make war for pleasure, nor for the sake of amusing yourself with improper young women.'

In his resentment Count von Falsberg resolved to revenge himself on the village. Seeking a pretext which would justify the utmost severity, he sent for the priest and ordered him to have the church bell rung at the Marquis von Eyrik's funeral. Contrary to his expectation the priest received his instructions with exemplary docility and deference. And when the body of Mademoiselle Fifi, borne by soldiers, and preceded, followed, and surrounded by yet more soldiers, all carrying loaded rifles, was conveyed from the château to the cemetery, the church bell spoke for the first time. It tolled the funeral knell with a certain blitheness, as if in response to the caress of a friendly hand. It rang again that evening, and the next day, and every succeeding day, chiming away to heart's content. And even during the night it sometimes began to oscillate all by itself and to utter a gentle tinkle through the darkness, as if possessed by a mysterious gaiety and vibrating under some secret influence. The peasants declared that it was bewitched, and no one except the priest and the sacristan ventured near the belfry.

The explanation, however, was simple. An unhappy girl was hiding there, in anguish and solitude, ministered to in secret by those two men. She remained concealed there till the departure of the German troops. Then, one evening, the priest borrowed the baker's wagonette, and himself drove his captive as far as the gates of Rouen. There he kissed her, and she alighted. She made her way back to her old establishment, whose mistress had given her up for dead.

Some time afterwards she was rescued by a man whose patriotism outweighed his prejudices. Loving her first for her noble deed and afterwards for her own sake, he married her and made of her a lady, no less deserving than many another.

A DUEL

The war was over. The Germans had occupied France, and
the country lay quivering like a vanquished wrestler under the
knee of the conqueror. The first trains from horror-stricken,
famished, despairing Paris crawled slowly along through
villages and countryside in the direction of the newly established
frontiers. The first batches of travellers gazed through the
windows at the devastated plains and burnt-out hamlets. At
the door of every house left standing, there were Prussian
soldiers in black helmets with copper spikes, sitting astride their
chairs and smoking their pipes. Others were chatting or helping
with the work as if they were members of the family. In every
town on the railway line whole regiments could be seen drilling
in the square, while now and then a guttural word of command
could be heard above the rumbling of the wheels.

Monsieur Dubuis had served in the National Guard throughout the siege of Paris, and was now on his way to Switzerland to
join his wife and daughter, whom he had prudently sent out of
the country before the German invasion. Neither hunger nor
hardship had reduced the ample girth of this wealthy, peace-
loving tradesman. He had endured all the terrible tribulations
with despairing fortitude, coupled with bitter comments on the
barbarity of man. Although he had done duty on the ramparts
and had mounted guard on many a freezing night, it was only
now, when the war was over and he himself on the way to
Switzerland, that he first set eyes on the Prussians. With horror
and resentment he beheld these armed and bearded foreigners,
who were making themselves at home on the soil of France, and
he felt within his soul a fever of helpless patriotism and at the
same time a strong impulse towards prudence, that newly
acquired instinct, which we have never shaken off.

His compartment was shared by two Englishmen as stout
as himself. They were bent on sight-seeing and surveyed all
things with calm, inquiring eyes. They conversed in their own
language, now and then referring to their guide book, and reading
extracts aloud, in order to identify the places to which it referred.

The train drew up in the station of a little town, and a Prussian officer, with much clanking of his sword, climbed up the steps into the compartment. He was tall, wore a tightly fitting uniform, and was mantled up to the eyes by a flaming red beard. His face was bisected horizontally by a long moustache of paler hue, which stuck out on either side. With smiles of gratified curiosity the two Englishmen at once set to work to study him, while Monsieur Dubuis pretended to be absorbed in his newspaper. He shrank into his corner, like a thief confronted with a policeman. When the train went on, the Englishmen resumed their conversation and their efforts to identify the exact position of each battlefield. As one of them was pointing out a distant village, the Prussian officer, flinging out his long legs and lolling back in his seat, remarked in Teutonic French:

'I killed twelve Frenchmen in that village over there, and took more than a hundred prisoners.'

'Aoh! and what is the name of the village?' asked the Englishmen with lively interest.

'Pharsbourg,' replied the Prussian. 'You should have seen me take those rascally Frenchmen by the ears.'

And he stared at Monsieur Dubuis with an insolent smile on his bearded face.

The train trundled along, past village after village in enemy occupation. German soldiers could be seen on every road, in every field, at every station exit, and conversing outside the cafés. They covered the earth like the locusts of Africa.

The Prussian stretched out his hand.

'If I had been in command, I should have taken Paris and burnt it to the ground and killed every man, woman, and child. No more France!'

'Aoh, yes,' murmured the Englishmen, with perfunctory politeness.

'In another twenty years,' the officer continued, 'the whole of Europe will be ours. Prussia is stronger than all the rest.'

The Englishmen were ruffled and made no reply. All expression vanished from their faces, which looked like waxen masks between their drooping whiskers. The Prussian officer burst out laughing. Still lolling back in his seat, he continued to utter his taunts. He scoffed at abject France, and insulted the prostrate foe. He sneered at Austria, vanquished in a previous war. He poured ridicule on the desperate but vain resistance offered by various provincial departments; on the militia and the ineffectual artillery. He declared that Bismarck intended to build an iron city with the captured guns. Presently he shoved his boots up against the thigh of Monsieur Dubuis, who crimsoned to the ears and looked away. The Englishmen seemed oblivious to everything around them, as if, of a sudden, they were once more secluded within the confines of their island, far from the clamour of the outer world.

The officer pulled at his pipe and said, with a look at the Frenchman:

'You haven't any tobacco on you?'

'No, sir,' replied Monsieur Dubuis.

'I 'll trouble you to get out at the next stop and buy me some. I 'll give you a tip,' he added with another guffaw.

The train whistled and began to slow down. It passed some charred station buildings and drew up. The German opened the carriage door and seized the Frenchman by the arm.

'Do as I told you and be quick about it.'

The station was occupied by a detachment of Prussian troops. More soldiers were standing at the wooden barriers looking on. The engine gave a warning whistle. Monsieur Dubuis hurriedly jumped down on to the platform, and, disregarding the gesticulations of the stationmaster, sprang into the next compartment. He found himself alone. His heart was beating so violently that he had to unbutton his waistcoat. Panting for breath he mopped his forehead. Presently the train halted at another station. Immediately, the Prussian officer appeared at the door of the compartment and entered. Close upon him followed the two Englishmen, actuated by curiosity. The German took the seat opposite the Frenchman. He was still laughing.

'So you declined to carry out my order?'

'Yes, sir,' replied Monsieur Dubuis.

The train began to move.

'Well, I shall have to cut off your moustache to fill my pipe.'

So saying the German stretched out his hand towards his neighbour's face. Impassive as ever, the two Englishmen watched the proceedings with their calm gaze. The German clutched at the Frenchman's moustache and began pulling it. Dubuis struck up his arm with the back of his hand, and seizing him by the collar hurled him on to the seat. Beside himself with rage, his temples swelling, his eyes suffused with blood, he kept a strangle-hold on his enemy with one hand, while savagely pounding his face with the clenched fist of the other. The Prussian struggled; he tried to draw his sword and to grapple with his adversary, who was on top of him, pinning him down with the sheer weight of his vast bulk. Never pausing to take breath, he kept launching his blows, hardly knowing where they fell. Blood was flowing freely. Half-throttled, the German was groaning and spitting out broken teeth. But he could not shake off this angry fat man who was pommelling him. The Englishmen had left their seats to obtain a closer view. Agog with joy and excitement they stood looking on, ready to lay a wager on one or other of the combatants. Exhausted by his exertions, Monsieur Dubuis suddenly stood up and without a word resumed his seat.

The Prussian was too bewildered, too overcome with pain and surprise, to fly at his enemy's throat. When he recovered his breath he exclaimed:

'I challenge you to a duel with pistols. If you refuse I 'll kill you on the spot.'

'I 'll meet you whenever you please,' replied Monsieur Dubuis.

'Here we are at Strasbourg,' returned the German, 'I will find two brother officers to act as my seconds. There will be time before the train goes on.'

Monsieur Dubuis, who was puffing as vigorously as the loco-motive, turned to the two Englishmen.

'Will you act as my seconds?'

'Aoh, yes!' they exclaimed in one breath.

The train halted. Within a minute, the Prussian had found two brother officers, who produced a pair of pistols, and the party set out for the ramparts. The Englishmen, anxious not to lose the train, kept pulling out their watches; they insisted on hurrying and on settling the preliminaries without waste of time. Monsieur Dubuis had never before had a pistol in his hand. He was stationed at a distance of twenty paces from his opponent.

'Are you ready?' asked one of the seconds.

As he signified his assent Dubuis noticed that one of the Englishmen had put up his umbrella to protect himself from the sun. A voice rang out:

'Fire!'

Without pausing to take aim Monsieur Dubuis pressed the

trigger, and to his utter amazement saw his adversary reel, throw up his arms, and pitch forward on his face. He had shot him dead.

'Aoh!' exclaimed one of the Englishmen, in a voice quivering with exultation, gratified curiosity, and genial impatience. His companion, who still held his watch in his hand, seized Monsieur Dubuis by the arm and hurried him along at a run in the direction of the railway station, while his friend, his elbows close to his side, his fists doubled up, marked time:

'One, two, one, two.'

Trotting along in line, regardless of their corporations, the trio resembled three droll figures in a comic paper. Just as the train was starting, they jumped into their carriage. The two Englishmen took off their travelling-caps, waved them in the air, and gave three hearty cheers. Then both of them solemnly shook hands with Monsieur Dubuis, and retired to their own corner of the carriage.

ST. ANTHONY
(*Saint-Antoine*)

PEOPLE called him Saint-Antoine—St. Anthony—partly because Antoine happened to be his name, partly perhaps because he was a jolly companion, a stout trencherman, and a hearty drinker, with a turn for practical joking and an eye for a petticoat, and this despite the fact that he was over sixty. A peasant of the Caux district, he was tall and florid, with a well developed chest and stomach, perched on a pair of long legs, which seemed too lean for his ample frame. He was a widower, and, except for a maidservant and two labourers, lived alone on his farm, which he managed with much shrewdness. Careful of his own interests, he had an excellent head for business, and for everything relating to stockraising and agriculture. He had two sons and three daughters, who had married well and lived in the neighbourhood. Once a month they all came to dinner with their father. He was famous for his strength throughout the district. 'As strong as St. Anthony' had become a household word.

At the time of the Prussian invasion, St. Anthony, sitting in the village pothouse, vowed he would eat an army. Like all true Normans, he was a braggart, with a braggart's underlying streak of cowardice. He thumped the table with his fist till it shook and the glasses and cups danced about. Red in the face, a cunning gleam in his eyes, he shouted with pot-valiant ferocity:

'I must eat them up. By God I must!'

He never dreamt that the Prussians would penetrate as far as Tanneville. After he had heard that they had reached Rautôt, he never left the house, but stayed at the little window of the kitchen, keeping his eye continually on the high road and expecting every minute to see bayonets pass by. One morning, as he and his household were at their soup, the door was thrown open and Monsieur Chicot, the mayor of the Commune, entered, followed by a soldier in a black helmet with copper spike. St. Anthony sprang to his feet, while his servants looked on, expecting to see him annihilate the Prussian. But he merely shook hands with the mayor, who explained the situation to him.

'Here's one for you, St. Anthony. They arrived last night. Mind you don't play the fool. They threaten to shoot the lot of us and burn the whole place down, if the least little accident occurs. Now I've warned you. Give him something to eat. He seems a decent lad. Good-bye. I have to see the others. There are enough to go round.'

He took his departure.

With haggard face, St. Anthony stared at his Prussian. He was a stout youth, with sleek, white skin, blue eyes, fair hair, and bearded to the cheekbones. He seemed a stupid, shy, good-humoured sort of fellow. The astute Norman took his measure in a moment and, with a feeling of relief, motioned him to a seat.

'Will you have some soup?' he asked.

The foreigner did not understand, and with sudden effrontery, Anthony thrust a brimming plateful under his nose.

'Here, lap that up, you fat swine.'

'Ja,' replied the soldier and fell to greedily, while the farmer, feeling that he had saved his face, winked at his servants, who were making strange grimaces, divided between terror and suppressed laughter.

When the Prussian had gulped down his soup, St. Anthony gave him a second plateful, which he likewise disposed of, but he refused a third helping in spite of the farmer's persistence.

'Come, stow it away,' he urged him. 'We'll fatten you up, you swine, you, or I'll know the reason why.'

All that the soldier grasped was that he was to be nourished to his heart's content. He gave an amiable smile and signified that he could hold no more. With an assumption of familiarity, St. Anthony patted his Prussian on the stomach.

'My porker is as tight as a drum,' he remarked.

Then he was suddenly convulsed with speechless mirth and turned an apoplectic red. Such a funny idea had occurred to him that he almost choked with laughter.

'I've got it. I've got it,' he gasped. 'St. Anthony and his pig. There you see the pig.'

The three servants joined in his laughter. The old man was so tickled that he called for a bottle of his best brandy and treated them all. They drank to the Prussian, who smacked his lips in polite appreciation.

'Great stuff, what?' the former roared at him. 'You don't get liquor like that at home, do you, Pig?'

From that day onwards, old Antoine never stirred without his Prussian. He had taken a line of his own. This was his private form of revenge, a revenge that was a credit to such an inveterate humorist. Though in the grip of mortal terror, the whole countryside rocked with laughter at St. Anthony's jest, when the conquerors' backs were turned. When it came to practical joking, nobody could compare with him. No one else had such notions. What a wag the fellow was! Every afternoon he called on the neighbours, arm in arm with his German, whom he introduced with some facetious remark.

'Here he is,' he exclaimed, clapping him on the shoulder. 'Here's this pig of mine. Take a look at him. Isn't he fattening nicely?'

The yokels would grin with delight:

'Isn't the old boy killing?'

'I'll sell him to you for three pistoles, Césaire.'

'Done with you, Antoine, and you shall help us to eat the sausages.'

'No, one of his trotters for me. Just feel him. Solid fat all through.'

The rustics winked at one another, but were careful not to laugh too uproariously for fear the Prussian should begin to suspect that they were poking fun at him. Antoine, however, grew more daring every day. Pinching the man's thighs and slapping him on the back, he would remark:

'Nothing but solid fat and crackling.'

He would pick up his Prussian in herculean arms that could lift an anvil.

'He weighs a good six hundred and there's no waste about him.

He induced the neighbours to offer food to his pig wherever he went. This became the chief entertainment of the day.

'It doesn't matter what it is,' he remarked. 'He'll eat anything.'

They would set before him bread and butter, potatoes, cold stew, and pork sausages, which suggested the witticism:

'Your own, and very choice.'

Gratified by these attentions, the dense, good-humoured German accepted whatever was offered him and would make himself ill, rather than give offence by refusing. He was certainly putting on flesh. To St. Anthony's delight, his uniform was becoming too tight for him.

'You know, Pig,' he said to him, 'they 'll have to get you a
new sty one of these days.'

The two had really become the best of friends. When
business took the old man about the neighbourhood, the Prussian
always insisted on accompanying him, simply for the pleasure
of his society.

It was bitter weather and freezing hard. The terrible winter
of 1870 was destined, it seemed, to visit France with every kind
of tribulation. Old Antoine, who looked ahead and never
missed an opportunity, found that his stock of manure was
insufficient for the spring ploughing. So he bought a midden
belonging to a neighbour who was short of cash. He arranged
to go over every evening and remove a cartload at a time.
Daily, at dusk he set out for Haule's farm, which was about
a mile away, with his faithful pig trotting beside him. Feeding
the brute had become an entertainment to which all the country
people came flocking, as they did to High Mass on Sundays.
But the soldier's suspicions had been aroused, and sometimes,
when the laughter became too boisterous, his eyes would roll
uneasily and flash with an angry gleam. One day when he had
eaten till he could eat no more, he refused to touch another
morsel, and attempted to get up and go away. But St. Anthony
caught him with a turn of the wrist, and putting his powerful
hands on his shoulders, forced him so roughly back into his chair
that it collapsed under him. This mishap was received with
peals of laughter.

Beaming all over, Antoine helped his pig on to his legs and
pretended to minister to his injuries. Then he exclaimed:

''Pon my soul, if you won't eat, you shan't refuse to drink.'

He sent to the inn for brandy. The soldier rolled his eyes
resentfully, but did not reject the liquor. On the contrary, he
drank all that was offered him, while, to the delight of the bystanders, Antoine drank level with him. Red as a tomato, his
eyes burning, the Norman filled and refilled the glasses, and as
he tossed off his own, he bawled out:

'Here 's to you.'

Without a word, the Prussian gulped down glass after glass.
It was a match, a duel, a battle. Which of the pair would
outlast the other? When the litre of brandy was drained
to the last drop both had reached the end of their tether.
Yet neither could claim the victory. Honours were even.

There was nothing for it but to resume their bout on the following day.

The two men reeled out of the house and turned homewards, walking beside the loaded cart, which the horses dragged slowly along. It was beginning to snow. There was no moon, and the night was dark save for the melancholy glimmer rising from the dead whiteness of the plains. The cold seized upon the pair and made them more drunk than ever. Disgusted at not having scored a victory, St. Anthony relieved his feelings by pushing against the Prussian's shoulder and trying to upset him into the ditch. The soldier kept backing away from these onslaughts, and each time he muttered some German words in angry tones, which sent the peasant into loud guffaws. Finally the Prussian lost his temper, and just as Antoine was preparing to jostle him again, he dealt him such a tremendous blow with his fist that the gigantic Norman staggered. Thereupon the old man, who was maddened by the brandy he had drunk, seized the soldier round the body, shook him for a few moments, as if he were a small child, and flung him clean across the road. Elated by this feat, he folded his arms and indulged in a new outburst of laughter. The soldier had lost his helmet. Bareheaded, he sprang to his feet and drawing his sword rushed upon old Antoine. The peasant at once seized his whip by the middle —a huge, straight whip of hollywood, immensely tough and supple. Sure of killing his man, the Prussian came on with his head down and his weapon held straight out in front of him. But old Antoine caught hold of the blade, which was pointing full at his stomach, thrust it aside, and brought the handle of his whip sharply down on his enemy's temple. The Prussian collapsed at his feet. Dazed and distraught with horror, old Antoine stared at the body, which lay face downwards, at first twitching convulsively, then lapsing into immobility. He stooped down, turned it over, and stood gazing at it. The German's eyes were closed, and a trickle of blood oozed from a gash on the temple.

Dark though it was, old Antoine could see the brown stain that the blood left upon the snow. Utterly dismayed he lingered there, while the horses continued to move slowly onwards with the loaded cart. What was he to do? He would be shot. His farm would be burnt and the whole countryside laid waste. What was to be done? How was he to hide the corpse, conceal the murder, outwit the Prussians? In the deep hush that brooded over the snowy landscape, he could hear the sound of distant voices. Panic-stricken, he picked up the helmet, and replaced it on his victim's head. Then clasping him round the loins he hoisted him up, ran with him after the cart, and deposited his burden on the top of the manure. Once home was reached he could think out his next move. He walked slowly along, racking his brains, but to no purpose. He fully realized his predicament, and gave himself up for lost.

When he entered the yard a light was showing at an attic window; the maid was still awake. He backed the cart smartly till it stood on the brink of the manure pit. Reflecting that when the load was turned out the body, now lying on the top, would be deposited underneath the heap in the bottom of the trench, he tipped up the cart. As he had foreseen, the corpse was completely buried beneath the manure.

Antoine smoothed the heap over with his pitchfork, which he then stuck in the ground beside it. Calling one of the farm-hands, he bade him put the horses in the stable. Then he betook himself to his own room, and went to bed, still trying to decide upon his next step. Not a single idea occurred to him. Lying quietly between the sheets he felt his terror growing upon him. He would certainly be shot. He was sweating with fear and his teeth were chattering. At last he could stand it no longer. Shivering all over, he rose, and went down to the kitchen. He took the brandy bottle from the cupboard, and returned with it to his room. He drank two large glasses straight off. A new wave of intoxication succeeded the first, but it in no way allayed his agony of mind. What a God-forsaken fool he was to have landed himself in such a quandary!

He walked up and down the room, casting about for subterfuges, explanations, evasions. Every now and then he would take another pull at the brandy to put some heart into him. But not a plan, not the ghost of a plan, suggested itself. Towards midnight his watchdog Dévorant, a brute with a strain of wolf in him, broke out into deathlike howls. Old Antoine shivered to the marrow of his bones. Each time his dog began his lugubrious, long-drawn cry, a shudder of horror ran all over him. Worn out, distracted, aching in every limb, he collapsed into a chair, and listened anxiously for Dévorant to lift up his voice again. He was shaken by every tremor with which panic afflicts the quivering nerves. The clock in the room below struck five. The dog never ceased his howling, and the old man was beside himself. At last he got up, intending to let him off the chain in the hope of silencing him. He went downstairs, opened the door, and plunged into the darkness. It was still snowing. Against the background of unrelieved white, the farm buildings stood out like great splashes of black. Antoine made his way to the kennel. The dog was straining at the chain. As soon as he was released he gave one spring; then, his coat bristling, his legs rigid, his fangs bared, he stopped dead, with his head turned towards the dunghill.

'What's up with you, you brute?' gasped Antoine, who was trembling from head to foot.

He took a few steps forward, and peered into the vague gloom of the shadowy yard. There he beheld, seated upon the dung-hill, a figure, the figure of a man. Panting and aghast he gazed at the apparition. Then his eyes lighted on the handle of the pitchfork planted in the ground beside him. He snatched it up, and in one of those transports of terror that inspire even cowards with boldness, he dashed forward to investigate. It was he; it was the Prussian. Covered with mire, he had crawled out from beneath the manure, where he had lain till warmed and revived. Mechanically he had sat himself down on the midden. Befouled with blood and filth, stupefied with drink, stunned by the blow and exhausted by his wound, there he had remained with the snowflakes powdering him all over. He caught sight of Antoine, and, too dazed to grasp the situation, he tried to get up. But as soon as the old man recognized the soldier, he began to foam at the mouth like a rabid animal.

'You swine, you!' he gabbled. 'Not dead, aren't you? You'd give me away, would you? You wait . . . you wait.'

He flew at the German. Lifting his pitchfork like a lance, he drove it with all the force of both arms into the man's chest, plunging the four iron prongs in up to the socket. Uttering a long-drawn moan, the soldier fell backwards, while the old peasant drew out his weapon and thrust it again and again into belly, stomach, throat, stabbing with the rage of a madman, riddling the quivering body from head to foot while the blood gushed out in violent spurts. At last, breathless with the fierceness of his exertions, sobered by the fact of the murder, he desisted, and drew deep breaths of air into his lungs. Then, as the cocks in the henroost began to crow and daybreak was at hand, he set to work to bury his victim. He scooped out a hole in the dunghill, till he reached the soil below, and dug yet deeper, working in frenzied haste, in a fury of energy, with violent movements of limbs and body. When the pit was deep enough, he rolled the corpse into it with the aid of his pitchfork, shovelled back the earth, trod it down carefully, and replaced the manure. He smiled, as he watched the swiftly falling snow completing his task and covering up all trace of the deed with a veil of white. Finally he stuck the pitchfork back on the dunghill and returned to his room. The brandy bottle, still half-full, was standing on the table. He drained it at one draught, threw himself on his bed, and fell into a profound sleep.

He woke perfectly sober, his mind calm and alert, able to grapple with the situation and to anticipate every development. Within an hour he was scouring the country for news of his soldier. He sought out the German officers and asked why they had taken his man away from him. Their friendship was so universally known that not a soul suspected him. He actually gave a direction to the investigations by remarking that the Prussian used to go out every night running after girls.

An old retired gendarme, who kept an inn in the next village and owned a pretty daughter, was arrested and shot.

JULIE ROMAIN

A YEAR ago last spring I was wandering on foot along the Mediterranean coast. What can be more delightful than to let the fancy roam, while, caressed by the wind, you swing along, skirting the mountain-side that overlooks the sea? The dreams that haunt you! The illusions, the romances, the adventures that flit through the soul of the rover, in the course of a two-hours' tramp! Hopes innumerable, vague and beguiling, are breathed in with the wind, with the balmy, quickening air, and awake in the heart a hunger for happiness, which keeps pace with the physical appetite, stimulated by the exercise. Ideas, swift and enchanting, soar into the air and sing like birds.

I was following the long road that runs from St. Raphael into Italy, or rather that theatrical, ever-changing panorama, which seems the ideal setting for all the great love poems of earth. And I reflected how, from Cannes, where all is ostentation, to Monaco, a mere gambling hell, not a soul comes to this region except to swagger about and squander money. Beneath that exquisite sky, in that garden of roses and orange blossom, every form of degrading vanity, vulgar display, and base greed is manifested, and the human spirit is exhibited in all its servility, ignorance, arrogance, and cupidity.

On the margin of one those adorable bays which are revealed at every turn of the road, I suddenly caught sight of a group of four or five villas lying at the foot of the mountain and fronting the sea. The background was a wilderness of pine-woods running far inland, in two deep valleys with no apparent path or outlet. One of these chalets was so charmingly pretty that I paused outside the door to admire it. It was a small white house with brown woodwork, covered to the eaves with climbing roses. And such a garden! It was a carpet of flowers of every hue and form, all growing together in studied and charming confusion. Flowers sprang up all over the lawn and clustered on either side of the steps leading up to the terrace, while from every window trails of blue or yellow blossom

hung down over the dazzling façade. The terrace, which had
a stone balustrade and ran the whole length of the house, was
festooned with great crimson bell-flowers like splashes of blood.
At the back, a long avenue of flowering olive trees stretched
away to the foot of the mountain. 'Villa d'Antan' was inscribed
on the door in small gold letters. What poet or fairy, I wondered, dwelt in this Paradise? What inspired recluse had
discovered this retreat and created this dream of a house, set
in the heart of a posy?

A few steps farther on I saw a man breaking stones by the
roadside, and I asked him who owned this gem of a place.

'Madame Julie Romain,' was the reply.

Julie Romain! Long ago, in my childhood, I had heard
endless stories about her, great actress that she was, the rival
of Rachel. Never was woman more admired. Never was
woman more beloved—that above all, beloved! Oh, the duels,
the suicides, of which she was the cause! The fame of her
romantic adventures! But how old was the enchantress now?
Sixty? Seventy? Seventy-five? Julie Romain here in this
house! The woman, who was worshipped by the greatest
musician and the subtlest poet of our country. I was only
twelve at the time, but I can still remember the wave of excitement that swept all over France, when she fled to Sicily with
one lover, after her shattering rupture with the other. It was
after a first night, when the audience had acclaimed her for half
an hour on end and had recalled her eleven successive times.
She and the poet eloped together, travelling by postchaise, as
was then the custom. They crossed the sea to that legendary
island, daughter of Greece, there to revel in their love in the
shade of the Conca d'Oro, the great orange groves which
surround Palermo.

They had climbed Etna, so the story ran, and, cheek to cheek,
their arms round each other, had leaned over the monstrous
crater, as if they would fling themselves into its fiery jaws.

He was dead, the poet, the maker of verse so disturbing, so
penetrating, so profound, that it had thrown a whole generation
off its balance; so subtle, so mysterious, that it had revealed
a whole new world to a new race of poets. And he, the deserted
rival, he too, was dead, who for her sake had created music
that still lingered in the memory of men, rhapsodies full of
triumph and despair, at once heart-rending and maddening.

And she, Julie Romain, was there, in that house with its veil of blossom. I did not stop to think, but rang the bell. The door was opened by a young footman, an awkward lad of eighteen with coarse hands. I scribbled a neat little compliment on my visiting card, accompanied by an ardent petition that she would deign to receive me. Possibly she knew my name and would open her door to me. After a brief absence the footman returned and invited me to follow him. He showed me into a prim, neat drawing-room in the style of Louis Philippe, where a little maid-servant of sixteen, slim of figure, but of no beauty whatever, was removing, in my honour, the dust sheets from the heavy, formal furniture. On the walls hung three portraits, one representing the actress in one of her roles, one the poet in the long, close-fitting frock-coat and ruffled shirt of his day, the third the musician, seated at the clavecin. Golden-haired and charming, though with the mincing airs of that day, she looked down, with a smile on her gracious lips and in the depths of her blue eyes. It was a careful, delicate, elegant, restrained piece of work. All three portraits seemed to be posing for the benefit of posterity. The whole atmosphere of the room was eloquent of bygone days and departed friends.

A door opened and a tiny figure glided into the room. It was an old, old lady, with white eyelashes and bandeaux of white hair, a little white mouse of a woman, swift and stealthy in her movements. She gave me her hand.

'Thank you,' she said in a voice still clear and fresh and thrilling. 'How kind of you men of to-day to remember the women of the past! Pray be seated.'

I told her how much her house had charmed me; how I had asked the owner's name, and, on hearing it, had been unable to resist the temptation to ring at her door.

'I appreciate your visit all the more,' she replied, 'because it is the first of its kind ever paid me. When your card with its graceful message was brought to me I was as startled as if an old friend, dead these twenty years, had suddenly been announced. I myself am dead now, as good as dead. No one remembers me, no one will give me a thought, until the day when I really die. Then for three days the newspapers will be full of Julie Romain, anecdotes about her, incidents, reminiscences, enthusiastic praises. And that will be the end of me.'

She paused for a moment.

'It won't be long now,' she resumed. 'A few more months, or days perhaps, and of this tiny little woman there will be nothing left save a tiny little skeleton.'

She raised her eyes to her own portrait, which smiled at her, smiled at the little old lady, who was such a caricature of her youthful self. Then Julie Romain glanced at her two lovers, the scornful poet and the inspired musician. They seemed to ask each other: 'What is this old wreck to you and me?'

An indefinable, poignant, overwhelming sadness clutched at my heart, the sadness of lives outworn, still struggling in a flood of memories, like men drowning in deep waters. From my chair I could see a string of smart carriages with their freight of young, pretty, wealthy women and smiling, complacent men, travelling swiftly along the road from Nice to Monaco. Her glance followed mine and she guessed my thoughts.

'One can't have one's life twice over,' she murmured with a smile of resignation.

'But how wonderful yours must have been!' I cried.

'Wonderful and sweet,' she sighed. 'That is why I regret it so bitterly.'

I saw that she was longing to talk about herself, and with the utmost tenderness, as if touching on an aching wound, I drew her out. She spoke of her triumphs and raptures, of her friends of her whole dazzling career.

'To what do you attribute your keenest joys, your purest happiness? To the stage?'

'Oh, no,' she replied, so vehemently that I smiled.

With a mournful glance at the portraits of the two men, she added:

'I owed it all to them.'

'Which of the two?' I could not refrain from asking.

'Both. Sometimes I actually find myself confusing them a little in my mind. And of one of them, nowadays, I cannot think without remorse.'

'Then really your gratitude is due, not so much to them, as to love itself. They were merely its interpreters.'

'Yes, but what interpreters!'

'Has it ever occurred to you that perhaps another man might have loved you equally well, if not better, a plain man, who would have devoted to you his whole life, his whole heart, all his thoughts, all his hours, and all his being? With those two you had a pair of formidable rivals, Music and Poetry.'

'Never!' she exclaimed, in that voice of hers, so youthful still with its soul-stirring appeal. 'Another man might have loved me more, but he could never have loved so exquisitely. They sang to me the music of love, those two, as no one else on earth could sing it. Ah, how intoxicating it was! Who else is there, in all the world, able to discern in sounds and words the wonders they found there? Is mere love enough, without the art that can glorify passion with all the poetry and music of heaven and earth? They knew the secret, those two, of driving a woman distraught with verse and melody. Perhaps you are right. There may have been more illusion than reality in our passion. But it is the illusions that waft you to the skies, while the realities bind you to earth. Other men may have loved me more, but it was these two who taught me to know and understand and worship love.'

Her tears began to flow. She wept silently, despairingly. I pretended not to notice and gazed into the distance.

'You see,' she resumed after a pause of several minutes, 'with most people, the heart grows old with the body. But with me that is not so. My poor body is sixty-nine, but my poor heart is twenty. And that is why I live here all alone, with my flowers and my dreams.'

Another long silence ensued. She recovered her composure, and said with a smile:

'How you would laugh, if you knew . . . if you knew . . . how I spend my evenings . . . when the weather is fine. I am quite ashamed of myself. But I am sorry for myself, too.'

Plead as I might, she refused to reveal her secret, and I rose to take my departure.

'So soon!' she exclaimed.

I told her I was dining at Monte Carlo.

'Won't you stay and dine with me?' she asked hesitatingly. 'It would give me such pleasure.'

I accepted her invitation with alacrity. Overjoyed, she rang for the little maid, and when she had given some orders, she took me all over the house. A conservatory full of shrubs, opening off the dining-room, commanded the whole extent of the long avenue of orange-trees, which stretched away to the foot of the mountain. A low chair, hidden away among the plants, led me to assume that the old lady often sat there. We strolled into the garden to admire the flowers. Dusk was slowly falling. It was one of those mild, still evenings, when earth gives forth all its perfumes.

It was almost dark when we sat down to table. We lingered long over an excellent dinner, and the two of us became fast friends, as soon as she realized the depths of sympathy she had stirred within my heart. She sipped a couple of fingers of wine, as they used to say, and became more confiding and expansive.

'Come and look at the moon,' she said. 'I love the moon, the friendly moon. She witnessed my keenest joys. I feel as if all my memories were stored within her. I have only to gaze at her for them all to come back to me. And then . . . sometimes . . . of an evening . . . I treat myself to such an enchanting little scene . . . perfectly idyllic . . . perfectly idyllic . . . if you only knew. But no, you would laugh at me. I simply couldn't . . . I shouldn't dare . . . I really shouldn't.'

'Come, come,' I pleaded. 'Why won't you let me into the secret? I promise not to laugh . . . I swear I won't. Now, do.'

As she still hesitated, I caught her hands in mine, those pitiful little hands of hers, so thin and cold, and I kissed each in turn over and over again, just as they used to do, her two lovers in bygone days. She was moved.

'You promise not to laugh?' she asked irresolutely.

'I swear it.'

'Very well, then, come along.'

She rose from the table, and as the young footman, an ungainly object in his green livery, drew back her chair she whispered something in his ear in a low hurried voice.

'Certainly, madam, immediately,' he replied.

She took my arm and drew me into the conservatory.

The avenue of orange trees was a delight to the eyes. Straight down the centre, the full moon, now risen, shed a narrow track of silver, a long shaft of light, which glided through the dark domes of the trees and fell upon the yellow sand. All the trees were in blossom and the night air was laden with their sweet heady perfume. Among the sombre foliage, thousands of fireflies were twinkling and glittering like star dust.

'What a setting for a love scene!' I exclaimed.

'Yes, isn't it? Isn't it? You shall see.'

She made me sit down beside her.

'How a night like this,' she sighed, 'makes one regret one's youth. But you care for none of these things, you modern materialists, you speculators, merchants, and business men. You have even lost the art of talking to us. By "us" I mean the young of my sex. Love affairs have degenerated into vulgar intrigues, which often originate in an unconfessed dressmaker's bill. If the bill seems to you more than the woman is worth, you beat a retreat. But if you rate her higher, you foot the bill. Pretty customs! Pretty love-making!'

She took my hand.

'Look!' she murmured.

I gazed bewildered and entranced.

From the far end of the avenue, down the path of moonlight, came a youthful pair, their arms around each other. It was charming to see them, as they tripped along, entwined, now bathed in pools of radiance, now plunged again in shadow. The boy wore a suit of white satin in eighteenth-century style and a hat with a sweeping ostrich feather. The girl had a gown with panniers, and her powdered hair was piled high on her head, after the fashion of the fair ladies of the Regency. A hundred paces away, they halted in the middle of the avenue and cere-moniously embraced. Suddenly I recognised the two young servants, and I was seized by one of those terrible paroxysms of mirth that rend one's very vitals. But not a sound escaped my lips. Convulsed with agony, I choked back my laughter, as a man whose leg is being amputated represses the screams that force their way through throat and jaws.

But as soon as the two young people retreated towards the far end of the avenue, they recovered their charm. They drew ever farther away, until they vanished like a dream and were lost to sight. The avenue looked very desolate without them.

I, too, took my departure, for I had no wish to see them again, and I feared that it might be unduly prolonged, this scene which conjured up the past, the whole histrionic, passionate, delusive, seductive past, with its specious glamour, its genuine charm, which could still stir the pulses of this ancient tragedy queen, this worn-out breaker of hearts.

THE UMBRELLA

(*Le Parapluie*)

MADAME OREILLE was a frugal soul. She knew the precise value of a *sou*, and was armed with a whole quiverful of rigorous maxims relating to the multiplication of money. Her maid found it no easy matter to feather her nest, while Monsieur Oreille had great difficulty in squeezing pocket-money out of his wife. Although the pair were comfortably off and had no children, it was pain and grief to Madame Oreille to part with her shining silver. Each coin seemed to be wrung from her very heart, and whenever she had to meet some substantial, but unavoidable, expense, it cost her a sleepless night.

'You really might launch out a little,' urged Monsieur Oreille again and again. 'We never live up to our income'

'It is better to be on the safe side,' was her invariable rejoinder. 'One never knows what may happen.'

She was a neat, wrinkled little woman of forty, with an uncertain temper. Her husband was continually fretting at the hardships she imposed on him, especially at certain galling incidents which wounded his vanity.

He had a post as head clerk at the War Office, which he retained in deference to his wife's wishes, thereby increasing their already redundant revenues. For the last two years he had come to office with the same patched old gamp, which had become a standing joke with his brother clerks. At last he could stand their chaff no longer, and insisted on Madame Oreille's buying him a new one. She invested eight francs fifty in an umbrella which was being sold for advertising purposes by one of the big shops. There were thousands of these umbrellas scattered all over Paris. Recognizing it at once, the other clerks laughed louder than ever and Oreille suffered agonies. But this purchase proved a bad bargain and within three months it was worn out, to the vast amusement of the entire Ministry. It actually became the subject of a song, which could be heard from morn till night, from basement to attic, throughout the whole building. In a fit of exasperation, Oreille ordered his wife to spend twenty francs on a new umbrella of the finest silk, and to produce the bill in evidence. She compromised on one at eighteen francs, and, crimson with mortification, handed it over to her spouse.

'There,' she cried, 'that has got to last you at least five years.'

The exultant owner scored an immense success at the office. When he returned home that evening, his wife shot an uneasy glance at the umbrella.

'You shouldn't keep the rubber band fastened,' she said, 'that's the way to cut the silk. You had better take care of it. I shan't buy you another in a hurry.'

She took it out of his hands, undid the button and shook out the folds. Then, petrified with horror, she stood and gazed at it. Right in the middle of the umbrella there was a round hole, the size of a farthing, which had evidently been burnt by a cigar end.

'Just look at that!' she gasped.

'What is the matter?' asked her husband placidly, without turning his head. 'What are you talking about?'

Her indignation almost choked her.

'You . . . you . . .' she stammered. 'You've gone and burnt . . . a hole in your . . . in your new umbrella. You . . . you must be crazy. Do you want to ruin us?'

He could feel the blood ebbing from his cheeks.

'What did you say?' he exclaimed, turning round.

'I tell you, you've burnt a hole in your new umbrella. Just look at it.'

With that she flew at him as if to strike him, violently thrusting the little round hole under his very nose. He stared at it in horror.

'How on earth did that happen?' he faltered. 'I know nothing about it. It wasn't my doing, I swear. I can't understand it at all.'

'Oh, I know!' she retorted. 'I wager you were fooling about with it at the office, opening it and showing it off.'

'Well I did open it once, but only to show them what a beauty it was. That was all, I assure you.'

Stamping with rage, she treated him to one of those scenes of wedded life which, to a man of peace, render the domestic hearth more formidable than a battlefield under a hail of bullets. She mended the hole with a scrap of silk from the old umbrella, which was of a different colour. The next morning, with chastened mien, Oreille set out for the office with his patched-up treasure. He put it away in his cupboard and relegated it, like any other painful memory, to his subconscious mind.

As soon as he returned home that evening, his wife snatched the umbrella out of his hands, and opened it to satisfy herself as to its condition. What was her horror at the lamentable spectacle that met her gaze! The whole cover was riddled with tiny holes, which were evidently burns. It was as if the glowing ashes of a pipe had been emptied all over the silk cover. The umbrella was a ruin, a hopeless ruin. Speechless with rage, she stared at it, while her husband surveyed it, dazed with horror and consternation. Their glances met. Then his eyes fell. Right in his face she hurled the pitiful remains.

'You wretch!' she screamed, her powers of speech restored by a paroxysm of rage. 'You wretch! You did it on purpose. But I'll pay you out. You shall never have another.'

A fresh scene was enacted. After the tempest had raged for an hour, he at last obtained a hearing. He vowed he had no idea how this thing had come to pass. It must have been an act of jealousy or revenge. A ring at the door brought relief. It was a friend, who had been invited to dinner. Madame Oreille laid the matter before him. As for buying a new umbrella, that, she declared, was out of the question. Her husband should never have another.

'But then, Madame Oreille,' her guest wisely objected, 'his clothes will get spoilt, and that will be even more serious.'

'Very well,' exclaimed the little woman, still fuming with rage, 'he can have a servant's umbrella. I'll never get him another silk one.'

This pronouncement roused Oreille to rebellion.

'In that case I warn you I shall send in my resignation. Nothing will induce me to go to the office with a servant's umbrella.'

'Why not have this one re-covered?' suggested their visitor. 'It wouldn't be expensive.'

'It would cost at least eight francs,' snapped Madame Oreille. 'Eight francs plus eighteen, that makes twenty-six. Twenty-six francs for an umbrella, why, it's outrageous. It's madness.'

The friend, who was a poor man, had a sudden inspiration.

'Get it out of your insurance company. They always pay compensation for anything burnt, provided that it happened on your own premises.'

This suggestion worked like a charm. After a moment's reflection Madame Oreille turned to her husband.

'To-morrow, on your way to the office, you can take the umbrella to the Maternelle, show them the damage, and put in a claim for compensation.'

Monsieur Oreille jumped.

'I should never have the face to do such a thing. After all, it's only a matter of eighteen francs. It won't ruin us.'

Happily the next day was fine, and he went to the office carrying a walking-stick.

All by herself at home, Madame Oreille could not cease from brooding over her vanished eighteen francs. The umbrella lay on the dining-room table and she kept hovering round it, unable to come to a decision. She was obsessed by the idea of the insurance company, yet she dreaded the mocking glances of the clerks at the office. She was timid in society, and had a habit of flushing at the merest trifles, while she never felt at ease in conversing with strangers. Yet her sorrow for her eighteen francs tormented her like an aching wound. In vain she tried to banish it from her mind. The memory of her loss rankled unceasingly. What was she to do? Hour followed hour, and she was still irresolute. Suddenly, like a coward screwing up his courage, she decided to take action.

'I'll go, and we'll see what happens.'

First, however, the umbrella had to be dealt with, so that the disaster should appear irreparable and the case conclusive. From the mantelpiece she took a match, and between two ribs of the umbrella she burnt a great hole the size of her hand. Then she dexterously rolled up the remains of the silk, fastened the elastic band round it, put on shawl and hat, and hurried off to the Rue de Rivoli, where the insurance company had its office. The nearer she drew, the more her pace slackened. What was she to say? And what answer would she receive? She glanced at the numbers above the doorways. There were still another twenty-eight houses. Good! That gave her time to think. She walked ever more slowly, till, with a sudden jump, she saw a door, bearing in golden letters the inscription: 'La Maternelle, Fire Insurance Company.' She was there already!

Confused and diffident, she paused a moment. Twice she walked past, and twice she retraced her steps.

'Well, it has to be done,' she told herself. 'The sooner it's over the better.'

As she crossed the threshold and entered the office she could feel her heart beating wildly. A counter ran all round the immense room and at each little aperture in the grating a man's head was visible, while the rest of his person was screened by lattice-work. She advanced towards a man who was passing through the room, carrying some papers.

'Excuse me, sir,' she murmured in low, trembling tones. 'Could you tell me to whom to apply for compensation in the case of damage by fire?'

'The first floor, on the left,' he replied in a resonant voice. 'The accident department.'

More flustered than ever by his answer, she longed to run away without another word and sacrifice her eighteen francs. Then she drew fresh courage from the idea of all that money. Panting for breath, pausing at every step, she climbed the stairs. She knocked at a door on the first floor. A ringing voice bade her enter and she stepped into a spacious room, where three men, all with ribbons in their buttonholes, were standing in a group, immersed in a serious discussion.

One of the men turned to her.

'What can I do for you, madam?'

She could hardly bring out the words.

'I've come,' she stammered. 'I've come . . . about an accident.'

The man motioned her politely to a chair.

'Pray be seated, madam. I shall be at your disposal in a minute or two.'

The interrupted conversation was resumed.

'In your case, gentlemen,' said the manager, 'the Company does not hold itself liable for a sum exceeding four hundred thousand francs. We cannot admit your claim for a further hundred thousand. Besides, the valuation . . .'

'That will do, sir,' broke in one of the others. 'The court will decide. We need not prolong the interview.'

After an exchange of ceremonious bows the two claimants left the room. Had she dared, she would have followed their example, joyfully sacrificing everything, if only she could escape. But it was too late. The manager rejoined her and said with a bow:

'I am at your service, madam.'

'I 've come,' she gasped with a painful effort, 'I 've come . . . about this.'

In frank astonishment he looked down at the object she presented to his gaze. Her trembling fingers fumbled at the elastic band. After several attempts she succeeded in unfastening it, and hastily shook out the mutilated remains of the umbrella.

'It looks in a bad way,' remarked the manager sympathetically

'It cost me twenty francs,' she said tentatively.

He seemed surprised.

'Really? as much as that?'

'Yes, it was a very good one. I wanted you to see for yourself what a state it 's in.'

'There 's no doubt about it,' he rejoined. 'But I fail to understand what it has to do with me.'

With a sinking heart she wondered whether the company refused to pay compensation for such trifling damages.

'You see,' she stammered. 'It has been burnt.'

'Evidently,' he replied, without attempting to refute her statement.

At this words failed her. She sat there gaping at him, until she suddenly realized that she had omitted to give her name.

'I am Madame Oreille,' she hurriedly informed him. 'We have taken out an insurance policy with the Maternelle, and I wish to put in a claim for compensation.'

To forestall the possibility of an unqualified refusal on his part she hastened to add:

'I am only asking you to have the umbrella re-covered.'

'But, madam,' he protested, greatly perplexed, 'we do not deal in umbrellas. We cannot undertake repairs of this description.'

The little woman felt her natural combativeness reviving. There was to be a tussle. Well, she was ready. She was no longer afraid.

'I am only asking you to pay for the repairs. I can get it re-covered myself.'

The manager seemed taken aback.

'Really, madam, it is such a small matter. We are never

asked to pay compensation for such trifling accidents. You must admit that we cannot be expected to replace handkerchiefs, gloves, brooms, old slippers, and all the little odds and ends that are liable to be burnt at any moment of the day.'

She felt her cheeks flushing with rising temper.

'Last December, sir, we had a chimney on fire and it cost us five hundred francs to repair the damage. Monsieur Oreille never asked the company for a farthing. So it is only fair that you should pay for my umbrella.'

The manager smiled at the transparent fiction.

'You cannot deny, madam, that it is very surprising of Monsieur Oreille, after making no claim for damages amounting to five hundred francs, to ask for five or six francs compensation for an umbrella.'

'I beg your pardon,' she said brazenly. 'The five hundred francs were Monsieur Oreille's concern. The eighteen francs came out of Madame Oreille's purse, which is a very different matter.'

Realizing that he would never get rid of her without wasting his whole day, he said resignedly:

'Will you kindly tell me how the accident came about?'

Confident now of victory, she began her story.

'It was like this, sir. In the hall, we have a bronze receptacle for umbrellas and walking-sticks. I came in the other day and put my umbrella into the stand. Just above it, I must tell you, there is a little shelf for candles and matches. I stretched out my hand and took four matches. The first one would not strike. The second flared up and went out and so did the third.'

'Government matches, I suppose?' broke in the manager facetiously.

'Possibly,' she replied, without noticing his joke. 'The point is that with the fourth match I lighted my candle. Then I retired to my room and went to bed. A quarter of an hour later, I thought I could detect a smell of burning. I am always afraid of fire. If we ever have one, it certainly won't be my fault. Ever since that chimney I told you about, I've lived in mortal terror. So I got up, left the room, and hunted high and low, sniffing about like a dog when it's hunting. At last I discovered that it was my umbrella that was burning. No doubt one of the matches had fallen into the folds. You see what a state it is in. . . .'

The manager bowed to the inevitable.

'What amount do you claim, madam?'

She did not venture to name her figure and remained silent.

'I leave it to you,' she said at last, anxious to appear magnanimous. 'You can have it repaired for me.'

'We cannot do that, madam. Kindly fix your own figure.'

'Why . . . I should think . . . No, sir, listen to me. I don't wish to make any profit out of you. This is the fairest way. I will take my umbrella to a shop, have it re-covered with good, hard-wearing silk and bring you the bill. Will that do?'

'Admirably. Then the matter is settled. Here is a note for the cashier, who will refund to you the cost of the repairs.'

He handed her a card. She clutched it, rose from her chair and muttering words of thanks, hurried from the room, for fear he should change his mind.

After this victory, she tripped gaily along the street, hunting for an umbrella shop of promising exterior. When she came to one that looked sufficiently expensive, she marched boldly in and said in authoritative tones:

'I wish to have this umbrella re-covered with the finest silk. Use the best material you have. I don't mind what it costs.'

BOITELLE

OLD Antoine Boitelle had the monopoly of all the unsavoury work of the neighbourhood. Whenever there was a pit, a midden, cesspool, a drain, or other deposit of filth to be cleaned out, he was always the one to be sent for. In clogs encrusted with dirt, he would come along with his scavenger's apparatus, and set to work, grumbling all the time at his occupation. When he was asked why he followed so repulsive a calling, he replied with resignation:

'Bless me, I've got my children to feed. It's better paid than most jobs.'

He had actually fourteen children. If you asked him what had become of them all, he would answer with an air of indifference:

'I've eight of them at home. One is in service, the other five are married.'

When questioned as to whether they had made good matches, he would reply with warmth:

'I didn't stand in their way. I've never stood in their way in anything. They married to please themselves. People oughtn't to be crossed when they take a fancy into their heads. It turns out badly. I shouldn't be the village scavenger now, if my parents hadn't crossed me. I should have had a trade like anybody else.'

This is the story of how his parents crossed him. It was when he was stationed at Havre doing his military service. He was no brighter than other people, and no duller, though perhaps a trifle simple-minded. When he was off duty, his great pleasure was to wander about on the quay, where the bird-fanciers congregated. Sometimes alone, sometimes with a townee, he would stroll slowly along past the cages of green-backed, yellow-polled parrots from the Amazon; grey-backed, red-polled parrots from Senegal; enormous macaws, looking as if they had been reared in hot-houses, with their plumage gay as flowers, their crests, and their aigrettes; parakeets of all sizes, so brilliant that they seemed to have been painted, with infinite care, by a god turned miniaturist; and the tiniest little birds hopping about, red, yellow, blue, and all the colours of the rainbow, all of them mingling their cries with the noises of the quay, and adding, to the hubbub of ships unloading, the crowds of people, and the traffic, a violent shrill, ear-splitting, deafening clamour, as of some far-off enchanted forest.

With open eyes and open mouth, his teeth flashing in an enraptured grin, Boitelle would linger by the captive cockatoos, who bobbed their white or yellow topknots at the sight of his bright red trousers and the metal fastenings on his belt. When he came across a talking parrot, he would ask it questions, and if the bird was so obliging as to answer him and converse, he was pleased and happy for the rest of the day. Watching the monkeys was yet another joy, and he could think of no greater bliss for a wealthy man than to own such pets, as ordinary mortals keep cats and dogs. This peculiar taste for the exotic was in his blood, like a taste for hunting, healing, or preaching in others. As soon as the barrack gates were open, he could not keep away from the quay. It was as if some irresistible attraction drew him thither.

One day he was watching, almost in ecstasy, a huge macaw, which was ruffling its plumage, and bowing and straightening itself like a courtier performing his reverences in the presence of the king of the cockatoos, when the door of a small café, adjoining the bird-fancier's shop, opened, and he saw a young negress with a red bandanna round her head appear on the threshold, sweeping the dust and old corks out into the road. Boitelle's attention was instantly divided between the two, the woman and the bird, and he would have been puzzled to decide which of the two he regarded with more wonder and admiration. After she had cleared out the rubbish from the café, the negress looked up, and she, for her part, was dazzled by the soldier's uniform. She stood facing him with her broom in her hands, as if presenting arms, while the macaw continued its obeisances. After a few moments, the soldier felt embarrassed by these attentions and moved away, though slowly enough to avoid the appearance of beating a retreat.

But he came again. Nearly every day he passed in front of the Café des Colonies and often, through the window, he caught a glimpse of the little blackamoor, serving the sailors from the harbour with beer or spirits, and frequently, when she saw him, she would step outside. Soon, although they had never exchanged a word, they smiled at each other like old acquaintances. Boitelle's heart would leap at the sight of the dazzling row of teeth between the girl's dark lips. One day he entered the café and found to his surprise that she talked French like anybody else. The bottle of lemonade, of which she accepted a glass, lingered in the soldier's memory as something peculiarly delectable. He fell into the habit of dropping into the little café in the harbour and absorbing as many syrupy potions as his pocket permitted. To him there was a charm, a joy which never left his thoughts, in the sight of the little waitress's black hand pouring the liquid into his tumbler, while her teeth flashed a brighter smile than her eyes. After meeting for a couple of months, they became fast friends. At first he was surprised to discover that his negress had the same correct ideas as the girls at home, and a due respect for thrift, industry, religion, propriety. But he liked her all the better for it and became so much enamoured that he was anxious to marry her. When he told her of his project, she danced for joy. She happened to possess a little money, left to her by an oyster woman, who had taken pity on her, when, a child of six, she had been deposited on the quay at Havre by an American sea-captain. A few hours after leaving New York, the captain had found her huddled up on some bales of cotton in the hold of his ship. On his arrival at Havre he had handed her over to the oyster woman, who felt sorry for this little black creature, stowed away on the ship for some unknown reason. After the death of her benefactress, the negro girl had taken a place as servant in the Café des Colonies.

'We'll get married,' said Antoine, 'that is if the parents don't object. I won't go against their wishes, you know, never. But I'll drop a hint, next time I go home.'

Accordingly, the following week he took twenty-four hours' leave and went to see his family, who worked a small farm at Tourteville near Yvetot. He waited till the after-dinner coffee, laced with spirits, had produced its mellowing effect upon their hearts, and then informed his parents that he had met a girl who was so completely to his mind in every respect that there was no one else in the whole world to suit him so perfectly. At this avowal, the old people at once grew cautious and asked him for details. He kept nothing from them except the colour of her complexion. She was a servant, he told them, without much fortune, but capable, thrifty, clean, well-conducted and sensible. All these virtues were more profitable than money, which a bad housewife would only fritter away. And then she was not quite penniless. She had a nest-egg, bequeathed to her by the woman who had brought her up, a tidy little sum, almost enough for a dowry, fifteen hundred francs in the savings bank. Impressed by his dissertation, and disposed moreover to trust his judgment, the old people were on the point of yielding, when he broached the delicate topic of her colour.

'There's only one thing you might object to,' he began with a constrained smile, 'she's not a white woman.'

At first they did not grasp his meaning, and he had to explain, at great length and as tactfully as possible, for fear he should prejudice them, that she sprang from that dusky race of which they had seen specimens only in Épinal colour prints. At this they were as much disconcerted, perplexed, and alarmed as if he had suggested a union with the devil.

'Black!' gasped his mother. 'How black do you mean? All over?'

'Yes. Of course. Just as you're white all over.'

'Black!' chimed in his father. 'As black as a cooking pot?'

'Well, perhaps not quite,' replied his son. 'She is black, but not black enough to put you off. The curé's cassock is black, but it looks no worse than a white surplice.'

'Are there people blacker than she in her own country?'

'Why, yes,' he replied with conviction.

The worthy man, however, shook his head.

'It must be unpleasant.'

'It's no more unpleasant than anything else. Why, you get used to it in no time.'

'Doesn't a skin like that come off on the linen?' asked his mother.

'No more than your own. Don't you see, it's her proper colour.'

They continued to ply him with questions, and finally it was agreed that they should see the girl before anything was settled. Their son, whose term of service expired the following month, was to bring her to the farm, and while they were talking they could have a good look at her and decide whether or no she was too black to be admitted into the Boitelle family. It was arranged that on Sunday, the twenty-second of May, the day on which he obtained his discharge, Antoine should take his beloved to Tourteville. In honour of this visit to her lover's parents, she put on her best and most startling clothes, in which yellow, red, and blue predominated, making her look as if beflagged for a national holiday. On the departure platform at Havre many glances were directed at her, and Boitelle felt proud to be giving his arm to a person who attracted so much attention. Seated beside him in the third-class railway carriage, she created such a sensation among the peasants that those in adjoining compartments stood up on their seats to stare at her over the wooden partitions. At the sight of her, a child began to cry with terror, while another hid its face in its mother's apron. All went well, however, till they reached Yvetot. As the train slowed down and steamed into the station, Antoine suddenly felt uneasy, as he used to do before an inspection, when he had omitted to study his drill book.

Leaning out of the window, he recognized his father in the distance, standing by the horse and trap, with the reins over his arm, while his mother had come right up to the trellis-work which the station-master had put up to keep out trespassers. He was the first to alight, and handed his sweetheart out of the train. Then, as erect as if he were escorting a general, he advanced towards his family. When she saw this black and bedizened female coming towards her with her son, the mother was so overcome that she could not open her mouth, while the father could hardly hold the pony, which kept plunging with fright, either at the locomotive or at the negress. Antoine, however, seized with pure joy at the sight of his old parents, rushed at them with open arms, and saluted first his mother, then his father, with sounding kisses, regardless of the panic-stricken pony. Then turning to his companion, whom the passers-by stopped to stare at in amazement, he introduced her.

'Here she is. You know I told you she was not very taking at first sight, but really and truly you 've only to know her, and you 'll find that there 's nobody in the world to beat her. Say "how do you do" to her, or she 'll feel hurt.'

Almost beside herself with embarrassment, Mother Boitelle dropped a kind of curtsy, while the father took off his cap and muttered:

'At your service, miss.'

Without further delay they all climbed into the trap, the two men sitting on the seat in front, the two women behind on chairs, which shot them up into the air at every bump in the road. No one uttered a word. Antoine nervously whistled a barrack-room tune; his father whipped up the pony, while his mother kept stealing furtive glances out of the corner of her eye at the negress, whose forehead and cheeks shone in the sun like well-polished shoes.

Anxious to break the ice, Antoine turned round.

'Aren't you two going to talk to each other?'

'Time enough for that,' replied the old dame.

'Why don't you tell her the story about your hen and the eight eggs?'

This was a favourite joke in the family. But as his mother's emotions still kept her tongue-tied, Antoine made himself spokesman and, laughing heartily, related that singular incident. His father, who knew the story off by heart, brightened up at the first words; his wife soon followed his example, and when he came to the climax, the negress herself suddenly burst into such peals of ringing, resonant, and torrential laughter that the pony, in its excitement, broke into a brief gallop. The barriers were down and they all talked freely. They reached home and scrambled out of the trap. Antoine at once took his sweetheart up to the bedroom, where she removed her gown, so as not to spoil it while preparing a succulent dish of her own, in the hope of captivating the old people with an appeal to their appetites. In the meantime Antoine drew his parents outside the door and asked with beating heart:

'Well, what do you think of her?'

His father held his peace, but his mother declared:

'She's too black. No, really, it's too much. She gives me the creeps.'

'You'll get used to her,' said Antoine.

'I dare say, but not just at first.'

They went indoors, and the good soul was touched when she saw the negress busying herself in the kitchen. An active woman still for her years, she turned up her skirts and lent a hand.

They sat long over an excellent meal and were all very merry. When the party was setting out for a stroll, Antoine took his father aside:

'Well, father, what do you think of her?'

But the old peasant was never one to commit himself.

'I haven't made up my mind. Ask your mother.'

Antoine rejoined his mother and made her fall back with him.

'Well, mother, what do you think of her?'

'My poor boy, really she is too black. If only she were just a little less so, I wouldn't stand in your way. But it's too much. She's like Satan.'

He did not press her. He was aware that the old dame never gave in. But he felt a tempest of grief surging up within his heart. He wondered what he had better do, what inducements to attempt, and he marvelled that his negress had failed to captivate them as speedily as she had won his own heart. Slowly the four wandered through the cornfields, gradually lapsing again into silence. Whenever they skirted an enclosure, the farmer came to the gate, the youngsters scrambled up the banks, and every one rushed into the road to see the blackamoor young Boitelle had brought home. From a distance people could be seen racing across the fields, as if they had heard the beating of a drum advertising a freak show. Aghast at the sensation their appearance created throughout the neighbourhood, the old couple hurried on together, far ahead of their son and his companion, who was asking him what his parents thought of her. Hesitatingly he replied that they had not yet made up their minds. Their arrival in the village square was the signal for an excited rush from every house, and at the sight of the steadily increasing crowd, the two old people took to their heels and made for home, while Antoine, boiling with rage, his sweetheart on his arm, strode majestically onwards under the wide-eyed gaze of the spectators. He felt that this was the end, that there was no hope, that he would never be married to his negress. She, too, realized the truth.

As they drew near the farm, both of them were dissolved in tears. They went indoors, and as before, she removed her gown and helped the mother in her household tasks. She followed her everywhere, into the dairy, the stable, the henhouse, and did most of the work herself.

'Let me do that, Madame Boitelle,' she kept saying, till by the evening the old woman's heart was touched, though she still remained inexorable.

'She's a good girl, all the same,' she remarked to her son.

'What a pity she's so black.   But really it is too much.   I couldn't put up with her.   She must go away again.   She's too black.'

Antoine had to break it to his sweetheart:

'She won't have it.   She thinks you're too black.   You will have to go away again.   I'll see you to the station.   But never mind.   Don't worry.   I'll have a talk to them when you've gone.'

He took her to the station, doing his best to cheer her.   Then he kissed her and put her into the train, and with tear-swollen eyes watched till it was out of sight.

Plead as he might with the old people, he could not gain their consent.   He never told this story, which was common property in the village, without adding:

'Ever since that day I haven't had the heart for anything. I couldn't get interested in any kind of work.   And so I became what I am now, a scavenger.'

'Still, you married,' someone would remark.

'Yes, and I can't say I didn't care for my wife, considering I've had fourteen children by her, but she's not the same as the other one, not she, oh no.   The other one, you see, my negress, she had only to look at me and I would feel a sort of thrill . . .'

THE DEVIL

(*Le Diable*)

DOCTOR and peasant stood facing each other, while the peasant's old mother, who lay in bed, dying, looked at the two men, and listened to their conversation. She was calm, clear-headed, resigned. She knew that she was going to die. But she accepted the fact. She was ninety-two. Her time was up.

The July sun poured in through the open windows and doorway. Its burning rays fell upon the brown, uneven, earthen floor, which the sabots of four generations of peasants had trodden. Grilling puffs of wind brought in with them the odours of the fields: of grass, of wheat, of leaves, burning under the noontide heat. The grasshoppers were shrilling themselves hoarse; the whole countryside was filled with their rapid chirping, not unlike the noise made by those wooden crickets which are sold to children at fairs.

The doctor's voice became more emphatic.

'Honoré, you cannot leave your mother by herself in the condition she is in. She may die at any moment.'

Honoré, very woebegone, replied:

'All the same, I've got to get in my wheat. It has been lying on the ground too long already. It's just the weather for it. What do you think, mother?'

The old woman, though on the point of death, was still in the fierce grip of Norman avarice. She nodded a silent assent. Her son must go and get in his wheat, and leave her to die by herself.

The doctor stamped his foot with annoyance.

'You're nothing but a brute, I tell you, and I won't allow you to do any such thing, understand that. If you've got to get your wheat in to-day, you must send for the Rapet woman, and make her look after your mother. I insist upon it, and if you don't do as I tell you, I'll let you die like a dog when it's your turn to fall sick. Remember that!'

Honoré, a tall, lean, slow-moving rustic, was tortured by

conflicting emotions. He was afraid of the doctor; on the other hand, he had a violent passion for economy. He hesitated; he made calculations. Finally he asked diffidently:

'How much does the Rapet woman ask for nursing?'

'How should I know?' the doctor said. 'It depends on how long you keep her. Make your own arrangements with her, for goodness' sake. But understand that I must have her here within the hour.'

'I'm going, I'm going,' said Honoré, having made up his mind at last. 'You can rest easy, doctor.'

The doctor gave a parting admonition:

'Now you look out for yourself, my man. It's no joke when I get my back up, I tell you.'

Left alone with his mother, Honoré turned to her and said in a tone of resignation:

'I'm going to fetch Mother Rapet, as that fellow insists on it. Keep easy till I come back.'

Then he followed the doctor out of the house.

Mother Rapet was an old woman who did ironing. She also looked after people who were dying in the parish and its vicinity, and watched the bodies after death. The instant she had finished sewing up her customers in the sheet which they were never to cast off, she set about her other task of ironing sheets for the living. Her face was wrinkled like a last year's apple. She was spiteful, envious, and of an avarice which was hardly human. She was bent double, as if she had broken her back with eternally running the iron backwards and forwards over the linen. As for death-beds, it was almost as if she had developed a hideous and morbid passion for them. Her only topics of conversation were the people whom she had seen die, and the different death-beds at which she had been present. In great detail, and never varying by a single word, she would relate these occurrences, with the accuracy of a marksman describing each individual shot.

When Honoré Bontemps entered her house, he found her mixing blue in a tub for the village girls' collarettes.

'Well, how do you do, Mother Rapet?' he said. 'Is everything all right with you?'

Turning towards him, she replied:

'So so, so so. And you?'

'Oh, I'm all right. It's my mother who is not doing so well.'

'Your mother?'

'Yes. My mother.'

'What's wrong with your mother?'

'She's going to turn up her toes, that's what's wrong with her.'

The old hag took her hands out of the water; the bluish, transparent drops trickled down to her finger-tips and fell back again into the tub. With suddenly aroused interest, she exclaimed:

'Is she as low as that?'

'The doctor says she won't last out the afternoon.'

'Ah, then, she must be far gone.'

Honoré hesitated. He had a proposal to make, but he could hardly tackle the business without certain preambles. He searched for an opening, but finding none, came straight to the point.

'How much will you take for looking after her till the end? We are far from well off, as you know. I can't so much as pay for a woman to do the work. That's just what has done for my mother, my poor mother. Too much bustle, too much work. She was ninety-two, but she did the work of ten. They don't make women like that nowadays.'

Mother Rapet replied gravely:

'I have two prices. For the rich, two francs a day and three francs a night. For the poor, one franc a day and two francs a night. I'll charge you one and two.'

Honoré thought this over. He knew his mother well. He knew her tenacity, her vitality, her powers of resistance. She might last a whole week, whatever the doctor's opinion was. He replied firmly:

'No. I'd rather you made me a fixed price, to include the whole job. It's a risk whichever way you take it. The doctor says she's going to die immediately. If that happens, so much the better for you, so much the worse for me. On the other hand, if she lasts another day or even longer, so much the better for me, so much the worse for you.'

Mother Rapet looked at him in surprise. She had never yet treated a death on a time-contract. Tempted by the speculative risk, she hesitated. Then a suspicion of trickery crossed her mind, and she replied:

'I can't say until I've seen your mother.'

'Come and see her then.'

She dried her hands and followed him forthwith. On the way to Honoré's house they were silent. She scuttled along, while he lengthened his stride, as if he had to cross a gutter at each step. Overcome by the heat, the cows were lying in the fields. As the old woman and the peasant passed by, the cattle raised their heads and lowed gently, as though asking for fresh grass. When they were close to their destination, Honoré Bontemps murmured:

'Anyhow, suppose it's all over by this time?'

His unconscious desire that this should be the case was perceptible in the tone of his remark.

The old woman, however, was not dead. She was lying on her back, in her truckle-bed, with her hands resting on the purple coverlet of printed calico. They were hideously thin and gnarled; doubled up with rheumatism, overwork, and the incessant tasks of wellnigh a century. They reminded one of uncanny animals such as crabs.

Mother Rapet went up to the bed and had a good look at the dying woman. She felt her pulse, passed her hand over her chest, listened to hear what her breathing, asked her some questions in order to hear what her voice was like. After she had studied her again for a long time, she went outside, followed by Honoré. She had quite made up her mind that the old woman would not last till nightfall.

'Well?' asked Honoré.

'Well,' replied Mother Rapet. 'She will last two days, perhaps three. My charge is six francs, inclusive.'

'Six francs! Six francs!' he exclaimed. 'Are you out of your wits? I give you my word she'll only last five or six hours, not a minute more.'

The dispute was conducted on both sides with extreme ferocity and at great length. However, the nurse threatened to leave him, and realizing that time was passing and that his wheat could not gather itself in without his assistance, he accepted her terms.

'Very well, then, six francs. And that includes everything up to the lifting.'

'Six francs it is.'

He made off with great strides in the direction of his field, where the reaped wheat was lying under the oppressive harvest sun. Mother Rapet went back into Honoré's house. She had brought some work with her. She always worked industriously by the bedside of the dead or the dying, sometimes for herself, sometimes for the family of the patient, if they would pay her a little extra for the double job. Suddenly she addressed the dying woman.

'Of course you 've had your Sacraments, Madame Bontemps?'

Madame Bontemps shook her head. Mother Rapet, who was very pious, got up with alacrity.

'Lord God, is it possible? I 'll go and fetch the priest.'

She dashed off headlong to the curé's house, running so quickly that the small boys on the village square thought something serious had happened. The priest came along at once. In front of him went a choir-boy ringing a bell to announce the passing of the Host. The landscape brooded under the burning sun. Some men, who were working at a little distance, took off their wide-brimmed hats and waited until the white surplice of the curé was lost to sight behind a farm. Women, who were lifting the sheaves, straightened themselves, and made the sign of the cross. A few black hens, terrified by the procession, fluttered along the ditches, until they found some well-known gap in the hedge through which they disappeared. A colt, tethered in a meadow, took fright and started running round and round at the end of his tether, kicking up his heels. The choir-boy in his red cassock trotted along, and the priest, who was wearing a biretta, followed him, murmuring prayers with his eyes on the ground. Last of all came Mother Rapet, head down, bent double, as if in the act of worship. She had clasped her hands, as though she were in church.

Honoré caught sight of them from a distance and asked:

'Where is our curé going?'

His labourer, who was more intelligent than his master, replied:

'He is taking the Sacrament to your mother, of course.'

Honoré expressed no astonishment.

'Like enough,' he said, and went on with his work.

Mother Bontemps made her confession, received absolution, and communicated, and the priest took his departure, leaving the two women alone in the suffocating cottage. Mother Rapet presently began to take stock of her patient. She was wondering how long she would take in dying.

Daylight was waning. The air became cooler. It entered the room in brisker puffs. The cheap coloured print, that was fixed to the wall by two pins, fluttered in the breeze. The little window curtains, once white but now yellow and fly-blown, had the appearance of wanting to fly away, of struggling to free themselves, like the old woman's soul.

Mother Bontemps lay motionless, with her eyes open, seeming to await with indifference the death that was so imminent and yet so slow of coming. Her throat was a little constricted and her breath was drawn with a slight whistling sound. Soon it would cease altogether; there would be one woman less in the world, and no one would miss her.

Honoré came in at dusk. Approaching the bed, he saw that his mother was still alive.

'How goes it?' he asked, exactly as he used to do when she was a little out of sorts. Then he sent Mother Rapet away, bidding her come without fail at five o'clock on the following morning. The old nurse did in fact return at daybreak. Honoré was having some soup before going out to his fields; he had prepared it himself.

'Is your mother dead yet?' the nurse asked.

With a sly twinkle in his eyes he replied:

'If anything, she is better.'

And off he went.

Mother Rapet became uneasy. She went close up to the dying woman, who seemed in precisely the same state as the day before; listless, impassive, with her eyes open, and her hands doubled up on the coverlet. Mother Rapet saw that in this condition she might last for two days, four days, even a week. Her avaricious heart was wrung by apprehension, and she felt furiously angry with the sharper who had tricked her, and with this woman who refused to die. None the less she set about her work, but she kept a steady gaze fixed on the countenance of Mother Bontemps. Honoré came in for dinner. His face wore a satisfied, almost a bantering expression. Presently he went out again. He was certainly getting in his wheat under ideal conditions.

Mother Rapet was losing her temper. Every moment that slipped past seemed now to her like stolen time, stolen money. She had a desire, a mad desire, to seize her by the throat, the tiresome, pig-headed, stubborn old thing. Just a little squeeze and she would stop that short, quick breathing which was robbing her of her time and her money. She reflected, however, that this would be a risky thing to do. Other schemes occurred to her. She approached the dying woman and asked her:

'Have you seen the Devil yet?'

'No,' replied Mother Bontemps.

The nurse then began to tell stories calculated to terrify the feeble intelligence of the expiring woman. She declared that the Devil always appeared to the dying just a few minutes before the end. He had a broom in his hand, a three-legged cooking-pot on his head, and he uttered loud yells. Once you had seen him, you were through with everything. You had only a few moments to live. She gave the names of all the people to whom the Devil had already appeared that year: Joséphine Loisel, Eulalie Ratier, Sophie Padagnau, Séraphine Grospied. All this had its effect on Mother Bontemps. She grew nervous, fidgeted with her hands, and tried to turn her head so as to see into the far end of the room.

Mother Rapet suddenly disappeared behind the curtains at the foot of the bed. From the wardrobe she took a sheet and wrapped herself in it. On her head she placed an inverted cooking-pot, with three short curved legs, which stood out exactly like three horns. She seized in her right hand a broom and in her left a tin bucket, which she threw up in the air, letting it fall with a horrible clatter. Then she climbed up on a chair, raised the curtains again, and showed herself to the patient. She gesticulated, she uttered shrill cries inside the iron pot which hid her face, and, like the devil in a Punch and Judy show, she shook her broom at the old peasant woman, now on the verge of death. In horror, with the expression of one crazed with fear, Mother Bontemps made a superhuman effort to scramble out of bed and run away. She managed to raise her shoulders and chest. But after this effort she fell back with a great sigh. All was over.

With perfect tranquillity, Mother Rapet put all her properties back in their right places: the broom in the corner of the wardrobe, the sheet inside, the saucepan on the hearth, the tin bucket on the floor, and the chair against the wall. Then she proceeded to the actions which her profession demanded. She shut the wide-staring eyes of the dead woman; she placed a dish on the bed, filled it from the holy-water basin, and dipped into it the sprig of box which was nailed above the chest of drawers. Then she fell on her knees and set about a fervid repetition of the prayers for the dead. She knew them by heart, that being part of her trade.

When Honoré came back from the harvest field at dusk, he found Mother Rapet on her knees. He entered forthwith into calculations. She had been three days and one night nursing his mother. That made a total of five francs, whereas he now had to give her six.

'I lost one franc over that,' he reflected.

THE OLIVE GROVE

(*Le Champ d'Oliviers*)

I

THE small Provençal port of Garandou is situated at the head of the Bay of Pisca, which lies between Marseilles and Toulon.

Catching sight of the Abbé Vilbois's boat on its way home from the fishing grounds, the men at the village came down to the shore to lend a hand in beaching it. The abbé was alone in the boat, and he handled his oars with the skill of a born sailor and with an energy surprising in a man of fifty-eight. His sleeves were turned up over his muscular forearms; the top buttons of his cassock were undone and the skirts tucked up between his knees. His three-cornered hat lay beside him on the thwart, and his head was protected from the sun's rays by a cork bell-helmet with a white cover. He looked like one of those priests of tropic climes, stout fellows, not without eccentricity, who suggest a capacity for adventure rather than for priestly functions.

From time to time he stopped to cast a glance over his shoulder and make sure of his landing-place. Then, resuming his oars, he rowed with strong rhythmic strokes, to show these southern lubbers yet again how men of the North handle their sculls.

Under the compulsion of his vigorous strokes, the boat reached the shore and glided on its keel up the sloping sand, as though bent upon reaching the top of the beach. When it came to a stop the five men who had been watching the boat's approach came down with obvious pleasure to give their priest a friendly greeting.

'Well, your reverence, what luck?' one of them asked in a strong Provençal accent.

The Abbé Vilbois shipped his oars, removed his cork helmet, put on his three-cornered hat, turned down his sleeves, and buttoned up his cassock. With this attention to the proprieties he resumed his pastoral dignity.

'Not too bad. Three bass, two muraenas, and some *girelles*.'

The fat bass, the flat-headed, repulsive, snake-like muraenas, the *girelles* with their stripes of violet and orange-gold, lay in the bottom of the boat, and the five fishermen came nearer and bending over the gunwale, inspected the catch with the air of experts.

'I'll take them up to your cottage, your reverence,' one of them volunteered.

'Thank you, my man.'

The priest shook hands all round and set off homewards, with one of the fishermen following him. The others stayed behind and busied themselves about the boat.

The abbé walked with long, slow strides. Energy and dignity characterized his bearing. He was still heated from his exertions at the oars, and whenever he passed under the shade of the olive trees, he removed his hat, so as to allow the evening air, which was tempered by a slight breeze from the open sea, to play upon his head, upon his stiff, close-cropped, white hair, and upon the square-set countenance, which suggested the soldier rather than the priest. Presently he came in sight of the village, which was situated on rising ground in the midst of a wide, flat valley-bottom, sloping towards the sea.

It was a July evening. The declining sun had almost reached the serrated crest of the distant hills. The dazzling rays fell upon the white road, which was thick with dust. The priest's shadow, prolonged by the sloping beams, fell diagonally across the path. His three-cornered hat, magnified to an inordinate size, cast on the adjoining fields a huge black blot which danced now on the tree trunks, now on the ground, now in and out amongst the olives.

In summer these southern roads have a mantle of dust, as fine as flour. Disturbed by the abbé's feet, it rose like a cloud of smoke about his cassock, and covered the skirts with a grey layer, gradually increasing in density. He was cooler now. Thrusting his hands into his pockets he walked on, with the strong, steady gait of a mountaineer ascending a slope. His calm eyes scanned the village, his own village, where he had been for twenty years parish priest. He had chosen it himself, and had obtained the charge of it as a special favour. In it he proposed to end his days. Its cottages lay on the slope of the hill, in the form of a great pyramid, the apex formed by the church with its two square, ill-matched towers of brown stone, their ancient outlines suggesting the defences of a stronghold rather than the belfries of a sacred edifice.

The abbé was pleased with his catch. In the eyes of his parishioners, it constituted yet another small triumph on the part of one whose special claim to their respect lay in the fact that he had probably, despite his age, the finest muscular development of any man in that countryside. He could snip a flower-stalk with a pistol bullet; he practised feats of swordsmanship with his neighbour the tobacconist who was an old master-at-arms; and he was the finest swimmer along that coast. These innocent vanities were now his greatest pleasures in life.

There had been a time when he was a well-known figure in the social world. But the Baron de Vilbois, that mirror of elegance, had in his thirty-second year taken Holy orders, in consequence of an unhappy love affair.

The ancient family of Picardy, royalist and Catholic, from which he sprang, had for many centuries sent its scions to the army, the magistrature, or the priesthood. His earliest impulse, at the prompting of his mother, was to take Holy orders, but reconsidering this on his father's advice, he decided instead to go to Paris, study law, and thereafter find some serious employment about the courts. While he was still engaged in his studies, his father succumbed to pneumonia contracted while shooting in the marshes, and his mother, who was overwhelmed by grief at his loss, died shortly afterwards. Having thus suddenly inherited a substantial fortune, he renounced his project of making a career for himself and surrendered to the charms of a life of idle opulence.

He was attractive and intelligent, but his mind was bounded by certain fixed beliefs, traditions, and principles which, like his muscles, he had inherited from ancestral squires of Picardy. He created a good impression, was well received in serious circles, and enjoyed life like a popular young man of sound principles and ample means.

Then came the unexpected. At the house of a friend he met on several occasions a young actress, who, while still in her novitiate at the Conservatoire, had made a startlingly successful first appearance at the Odéon. The Baron de Vilbois fell in love with her with the violence and headlong passion of a man whose natural temperament leaves him at the mercy of his ideals. This sudden passion was conceived when he saw her steeped in the glamour of the romantic role in which she had, on the day of her début, scored so notable a triumph.

She was pretty, but had an ingrained perversity of character. Her face wore an innocent and childlike expression, which he called her angel look. She succeeded in reducing him to abject slavery. She transformed him into one of those ecstatic madmen, whom the glance of a woman's eyes, the flutter of her skirts, can thrust into the fiery furnace of inextinguishable passion. He made her leave the stage. She came to live with him, and for four years he loved her with ever-increasing ardour. In spite of his noble birth and the aristocratic traditions of his race, he would eventually have made her his wife, had he not one day discovered that she had for long been deceiving him with the friend who had first brought them together.

This revelation was the more grievous from the fact that she was expecting to become a mother, and he was only awaiting the birth of the child as a deciding factor in his intention to marry her. He had come upon some letters in a drawer, and confronting her with these proofs, he reproached her for her faithlessness, her treachery, her shamelessness, with all the brutality of his semi-barbaric nature.

She was, however, a true child of the Paris streets, as impudent as she was immodest. Convinced of the sureness of her hold both on the baron and his rival, and endued moreover with the hardihood of these women of the lower class, who in sheer effrontery perch themselves on the top of the barricades, she defied him and flung back his insults. When he lifted his hand to strike her, she paraded her figure before him.

He checked himself. Pale with the thought that the polluted flesh, the vile body, of so foul a creature enshrined his child, he hurled himself at her, intending to destroy the pair of them, to annihilate in a single blow his twofold shame. Overwhelmed with terror she gave herself up for lost. Felled by a blow of his fist, she saw his heel ready to crush her and the budding life within her, and as she stretched out her hands to ward off his fury, she cried out:

'Don't kill me. The child is not yours. It is his.'

He started back, in such a state of stupefaction and consternation that, like that menacing heel, his wrath was stayed.

'You . . . you . . . What's that you say?' he stammered.

She had caught the threat of murder, not only in his eyes, but in his terrifying gestures.   Crazed with fear she repeated:

'It is not yours.   It is his.'

Utterly bewildered, he muttered between clenched teeth:

'The child?'

'Yes.'

'Liar!'

Again he raised his foot to stamp on her.   She had struggled to her knees, and was trying to move back out of his reach, but all the time she kept stammering:

'I tell you it is his.   If it was yours, shouldn't I have had it long ago?'

This argument struck home with all the force of truth.   In one of those lightning flashes of thought, which combine every process of reasoning with illuminating lucidity and are at once precise, irrefutable, conclusive, and irresistible, he was possessed by the conviction that he was not the father of that wretched unborn brat.   In a moment his fury abated.   Tranquil, calm, almost appeased, he renounced his intention of destroying this wanton creature.

In quieter tones he said:

'Get up.   Off with you.   Never let me see you again.'

Utterly defeated, she docilely removed herself, and he never saw her again.   He too departed.   He made his way southwards, to the land of sunshine, and finally came to a halt at a village situated on a knoll in a broad valley, by the shores of the Mediterranean.   He found, facing the sea, an inn which attracted him, and taking a room there, he went no farther.   Here he remained for eighteen months in complete isolation.   Sunk in mortification and despair, he was for ever haunted by devastating memories of the woman who had betrayed him; he recalled her charm, her fascination, her mysterious witchery, and he never ceased yearning for her presence and for her caresses.

As he wandered among the Provençal valleys, where the sun's rays filtered down through the grey-green olive leaves, his tortured brain was racked by these obsessions.   This melancholy solitude had, however, the effect of bringing back to him the pious predilections of his youth.   Very gently, with their ardour a little sobered, they stole back into his heart.   Religion, which had once appealed to him as a shelter against the unknown perils of life, he now viewed as a refuge from its tortures and deceptions.

He had never lost his habit of prayer, and in his desolation he clung to it. He would often go at twilight and kneel in the darkening church where the lamp, the sacred guardian of the sanctuary, the symbol of the Divine Presence, shed its solitary ray from the recesses of the choir. To his God he confided his anguish, to Him he told his troubles, asking of Him pity, succour, protection, consolation. The increasing fervour wherewith he repeated his daily orisons, was evidence of the growing depth of the emotion which prompted them. Bruised and corroded by his passion for a woman, his heart still remained tender, impressionable, eager for love. Constant in prayer, living a hermit's life, and growing ever more assiduous in the practice of piety, he surrendered himself to the secret communion which unites devout souls to the Saviour, who comforts the wretched and draws them to Him. The mystic love of God entered into him, and his baser affections were subdued. His thoughts turned again to the projects of his early youth, when he had dreamed of giving his virgin heart to the Church. He now decided to offer upon the altar his broken life. He accordingly took Holy orders.

Family interest procured for him the appointment of parish priest to the Provençal village in which chance had cast him up. He consecrated the greater part of his wealth to charitable works, only retaining sufficient to enable him to be of practical assistance to the poor of his parish during the remainder of his life. Thus he found a refuge in a tranquil existence of pious observances and of devotion to his fellow-creatures.

His views were narrow, but he was a good priest, although in his manner of guiding his flock there was more of the soldier than the pastor. The forest of life is full of by-ways which lead us astray. Erring humanity wanders blindfold in a labyrinth of instincts, preferences, and desires. He drove, rather than led, his people into the right path. But in his new sphere he still retained many of his former tastes. Violent exercise appealed to him as strongly as ever. He enjoyed the nobler forms of sport and the practice of arms. But he shrank from all women with the instinctive fear of a child when confronted with some danger which it cannot understand.

II

The fisherman who followed the abbé had the true southerner's irresistible desire to talk. But the abbé kept his flock in good order, and the man was afraid to begin. At last, however, he ventured a remark.

'You are quite comfortable in your little shanty, your reverence, I hope?'

This cottage of the abbé's was one of those tiny buildings in which people from Provençal towns and villages take up their quarters in the summer for the sake of the country air. His official residence was built up against the walls of the church, right in the centre of the parish, and was uncomfortably small. He had accordingly rented this cottage in a field at five minutes' distance from the parsonage. Even in summer he did not occupy it regularly, but spent a few days there from time to time, in order to immerse himself in the peace of the country and also to practise pistol-shooting.

'Yes, my friend,' he replied to the fisherman, 'I'm quite comfortable there.'

The little, pink-washed cottage came into view. It stood in an unwalled field, which had been planted with olive trees, and it looked as if it had sprung up like a Provençal mushroom. The branches and leaves of the olive trees cast a dappled pattern of striped and criss-crossed shadows upon the walls of the house. Outside the door his buxom housekeeper was laying a small table with methodical slowness, making a journey into the house for each separate article she placed upon it—the cloth, the plate, the napkin, the tumbler, and the hunk of bread. She wore the little Arlesian bonnet, a cone of black silk or velvet trimmed with a white mushroom-shaped ornament. When the abbé arrived within earshot, he called out to her. She looked round and recognized her master.

'Oh, it's you, your reverence, is it?'

'Yes. I've brought home a fine catch. You must set to work and fry a bass for me. Cook it in butter, just butter, you understand.'

The servant came nearer and with the eye of a connoisseur examined the fish which the boatman was carrying.

'There is a chicken and rice all ready for you,' she said.

'Never mind. Fish don't improve with keeping. I'll in-

dulge in a little orgy for once. I don't often do it. And after
all it isn't a mortal sin.'

The woman picked out the bass from the rest of the fish.
As she turned away with it, she said:

'There has been a man asking for you. He came three
times.'

'A man? What sort of man?' the abbé asked with indifference.

'Well, his looks were no recommendation.'

'A beggar?'

'I dare say. He might be that. To me he had more the
look of a *maoufatan.*'

The Abbé Vilbois laughed when he heard this Provençal
word, signifying malefactor or vagabond. He knew that
Marguerite, who was a timorous soul, could never live in the
cottage without imagining all the time, and especially at night,
that they were going to be murdered.

The abbé dismissed the sailor with a few coppers, and then,
having preserved the dainty habits of his unregenerate days,
he went to wash his face and hands.

Marguerite was in the kitchen scraping the bass from tail to
head with a knife, and the scales, slightly tinged with blood,
came away like tiny, silver sequins.

'There he is again,' she called out.

The abbé turned towards the road, and to be sure there was
the man, slowly approaching the house. Even from a distance
his clothes seemed to be in a dreadful condition.

'Upon my soul,' reflected the abbé, 'Marguerite is right.
He has all the appearance of a *maoufatan.*'

While awaiting the stranger, he continued to smile at the
recollection of his handmaiden's terror.

The unknown man approached with his hands in his pockets.
He strolled leisurely along, and kept his eyes fixed on the
priest. He was young, and had a fair, curling beard, and his
hair waved under the brim of a soft felt hat which was so dirty
and battered that the original colour and shape were undis-
cernible. He wore a long brown overcoat; the bottoms of his
trouser legs were frayed, and he had on his feet a pair of rope-
soled canvas shoes, which gave him the furtive, disquieting
gait of a prowling thief. Arrived within a few paces of the
abbé, he raised his hat with a touch of the theatrical, and

revealed a face which, though branded with the marks of debauchery, was not ill-favoured. The crown of his head was bald, which in a man, whose age certainly did not exceed twenty-five, was a sign either of an enfeebled constitution or of precocious vice.

The priest, too, took off his hat. He was intuitively aware that this person was neither the ordinary vagabond or out-of-work, nor the habitual offender, who drifts from prison to prison, and can lay his tongue to naught save the mysterious jargon of the jail-bird.

'Good evening, monsieur,' said the stranger.

The abbé replied with a simple 'Good evening,' not wishing to use the word *monsieur* to this dubious-looking tatterdemalion. The priest and the young man looked each other up and down, and under the vagabond's scrutiny the Abbé Vilbois experienced a sensation of discomfort. He felt as if he were confronted with some mysterious hostility, and he was seized by one of those curious presentiments which send a thrill of apprehension through the human frame.

At last the vagabond broke the silence.

'Well, do you remember me?'

'Remember you?' replied the abbé in great astonishment. 'Certainly not. I don't know you at all.'

'Ah, you don't know me at all. Just take another look at me.'

'It's no use my looking at you. I've never set eyes on you before.'

'That is true,' the other assented in ironic tones. 'But I am going to show you someone whom you will have no difficulty in recognizing.'

He put on his hat and unbuttoned his overcoat, revealing his bare chest. A red belt was fastened round his lean waist and served to keep his trousers in position. Out of his pocket he took an envelope, mottled with every possible variety of stain, one of those preposterous envelopes, treasured by wandering outcasts in the lining of their clothes, and containing documents, genuine or forged, stolen or honestly come by, which are to their owners precious guarantees of personal liberty against the patrolling gendarme. From it he drew forth a photograph of the old-fashioned cabinet size. It was yellow and faded, having been carried for many a day in contact with the defiling warmth of his body. He raised the photograph to the level of his face and then said:

'What about this one?'

The abbé came two steps nearer. He turned pale with consternation, for the portrait was his own. It had been taken for the woman whom he had loved long ago. He was too bewildered to reply, and the vagabond pressed his question.

'Do you recognize it?'

'I do,' faltered the priest.

'Who is it?'

'It is myself.'

'It is really you?'

'Undoubtedly.'

'Well then, look at me and at your likeness. Look at the two of us side by side.'

The miserable abbé had already realized that these two faces, the one in the photograph and the mocking countenance beside it, were as like as two brothers. Still he did not understand.

'Tell me what you want of me,' he stammered.

In venomous tones, the stranger replied:

'What do I want of you? What I want is that you should first of all acknowledge me.'

'Acknowledge you? But who are you?'

'Who am I? Ask any passer-by, ask your servant, ask the mayor of this place. Show him this photograph, and I tell you he will laugh. Ah! you don't want to admit that I am your son, my reverend papa?'

The elder man raised his arms to heaven with the gesture of a biblical patriarch in despair.

'It is not true,' he groaned.

The young man came up close to him, so that they stood face to face.

'Oh, indeed, not true, isn't it? None of your lies, my friend. Understand that.'

The expression on his face was menacing. His fists were clenched. His voice rang out with such conviction that the abbé, as he yielded ground before him, wondered whether it was himself or the stranger who was mistaken. But again he asserted:

'I never had a child.'

'Or a mistress either, I suppose,' the other retorted.

With courage and dignity the abbé replied in three words:

'A mistress, yes.'

'And when you sent her away was she not about to become a mother?'

At these words the ancient anger, which he had smothered twenty-five years before, blazed up again. It had never been fully extinguished; through the years it had lain in the depths of the lover's heart, where he had walled it up, building over it a crypt of faith, of resignation, of renunciation. But in one moment the flames broke through. Beside himself he cried out:

'I turned her away because she was unfaithful to me. The child was of another man's begetting. Had it not been so I should have killed her, and you along with her.'

The young man was taken aback by the abbé's vehemence. It was his turn to be surprised, and his reply was couched in more subdued tones.

'Who told you that you were not the child's father?'

'She, she herself, as she defied me.'

The vagabond did not dispute this statement. He merely remarked, with the casual air of a ruffian who is giving his verdict on a case:

'Well, it was mamma's mistake. She was bluffing you, that's all.'

His outburst of rage having subsided, the abbé became more master of himself.

'Who told you that you were my son?' he questioned him.

'My mother. On her deathbed. If you want more evidence look at this.'

Again he held out the photograph. The abbé took it and slowly, minutely, compared his old likeness with the face of this unknown tramp. His heart was brimming over with anguish. But he could doubt no longer. The man who stood before him was in very truth his son.

His soul was wrung with agony, with inexpressible emotion that tortured him, like remorse for a sin committed long ago. With the help of his actual knowledge and his own conjectures he recalled the brutal scene of that separation. It was to save her life, which was threatened by the man whose pride she had outraged, that the deceitful and perfidious woman had hurled this lie at him. The lie had done its work. And a child, his child, had been born, and had grown up into this squalid tramp, who stank of vice, as a he-goat stinks of animalism.

'Will you take a turn with me,' said the abbé, 'so as to get the matter a little clearer?'

'Why certainly,' sneered the other. 'That's the very thing I have come for.'

They walked side by side through the olive grove. The sun had set, and the sudden chill that comes with twilight to these Mediterranean shores, descended on the countryside like a cold invisible shroud. The abbé shivered. Raising his eyes suddenly, as he was wont to do while officiating at divine service, he saw all around and above him, quivering between him and the heavens, the grey-green foliage of the sacred tree, whose tenuous shadow had screened the greatest of all agonies, Christ's one and only manifestation of weakness.

A brief, despairing prayer gushed from him, not in spoken words, but framed with that inner voice which does not pass the lips, the voice wherewith the believer implores his Saviour to succour him.

'Then your mother is dead?' he asked, turning to his son.

When he said these words his heart was wrung with yet another pang. He felt that strange, physical agony of a man who cannot forget, a cruel reminder of the torture he had once undergone. Or, now that she was dead, was it not rather a thrill of that brief intoxicating youthful bliss, of which no trace remained in his heart, save the scar of an ancient wound?

'Yes, my mother is dead,' replied the young man.

'Was it long ago?'

'Three years.'

A fresh suspicion flashed across the priest's mind.

'Why didn't you come to see me sooner?' he asked.

The young man hesitated a moment before replying.

'I hadn't a chance. There were . . . h'm . . . obstacles. But will you pardon me if I postpone my confidences for a little. I shall make them as detailed as you please. But in the meantime I must tell you I have had nothing to eat since yesterday morning.'

The abbé was smitten by a sudden shock of compassion. He stretched out his hands and said:

'My poor boy!'

The young man's slender trembling fingers were clasped by the strong hands held out to him. He replied, with the air of cynical mockery which was habitual with him:

'That's all right. I reckon we'll come to an understanding after all.'

The abbé turned towards the house.

'Let us go in to dinner,' he said, and he suddenly thought, with an instinctive thrill of strange, confused pleasure, of the fine fish he had so opportunely caught, and of Marguerite's chicken and rice. The two dishes would make a splendid meal for the wretched youth.

Marguerite had by this time become uneasy and was inclined to be peevish. She was waiting in front of the door.

'Marguerite,' the abbé called out, 'take the table into the dining-room and lay covers for two. As quickly as possible, please.'

Such was Marguerite's consternation at the idea of her master dining in the company of such an unmistakable ruffian that she stood paralysed; so the abbé set to work himself, and began to remove the knives and forks into the room, which occupied the entire ground-floor of the house. Five minutes later he and the vagabond were seated opposite each other, with a tureen of steaming cabbage-soup between them.

III

The broth was ladled out, and the visitor set to without delay. He plied his spoon busily and swallowed down his soup with avidity. But the abbé had no appetite. He slowly sipped the savoury liquid, but left the bread in his plate untouched.

'What name do you go by?' he suddenly asked.

The other laughed. The process of satisfying his hunger had raised his spirits.

'Paternity unknown,' he said. 'So the only family name I have is that of my mother, which doubtless you have not forgotten. I have, however, two Christian names which, I may venture to say, do not suit me at all: Philippe-Auguste.'

The abbé had a feeling of constriction in his throat. Turning pale he asked:

'Why did they give you those names?'

The vagabond shrugged his shoulders.

'You ought to be able to guess. When my mother left you she wanted to make your rival believe that he was my father.

He did believe it, until I was fifteen or thereabouts. At that age I began to have a suspicious likeness to you. So the dirty dog denied paternity. Still, there I was, with his two names. If I had only had the luck not to resemble any one in particular, or if I had merely been the son of some third scallywag, who had kept out of the way, I should now be calling myself the Vicomte Philippe-Auguste de Pravallon, whose relationship had been somewhat tardily recognized by his father, the count of the same name. I have baptized myself since then, however, and call myself "No-luck-at-all."'

'How did you find out all these facts?'

'Because they conducted their controversies in my presence. Plain-speaking it was, I can tell you. Ah! that's the sort of thing that teaches you what life is.'

Much as the abbé had suffered during the preceding half-hour, the feelings that now swept over him had fresh poignancy, an enhanced power to torture him. He felt as if he were choking, with an oppression that would become stronger and stronger until it killed him. It arose not so much from the bare facts to which he was listening, as from the way in which they were recounted; from something in the face of the dissolute wretch who narrated them, which endued them with disgusting significance. Between him and this creature, who was his son, he began to realize that there lay a trench brimming with moral filth, with a foulness that is mortal poison to a healthy mind. And that was his son! As yet he could hardly believe it. He must have all the proofs, every possible proof. He must learn all, he must listen, understand, and endure each pang. Again he thought of the olive-trees that surrounded his little house. And again the prayer came to his lips:

'O God in heaven, succour me.'

Philippe-Auguste had finished his plate of soup.

'Is that all there is to eat?' he asked.

The kitchen was built on to the house, and Marguerite could not hear the abbé when he called. He used to summon her with a few strokes upon a Chinese gong which hung just behind his chair. He took the leather-covered gong-stick and struck the round disk of metal two or three times. The sound, feeble at first, grew louder and harsher till the tones rang out sharp, shrill, ear-piercing, with the plaintive clang of bronze.

Marguerite answered the summons. Her face was rigid with

disapproval. She cast furtive glances at the *maoufatan*, as though, with the instinct of a faithful hound, she had some presentiment of the tragedy that hung over her master. She brought in the dish with the grilled bass, which diffused a fragrant odour of melted butter.

The abbé divided the fish lengthways with a spoon and offered the back fillet to the son of his youth.

'I have just caught this fish myself,' he declared, with a touch of pride, which emerged through his distress.

Marguerite had remained in the room.

'Fetch some wine. The best wine. The white wine of Cap Corse,' the abbé ordered.

She made a gesture which almost threatened disobedience, and he had to repeat his order in a severe tone.

'Come now. Fetch the wine. Two bottles.'

When he had the rare pleasure of offering wine to a guest, he always indulged in a bottle himself. Radiant with expectation, Philippe-Auguste murmured:

'First-rate! It 's a long time since I had a meal like this.'

Marguerite came back in a couple of minutes, but to the abbé, who was now consumed, as by the flames of hell, by a necessity to know the whole truth, the time of her absence seemed as long as two eternities.

After the bottles were uncorked, Marguerite lingered on in the room with her eyes fixed upon the stranger.

'You may go,' said the abbé.

She pretended not to hear him.

'I asked you to leave us,' the abbé said peremptorily, and at that she took herself off.

Philippe-Auguste devoured the fish with voracious rapidity. His father, watching him, observed with increasing amazement and chagrin how deeply the face, which was so like his own, was branded with the marks of degradation. He himself could not eat the morsels of fish which he put into his mouth and continued to masticate. His throat felt constricted; he could not swallow. A thousand questions thronged into his mind, and he kept searching for the one which would elicit the answer he was most eager to provoke. Finally, in a low tone, he asked:

'Of what did she die?'

'Consumption.'

'Was she ill for long?'

'About eighteen months.'

'What brought it on?'

'They couldn't say.'

A silence fell on them and the abbé continued to reflect. His ignorance weighed on his mind. There was so much that he was now eager to hear. He knew nothing of what had happened to her since the day when, after he had been within an ace of killing her, he had sent her away. It was true that for many years he had lost all desire to learn. He had resolutely cast her and his days of happiness into the gulf of oblivion. But, now, at the news of her death, he was seized with a desire to know all, a desire fraught with the jealousy, almost with the ardour, of a lover.

'She was not alone at the time?'

'No. She was still living with him.'

'With him? With Pravallon?' the abbé asked, with a start.

'Why, yes.'

So the same woman, who had betrayed and deceived him, had lived for over thirty years with his rival. The next question came involuntarily to his trembling lips.

'Were they happy together?'

Philippe-Auguste replied, with a sneering laugh:

'Well, yes. They had their ups and downs. They would have got on all right if I hadn't been there. I was always the fly in the ointment.'

'Why so?'

'I've told you that already. Till I was about fifteen he thought I was his son. But the old boy was no fool. He noticed the resemblance of his own accord, without help from anybody, and then there was a to-do. I used to listen at the keyhole. He accused my mother of having let him down, and she said: "Well, was it my fault? You knew very well that I was the other man's mistress at the time you took me on." The other man was you.'

'Ah! then they used to speak of me sometimes?'

'Yes, but they never mentioned your name in my presence except at the end, right at the end, during the last few days, when my mother felt she was going. And even then they didn't trust each other.'

'And you . . . you learned pretty early that your mother's position was irregular?'

'What do you think? I'm no greenhorn. For that matter, I never was one. As soon as a man begins to know a bit of the world, he gets the hang of a situation like that.'

Philippe-Auguste was helping himself freely to the wine. His eyes were lit up and he was yielding to the rapid intoxication that overtakes a half-starving man. The abbé noticed this, but did nothing to check him. He reflected that drunkenness sapped a man's self-control and induced him to talk more freely. He accordingly refilled the young man's glass.

Marguerite brought in the chicken and rice, and placed it on the table. Then she fixed her gaze anew upon her master's disreputable guest.

'He's drunk, your reverence. Only look at him,' she said indignantly.

'Kindly leave us alone,' replied the abbé. 'And go away.'

She slammed the door as she went out.

The abbé turned to his guest.

'Tell me what your mother used to say about me.'

'Oh, just the sort of thing they always say when they leave a man in the lurch. She said you weren't easy to get on with, and you got on her nerves, and you would have made her life very difficult with your queer notions.'

'Did she often say that?'

'Yes. Sometimes she wrapped it up so that I shouldn't understand it, but I could always guess.'

'How did the two of them treat you?'

'Very well, at first. Very badly, afterwards. As soon as my mother saw that I was queering her pitch she bundled me out.'

'How did she manage that?'

'How? Oh, quite easily. I went a bit on the loose when I was sixteen or so, and the dirty sweeps stuck me into a reformatory, to get rid of me.'

He put his elbows on the table, rested his cheeks on his hands, and, his brain being turned with the wine, he suddenly yielded to that irresistible impulse which drives a drunken man to indulge in fantastic boasts. He smiled. And in his smile there was an attractiveness, a feminine grace, and at the same time, an element of perversity, which the abbé recognized. Not only did he recognize it, but he again felt the charm of it, hateful yet insidious, which had formerly conquered and destroyed him.

At that moment it was the likeness to his mother that was noticeable. The resemblance did not lie in the actual features, but in that expression, so captivating, so insincere, in the seductiveness of that treacherous smile, which parted his lips, merely that they might give vent to all the vileness that lay behind them. Philippe-Auguste pursued his narrative.

'Ah! It was a queer life I led after I left the reformatory! Any great novelist would pay me well to tell him all about it. I assure you, the elder Dumas with his *Monte Cristo* never imagined anything weirder than the things that happened to me.'

He fell into a silence. His face wore the portentous gravity of the meditative drunkard. Then he began to speak again, with deliberation.

'If you want a boy to turn out well, you should never send him to a reformatory, whatever he has done. He learns things there. I picked up a notion or two myself, but they didn't work. I was racketing about one evening with three pals. We were all a bit sprung. It was about nine o'clock on the main road, near the Folac ferry. I came across a carriage with all the occupants sound asleep. They consisted of the driver and his family, people from Martinon who had been dining in town. I took the horse by the reins, led him up on to the ferryman's barge, and then I pushed the barge off into deep water. The driver of the carriage, disturbed by the noise I made, woke up, and suspecting nothing, whipped up his horse. Off goes the horse, and down goes the carriage into the river. Every soul was drowned. My pals gave me away. They were willing enough to laugh while they saw me performing my little joke. Of course, it never occurred to any of us that the thing would turn out so badly. Just for the fun of it, we thought we would give those people a ducking. On my honour I didn't deserve to be punished for it. However, I did worse things later on, and took my revenge that way. But they are hardly worth the trouble of telling you. I'll just tell you one of my exploits, the latest, because I'm sure you'll be delighted with it. I avenged you, my dear papa!'

The abbé could not eat another morsel. He merely gazed at his son with horrified eyes.

Philippe-Auguste was about to resume his narrative, when his father interrupted him, and asked him to wait one moment. He turned and struck the strident Chinese gong, and Marguerite entered immediately. He issued his orders to her in so harsh a tone that she cowered before him in terrified obedience.

'Bring in the lamp and the rest of the food. After that, don't come in again, unless I strike the gong.'

She went out, and presently returned carrying a white porcelain lamp with a green shade. Then she brought in a large piece of cheese and some fruit, set them on the table, and retired.

'Now,' said the abbé in resolute tones, 'I am ready. Go on.'

Philippe-Auguste calmly helped himself to the dessert and to another glass of wine. The second bottle was nearly finished, although the abbé had hardly touched it. The young man's speech was thick and heavy with the food and wine he had consumed. He stammered as he told his story.

'Well, this was my latest . . . pretty hot stuff . . . I had come back home, and I stayed on in the house because those two were afraid of me . . . yes . . . afraid . . . Ah, people had better not play the fool with me . . . I don't care what I do when I get my back up . . . You know . . . they were living together and yet not together. He had two houses, a senator's house and another for his mistress. But he spent most of his time with my mother because he was no longer able to do without her. Oh, my mother was a cunning one, and clever. She was the one to keep a hold on a man. She had that fellow in her power, body and soul, and she held on to him to the last day of her life. What fools men are! Well, I was at home and I got the whip-hand over them by making them afraid of me. I tell you, I 'm a nailer at wriggling out of trouble when it has got to be done, and if it comes to dodges and tricks, or force either, I 'm afraid of nobody. My mother fell ill and he put her into a fine house near Meulan. It stood in the middle of a park as big as a forest. That lasted about eighteen months, as I told you. Then we saw that the end was near. Pravallon used to come from Paris every day to see her, and his grief was genuine. It really was. One morning they had been talking for about an hour and I was wondering what they could be jabbering about for such a long time, when they called me in, and my mother said to me:

'"I am going to die very soon and there is a secret I wish to tell you, although the count thinks I oughtn't to." She always called him "the count" when she referred to him. "Your father is still alive, and I am going to tell you his name."'

'I had asked her times out of number to tell me this . . . times out of number . . . the name of my father . . . times out of number . . . and she had always refused. I believe one day I boxed her ears to make her speak, but even that was no good. In order to get rid of me, she declared that you had died a pauper, that you were a nobody, a casual error of her young days, a girlish blunder. She reeled it all off so plausibly that I believed every word about your death.

'"Your father's name," she said.

'Pravallon was sitting there in an arm-chair and he called out just like this, three times:

'"You are wrong, you are wrong, you are wrong, Rosette."

'My mother sat up in bed. I can see her still, with her flushed cheeks and bright eyes. In spite of everything she was very fond of me, and she said:

'"Then you must do something for him, Philippe."

'She used to call him Philippe and me Auguste.

'He began to shout like a madman.

'"For that blackguard? For that worthless wretch, for that jail-bird, for that . . ."

'He found as many names for me as if he had spent all his life thinking them out.

'I was getting a bit annoyed, but my mother made me keep quiet. She said to him:

'"You want him to die of hunger. You know that I have nothing to give him."

'Not in the least perturbed, he replied:

'"Rosette, for thirty years I have given you thirty-five thousand francs a year. That makes more than a million francs. Thanks to me you have lived the life of a woman of wealth, you have been cherished, and I venture to maintain, happy. I owe nothing to this wretch who has spoiled our last years together, and from me he shall have not a farthing. It is useless your insisting. Tell him his father's name if you wish. I disapprove, but I wash my hands of him."

'Then my mother turned to me. I was just thinking to myself: "That's all right. Now I shall discover my real father. If he has money, I'm saved."

'My mother continued:

'"Your father, the Baron de Vilbois, passes now under the name and title of the Abbé Vilbois, parish priest of Garandou, near Toulon. He was my lover and I left him and came to the count."

'Then she told me the whole story. She omitted, however, to let me know that she had fooled you over her child's paternity. Women are women, you know. They can't ever tell the whole truth.'

He sniggered cynically, hardly aware of the vileness of his own utterances. He drank some more wine, and then, with the same expression of amusement on his face, went on with his story.

'My mother died two days . . . two days later. He and I both followed her coffin to the cemetery. Funny, wasn't it? He and I. And the three servants. That was all. He wept like a cow. We were standing side by side. Any one would have taken us for father and son. Then we went back to the house. We two, alone. I was thinking to myself that I would have to clear out. I had just fifty francs. Not another farthing. What possible way was there for me to be revenged on him? He touched me on the arm and said:

'"I want to speak to you."

'I followed him into his office-room. He seated himself at his table and then, spluttering through his tears he told me that he didn't mean to be as hard on me as he had said to my mother. He begged me not to make myself a nuisance to you. But that —that lies between you and me. He offered me a banknote of a thousand . . . a thousand francs. What use was a thousand-franc note to a man like me? I noticed that he had a whole heap of them in his drawer. When I caught sight of those banknotes I felt like sticking a knife into him. I stretched out my hand to take the note he was offering me, but instead of accepting his alms I jumped on the top of him, I threw him down on the floor, and squeezed his throat till his eyes nearly popped out of his head. I didn't loosen my grip until he was nearly done. Then I gagged him, tied him up firmly, stripped his clothes off him, and then turned him over on his face. Ha ha ha! I avenged you properly.'

Philippe-Auguste choked with mirth till he coughed. His upper lip was curled with cruel gaiety, and again the Abbé Vilbois recognized the smile he had known so well in bygone years, the smile of the woman who had lured him to destruction.

'And after that?'

'After that—ha ha ha!—there was a great fire in the chimney-place. It was December, very cold; that's what killed my mother. It was a big coal fire. I took the poker and made it red-hot, and then I branded him all over the back with crosses, eight or ten of them, I don't remember how many, and then I turned him over again and branded his belly. Wasn't that a good joke, papa? That's how they used to brand the convicts in old times. He squirmed like an eel, but he couldn't say a word. I had him well gagged. Then I took the banknotes, twelve of them; and that made thirteen, counting my own; an unlucky number for me. Then I cleared out, after telling the servants they were not to disturb their master until dinner-time because he was asleep. Considering that he was a senator I was convinced that he would keep his mouth shut for fear of the scandal. But I made a mistake there. I was arrested four days later in a Paris restaurant, and I got three years' imprisonment. That is the reason why I couldn't come sooner to look you up.'

He took another drink. Stuttering so badly that he could hardly bring out his words, he said:

'Now then . . . papa . . . my reverend papa . . . what a joke to have a parish priest for a papa! Ha ha! You'll have to be nice to me, very nice to little me, because I'm rather unusual . . . and I served him out . . . I did . . . quite handsomely . . . that old boy . . .'

The Abbé Vilbois now felt himself roused by this loathsome creature to the same fury that had maddened him when confronted by the woman who had betrayed him. In the name of God, he had given absolution for many sins, for shocking secrets, which had been whispered to him in the mystery of the confessional. But now in his own person, he had neither pity nor pardon. He no longer invoked that God of mercy, helpfulness, and compassion, for he realized that the protection of neither God nor man will avail to save, on this earth below, those who are the victims of such dread mischances. All the ardour of his passionate heart, all the rage of his fiery temper, which he had restrained in virtue of his holy office, burst forth into irresistible revolt against this wretch who was his son; against the resemblance he bore not only to his father, but to his mother, to that unworthy mother who had conceived him after her own nature; against the fatality which riveted his scoundrel to his parent, as the cannon-ball is riveted to the ankle of the galley-slave. Roused by this shock from the dreamy piety and tranquillity of five-and-twenty years, he faced the situation and foresaw the future with sudden lucidity. He realized that he must use the strong hand with this ruffian, and terrify him at the first onset. His jaws were clenched in fury. Forgetting that the man was drunk, he said:

'Now that you have told me all, you can listen to me. You will leave this village to-morrow morning. You will go to a place which I shall indicate to you, and you will not leave that place without my orders. I shall make you an allowance which will be enough for you to live on. It will be small. I am a poor man myself now. If you disobey my orders on any single occasion, I shall stop my remittances, and you will have to deal with me personally.'

Stupefied with drink as he was, Philippe-Auguste understood the threat. The criminal in him suddenly rose to the surface. Venomously, between hiccups, he spat out these words:

'Ah, papa . . . mustn't do that . . . papa is a parish priest . . . I've got you . . . under my thumb . . . you'll sing small, like the rest of them.'

The abbé started. He felt in his old, but still herculean muscles, an invincible impulse to seize this monster, to bend him like a twig, and show him that he must give way. He seized the table, and shook it, and hurled his words right into the vagabond's face:

'Have a care. I warn you. Have a care. I'm afraid of no man . . .'

The drunken man lost his balance and rocked from side to side in his chair. Realizing that he was on the point of falling, and that he was in the abbé's power, he stretched forth his hand towards a knife which lay on the table-cloth. The gleam of murder in his eyes was unmistakable. The Abbé Vilbois saw the movement and pushed the table with such force that his son fell over backwards and lay at full length on the floor. The lamp upset, and the room was in darkness. There was a jingling of wine-glasses, and for a few seconds the clear bell-like notes vibrated through the room. Then came a rustling sound as of some soft body crawling along the paved floor. And after that, silence.

With the breaking of the lamp darkness had descended upon

them, so sudden and unexpected and profound, that both men
were aghast as at some terrifying accident. The drunkard,
cowering against the wall, never stirred. The abbé remained
seated in his chair. The deep night in which he was plunged
had the effect of subduing his anger. The veil of blackness that
had fallen upon him immobilized his raging impulses. And
gradually other thoughts took possession of him, thoughts as
dark and gloomy as the enveloping obscurity.

Silence. Silence as impenetrable as the silence of a walled-in
tomb. A silence of death. No sound came from without; not
so much as the rolling of a distant carriage-wheel, or the barking
of a dog; not even the whispering passage of the wind through
the olive branches or along the walls.

This silence lasted for a long, long time, perhaps an hour.
Then suddenly the gong rang out. Once only it sounded,
smitten by a hard, sharp, vigorous stroke. On the top of that
came the crash of a fall, and of the upsetting of a chair.

Marguerite, who had been all the time on the alert, came
running in from the kitchen, but when she opened the dining-
room door she started back in terror from the impenetrable
darkness. A trembling seized her, her heart beat fast, and in
fear-stricken tones she gasped:

'Master, where are you? Speak.'

There was no reply. Nothing stirred in the room.

'Good Heavens,' she thought. 'What have they been doing?
What has happened?'

She had not the courage either to advance into the room or to
go back to the kitchen for a light. Her limbs shook under her;
she would have given the world to be able to escape, to run
away, to scream. But all she could do was to keep on saying:

'Master, where are you? Speak. It is Marguerite.'

Then, despite her fears, a sudden and instinctive desire to
come to the help of her master surged up within her. She was
inspired with that panic-stricken courage which sometimes comes
to women in such moments, and renders them capable of
heroic actions. Running to her kitchen, she came back with a
lamp. She stopped on the threshold of the dining-room and
looked in. The first thing she saw was the stranger lying at
full length on the floor, close to the wall He was sleeping, or
feigning sleep. Next she noticed the overturned lamp. And
last of all, under the table, she saw the feet and legs of the abbé,

in their black shoes and stockings. He had seemingly struck the gong with his head and had then collapsed on to his back on the floor.

She was trembling in every limb.

'Good God!' she said again and again. 'Good God! What has happened?'

Timidly and slowly she went forward into the room. Her feet slipped on something slimy and she nearly came down. She stooped and examined the red flagstones. All about her feet she saw a crimson fluid, which trickled in the direction of the door. It was blood.

She hurled away the lamp so that she might see no more. Beside herself with horror, she fled from the house, out into the open country, and made for the village. In her blind flight she kept running into the trunks of the olive-trees. She screamed as she ran, and her eyes were fixed on the distant lights of the village. Her shrieks pierced the darkness like the sinister cry of the screech-owl, and she went on shouting:

'Le maoufatan, le maoufatan, le maoufatan!'

When she reached the outlying houses of the hamlet the frightened villagers ran out and gathered round her, but she had completely lost her head and could not answer their questions. She was still struggling with overwhelming terror. But they gathered that some disaster had occurred in the abbé's house among the olives, and the men snatched up weapons and ran to the help of their priest.

The abbé's pink-washed cottage in the olive orchard was invisible in the dark and silent night. When the solitary lamp which lighted its one window had been extinguished, like the closing of an eye, the house was plunged in shadow, lost in the darkness, undiscoverable by any one save a native of the country. Presently the lanterns, which were carried close to the ground, could be seen approaching the house, across the plantation of olives. The long yellow streaks of light shot over the parched grass. Under the distortion of these rays the gnarled trunks of the olives took on the semblance of monsters, of a hell-brood of serpents, interlaced and writhing. In the farthest flashes of light there suddenly rose out of the darkness a phantom shape, which presently revealed itself as the low right-angled wall of the pink-washed house, its colour showing up in the glow of the lanterns. These were carried by peasants, who formed an escort to the two gendarmes, armed with revolvers, to the rural policeman and the mayor. Marguerite was with them, but had to be supported on either side, being on the verge of collapse. There was a momentary recoil before the dark and terrifying cavern beyond the doorway. But the sergeant seized a lantern and entered the house, while the others followed him.

Marguerite's story was true. The blood, now coagulated, spread like a carpet on the floor. It had reached as far as Philippe-Auguste; his legs and one of his hands were crimson with it.

Father and son slept.

The abbé's throat was cut. Philippe-Auguste was plunged in drunken sleep, but his father's sleep was the slumber of eternity. The two gendarmes threw themselves upon the son and clasped the handcuffs round his wrists before he had time to wake up. When he came to himself he rubbed his eyes. He was still in the stupor of intoxication. At the sight of the abbé's corpse he seemed frightened and bewildered.

'Why did he not make his escape?' the mayor asked.

'He was too drunk,' the sergeant replied.

Every one present agreed with him. It would never have occurred to any of them that the Abbé Vilbois might perhaps have died by his own hand.

LOST AT SEA

(*Le Noyé*)

EVERY one at Fécamp knew the history of Mother Patin. One thing was certain: she had not been happy with her husband, who in his lifetime had thrashed her as wheat is thrashed in a barn.

Many years before, though she was a penniless lass, he had taken her to wife, because she was pretty and attractive. Patin, who at that time was master of a fishing boat, was a good sailor, but a brute. He used to go to old Auban's liquor shop, where his usual allowance was four or five small glasses of spirits. However, when he had had a good catch he would take eight or ten, or even more, if, as he put it, he was feeling cheerful. The customers were served by Auban's daughter, a pleasant-looking dark-eyed girl, who attracted custom to the house by her appearance only, for there had never been any gossip at her expense.

When Patin came to the liquor shop he at first contented himself with looking at the girl. He might make a few quiet and respectful remarks to her, but he never went beyond the limits of propriety. His first glass of brandy, however, added to her attractiveness; with the second glass he was winking at her; with the third he was saying: 'If you only would, Mademoiselle Désirée . . .,' without finishing the phrase. With the fourth glass he was snatching at her skirt and trying to kiss her; and when he got as far as his tenth old Auban sent his daughter away and served the remaining drinks himself.

Auban was an old hand at the game of keeping licensed premises, and was up to all the tricks of the trade. He would keep his daughter moving about among the tables, to provoke the consumption of liquor, and Désirée, who had learnt a thing or two from the old man, had a merry smile and a roguish eye, and as she exchanged pleasantries with the topers, did not forget to exercise the attraction of her sex.

Patin was so constant a frequenter of Auban's shop that Désirée's face became very familiar to him. Even when he was in his boat, casting his nets in the open sea, whether the weather was windy or calm, the night dark or moonlit, his mind would dwell on her. He thought of her, when he was seated in the stern of his boat with his hand on the tiller, while his four shipmates were dozing with their faces on their arms. And when he saw her in those reveries she was always smiling at him, raising her shoulder to pour out for him a glass of the amber-coloured brandy, and then, as she left him, saying:

'There! Is that what you want?'

So constantly did he have her in his mind and eye, so fiercely did he desire to make her his wife, that at last he could bear it no longer, and demanded her hand in marriage.

He was well off, owning his boat and nets, as well as a house at the foot of the slope on the Retenue, whereas old Auban had nothing. His offer was therefore accepted with alacrity, and the wedding took place with the least possible delay, both parties being anxious for the affair to be consummated, though for different reasons.

However, hardly three days had elapsed since the marriage ceremony, when Patin began to wonder how on earth he had come to believe that Désirée was different from any other woman. To be sure, he reflected, he must have been crazy to get himself tied up with a penniless wench who had lured him on with her brandy. Brandy indeed! He would wager that she had doctored the stuff with some drug or other for his benefit. For whole tides, he never ceased swearing. He bit through the stem of his pipe; he bullied his crew; he vented every curse he knew against things in general, and spat out the remains of his rage upon the fish and lobsters, as he drew them one by one out of the net. He could not throw them into the hampers without obscene oaths.

When he reached home, his wife, Auban's daughter, was always there within reach of word or blow, and he quickly learnt to treat her as the most contemptible of created things. Désirée was accustomed to her father's barbarity, and accepted her husband's insults with a resignation which exasperated him to fury. At last came a night when he gave her a beating, and after that her existence with him was terrible indeed.

For the next ten years, a favourite theme of conversation on the Retenue was the thrashings Patin gave his wife, and the foul language he hurled at her head on every possible occasion.

He really had a special gift of profanity; he was never at a loss for oaths and he roared them with a resounding zest, which no other man in Fécamp could rival. The moment his boat came into view at the entrance of the port, people were on the alert for the first broadside, which he would launch from the deck to the jetty, as soon as he caught sight of his wife's white bonnet. He would be standing in the stern of his boat, with his hand on the tiller, and his eyes watching the bow and the sail. It might be a day when the sea was running high, and all his attention taken up by the difficulty of piloting his boat through the narrow passage; a ground swell might be sending its mountainous rollers through the neck of the harbour; it was all one to him. He scanned the group of women who were awaiting their husbands on the spray-lashed jetty, and tried to pick out his wife, old Auban's daughter, the beggarly trash. The moment he saw her, he would, in spite of the uproar of wind and waves, launch at her a torrent of abuse, in such a terrifying bellow, that the bystanders could not help laughing, much as they pitied the victim. When the boat came alongside the quay he had a way of discharging his ballast of good manners, to use an expression of his own, while he was unloading the catch of fish, which brought all the scamps and unemployed of the port hanging about his mooring-ropes. Sometimes the insults were brief and terrible, like cannon-fire; sometimes they were like a rolling peal of thunder, which lasted for five minutes. It was such a hurricane of bad language that he seemed to have all the storms of God stored in his lungs. When he stepped ashore and came face to face with his spouse in the midst of a throng of fish-wives and inquisitive bystanders, he raked out from the bottom of the hold a whole new cargo of insults and wounding speeches, which he inflicted on her while they were going homewards, she leading, he following, he cursing, she weeping. As soon as he was alone with her, he cuffed her on the slightest pretext. Any excuse was good enough to justify a blow, and once he had started, he could not stop. And all the time he spat into her face the reason of his hatred. At every box on the ear, at every thump with his fist, he shouted:

'Ah, you beggar, you pauper, you empty-belly, I made a

proper fool of myself when I rinsed my teeth with your swindling father's rot-gut liquor.'

The poor woman lived in an atmosphere of never-ceasing terror, continually panic-stricken, soul and body, in bewildered expectation of new outrages and thrashings.

This state of affairs endured for ten years. She became so cowed that she could not talk to any one without turning pale. Her thoughts were occupied exclusively with the blows that menaced her. She became as thin and yellow and dry as a smoked fish.

II

One night when her husband was at sea, she was suddenly awakened by the fierce growling of the wind at its first onset, like a dog slipped from the leash. She sat up in bed, in terror; then the sound died away and she lay down again. Almost immediately there came from the fire-place a roar, which shook the whole house. Presently the whole sky seemed to be filled with it, as if a herd of wild beasts were careering across the void, panting and bellowing. She sprang out of bed and ran down to the harbour. Other women were hurrying thither from all sides, bringing lanterns, and men came running up. All of them looked at the sea and saw the foam on the summits of the waves, flashing white through the darkness.

The storm lasted for fifteen hours. Eleven fishermen never came home. Patin was one of them. Fragments of Patin's boat, the *Jeune-Amélie*, were washed up near Dieppe and the bodies of his crew somewhere near Saint-Valéry. But Patin's body was never found. The hulk of the *Jeune-Amélie* seemed to have been cut in two. Possibly there had been a collision. In that case the other boat might have picked him up, alone of all the crew, and sailed away with him.

Gradually she accustomed herself to the idea that she was a widow. But for all that she was still startled whenever a neighbour, or a beggar, or a travelling pedlar suddenly entered her house.

One afternoon about four years after the disappearance of her husband, she was walking along the Rue aux Juifs, and she stopped before the house of an old sea-captain, recently deceased, whose effects were being auctioned. Just as she was passing, a green parrot with a blue head was put up for sale. The bird regarded the bystanders with an air of mingled apprehension and disgust.

'Three francs!' cried the auctioneer. 'A bird that talks like a lawyer. Three francs.'

A friend of Désirée's jogged her elbow.

'You ought to buy that,' she said. 'You can afford it. It would be company for you. It's worth more than thirty francs, that bird is. You could always sell it again for twenty or twenty-five.'

'Four francs, ladies, four francs,' continued the auctioneer. 'He sings vespers and preaches like a parish priest. He is a phenomenon, a miracle.'

Désirée raised the bidding to four francs fifty centimes, and at that price the bird, along with a small cage, was knocked down to her. When she opened the wire door of the cage to give the bird a drink, it jabbed her finger with its hooked beak, which cut through the skin and drew blood.

'Ah, he's a bad one,' she said.

However, she gave him some hemp-seed and maize, and then left him alone to preen his feathers, which he did, while slyly taking stock of his new house and mistress.

Daylight was just breaking on the following morning when Madame Patin heard, as clearly as possible, a human voice, a strong, sonorous, rolling voice. It was the voice of Patin.

'Will you get up, you slut?'

Now, her late husband had been in the habit, the moment he opened his eyes in the morning, of shouting these very words in her ear, and well she knew them. On hearing them again her terror was such that she hid her head under the blankets. Huddled up, trembling all over, her back braced to receive the blows which she was momentarily expecting, she hid her face in the pillow.

'God in heaven,' she murmured, 'he has come back! God in heaven, here he is! Oh, my God!'

Several moments elapsed, but no further sound broke the silence of the room. Shuddering, she put her head out of the bed. She was convinced that he was there, watching her and really to strike. But she saw nothing; nothing but a ray of sunshine coming through the window pane.

'He must be hiding,' she thought.

She waited for a long time and gaining a little confidence, she reflected:

'He hasn't shown himself, so I must have been dreaming.'

She was just closing her eyes again, when suddenly the furious voice of Patin broke out anew quite close to her, like a clap of thunder.

'Are you going to get up, you b——?'

She bounded out of bed, prompted by the passive obedience of a woman who has been beaten unmercifully; who still, after four years, remembers, and for the rest of her life will always remember, and who will never fail to do the bidding of that terrible voice.

'Here I am, Patin,' she replied. 'What do you want?'

There was no reply.

Distraught, she gazed around. Then she searched everywhere; in the wardrobes, up the chimney, under the bed. But she found nobody.

In anguish and bewilderment, convinced that Patin's disembodied soul was there by her side, and had come back in order to torment her, she sank into a chair. Then suddenly she remembered the hayloft, which could be reached by means of an outside ladder. To be sure, Patin must have hidden himself in the loft, so as to come upon her by surprise. No doubt he had been kept prisoner by savages on some distant shore and had not been able to escape sooner. But now he had come back, wickeder than ever, as she could tell from the tone of his voice.

She looked up at the ceiling and asked:

'Are you up there, Patin?'

But there was no reply.

Then she went outside. Her heart was palpitating in an agony of dread. But she climbed the ladder, opened the granary window, looked in, and saw nothing. She entered the loft, searched it, and found no sign of him. She sat down on a truss of straw and began to weep. But in the midst of her sobs she was pierced through and through by poignant and supernatural terror. From the room below she heard Patin making remarks.

He seemed in less of a temper, and less excited.

'Dirty weather,' he observed. 'High wind. Dirty weather. I haven't had my breakfast yet. Curse it.'

She called aloud through the ceiling:

'I am here, Patin. I 'm coming to make your soup. Don't get angry. I 'm coming.'

She ran down the ladder and into the house. There was nobody there. She felt the weakness of death come over her. She was on the point of rushing out of doors to ask help of the neighbours when the voice cried out quite close to her ear:

'I haven't had my breakfast yet. Curse it.'

The parrot, in its cage, had its round, sly, wicked eye fixed on her.

Bewildered, she gazed on the bird.

'Ah, it was you!' she murmured.

The parrot spoke again. He moved his head up and down and said:

'Wait, wait, wait. I 'll teach you to be lazy.'

What were the emotions that now seized upon her? She felt, she believed, that it was really the dead man who had come back. He had concealed himself in the plumage of this bird. Soon he would begin again to torture her as of old; he would swear at her the whole day long, he would bite her, and shout insults at her, so that all the neighbours would gather round and laugh at her.

She rushed to the cage, opened it, and grasped the bird. In self-defence the parrot tore her skin with beak and claws. But Madame Patin held on to it with all the strength of both hands. She threw herself down and rolled on the floor with the bird underneath. With the frenzy of one possessed, she mangled it, until it was mere pulp, a small feathery green mass, which moved no more, spoke no more, but hung limply from her hands. Then she wrapped the dead bird in a duster as in a shroud, and, still in her chemise and with bare feet, crossed the quay on which the waves were beating. Shaking out the duster, she dropped into the sea this small, dead thing, which looked like a handful of grass. Then she returned to her house and fell on her knees before the empty cage, and, beside herself with agitation over what she had done, sobbing as though she had committed some horrible crime, she implored God to pardon her.

THE HOSTELRY

(*L'Auberge*)

AT the foot of the glaciers, in those naked and rock-bound *couloirs* which indent the snow-clad ranges of the High Alps, you will find every here and there a guest-house. These little hostelries are constructed of timber and are all built very much to the same pattern. The Schwarenbach Inn was one of them.

The Schwarenbach served as a refuge to travellers attempting the passage of the Gemmi. For the six summer months it remained open, with Jean Hauser's family in residence; but as soon as the early snows began to accumulate, filling the valley and rendering the descent to Leuk impracticable, Jean Hauser with his three sons and his wife and daughter quitted the house, leaving it in charge of the old guide Gaspard Hari and his companion, together with Sam, the big mountain-bred dog. The two men, with the dog, lived in their prison of snow until the spring arrived. They had nothing to look at, except the vast white slopes of the Balmhorn. Pale glistening mountain peaks rose all round them. They were shut in, blockaded, by the snow; it lay on them like a shroud, growing ever deeper and deeper until the little house was enveloped, closed in, obliterated. The snow piled itself upon the roof, blinded the windows and walled up the door.

On the day on which the Hauser family took their departure for Leuk, the winter was close at hand, and the descent was becoming dangerous. The three sons set off on foot leading three mules laden with household belongings. Behind them followed the mother, Jeanne Hauser, and her daughter Louise, both riding the same mule. Last came the father and the two caretakers. The latter were to accompany the family as far as the beginning of the track that leads down the mountain-side to Leuk.

The party first skirted the edge of the little lake, already frozen, in its rocky hollow in front of the inn; then they proceeded along the valley, which lay before them, a white sheet of

snow, with icy peaks dominating it on every side. A flood of
sunshine fell across the whiteness of this frozen wilderness,
lighting it up with a cold, blinding brilliance. There was no
sign of life in this sea of mountains; not a movement could be
seen in the limitless solitude; not a sound disturbed the profound
silence.

Gradually the younger of the guides, Ulrich Kunsi, a tall long-
limbed Swiss, forged ahead of the two older men and overtook
the mule on which the two women were riding. The daughter
saw him as he approached, and there was sadness in the glance
with which she summoned him to her side.

She was a little peasant girl, with a complexion like milk.
Her flaxen hair was so pale that one might fancy it had been
bleached by prolonged residence amongst the snows and glaciers.

On overtaking the mule on which Louise and her mother were
riding, Ulrich Kunsi placed his hand on its crupper and slackened
his pace. The mother began talking; she expounded in infinite
detail her instructions for wintering. It was the first time that
Ulrich had stayed behind. Old Hari, on the other hand, had
already accomplished his fourteenth hibernation under the snow
that covered the Schwarenbach Inn.

Ulrich listened, but without any appearance of grasping what
was said. He never took his eyes off the daughter. Every now
and then he would reply: 'Yes, Madame Hauser.' But his
thoughts seemed far away, and his face remained calm and
impassive.

They reached the Daubensee, which lies at the foot of the
valley. Its surface was now a vast level sheet of ice. On the
right, the rocks of the Daubenhorn, dark and precipitous, rose
above the vast moraines of the Lemmern Glacier, and the
Wildstrubel towered over all.

As they approached the Gemmi saddle, from which begins the
descent to Leuk, they suddenly beheld, across the deep wide
valley of the Rhône, the prodigious sky-line of the Valais
Alps, a distant multitude of white peaks of unequal size,
some pointed, some flattened, but all glistening in the rays
of the sun.

There was the two-horned Mischabel, the majestic mass of
the Weisshorn, the lumbering Brunnegghorn, the lofty and fear-
inspiring Cervin, which has killed so many men, and the Dent-
Blanche, monstrous yet alluring. Below them, in an enormous

hollow at the foot of terrifying precipices, they caught sight of Leuk, so far away from them that the houses seemed like a handful of sand, thrown down into the vast crevasse, which has at one end the barrier of the Gemmi, and at the other, a wide exit to the Rhône valley.

They had reached the head of a path, which winds downwards, in serpentine coils, fantastic and extraordinary, along the mountain-side, until it reaches the almost invisible village at the foot. The mule stopped and the two women jumped down into the snow. By this time the two older men had overtaken the rest of the party.

'Now, friends,' said old Hauser, 'we must say good-bye till next year. And keep your hearts up.'

'Till next year,' replied Hari.

The men embraced. Madame Hauser gave her cheek to be kissed and her daughter followed her example. When it was Ulrich Kunsi's turn to kiss Louise, he whispered in her ear:

'Don't forget us up on our heights.'

'No,' she replied in tones so low that he guessed, rather than heard, the word.

'Well, well, good-bye,' said old Hauser again. 'Take care of yourselves.'

He strode on past the women and led the way downwards. All three were lost to view at the first bend in the track. Gaspard and Ulrich turned back towards the Schwarenbach Inn. They walked slowly and in silence, side by side. They had seen the last of their friends. They were to be alone, with no other companionship, for four or five months.

Gaspard Hari began to tell Ulrich about the previous winter. His companion then had been Michael Carol; but accidents were likely to happen during the long solitude, and Michael had grown too old for the job. Still, they had had a pretty good time together. The secret of the whole thing was to make up your mind to it from the beginning. Sooner or later one invented distractions and games and things to while away the time.

With downcast eyes Ulrich Kunsi listened to his companion, but his thoughts were following the women, who were making their way to the village, down the zigzag path on the Gemmi mountain-side.

They soon caught sight of the distant inn. It looked very tiny, like a black dot at the base of the stupendous mountain of snow. When they opened the door of the house, Sam, the great curly-haired dog, gambolled round them joyfully.

'Well, Ulrich, my boy,' said old Gaspard, 'we have no women here now. We must get dinner ready ourselves. You can set to and peel the potatoes.'

They sat down on wooden stools and began to prepare the soup. The forenoon of the following day seemed long to Ulrich Kunsi. Old Hari smoked his pipe and spat into the fireplace. The younger man looked through the window at the superb mountain, which rose in front of the house. In the afternoon he went out, and pursuing the road he had taken the previous day, he followed the tracks of the mule on which the two women had ridden. He arrived at last at the saddle of the Gemmi, and lying prone on the edge of the precipice, gazed down on Leuk. The village, nestling in its rocky hollow, had not yet been obliterated by the snow. But there was snow very near. Its advance had been arrested by the pine forests which guarded the environs of the hamlet. Seen from a height, the low houses of the village looked like paving-stones set in a field.

Ulrich reflected that Louise Hauser was now in one of those grey cottages. Which one was it? he wondered. They were too remote to be separately distinguished. He had a yearning to go down there, while it was still possible. But the sun had disappeared behind the great peak of the Wildstrubel, and Ulrich turned homewards. He found Hari smoking. On Ulrich's return Hari proposed a game of cards, and the two men sat down on opposite sides of the table. They played for a long time at a simple game called brisque. Then they had supper and went to bed.

Subsequent days were like the first, clear and cold, without any fresh fall of snow. Gaspard passed his days watching the eagles and other rare birds which venture into these frozen altitudes. For his part, Ulrich went regularly to the Gemmi *col* to look down at the distant village. In the evening they played cards, dice, and dominoes, staking small objects to lend an interest to the game.

One morning, Hari, who had been the first to rise, called out to Ulrich. A drifting cloud of white foam, deep yet ethereal, was sinking down on them and on all around them, spreading over them slowly, silently, a cover which grew ever thicker and heavier. The snowfall lasted four days and four nights. The door and windows had to be cleared, a passage dug, and steps cut, to enable them to climb out on to the surface of powdery snow, which twelve hours of frost had made harder than the granite of the moraines.

After that they lived as in a prison, hardly ever venturing outside their dwelling. The household tasks were divided between them and were punctually performed. Ulrich Kunsi undertook the cleaning and washing up and keeping the house neat. He also split the firewood. Hari kept the fire going and did the cooking. These necessary and monotonous tasks were relieved by long contests at dice or cards. Being both of them of calm and placid temperament, they never quarrelled. They never went even as far as to display impatience or peevishness, or to speak sharply to each other, both having determined before-hand to make the best of their winter sojourn on the heights. Occasionally Gaspard took his gun and went out hunting chamois, and when he had the good luck to kill one it was high day and holiday in the Schwarenbach Inn and there was great feasting on fresh meat.

One morning Hari set forth on one of these expeditions. The thermometer outside the inn showed thirty degrees of frost. Hari started before sunrise, hoping to take the chamois by surprise on the lower slopes of the Wildstrubel.

Left to himself, Ulrich remained in bed until ten o'clock. He was by nature a good sleeper, but he would not have dared to give way to this proclivity in the presence of the old guide, who was an early riser and always full of energy. He lingered over his breakfast, which he shared with Sam, who passed his days and nights sleeping in front of the fire. After breakfast he felt his spirits oppressed, and almost daunted, by the solitude, and he longed for his daily game of cards with the unconquerable craving that comes of ingrained habit. Later, he went out to meet his comrade, who was due to return at four o'clock.

The whole valley was now of a uniform level under its thick covering of snow. The crevasses were full to the top; the two lakes could no longer be distinguished; the rocks lay hid under a snowy quilt. Lying at the foot of the immense peaks, the valley was now one immense basin, symmetrical, frozen, and of a blinding whiteness.

It was three weeks since Ulrich had been to the edge of the precipice from which he looked down at the village. He thought he would go there again, before climbing the slopes that led to the Wildstrubel. The snow had now reached Leuk, and the houses were lost under their white mantle.

Turning to the right, he reached the Lemmern glacier. He walked with the mountaineer's long stride, driving his iron-pointed staff down on to the snow, which was as hard as stone. With his far-sighted eyes he sought the small black dot which he expected to see moving, in the far distance, over this vast sheet of snow. On reaching the edge of the glacier he stopped, wondering whether old Hari had really come that way. Then, with increasing anxiety and quicker steps he began to skirt the moraines.

The sun was sinking. The snow was suffused with a tinge of pink, and over its crystalline surface swept sharp gusts of a dry and icy breeze. Ulrich tried to reach his friend with a call, shrill, vibrant, prolonged. His voice took its flight into the deathless silence, in which the mountains slept. It rang far out over the deep motionless undulations of frozen foam, like the cry of a bird over the waves of the sea. Then it died away. And there was no reply.

He walked on and on. The sun had sunk behind the peaks, and the purple glow of sunset still lingered about them, but the depths of the valley were grey and shadowy, and Ulrich was suddenly afraid. He had an idea that the silence, the cold, the solitude were taking possession of him, were about to arrest his circulation and freeze his blood, stiffen his limbs and convert him into a motionless, frozen image. With all the speed he could he ran back towards the inn. Hari, he thought, must have taken another way and reached home already. He would find him seated by the fire, with a dead chamois at his feet. He soon came in sight of the hostelry. There was no smoke issuing from the chimney. Ulrich ran yet faster, and when he opened the door of the house, Sam leaped up to greet him. But there was no Gaspard Hari.

In consternation Kunsi turned hither and thither, as though expecting to find his comrade hiding in a corner. Then he relighted the fire and made the soup, still hoping that he would look up and see the old man coming in. From time to time he went outside, in case there should be some sign of him. Night had fallen, that wan, livid night of the mountains, illumined only by the slender, yellow crescent of a new moon, which was sinking towards the skyline and would soon disappear behind the ridge.

Returning to the house Ulrich sat down by the fire, and while he was warming his hands and feet his thoughts ran on possible accidents. Gaspard might have broken a leg, or fallen into a hollow, or made a false step which had cost him a sprained ankle. He would be lying in the snow, helpless against the benumbing cold, in agony of mind, far from any other human soul, calling out for help, shouting with all the strength of his voice in the silence of the night.

How discover where he was? So vast and craggy was the mountain, so dangerous the approaches to it, especially in the winter, that it would take ten or twenty guides, searching for a week in all directions, to find a man in that immensity. None the less Ulrich made up his mind to take Sam and set forth to look for Gaspard, if he had not come back by one in the morning.

He made his preparations. He put two days' provisions into a bag, took his cramp-irons, wound round his waist a long, strong, slender rope, and inspected thoroughly his alpenstock and his ice-axes. Then he waited. The fire was burning with a clear flame; the great dog lay snoring in its warmth; the steady ticking of the clock, in its resonant wooden case, sounded like the beating of a heart. Still he waited, his ears straining to catch any distant noise. When the light breeze whispered round roof and walls, he shivered.

The clock struck the hour of midnight. Feeling chilled and nervous, he put some water on the fire to boil, so that he might have some steaming coffee before setting out. When the clock struck one he rose, called Sam, opened the door, and struck out in the direction of the Wildstrubel. He climbed for five hours continuously. He scaled the rocks with the help of his irons, and cut steps in the ice with his axe, always advancing steadily and sometimes hauling the dog after him up some steep escarpment. It was about six o'clock when he reached one of the peaks to which Gaspard often came in search of chamois. There he waited for the day to break.

The sky above became gradually paler. Then suddenly that strange radiance, which springs no one knows whence, gleamed over the great ocean of snow-clad peaks, stretching for a hundred leagues around him. The vague light seemed to arise out of the snow itself and to diffuse itself in space. One by one, the highest and farthest pinnacles were suffused with a tender rosy hue and the red sun rose from behind the great masses of the Bernese Alps. Ulrich Kunsi set forth again. Like a hunter, he bent down, searching for tracks and saying to his dog:

'Seek, old man, seek.'

He was now on his way down the mountain, investigating every chasm, and sometimes sending forth a prolonged call, which quickly died away in the dumb immensity. At times he put his ear close to the ground to listen. Once he thought he heard a voice and he ran in the direction of it, shouting as he ran, but he heard nothing more, and sat down, exhausted and despairing. About midday he shared some food with Sam, who was as weary as himself. And again he set out on his search. When evening came he was still walking, having accomplished fifty kilometres among the mountains. He was too far from the house to think of returning there, and too tired to drag himself along any further. Digging a hole in the snow, he curled up in it with his dog, under cover of a blanket, which he had brought with him. Man and beast lay together, each body sharing the warmth of the other, but frozen to the marrow none the less. Ulrich's mind was haunted by visions, and his limbs were shaking with cold. He could not sleep at all. When he rose, day was on the point of breaking. His legs felt as rigid as bars of iron; his resolution was so enfeebled that he almost sobbed aloud in his distress, and his heart beat so violently that he nearly collapsed with emotion whenever he fancied that he heard a sound.

The thought suddenly came to him that he too might perish of cold amidst these solitudes, and the fear of such a death whipped up his energy and roused him to fresh vigour. He was now making the descent towards the inn, and kept falling down from weariness and picking himself up again. His dog Sam, with one paw disabled, followed far behind, limping. It was four o'clock in the afternoon before they reached the Schwarenbach. Hari was not there. Ulrich lighted a fire, had something to eat, and then fell asleep, so utterly stupefied with fatigue that he could think of nothing. He slept for a long, a very long time. It seemed as if nothing could break his repose, when suddenly he heard a voice cry 'Ulrich!' He was shaken out of his profound torpor, and started up. Was it a dream?

Was it one of those strange summonses that disturb the slumber of uneasy souls? No. He could hear it still. That ringing cry had pierced his ear, had taken possession of his body, right to the tips of his sinewy fingers. Beyond all doubt, there had been a cry for help, an appeal for succour. Some one had called out 'Ulrich!' Then some one must be in the vicinity of the house. There could be no question about it. He opened the door and shouted with all his strength: 'Gaspard, is that you?'

There was no reply. The silence was not broken by sound, or whisper, or groan. It was night, and the snow lay all around, ghast'y in its whiteness.

The wind had risen. It was that icy wind which splits the rocks and leaves nothing alive on these forsaken altitudes. It blew in sharp, withering gusts, dealing death more surely than even the fiery blasts of the desert. Again Ulrich called out:

'Gaspard, Gaspard, Gaspard!'

He waited a little, but silence still reigned on the mountain side, and he was forthwith stricken by a terror which shook him to the very bones. He leaped back into the inn, closed and bolted the door, and with chattering teeth collapsed into a chair. He was now sure that the appeal for help had come from his comrade, at the moment when he was yielding up the ghost. He was as certain of that as one is of being alive or eating bread. For two days and three nights old Gaspard Hari had been wrestling with death in some hollow in one of those deep unsullied ravines, whose whiteness is more sinister than the darkness of underground caverns. For two days and three nights he had been dying, and at this very moment, whilst he lay at the point of death, his thoughts had turned to his comrade, and his soul, in the instant of gaining its freedom, had flown to the inn where Ulrich lay sleeping. It had exercised that mysterious and terrible power, possessed by the souls of the dead, to haunt the living. The voiceless spirit had called aloud in the over-wrought soul of the sleeper, had uttered its last farewell, or, perhaps, its reproach, its curse on the man who had not searched diligently enough.

Ulrich felt its presence there, behind the walls of the house, behind the door which he had just closed. The soul was prowling around. It was like a bird of night fluttering against a lighted window. Ulrich, distraught with terror, was ready to scream. He would have taken to flight, but dared not open the door.

And never again, he felt, would he dare to open that door, for the spectre would be hovering, day and night, round the inn, until the corpse of the old guide had been recovered and laid in the consecrated earth of a cemetery.

When day broke Ulrich regained a little confidence from the brilliance of the returning sun. He prepared his breakfast and made some soup for the dog, but after that he remained seated motionless in a chair. His heart was in agony; his thoughts turned ever to the old man, who was lying out there in the snow. When night again descended upon the mountains new terrors assailed him. He paced to and fro in the smoke-blackened kitchen, by the dim light of a solitary candle. Up and down he strode, and always he was listening, listening, for that cry, which had terrified him the night before. Might it not ring out again through the mournful silence of the outer world? He felt forlorn, poor wretch; forlorn, as never a man had been, here in this vast whiteness of snow, all alone, seven thousand feet above the inhabited world, above the dwellings of men, above the excitements, the hubbub, the noise, the thrills of life; alone in the frozen sky. He was torn by a mad desire to make his escape in whatsoever direction, by whatsoever means; to descend to Leuk, even if he had to hurl himself over the precipice. But he did not dare so much as to open the door; he felt sure that that thing outside, the dead man, would bar his passage, and prevent him from leaving his comrade alone upon those heights.

As midnight approached his limbs grew weary, and fear and distress overcame him. He dreaded his bed, as one dreads a haunted spot, but yielding at last to drowsiness he sank into a chair.

Suddenly his ears were pierced by the same strident cry that he had heard the previous night. It was so shrill that Ulrich stretched out his hands to ward off the ghost, and losing his balance fell backwards on to the floor. Aroused by the noise, the dog began to howl in terror, and ran hither and thither in the room, trying to find out whence the danger threatened. When he came to the door he sniffed at the edge of it, and began howling, snorting, and snarling, his hair bristling, his tail erect. Beside himself with terror, Kunsi rose and, grasping a stool by one leg, shouted:

'Don't come in. Don't come in. Don't come in or I'll kill you.'

Excited by his menacing tones, the dog barked furiously at the invisible enemy whom his master was challenging. Gradually Sam calmed down, and went back to lie on the hearth, but he was still uneasy; his eyes were gleaming and he was baring his fangs and growling. Ulrich, too, regained his wits; but feeling faint with terror, he took a bottle of brandy from the sideboard and drank several glasses of it in quick succession. As his mind became duller, his courage rose, and a feverish heat coursed along his veins. On the following day he ate hardly anything, confining himself to the brandy, and for some days after he lived in a state of brutish intoxication. The moment the thought of Gaspard Hari crossed his mind, he began drinking and did not leave off until he collapsed to the ground in a drunken torpor, and lay there face downwards, snoring and helpless. Hardly had he recovered from the effects of the burning and maddening liquor, when the cry 'Ulrich!' roused him, as though a bullet had penetrated his skull. He started to his feet, staggering to and fro, stretching out his hands to keep himself from falling, and calling to his dog to help him. Sam, too, appeared to be seized with his master's madness. He hurled himself against the door, scratching at it with his claws, gnawing it with his long white teeth, while Ulrich, with his head thrown back, his face turned upwards, swallowed brandy in great gulps, as though he were drinking cool water after a climb. Presently his thoughts, his memory, his terror, would be drowned in drunken oblivion.

In three weeks he had finished his entire stock of spirits. But the only effect of his inebriation was to lull his terror to sleep. When the means for this were no longer available, his fears returned with fresh ferocity. His fixed idea, aggravated by prolonged intoxication, gained force continually in that absolute solitude, and worked its way, like a gimlet, ever deeper into his spirit. Like a wild beast in a cage, he paced his room, every now and then putting his ear to the door to listen for the voice of Gaspard's ghost, and hurling defiance at it through the wall. And when, in utter weariness, he lay down, he would again hear the voice and leap once more to his feet. At last, one night, with the courage of a coward driven to bay, he flung himself at the door and opened it, to see who it was who was calling him, and to compel him to silence. But the cold air struck him full in the face, and froze him to the marrow. He slammed the door to again, and shot the bolts, never noticing that his dog had dashed out into the open.   Shivering, he threw some more wood on to the fire and sat down to warm himself. Suddenly he started.   There was someone scratching at the wall and moaning.

'Go away,' he said, terror-stricken.

The answer was a melancholy wail.

His last remaining vestiges of reason were swept away by fear.

'Go away,' he cried again, and he turned hither and thither in an effort to find some corner in which he could hide himself. But the creature outside continued to wail, and passed along the front of the house, rubbing itself against the wall.   Ulrich dashed to the oaken sideboard, which was full of provisions and crockery, and with superhuman strength dragged it across the room and set it against the door to act as a barricade.   Then he took all the remaining furniture, mattresses, palliasses, chairs, and blockaded the window, as if in a state of siege.   But the thing outside went on groaning dismally, and Ulrich himself was soon replying with groans not less lugubrious.   Days and nights passed, and still these two continued to answer each other's howls.

The ghost, as it seemed to Ulrich, moved unceasingly round the house, scratching at the walls with its nails in a fierce determination to break a way through.   Within the house Ulrich crouched with his ear close to the masonry, following every movement of the thing outside, and answering all its appeals with horrifying shrieks.   Then came a night when Ulrich heard no more sounds from without.   Overcome with fatigue, he dropped into a chair and fell asleep immediately.   When he awoke his mind and memory were a blank.   It was as if that sleep of prostration had swept his brain clean of everything. He felt hungry and took some food. . . .

The winter was over.   The passage of the Gemmi became practicable; and the Hauser family set forth on its journey to the inn.   At the top of the first long acclivity, the two women clambered up on to their mule.   They spoke about the two men, whom they expected presently to meet again.   They were surprised that neither of them had descended a few days earlier, as soon as the Leuk road was practicable, to give them the news of their long winter sojourn.   When they came in sight of the inn, which was still covered with a thick mantle of snow, they saw that the door and window were closed, but old Hauser was reassured by a thin column of smoke which was rising from the chimney. As he drew nearer, however, he saw on the outer threshold the skeleton of an animal. It was a large skeleton, lying on its side, and the flesh had been torn off the bones by eagles.

All three examined it.

'That must be Sam,' Madame Hauser said.

Then she called out for Gaspard, and from the inside of the house came a shrill cry like that of an animal. Old Hauser, too, shouted Gaspard's name. A second cry came from within. The father and his two sons thereupon endeavoured to open the door, but it resisted their efforts. They took a long beam out of an empty stable, and used it as a battering-ram. They dashed it with all their strength against the door, which gave way with the shriek of splintering planks. The sideboard fell over on the floor with a great crash, which shook the house, and revealed, standing behind it, a man whose hair came down to his shoulders, and whose beard touched his chest. His eyes were bright; his clothing was in rags.

Louise alone recognized him.

'Mother!' she gasped, 'it is Ulrich.'

And the mother saw that it was indeed Ulrich, although his hair had turned white.

He suffered them to come near him and touch him, but when they asked him questions, he made no reply. He had to be taken down to Leuk, where the doctors certified that he was insane.

The fate of old Gaspard was never known.

During the following summer Louise Hauser came near to dying of a decline, which was attributed to the rigours of the mountain climate.

A PORTRAIT

(*Un Portrait*)

'WELL, Milial,' said someone near me, accosting a friend.

I turned to look at this man of the name of Milial. I knew his reputation as a Don Juan, and had for a long time been anxious to make his acquaintance.

Milial was no longer young. His hair of lustreless grey was so thick that it looked like one of those fur caps worn in the far north, and his beard, which was of fine texture and long enough to reach his chest, had also a certain character of furriness. He was conversing with a woman, and his voice was pitched in low tones. As he talked he leaned towards her and looked at her with eyes which caressed her with gentle homage.

I knew what his life had been, or at least I knew as much as was common property. Several women had fallen madly in love with him, and dramas had occurred in which he had played the protagonist. His reputation was that of a man whose powers of seduction were so great as to be almost irresistible. Wishing to ascertain the source of this unusual fascination, I made inquiries of some of the women who were must enthu-siastic in his praise, and I observed that they always, after an effort to arrive at something definite, made the same vague reply:

'Oh, I don't know. It's just his charm.'

No one would have described him as particularly good-looking. He had none of the refinements of address with which the subduers of the feminine heart are supposed to be endowed. The problem interested me, and I began to wonder wherein lay his special attraction. Was he brilliant? No one quoted his epigrams or credited him with intelligence beyond the ordinary. Was it his eyes? Possibly. Or his voice? There are voices which are charged with a sensuous and irresistible witchery. They have, as it were, the perfume and the savour of exquisite viands, so that one hungers to listen to them; one absorbs the sound of them as if they were something delicious to eat.

A friend of mine was passing, and I said to him:

'Do you know Monsieur Milial?'

'Yes.'

'Will you introduce me to him?'

The introduction was effected, and Milial and I stood chatting together among the other guests. His conversation was agreeable and sensible, but conveyed no impression of intellectual superiority. It is true that his voice was agreeable, soft, caressing, and musical, but I had heard voices of a still more captivating quality. To listen to it was pleasing, just as it is pleasing to watch a charming stream gliding past. There was no mental strain involved in following him; there was no subtlety to excite the hearer's curiosity; one's interest was not stirred by the expectation of anything remarkable. Rather was his talk of a soothing character. It aroused neither a keen desire to challenge or contradict, nor any very ecstatic admiration. To reply to him was as easy as to listen to him. As soon as he made a remark, the answer came easily to the lips; observations flowed without effort, as though in response to some natural compulsion. One reflection occurred to me almost immediately. I had met him only a quarter of an hour ago, yet already he seemed to me like an old friend. His face, his gestures, his voice, his ideas, were as familiar to me as if I had known him for years. A few minutes of intercourse had sufficed to instal him definitely on an intimate footing with me. If he had demanded my confidence, I should have told him things about myself which ordinarily a man reveals only to his oldest comrades. There was assuredly an element of the mysterious in this. There are barriers set between all human beings, and these yield only one by one, as they are unlocked by the key of sympathy, or similar tastes, or harmony of intellectual culture, or constant association. But no such barriers seemed to stand between him and me, nor for that matter between him and other men and women whom chance threw in his path. At the end of half an hour, when we said good-bye, we were looking forward to meeting each other again, and he gave me his address, with an invitation to lunch with him two days later.

Having forgotten the hour, I arrived too soon. He had not yet come in. A silent and well-trained man-servant showed me into a fine drawing-room, which was furnished with sober and homely good taste. At once I felt as much at ease in it as if I had been in my own house. I have often observed the effect which rooms have upon the character and temperament. There are rooms which inevitably make one feel stupid; others, which rouse one to animation. A room may be well lighted, and decorated in white and gold, and yet it will make you melancholy. Another room will cheer you at once, although its furnishing may be of the soberest. Our eyes, like our souls, have their preferences and their aversions, for which there is no reason discoverable. Simply, secretly, furtively, these influences are imposed upon us. Just as the atmosphere of forest, sea, or mountain affects our physical condition, so does the harmony of furniture and walls, and the general scheme of decoration, act instantly upon our intellectual nature.

I took my seat upon a divan covered with silk cushions, and I at once felt as comfortably propped and supported as if these small, silk-covered sacks of feathers had been purposely arranged to fit the contours of my body.

Then I looked round me. There was not one garish article in the room. Everything was beautiful but unpretentious; the furniture was simple but choice; the Oriental curtains looked as if they had come from the interior of a harem, and not from the Louvre.

Facing me was a young woman's portrait. It was a picture of medium size, showing the head, the upper part of the body, and the hands, which held a book. She wore no hat. Her hair was dressed in simple bandeaux. On her lips was a smile, which had a trace of sadness. Whether because her head was uncovered, or because I was impressed by the naturalness of her poise, it is a fact that I never saw a portrait which seemed so much at home as this portrait in that room. Almost all the women's portraits I know are obviously posed. Either the subject is ostentatiously dressed, with a specially becoming coiffure; or she seems too obviously aware that she is posing, in the first place for the artist, and in the second place for those who will look at the portrait; or she has assumed an attitude of careless ease and is wearing a dress to correspond.

Some of the ladies stand erect and majestic, flaunting their beauty with an air of haughtiness which they would find it difficult to preserve for very long in the common exigencies of

life. Others have a self-conscious simper, although the canvas
condemns their features to immobility. There is not one of
them who has not some trifle such as a flower or jewel, a fold
of the gown or a curve of the lips, set there by the artist for
effect. Whether they wear a hat or a wisp of lace on the head,
or whether the hair is unadorned, one divines in them something that is not absolutely natural. What is it? Without
knowing the original it is impossible to say definitely. But the
affectation is there. The subject of the portrait has the air of
calling on strangers, on whom she desires to produce a good
impression. It is as if she wished to display herself to the
greatest advantage. Whatever her attitude may be, whether
unassuming or dignified, it is obviously studied.

But how about the portrait I was now studying? Clearly
this woman was in her own house, and alone, yes, absolutely
alone. Her smile was the smile of one who dreams in solitude
of something that is both sweet and sad. It was not the smile
of a woman conscious of an admiring gaze. She was so
thoroughly alone and at home, that she created a solitude,
an absolute solitude, in that large room. Alone she dwelt in
it, alone she sufficed to people it and animate it. Any number
of men and women might enter that room; they might speak,
and laugh, and even sing, but they could never break into her
sanctuary. Still she would smile the smile of solitude; still would
the room derive all its vitality from that face in the picture.

There was something unique in her expression. Steady,
caressing, her eyes rested upon me without seeing me. All
other portraits seem to know when they are being examined,
and to respond with eyes that see, and think, and follow us, and
never quit us, from the moment we enter the room until we
leave it. But the eyes of this portrait took no notice of me or
of any one else, although they were looking straight at me.
I recalled that curious line of Baudelaire:

Et les yeux attirants comme ceux d'un portrait.

It is the truth that these painted eyes which had once lived, and
were still perhaps living, attracted me irresistibly and filled me
with an emotion which was new and strange and potent. These
impenetrable eyes, shining out of that sombre picture, diffused
an infinite and tender charm. It was like the soft rustling of
the passing breeze. It was as seductive as a dying twilight sky

of lilac, rose, and azure; it was as full of gentle melancholy as the night which follows such a sunset. These eyes, which were created by a few strokes of the brush, hid in their depths the mystery of something that seems to be and is not, something that can reveal itself in a woman's glance, something that is the source of all the love that is born in us.

The door opened and Milial came in. He apologized for his lateness, I for my unduly early arrival. Presently I said to him:

'Is it indiscreet to ask whose portrait that is?'

'It is my mother's,' he replied. 'She died when she was quite young.'

Then it was that I understood the secret of my friend's irresistible attraction.

SHALI

(*Châli*)

FROM the depths of the easy-chair where he seemed to be dozing rose the quavering treble of old Admiral de la Vallée:

'I once had a little romance; it was a very curious affair. If you like I will tell you about it.'

Round his lips played that eternal smile of his, the twisted smile of a Voltaire, which had earned for him a reputation for devastating cynicism.

I

When I was thirty, and a lieutenant in the Navy, I was ordered off on an astronomical expedition into Central India. The British Government gave me every assistance and before long, attended by a small escort, I plunged into the heart of that strange country of marvels and prodigies.

It would take a score of volumes to do justice to my journey. I passed through regions of fabulous magnificence, where I was welcomed by princes of superhuman beauty in surroundings of unimaginable splendour. For two months I seemed to be living in a poem; riding on phantom elephants through realms of fancy and discovering fantastic ruins in the depths of enchanted forests. In cities that had all the glamour of a dream I beheld marvellous buildings, like jewels of exquisite workmanship, delicate as lace, massive as mountains, buildings so divine, so magical, so lovely, that a man falls in love with them as with a woman, and derives from their contemplation a sensuous, physical delight. In short, to quote Victor Hugo, I moved in a waking dream.

At last I reached my destination, Ganhara, once one of the most flourishing cities in Central India, but now in its decline. Its ruler was a wealthy potentate, the Rajah Maddan, a typically Oriental sovereign, despotic, violent, cruel, and at the same time generous; refined yet barbarous; gracious yet sanguinary; a blend of feminine charm and ruthless ferocity.

The city lies in the depths of a valley, on the shores of a little lake, which is girt with innumerable pagodas, their walls washed by its waters. From afar, the town appears a patch of white, gradually opening out as the traveller draws near and revealing one by one the domes, the minarets, the spires, the slender, airy pinnacles that lend such grace to Indian architecture.

About an hour's march from the city gates the rajah sent a guard of honour and a magnificently caparisoned elephant to meet me, and I was conducted with great pomp to the palace.

I asked to be allowed time to change into more ceremonial attire, but the rajah's impatience would brook no delay. He was eager to make my acquaintance and to discover my possibilities as a source of entertainment. The rest could wait. Passing through groups of bronzed, statuesque warriors in glittering uniforms, I was ushered into a great hall. Around the walls ran galleries, in which stood men sumptuously clothed and blazing with jewels. On a seat, like a common garden bench with no back to it, covered, however, with a magnificent carpet, I beheld a dazzling mass, a sort of couchant sun. This was the rajah, who sat there motionless in his robes of glaring canary yellow, waiting to receive me. He was decked with diamonds worth ten or fifteen millions of francs, while on his forehead, in solitary splendour, blazed that famous Star of Delhi, an heirloom of the illustrious dynasty of the Pariharas of Mundore, from whom my host claimed descent. He was a young man of about twenty-five, who, although of purest Hindoo stock, looked as if he had negro blood in his veins. He had large, set, somewhat vacant eyes, high cheek-bones, thick lips, a curly beard, a low forehead, and sharp, dazzlingly white teeth which he frequently showed in a mechanical smile. He rose to meet me and shook hands in English fashion. Then he made me sit beside him on his bench, which was so high that my feet barely touched the ground. It was an extremely uncomfortable perch.

He at once suggested a tiger hunt for the following day. He had a passion for hunting and for single combats, and he failed to understand how any one could possess other interests. He was evidently convinced that I had undertaken my long journey for the sole purpose of ministering to his amusement and of sharing his pleasures. As his good will was essential to the success of my mission, I did my best to humour him. He was so much gratified by my attitude that he insisted on showing me a fight between two champions and carried me off to a sort of arena in the interior of the palace.

At his command two copper-coloured combatants appeared, stark naked, with sets of steel talons, like sharp-pronged rakes, fastened to their hands. They set to immediately, each seeking to claw his adversary with his murderous weapon, until their dark skins were covered all over with hideous gashes dripping with blood. The fight lasted for a long time. Even when their bodies were one mass of wounds, they went on slashing each other. One man's cheek was in ribbons, while his opponent's ear was torn in three. The prince watched the proceedings with savage gusto. He quivered all over with delight, uttered low growls of satisfaction, and unconsciously mimicked all the movements of the combatants.

'Hit him!' he kept shouting. 'Let him have it!'

At last one of the champions sank to the ground unconscious and had to be removed from the blood-stained arena. It was over all too soon for the rajah, who heaved a deep sigh of disappointment and regret. He turned to me, anxious to hear my impressions. Concealing my disgust, I congratulated him warmly.

After this, he gave orders for me to be conducted to the Khoosh Mahal (Palace of Pleasures) where I was to be housed. Passing through the fairylike gardens that grace these regions, I reached my residence. One entire side of this jewel of a palace, which was situated on the borders of the royal park, was washed by the waters of the sacred lake of Vihara. It was a square building; and each of its four façades presented three tiers of galleries with exquisitely wrought colonnades. At each corner rose graceful turrets, some high, some low, some single, some in pairs, no two of them alike in size or form, and looking for all the world like natural flowers sprung from that exquisite plant of Oriental architecture. Each turret was capped with a roof of quaint design, like a coquettish head-dress. The massive central dome, from which arose an adorable, slender spike all in delicate open-work, reared towards the sky its cupola, like a swelling breast of white marble. The entire building from base to summit was covered with sculpture, with those exquisite arabesques that ravish the sight, those petrified processions of dainty figures, whose attitudes and gestures perpetuate the manners and customs of India.

The rooms were lighted by windows with perforated arches, opening on to the gardens. The marble floors were inlaid with onyx, lapis lazuli, and agate, in graceful designs of bouquets of flowers.

I had hardly time to change my dress, before a high official of the court called Haribadada, who had been especially appointed intermediary between the prince and myself, announced a visit from the monarch. The rajah appeared in his saffron robes, shook hands again, and began to converse volubly, continually pressing me for opinions, which I had great difficulty in producing. Presently he offered to show me the ruins of the old palace at the far end of the gardens.

It was a perfect wilderness of stone, and haunted by a tribe of large monkeys. As we approached, the male monkeys ran up and down along the walls making horrible grimaces at us, while the females scampered away with their babies in their arms. The king went into fits of laughter, pinched my shoulder to show his amusement, and sat down among the ruins, while all around us on every wall and ledge squatted white-whiskered monkeys putting out their tongues and shaking their fists at us. When he was tired of this entertainment His Saffron Majesty rose and, still keeping me beside him, gravely resumed his walk. He was much elated at having shown me such wonders the very day of my arrival, and reminded me of the great tiger hunt which had been arranged in my honour for the following day.

I took part in that hunt, in a second, a third, and a score of other hunts in succession, in the course of which we followed every species of beast which that country harbours—panther, bear, elephant, antelope, hippopotamus, crocodile, and heaven knows what else—at least one-half of the entire brute creation, until I was sick and tired of slaughter, utterly weary of the eternal sameness of the sport.

Eventually the rajah's enthusiasm subsided, and at my earnest entreaty, he allowed me a little leisure for my work. He now contented himself with loading me with gifts. He sent me jewels, wonderful fabrics, performing animals, all of which were presented by Haribadada with as deep a semblance of respect as if I had been the sun himself, though privately he regarded me with deep disdain.

Every day a procession of servants brought me, on covered

plates, portions of every dish served at the royal repasts. Every day I had to simulate ecstasies of enjoyment at some new entertainment devised for my amusement; dances of nautch girls; jugglers; reviews of troops, whatever spectacle suggested itself to the rajah, with his embarrassing ideas of hospitality, as calculated to impress me with the charm and splendour of his amazing realm. Whenever I was allowed a little time to myself I worked or went to watch the monkeys, whose company I infinitely preferred to that of the king.

One evening on my return from a walk I met Haribadada, looking very solemn, at my palace door. He informed me, in veiled language, that a present from his sovereign awaited me in my room, and he apologized on behalf of his master for his omission to supply long ago a want of which I must have been sensible. After this mysterious utterance he bowed and withdrew.

On entering my room I saw six little girls, lined up against the wall in order of height, stock still, all in a row like larks on a spit. The oldest of them was about eight and the youngest six. At first I did not grasp the purpose for which this infant school had been quartered on me; then I suddenly realized that it was a delicate attention on the part of the rajah.

I stood there utterly confused and ashamed, confronted with those mites, who gazed at me with their great, solemn eyes, as if already aware of the demands that might be made upon them. I had no idea what to say to them and longed to send them back, but to return a gift of the rajah's would have been construed as a mortal insult. There was nothing for it but to accept the situation and to keep the children in the palace. They stood perfectly still, staring at me, waiting for orders and trying to read my thoughts in my eyes. That infernal gift! How abominably it embarrassed me! I felt such a fool that at last I said to the eldest one:

'What is your name, child?'

'Shali,' she replied.

She was a marvel, this chit of a girl, her smooth skin tinged with the creamy tones of ivory; her face a long oval, pure of line as the face of a statue.

To see what she would say, and possibly with some idea of confusing her, I asked:

'Why are you here?'

In soft, melodious tones, she answered:

'I am here to do my lord's bidding.'

She had had her instructions, the little creature.

I put the same question to the youngest of the six, who, in a still more piping voice, enunciated clearly:

'Master, I am here to do your bidding.'

She was a darling, just like a little mouse. I caught her up in my arms and kissed her. Then I sat down on the floor, in Indian fashion, and made them group themselves around me, while I told them a fairy tale about genii, for I could speak their language tolerably well. They listened with rapt attention; thrilling with delight, shuddering with horror, holding up their hands at all the wonderful incidents I related.

When my story was ended I summoned Latchman, my confidential servant, and ordered him to bring sweets, sugar-plums, and cakes, which the children ate till they were nearly ill.

I was beginning to enjoy the humour of the situation and thought of all sorts of pastimes to amuse my little sultanas. One of these games, especially, was a huge success. I straddled my legs and my six babies ran through, one after the other, beginning with the smallest, and the tallest always bumped against me a little because she would never duck her head sufficiently. This sent them into shrieks of deafening laughter, till the low vaulted roofs of my sumptuous palace, roused to life and penetrated with childlike gaiety, rang with their youthful voices.

I took a keen interest in the arrangements of the dormitory where my six innocents were to sleep. At last I shut the door on them, leaving them to the care of four serving-women whom the rajah had sent as their attendants.

For a whole week I enjoyed playing papa to these puppets. We had glorious romps at hide-and-seek, hot cockles and puss in the corner, which sent them into raptures; every day I taught them another of these new and entrancing games.

My house was now like a girls' school. Arrayed in lovely silks and gold and silver brocade, my little friends ran like tiny human animals up and down the long galleries and flitted in and out of the silent halls, where the light fell softly through the arched windows.

The biggest of them, the child Shali, who was like a statuette of old ivory, became my particular pet. She was an adorable little creature, shy and gentle, yet merry, and soon she loved me with a passionate affection which I returned. The others continued to frisk about the palace like so many kittens, but Shali never left my side, except when I went to visit the rajah.

We spent delicious hours together among the ruins, surrounded by the monkeys, of whom we had made friends. She would sit quietly on my knee, her little sphinx-like head busy with its fancies, or thinking perhaps of nothing at all, but never losing the beautiful, graceful pose, inborn in that subtle, meditative race, the hieratical pose of sacred statues. I always brought a great copper dish of fruit, and the female monkeys, followed by their more timid young, would gradually come as close as they dared and sit round us in a ring, waiting for me to distribute my dainties. As a rule one of the male monkeys, bolder than the rest, would venture near me, holding out his hand like a beggar, and I would give him a tit-bit, which he at once took to his mate. At this, all the others broke into furious cries of jealousy and rage, and nothing would allay their appalling clamour until I had thrown each animal its share.

I was so much at home among the ruins that I thought of setting up my little apparatus and working there. But as soon as they caught sight of my brass mathematical instruments, the monkeys evidently took them for lethal weapons, and fled in all directions, uttering ear-piercing shrieks.

Often I spent the evening with Shali on one of the outer galleries overlooking the lake of Vihara. In silence we watched the radiant moon, scaling the steeps of heaven and casting upon the waters a veil of shimmering silver, and on the opposite bank, the tiny pagodas like a row of fairy mushrooms, their stems rising out of the ripples. I took my little darling's serious face between my hands and bestowed lingering caresses upon her ivory brow, upon her great eyes fraught with all the mystery of that ancient realm of story, upon her serene lips that parted as I kissed them. And I was thrilled with a sensation, vague, compelling, infinitely romantic, as if in the person of this child I embraced an entire race, that beautiful and mysterious race from which, it seems, all other races have sprung.

Meanwhile the rajah continued to heap gifts upon me. One day he sent me an unexpected offering, which excited Shali's passionate admiration. It was one of those common little boxes

made of cardboard with small shells glued all over the outside
and worth, in France, not more than a couple of francs. Out
there, however, it was of incalculable value, and doubtless the
first that had ever reached that country.

Smiling at the importance attached to this hideous knick-
knack emanating from some bazaar, I left it lying on a table.
Shali was never tired of gazing at it and admiring it with rapt
and reverent eyes.

'May I touch it?' she asked sometimes.

And when I had given her leave, she would raise and lower the
lid with infinite precautions, and with her delicate fingers, very
gently stroke the coating of small shells as if the mere feel of it
thrilled her to the heart with exquisite delight.

My work was now completed, and I had to think of my return.
I was a long time making up my mind, so loath was I to leave my
little friend. But at last I was obliged to tear myself away.
The rajah was in despair. He arranged a fresh series of hunts
and single combats, but after a fortnight of these diversions, I
protested that I could postpone my departure no longer and he
let me go.

Shali's farewells were heartbreaking. Clinging to me, her
face buried on my bosom, her whole form shaken with sobs, she
wept inconsolably. I did all I could to comfort her, but my
kisses were unavailing. With a sudden inspiration, I rose,
fetched the shell trinket box and put it into her hands.

'Take it. It's yours.'

Then, at last, I saw her smile. Her whole face glowed with
that deep inward rapture that manifests itself when some impossible dream suddenly comes true. She kissed me passionately.
But for all that she cried bitterly at the final moment of
parting.

After I had bestowed on my other little sultanas cakes combined with paternal kisses, I went my way.

II

After a lapse of two years, the vicissitudes of a sailor's career
brought me again to Bombay, where unforeseen circumstances
detained me. I was charged with another mission for which I
was specially qualified by my knowledge of the country and the
language. I completed my work with all possible dispatch, and

as I had still three months in hand, I decided to pay a short visit to my friend the Rajah of Ganhara, and my dear little Shali, whom I expected to find much changed.

The Rajah Maddan welcomed me with frantic ebullitions of delight. He had three champions done to death in my presence, and never left me for a single moment during the first day of my arrival. At nightfall, however, I found myself alone, and sent for Haribadada. After plying him with questions on many different subjects, with the idea of throwing him off the scent, I finally asked:

'And do you know what has become of that little Shali, whom the rajah presented to me?'

The minister's face clouded, and he replied, in great embarrassment:

'It is better not to mention her.'

'Why not? She was a charming little creature.'

'She turned out badly, my lord.'

'What, Shali? What became of her? Where is she?'

'What I mean is that she came to a bad end.'

'A bad end? Is she dead?'

'Yes, my lord. She was guilty of a vile action.'

I was deeply moved. My heart was beating violently, while a pang of agony shot through my breast.

'A vile action?' I echoed. 'What did she do? What happened to her?'

In ever deeper confusion, he faltered:

'It is better not to inquire.'

'But I insist upon knowing.'

'She robbed someone.'

'Shali? Whom did she rob?'

'You, my lord.'

'Me? What do you mean?'

'The day of your departure she stole from you the casket that the prince had bestowed upon you. She was caught with it in her hands.'

'What casket?'

'The one with the shells.'

'Why, I gave it to her!'

The Indian gazed at me in stupefaction.

'To tell you the truth, she swore by all that was holy that you had given it to her. But who could believe that you could possibly have bestowed the sovereign's gift upon a slave? So the rajah had her punished.'

'Punished? In what way? What did they do to her?'

'They tied her up in a sack, my lord, and threw her into the lake from that window, the window of this very room where we are at this moment, and where the theft was committed.'

My heart was wrung with the most terrible anguish I have ever endured. I motioned to Haribadada to leave me, so that he should not see my tears.

I spent the night in the gallery overlooking the lake—that same gallery where I had so often sat, with the poor child on my knee. And I thought of her lovely little body, now a mouldering skeleton, tied up in a canvas sack, down there in the depths of those black waters on which we used to gaze together.

In spite of the rajah's protests and his violent distress, I left the following day.

And now I verily believe that Shali is the only woman I ever loved.

IDLE BEAUTY

(*L'Inutile Beauté*)

I

A REMARKABLY smart victoria, drawn by a pair of splendid black horses, was waiting at the portico steps of the mansion. It was about half-past five in the afternoon, towards the end of June, and between the roofs of the houses that overlooked the courtyard appeared cheerful glimpses of warm, clear sky.

The Countess de Mascaret appeared on the steps, just as her husband came in at the carriage entrance. He paused a moment to gaze at his wife, and he turned a little pale. She was very beautiful, with her slender figure, her air of distinction, her large grey eyes, her black hair, the long oval of her face, and the warm ivory tints of her skin. Without one glance at him, as if she had not even noticed his presence, she stepped into the carriage. She moved with such perfect grace and breeding, that the shameful jealousy which had tortured him all these years once more stung him to the heart. He raised his hat and went towards her.

'You are going for a drive?'

'As you see.'

The words came grudgingly from her contemptuous lips.

'In the Bois?'

'Very likely.'

'Will you allow me to accompany you?'

'It is your carriage.'

He betrayed no surprise at the tone of her reply, but seated himself at her side and ordered the coachman to drive to the Bois.

The footman jumped up on the box, and the horses started off, snatching at the bit and prancing as was their wont, until they turned into the street. Husband and wife drove along in silence. He beat about for an opening, but her expression was so forbidding that he did not venture to address her. At last he stealthily slid his hand towards her gloved fingers and touched them as if by chance. The gesture with which she withdrew her

297

arm was so eloquent of resentment and aversion that he was dismayed, for all his arbitrary and tyrannical temper.

'Gabrielle,' he murmured.

'What do you want?' she asked without turning her head.

'I think you are adorable.'

She made no reply but leaned back in the carriage with an air of offended majesty. They were driving along the Champs-Élysées in the direction of the Arc de Triomphe de l'Étoile which, at the far end of the great avenue, swung upwards against a background of crimson sky. The sun was shedding a shimmering haze on the mighty archway and on the whole horizon. Two streams of carriages, with the light dancing on the brass and silver of the harness and the crystal of the lamps, were proceeding, one towards the park and one towards the town.

'My dear Gabrielle,' exclaimed the count.

Vexed beyond endurance, she replied irritably:

'Can't you leave me alone? Apparently I mayn't even have my carriage to myself now.'

He pretended not to hear.

'I have never seen you looking prettier.'

It was clear that her patience was at an end. With a bitterness she could not control, she retorted:

'How unfortunate that you should have noticed it! Because I assure you that I will have nothing more to do with you.'

Hurt and bewildered, he allowed his customary violence to gain the upper hand.

'What do you mean?' he rapped out, in a voice that suggested the brutal tyrant rather than the tender lover.

Although the sound of the wheels drowned their conversation, she lowered her voice:

'What do I mean? What do I mean? You are at your old games again. Do you want me to tell you what I mean?'

'Yes.'

'The whole truth?'

'Yes.'

'All my grievances against you, since I first became the victim of your ferocious egotism?'

He had turned red with surprise and chagrin.

'Yes, out with it!' he growled between his clenched teeth.

Tall and handsome, with broad shoulders and a great red beard, aristocrat and man of the world, he was generally considered an excellent husband and father. For the first time since they had left the house she turned and looked him straight in the face.

'Ah! you will hear some disagreeable truths, but I warn you that I am ready for every contingency and for every threat; I am afraid of no one now, least of all yourself.'

He returned her challenging gaze. In a voice that was already quivering with fury, he muttered:

'You must be mad.'

'No. But I refuse to remain the victim of the intolerable burden of maternity you have imposed upon me for the last eleven years. Like other women, I claim my right to enjoy my position in society.'

Again he turned pale.

'I don't know what you are driving at,' he stammered.

'Yes, you do. It is now three months since my last child was born. In spite of your efforts, I have kept my looks and even my figure, as you realized just now when you caught sight of me on the steps. So you think it is time I began again.'

'You must be crazy.'

'Not at all. I am thirty. We have been married for eleven years, and I have seven children. You intend this sort of thing to go on for another ten years. By that time you hope to have no further cause for jealousy.'

He seized her roughly by the arm.

'I won't have you talking to me like this.'

'You shall hear me out. I mean to have my say. If you attempt to stop me I shall raise my voice, so that the two men on the box can hear me. My one idea, in letting you come for this drive with me, was to have witnesses, whose presence would oblige you to listen to me and to control yourself. These are the facts. You have always been antipathetic to me, and I have never concealed my dislike. I have never lied to you. You married me against my will. Because you were very rich, you forced my parents, who were in difficulties, to give you my hand. In spite of my tears, they insisted on my marrying you. And so you bought me. I made up my mind to do my duty by you, to forget your intimidating and bullying ways, to become an affectionate companion and a devoted wife, and to love you as much as I possibly could. But as soon as I was in your power you grew jealous—jealous as no man has ever been, with an underhand, base, ignominious jealousy, a degradation for yourself, and an insult to me. I had not been married eight months before you suspected me of every conceivable act of treachery. And you actually let me see it. The shame of it! As you could not prevent me from being handsome and attractive, from being mentioned in drawing-rooms, and even in newspapers, as one of the prettiest women in Paris, you racked your brains for a plan to deprive me of all this admiration, and at last you hit upon the outrageous idea of making me spend my life in incessant child-bearing, until I should grow positively repulsive. Oh, you needn't protest! It took me a long time to discover it. But at last I began to suspect. You actually boasted of your scheme to your sister, who told me, because she was fond of me and was disgusted by your boorish brutality. What a life you led me all those eleven years! I was like a brood mare on a stud farm. And as soon as I was in that condition you yourself shrank from me in disgust, and I never saw you for months on end. I was dispatched to your country seat, to the back of beyond, there to produce my baby. When, proof against your designs, I returned as blooming and beautiful, as captivating as ever, still able to command the former admiration, just when I hoped for a little respite so that I might enjoy myself like any other young woman of rank and fortune, you were seized with the old jealousy and began to persecute me with the same revolting, vindictive desire which is even now tormenting you. It is not the desire to possess me—I should never have refused myself to you—but the desire to disfigure me.

'Then came a new and abominable development; it was something so obscure and mysterious that it took me a long time to discover it, but by dint of studying your thoughts and actions I have grown very shrewd. You became fond of your children, because of the peace of mind they secured for you in the months before they were born. Your affection for them is made up of your aversion for myself, of your ignoble suspicions, which thanks to them were temporarily allayed, and of the satisfaction with which you observed the signs of my condition. How often have I caught that gloating look in your eyes; and seen and understood. You love your children, not because they are your own flesh and blood, but because they represent so many triumphs over me, over my youth and beauty and charm, over the flattery which was paid to me openly and the compliments that were whispered in my presence. You are proud of them; you enjoy showing them off when you take them for drives in the brake in the Bois de Boulogne, and for donkey rides at Montmorency. You accompany them to matinées, so that people may see you with them and say to one another: "What a good father!"'

He had grasped her by the wrist and was squeezing it so savagely that she could not speak. She stifled a groan.

'I love my children, I tell you,' he muttered very low. 'What you have just told me is shameful in a mother. But you are my property. I am the master—your master. I can make any demands I please upon you, and at my own time. The law is on my side.'

He was trying to crush her fingers in his coarse masculine grip. Livid with pain, she vainly endeavoured to draw her hand from the vice-like hold that was bruising it. The tears rose to her eyes. She was gasping with agony.

'That will show you that I am the master,' he said, 'and stronger than you.'

He relaxed his grasp a little and she was able to command her voice.

'Do you consider me a religious woman?' she resumed.

'Why, yes,' he said in some surprise.

'Do you think I believe in God?'

'Yes, certainly.'

'Do you think I could tell you a lie, if I took an oath before the altar with the Host upon it?'

'Of course not.'

'Would you mind entering a church with me?'

'What ever for?'

'You will see. Will you come?'

'Yes, if you make a point of it.'

'Philip,' she called to the coachman.

The man, as if lending his ear to his mistress while keeping his eyes on his horses, moved his head slightly in her direction.

'Drive to the church of St. Philippe-du-Roule.'

The victoria turned back, just as it had reached the gate leading into the Bois de Boulogne. No further words passed between husband and wife, till the carriage drew up outside the church. The countess alighted and entered the building, followed by her husband, a pace or two behind. Without a moment's hesitation she advanced as far as the choir railing. There she fell on her knees, and prayed with her face hidden in her hands. She remained thus for an appreciable time, and presently the count, who was standing behind her, noticed that she was in tears. She was weeping silently like a woman over-whelmed with some supreme sorrow. Her grief seemed to sweep in waves over her body, each paroxysm ending in a low sob, which she at once repressed with her hand upon her lips.

When the count felt that the scene had lasted long enough he touched her on the shoulder. She started as if she had been stung. Rising from her knees, she looked deep into his eyes.

'This is what I have to say to you. I am not in the least afraid of you; you can do as you please; kill me, if you like. But one of your children is not your own. I swear it by God, who hears me. It was my one solitary act of vengeance upon you for your abominable masculine tyranny, and for the slavery of child-bearing to which you condemned me. Who was my lover? That you shall never know. You can suspect the whole world. But you shall never find out. I gave myself to him without love, without passion, simply for the sake of betraying you. By him, too, I became a mother. Which is his child? That, too, you shall never learn. I have seven children. You have ample scope for guessing. I always meant to tell you this some day in the distant future, because such a betrayal is no revenge unless the victim is aware of it. You forced me to confess to you this afternoon. That is all I have to say.'

She fled down the nave towards the door that opened on to the street. Every moment she expected to hear behind her the swift step of the husband she had defied, and to be felled to the ground by a murderous blow from his fist. But there was no sound, and she reached her carriage in safety. Convulsed with emotion, palpitating with terror, she jumped in and ordered the coachman to drive home. The horses set off at a rapid trot.

II

The countess shut herself up in her room and awaited the dinner hour, as a condemned prisoner awaits the moment of his execution. What would her husband do? Had he returned yet? Hasty, tyrannical, prone to every form of violence, what scheme of retaliation had he devised? The house was plunged in silence. She kept glancing at the hands of the clock. Her maid came to dress her for the evening; then left her to herself. Eight o'clock struck, and almost immediately afterwards there was a double knock at her door.

'Come in,' she cried.

It was, however, only the butler, who announced that dinner was ready.

'Has the count come in?'

'Yes, my lady; the count is in the dining-room.'

At first she thought of arming herself with a small revolver, which she had bought with a prevision of the crisis towards which her thoughts were tending. But she remembered that the children would be present, and took only her smelling salts.

When she entered the dining-room she found her husband standing by his chair, waiting for her. They nodded to each other and sat down, and the children followed their example. The three boys and their tutor, the Abbé Marin, sat on their mother's right, the three girls and Miss Smith, their English governess, on her left. The baby, who was only three months old, had been left in the nursery.

The three little girls with their fair hair and their blue frocks, trimmed with narrow white lace, looked like exquisite dolls. They were pretty children, who showed early signs of inheriting their mother's beauty. The eldest was ten, the youngest only three. Two of the boys had chestnut hair, while the eldest, who was nine, was dark. They promised to grow up tall, strong, and broad-shouldered. The whole family seemed sprung from the same vigorous and vital stock.

The abbé said grace, as was his custom when no strangers were present. When there were guests, the children did not come in to dinner.

In the grip of unexpected emotion the countess sat with downcast eyes, while the count scrutinized, now the three boys, now the three girls, his troubled, anxious gaze wandering from face to face. Suddenly, as he set down his glass, he snapped the stem, and the wine and water poured all over the cloth. The tiny crash made by this trifling mishap so startled the countess that she half-rose from her chair. For the first time that evening they glanced at each other. From that moment, in spite of themselves, in spite of the shock that convulsed them, body and mind, whenever their eyes met, their glances continued to cross like swords.

Conscious that an embarrassing situation had arisen, through some cause he could not divine, the abbé endeavoured to make conversation. He touched on various subjects, but his forlorn attempts elicited no response.

Like a tactful woman of the world the countess strove to second his efforts, but in vain. Such was her confusion of mind, that the right words eluded her. In the prevailing silence, broken only by the faint clink of silver and china, the sound of her own voice almost frightened her.

All at once her husband leaned towards her and said:

'Here, under this roof, surrounded by your children, will you swear that you told me the truth just now?'

Stung by the hatred that was seething in her veins, she met this challenge with the same undaunted spirit wherewith she had returned his glance. Raising her arms she stretched her right hand towards her sons, her left towards her daughters, and without a tremor in her voice, in calm, resolute tones, she answered:

'I swear by my children that I was speaking the truth.'

He sprang up, threw down his table-napkin with a passionate gesture, hurled his chair against the wall and without another word flung out of the room. She drew a deep sigh of relief, as if she had won the first round.

'Don't be frightened, my dears,' she said to the children in even tones. 'Your father heard some bad news this afternoon and he is still very much upset. He will get over it in a day or two.'

She began to talk to Miss Smith and to the abbé, and she petted the children, lavishing upon them all the tender words, the caresses, the little indulgences, that make a small heart swell with happiness. After dinner, she took all her flock into the drawing-room with her. She encouraged the elder children to chatter, told the younger ones stories, and when bedtime came, she dismissed them with long and lingering kisses. Then she retired to her own room.

She was sure that he would follow her thither and she sat up waiting for him. With her children no longer round her, she was determined to defend her rights as a human being, as she had fought for her social claims. The little revolver, which she had recently purchased, was loaded, and she hid it in the pocket of her gown. The clock struck hour after hour. Gradually all the sounds within the house died away. Through the tapestry-covered walls she could hear the distant and muffled sound of cab wheels, passing up and down the streets.

Full of energy and resolution, no longer afraid of him, ready for every emergency, she waited for him. She was almost triumphant in the thought that she had devised for him a torture which would embitter his every moment, until the end of his days.

The first glimmer of dawn stole in through the fringes of the window curtains. And still there was no sign of him. At last, in amazement, she realized that he would not come. She locked her door and shot the bolt, an additional safeguard, which had been affixed by her orders. Then she went to bed and lay with open eyes, pondering, utterly unable to divine his intentions.

When the maid came in with the early tea she brought her mistress a letter from the count. He informed her that he was going to travel for some time, and added, by way of postscript, that his lawyer had been instructed to provide her with sufficient money for her requirements.

III

It was at the Opera, during an interval between the acts of *Robert the Devil*. In the space behind the stalls groups of men were standing about, hat on head, their waistcoats revealing a wide expanse of white shirt-front, on which glittered golden or jewelled studs. They glanced up at the boxes which were occupied by ladies in evening dress, decked with pearls and diamonds, their exquisite faces and dazzling shoulders like hot-house flowers, blossoming forth beneath admiring glances, in an atmosphere of music blended with the hum of human voices. Two friends were standing and talking with their backs to the stage, and examining through their opera-glasses the bevy of beauty and fashion, genuine or meretricious, the jewels, the luxury, the pretentiousness, which, ranged around the great theatre, made so brilliant a display.

'Look at the Countess de Mascaret,' said Roger de Salins to his companion. 'She is as handsome as ever.'

Bernard Grandin focused his glasses on a lady in the box opposite to them. She was tall and looked in the flower of youth, while her radiant beauty seemed to attract admiration from every corner of the theatre. The ivory pallor of her complexion suggested a statue. Her tresses were black as night and crowned with a rivière of diamonds, which glittered like the Milky Way.

After he had gazed at her for some time, Bernard Grandin replied with playful conviction:

'As handsome as ever? I should just think she was!'

'About what age would she be?'

'Wait a minute. I can tell you exactly. I knew her as a child, and I saw her when she first came out. She must be . . . thirty . . . thirty-six.'

'Nonsense!'

'I am perfectly certain.'

'She looks twenty-five.'

'And she has had seven children.'

'It's incredible.'

'What is more, all seven of them are living, and she is a most devoted mother. I go there from time to time. It's a pleasant house, with a very peaceful and wholesome atmosphere. She has performed the miracle of reconciling social and domestic duties.'

'How extraordinary! And never a whisper about her?'

'Never.'

'But her husband? He's an odd fellow, isn't he?'

'Yes and no. Something may have passed between them. One suspects one of those little dramas of married life, of which one never really knows the facts, though one can hazard a guess.'

'What do you mean?'

'Well, I hardly know. Mascaret has become tremendously fast, after being an admirable husband. As long as he was steady, he had a shocking temper, and was thoroughly cross-grained and cantankerous. Since he has kicked over the traces, nothing seems to ruffle him. But one would think he had some secret trouble or sorrow, some perpetual worry. Unlike his wife, he has aged very much.'

The two friends exchanged some sage remarks concerning those vague, mysterious family troubles arising out of divergences of character or physical antipathies, which were not discernable at the outset.

'It is inconceivable that that woman should have borne seven children,' resumed Roger de Salins, who was still watching the countess through his glasses.

'Yes, and all in eleven years. After that she turned from the task of producing offspring to the more spectacular amusement of displaying herself—a phase which shows no sign of coming to an end.'

'These unfortunate women!'

'Why do you pity them?'

'Why? Just think, my dear fellow. Eleven years of child-bearing for a woman like that, what hell! All her youth, all her beauty, all her hopes of success, all her romantic dreams of a brilliant future, sacrificed to the abominable law of reproduction, which turns the normal woman into a mere machine for propagating the species.'

'What would you have? It's nature.'

'Yes. But I maintain that nature is our enemy. We have to be continually resisting her efforts to reduce us to the level of brutes. Whatever on this earth is seemly, comely, delicate, and poetic, we owe not to nature, but to man, to the human brain. Thanks to us, thanks to the poets, who have sung and interpreted and praised it; to the artists, who have idealized it, to the scientists, who, in self-delusion, have explained it and set forth ingenious reasons for its various phenomena, creation is redeemed by some touch of grace and beauty, some hint of indefinable charm and mystery. Nature has created none but rudimentary beings, swarming with germs of disease, doomed, after a few short years of animal development, to an old age hideous with all the infirmities and disabilities of human decrepitude. Mankind, it seems, is created only to reproduce itself in squalor, and then to die. . . . It is as if a cynical and perfidious creator had schemed to prevent man from ever ennobling, exalting, and idealizing his relations to woman. But man has invented love, not such a bad rejoinder to the wiles of Destiny, and has so adorned it with poetic fancies, that woman often forgets the gross facts. Some of us, who cannot accept these delusions, have invented vice and brought it to a fine art, which is another way of tricking Providence and rendering homage, however tainted, to beauty. But ordinary mortals beget children, like a pair of animals, mated by law. Look at that lovely creature! Isn't it outrageous to think that that jewel, that pearl of a woman, born to be beautiful, born to be admired, fêted and adored, has spent eleven years of her life in presenting the Count de Mascaret with offspring?'

Bernard Grandin remarked, with a smile:

'There's a great deal of truth in what you say. But few people would understand you.'

'Do you know my conception of Providence?' pursued de Salins, warming to his subject. 'I picture it as a monstrous and inscrutable instrument of fertility, which scatters millions of worlds through space, just like a fish scattering its spawn all over the sea. It creates, because creation is the divine function. But it works ignorantly. Blindly prolific, it has no notion of all the various combinations that arise out of the germs it has broadcasted. The human mind is simply a fortunate little accident which has somehow sprung from that haphazard fecundity; it is local, ephemeral, unpremeditated, doomed to disappear with the earth itself, and perhaps to emerge again here or elsewhere, different or identical, with new affinities that will manifest themselves in the course of these eternal re-births. It is thanks to our intelligence, that trifling accident, that we can never feel at home in a world which was not made for such as us, which was never intended to shelter, nourish, and satisfy reasoning beings. If we are really highly sensitive and highly civilized, we are condemned to a never-ending struggle against what are still called the designs of Providence!'

Grandin, who had long been accustomed to his friend's surprising outbursts of imagination, had listened with interest.

'Then you believe that human thought is a spontaneous by-product of blind, but supernatural, parturition?'

'Why, certainly. It is due to the fortuitous action of the nerve centres of the brain, analogous to the unforeseen chemical results of new combinations, to manifestations of electricity, produced by friction or unexpected contact, or to any other phenomena originating in the endless processes of fermentation and fertility which occur in living matter. My dear fellow, the proof is clear as daylight to any man who looks about him. If the human intelligence had been contrived by a reasoning creator, if it had been meant to develop as it has done into something utterly different from the instinct and stolidity of animals, and to become this thing so exacting, so questioning, so restless, so harassed, if this world had been destined to harbour man as he is to-day, it would never have been this cramped, inconvenient, little paddock, this cabbage patch, this kitchen garden, this rocky jungle-covered sphere, where your improvident Providence has planted us, to live naked in caves and under trees, feeding on the murdered corpses of brother animals, or on raw roots and herbs that grow in the rain and the sun. A moment's reflection will suffice to make it clear that the world was not made for creatures like us. The mind, which has unfolded and developed itself by some miracle of the nervous force of the brain cells, feeble, ignorant and confused though it is and always will be, dooms us intellectuals to miserable and perpetual exile upon earth.

'Consider the earth, as it was when it was first bestowed upon its denizens. It is obvious that it was planned, with its forests and its vegetation, simply for animals. What does it offer us? Nothing. But it supplies them with everything they need: caves, trees, foliage, springs, lairs, food and drink. Fastidious people, such as myself, can never feel at ease here. Only those who are near to the brute creation are happy and content. But the rest of mankind, the poets, the sensitive dreamers, the questing, restless souls? Alas for them! I am condemned to eat cabbages and carrots, and even, confound it, onions, turnips, and radishes; we are forced to accustom ourselves to such diet and to acquire a taste for it, because there is nothing else. But it is mere food for goats and rabbits, just as grass and clover are food for horses and cows. When I look at a field of ripe corn, I realize that the earth has brought it forth for the little beaks of sparrows and larks, and not for my benefit. When I eat bread, I am robbing the birds, just as when I eat poultry, I am robbing the weasel and the fox. Quail, pigeon, and partridge are the hawk's natural prey; just as sheep, goats, and cattle are that of the larger carnivora. They were never meant for us, though we batten on roast joints garnished with truffles, which the pigs have rooted out for us. The only business of animals here below is to keep alive. They are at home on this earth of theirs; they are sheltered and fed. They have only to crop the grass or to hunt and devour one another, according to their instincts. The Creator never foresaw gentleness and peaceful ways. He foresaw only the violent end of creatures, bent on destroying and devouring each other.

'As for us, what labour, effort, patience, ingenuity, imagination, industry, what talent, what genius, man has had to spend to make this conglomeration of stones and roots more or less habitable! Only think of all that we have done in spite of nature, in opposition even to nature, to construct a makeshift scheme of life, wholly unworthy of us, with a mere minimum of decency, comfort, and decorum. The more intelligent, the more highly civilized and refined we are, the more we have to resist and conquer the animal instincts, which are all that we owe to Providence. Remember that it was left to us to invent civilization, which includes amenities of every kind and description, from socks to telephones. Think of all the things we see and use every day of our lives.

'To sweeten our brutish lot, we have devised and created every sort of convenience: houses first, then dainty food, confectionery, pastry, wines, liqueurs, materials, clothes, adornments, bedding, mattresses, carriages, railways, and machines out of number. Besides all this, we have discovered the sciences, the arts, as well as writing and verse. Yes, we have created poetry, music, and painting. The ideal is our own conception, and so, too, are the delicate refinements of life, the apparel of women, the talents whereby men have at last contrived to invest life with a little glamour, to render less crude, less dreary, less rough, the existence of mere reproductive animals, for which alone divine Providence called us into being.

'Look round this theatre. It contains, does it not, a whole human society evolved by ourselves, which was never foreseen by Destiny, and is not recognized by it. It is intelligible to the human mind only; it is a frivolous, sensuous, intelligent diversion, invented solely for and by those small discontented, restless animals, you and me.

'Look at Madame de Mascaret. Nature intended her to dwell in a cave naked or wrapped in the skins of beasts. Isn't she better as she is? By the way, does any one know why, or how, her brute of a husband suddenly came to desert such an exquisite companion to run after hussies? Especially after he had been boor enough to inflict seven children upon her.'

'My dear fellow, that may be the real explanation. Perhaps he found the privilege too expensive. Considerations of domestic economy may have led him to the same conclusions as your principles of philosophy.'

The last act was signalled. The two friends removed their hats and resumed their seats.

IV

Driving home in their brougham after the opera, the Count and Countess de Mascaret sat side by side without exchanging a word. Suddenly the count broke the silence.

'Gabrielle!'

'What do you want?'

'Don't you think this has gone on long enough?'

'What?'

'The infernal torture you have inflicted on me for the last six years.'

'There's nothing I can do.'

'Won't you tell me even now which one it is?'

'Never.'

'Do you realize that I cannot look at my children, cannot have them round me, without feeling my heart crushed by the uncertainty. Tell me which of them it is. I swear not to revenge myself and not to treat the child differently from the others.'

'I have no right to reveal the secret.'

'Can't you see that I can stand this state of things no longer? I am obsessed by this thought, this question that I keep asking myself, this doubt that tortures me whenever I look at them. It is driving me mad.'

'Then you have really felt it?' she asked him.

'Terribly. Otherwise should I have endured the horror of living with you and the even worse horror of feeling, of knowing, that there is one among the children—which one I can't guess —who embitters my love for all the rest?'

'It has really caused you great suffering?'

He replied in a subdued voice, full of pain:

'I have told you day after day that I am enduring torments. Should I have come back and lived in the same house with you and them, if I did not care for the children? Ah, you have treated me abominably! My one soft spot is for my children, as you very well know. I am the patriarchal type of father, just as I was the patriarchal type of husband. I have always been a primitive man, obeying my natural instincts. You made me frantically jealous, I admit, because you were a woman of a different race, of different soul, and with other needs. Ah, I shall never forget the things you said to me! But from that day onwards, I have never cared for you. I did not kill you, because it would have meant destroying my only hope of ever discovering which of our . . . of your children is not mine. I have been patient, but I have suffered more than you could believe, because I dare not love them, except perhaps the two eldest. I dare not look at them, call them to me, kiss them; I cannot even lift one of them on to my knee without wondering whether this is the one. For six years I have treated you with courtesy, I may even say with indulgence and consideration. Tell me the truth. I swear that no one shall suffer for it.'

It was dark inside the brougham, but he thought that she seemed moved, and he felt that at last she was about to speak.

'I entreat you,' he pleaded. 'I implore you.'

'I may have been more to blame than you think,' she said. 'But I could not, I simply could not, continue that horrible existence of perpetual child-bearing. There was only one way of driving you from me. I lied before God; I lied when I swore by my children. I have never betrayed you.'

In the darkness he caught her by the arm, and crushed it, as he had done on that terrible drive to the Bois.

'Is this true?'

'It is true.'

In spite of his relief from anguish, he groaned:

'Ah, I shall only be plunged again into fresh doubts that will never end. When did you lie to me . . . then, or now? How can I believe you? Who could believe a woman after such an admission? Now I shall never know what to think. I would rather you had said: "It is Jacques," or "It is Jeanne."'

The carriage turned into the court-yard and drew up by the portico steps. The count stepped out of the brougham, and as was his wont, offered his wife his arm to conduct her up the steps. As they reached the first floor he said:

'May I continue our conversation for a few minutes?'

'Certainly.'

They passed into a small drawing-room, and a somewhat astonished footman was told to light the candles.

As soon as they were alone he resumed:

'How am I to know the truth? Time after time I have besought you to speak. But you have remained mute, inscrutable, inflexible, ruthless. And now to-day you tell me that you were lying. For six years you could let me believe a thing like that. No, it is to-day that you are lying. I cannot think why, unless it is out of pity for me.'

In tones of absolute sincerity she replied:

'If I had not lied, I should have had four more children in the last six years.'

'You, a mother, to talk like that!' he exclaimed.

'Ah, no,' she said. 'I do not consider myself the mother of children who have never been born. It is enough for me to be a mother to the children I have and to love them with all my heart. Women are civilized creatures. We are no longer mere females, whose only mission in life is to populate the earth. We refuse to accept that view.'

She rose, but he caught her hands.

'One word, one last word, Gabrielle. Tell me the truth.'

'I have told you the truth. I never betrayed you.'

He looked searchingly into that lovely face, into eyes as grey as the wintry sky. In her dark tresses, in the deep night of her jet-black hair, the rivière of diamonds glittered like the Milky Way. All at once he seemed to divine intuitively that this glorious creature was not merely a woman destined to perpetuate his race, but the strange and mysterious product of all the complex desires implanted in us in the course of centuries, desires diverted from their primitive and natural end, and blindly seeking a mystic beauty, elusive and half revealed. There are women whose loveliness serves but to inspire our dreams, who are adorned with all the poetry, the glamour, the voluptuousness, the seduction, the aesthetic charm, that civilization lends to their sex; living statues who inspire not only the fever of the senses, but spiritual yearnings.

Bewildered by this sudden and mysterious revelation, gropingly approaching the secret of his former jealousy and wondering confusedly what it all meant, he stood before her.

'I believe you,' he said at last. 'I feel that you have now told me the truth. I always had an idea that you were lying to me that day.'

'Then we are friends?' she asked, holding out her hand. He took it and raised it to his lips.

'We are friends. Thank you, Gabrielle.'

Still with his eyes upon her he left the room. He marvelled that she was still so beautiful, and he felt a strange emotion arising within him, an emotion which threatened his peace even more, perhaps, than his primitive passion of earlier days.

AN ENCOUNTER

(*Rencontre*)

IT was chance, the purest chance. On the evening of the princess's reception, every room in the house was thrown open, and the Baron d'Étraille, who was tired of standing, had entered a dim, empty bedchamber, opening off the brilliantly lighted drawing-rooms. Aware that his wife would not be ready to leave till daybreak, he was looking for an easy-chair where he could go to sleep. As he opened the door, he saw, in the middle of the spacious room, a wide bed with blue and gold hangings, suggesting a catafalque where love lay entombed, for the princess was no longer young. On the wall at the head of the bed, loomed a great patch of brightness, like a lake viewed from a lofty window. This was the princess's mirror, a trusty friend. It was festooned with dark draperies, which could be let down on occasion, but had often been drawn back. It appeared to be contemplating as a confederate the couch above which it hung. Round it seemed to hover memories and regrets, like ghosts of the dead that haunt old châteaux. The baron half expected to see, flitting across its smooth blank surface, exquisite reflections of rosy limbs, charming gestures of embracing arms.

Smiling and a little moved, the baron paused on the threshold of this bower of love. Suddenly in the depths of the mirror something stirred, as if the phantoms he had invoked were about to appear to him. He saw a man and a woman rise from their seat on a low divan, which was hidden in the gloom. As they stood there together, reflected in the gleaming crystal, their lips met in a farewell kiss. The baron recognized his wife and the Marquis de Cervigné. With all a strong man's self-control he turned and left the room. He waited till daybreak to escort the baroness home, but all desire for sleep had left him.

As soon as they were alone, he said to his wife:

'I happened to see you just now in the Princess de Raynes' bedroom. I need hardly explain myself further. I have no taste for recrimination and scenes, or for making myself ridiculous.

To avoid all that sort of thing, we will quietly arrange to separate. My lawyers will regulate your position according to my instructions. When you are no longer under my roof you will be free to do as you please. But as you will still bear my name, I warn you that if your conduct gives rise to any scandal, I shall have to take severe measures.'

She attempted to reply, but he silenced her, bowed, and withdrew to his own room. He was hurt and surprised, rather than sad. In the early days of their married life, he had been very much in love with his wife. Gradually, however, his passion had cooled, and though he still had a mild liking for the baroness, he followed the dictates of his roaming fancy, whether in society or in the theatrical world. The baroness was very young, barely twenty-four, small, unusually fair, and thin—almost too thin. She was one of those little Parisian dolls, dainty, spoilt, exquisite, coquettish, sufficiently intelligent, possessing charm rather than beauty.

'My wife,' remarked the baron confidentially to his brother, 'is very sweet and seductive . . . but there's nothing of her. She's like a glass of champagne, all froth. What there is of it is delicious, but there isn't enough.'

Busy with painful thoughts, he paced up and down his room. At times a gust of anger swept over him, and he felt a savage longing to break the marquis's neck or to go up to him in the club and punch his head. Then he realized that it would be bad form, that the laugh would be against himself rather than his supplanter, and that, after all, his resentment arose from wounded vanity rather than a broken heart. He went to bed, though he did not sleep. A few days later all Paris knew that a separation, by mutual consent, had been arranged between the Baron and Baroness d'Étraille on grounds of incompatibility of temper. The matter gave rise neither to rumours, gossip, nor conjectures.

To avoid embarrassing meetings he travelled for a year, spent the following summer at the seaside, and the autumn shooting, and did not return to Paris till the winter. Not once did he see the baroness. He knew, however, that there was no gossip about her. She was evidently careful to observe the conventions, which was all he asked of her. Bored with Paris, he set off again on his travels. Then he spent two years restoring his country seat, the Château de Villebosc; after this he gave a series of house parties, which whiled away at least fifteen months. At last, weary of that tedious form of entertainment, he returned to his mansion in the Rue de Lille, exactly six years after his separation from his wife. Now, at forty-five, with a tendency to stoutness and not a few white hairs, he was visited by that peculiar melancholy which afflicts men, once handsome, courted, and adored, who feel their fascinations waning day by day.

A month after his return to Paris he caught a chill, as he emerged from his club, and developed a cough. The doctor ordered him to Nice for the rest of the winter. Accordingly, one Monday evening he caught the Riviera express. He cut it so fine that when he arrived at the station the train was already in motion. He threw himself into the first carriage he saw with a vacant seat. The far corner was already taken, but its occupant was so closely muffled in coats and furs that he could not make out so much as the sex of his fellow traveller, who seemed a mere bundle of wraps. At last he gave up the problem and settled down for the night. He put on his travelling cap, tucked his rugs round him, lay back and went to sleep. It was daybreak when he awoke. He again shot a glance at his companion, who had not stirred all night and who still seemed fast alseep.

Monsieur d'Étraille seized the opportunity to make a hasty toilet. He brushed his hair and beard and did his best to efface the ravages which night inflicts upon the face of middle age.

'O glorious youth, how splendid are thy dawns!' quoth the poet.

Ah radiant youth, springing from its couch with glowing skin, bright eyes, hair shining with vital sap!

Ah melancholy awakening, when lack-lustre eyes, flushed, puffy cheeks, swollen lips, straggling hair and tangled beard invest the face with the drawn and weary aspect of age!

The baron opened his suit-case, took out his brush, and tried to make himself presentable. Then he waited.

The train whistled and came to a halt, which roused the baron's companion, who stirred a little. Presently the train went on. A slanting ray of sunshine penetrated into the carriage and glided across the sleeper, who moved again, and after a succession of little nods, like a chicken emerging from its shell, calmly unveiled and sat up. The mysterious traveller proved to be a woman, fair-haired, blooming, and remarkably pretty and plump.

The baron gazed at her in amazement. He could hardly believe his eyes. Really he could have sworn that it was . . . that it was his wife, but his wife so astonishingly altered . . . for the better. She had put on weight . . . quite as much as he himself . . . but in her case what an improvement it was!

She looked at him placidly as if she did not recognize him and calmly proceeded to lay aside her wraps. She had the poise of a woman who is sure of herself, the insolent complacency of one who awakes looking her best and freshest.

The baron lost his head completely.

Could it be his wife, or was it some other woman resembling her as closely as a sister? As it was six years since he had seen her, he might well be mistaken. She yawned, and he recognized her way of doing it. Again she turned to him and surveyed him with an expression of calm indifference, without a hint of recognition. Then she looked out of the window. Bewildered, terribly perplexed, he kept stealing glances at her, while he stubbornly awaited developments.

Confound it! of course it was his wife! How could he doubt it? No two women had a nose like that.

A thousand memories stirred within him, memories of past caresses, of tiny details of her person. There was that beauty spot on her hip which was matched with another on her back. How often he had kissed them! The old sense of intoxication stole over him, as he recalled the fragrance of her skin, her smile when she threw her arms round his neck, the soft inflections of her voice, and all her coaxing ways. But what a change! What a wonderful change! It was she and yet not she. She had matured and developed. She was more feminine, more seductive, more desirable . . . more exquisitely desirable than ever.

Then this unknown, this mysterious woman, met by chance in a railway carriage, was his, legally his. He had only to say to her: 'Come!' Once he had slept in her arms, and her love had filled his life. Now he had found her again, changed almost beyond recognition. It was she herself, but at the same time it was someone quite different; someone who had budded, ripened, bloomed after he had left her; and yet, for all that, it was his old love still.

Her pose was more studied; her features were more marked; her gestures, her smiles, more sedate, less playful; nevertheless each trait was familiar. Two women were blended in one; the strange, new element mingling freely with the cherished memory. It was a curious sensation, thrilling, intoxicating, tinged with the mystery of love and with delicious confusion. It was his wife, reincarnated in a new form, in a new body, which his lips had never touched.

After all, he reflected, in six years the human frame undergoes a complete change. Only the contours of the figure remain and even they are subject to alteration. The blood in our veins, our hair, our skin—everything is renewed, replaced.

When two friends meet after long absence, each is confronted with an entirely different person, though he bears the same name and the same individuality. The heart itself may change. Ideas may be modified, principles altered, so that in a space of forty years, by processes, gradual but insistent, we may be transformed four or five times from one personality into another utterly new.

Thus he mused, stirred to the very soul. Suddenly there flashed upon him the memory of that evening when he had surprised her in the princess's bedroom. He felt no thrill of anger. She, whom he now beheld, was no longer the same woman, the same slight, fragile, vivacious doll of those distant days.

What should he do? How should he address her? And did she recognize him?

When the train halted again he rose from his seat and bowed to her.

'Berthe,' he began, 'is there anything you would like . . . anything I can bring you?'

She looked him up and down without a shade of surprise, embarrassment, or resentment in her glance.

'No thank you,' she said with calm indifference, 'nothing at all.'

He left the carriage and walked up and down the platform, actuated by an impulse to move his limbs and to pull himself together, as if after a fall. He deliberated as to what he should do. Transfer himself to another carriage? No, it would look like flight. Court her, pay her attention? No, she would think he was asking her pardon. Be masterful? No, he would only seem a brute, and besides, surely he had forfeited his rights. He returned to the carriage.

During his absence, she, too, had made a hasty toilet, and was now leaning back in her seat, radiant and serene. He turned to her.

'My dear Berthe,' he began, 'as Fate has brought us together again in this curious way after six years of a separation which was perfectly amicable, need we continue to glare at each other like a pair of mortal enemies? Here we are, for better or for worse, shut in together, *tête-à-tête*. Personally I don't propose to go away. Wouldn't it be pleasanter to chat like . . . like . . . friends . . . for the rest of the journey?'

'Just as you please,' she rejoined calmly.

He was at a loss how to continue. Then plucking up his courage he took the seat beside her.

'I see I shall have to pay court to you,' he said ingratiatingly. 'Very well. It will be a pleasure, for you are looking enchanting. You have no idea how wonderfully you have improved in the last six years. There 's no woman to whom I owe such a thrill of delight as I felt just now when you slipped off your furs. Really I could never have believed such a change possible.'

'I can't say as much for you,' she replied without turning her head to look at him. 'You haven't worn at all well.'

'How unkind you are!' he replied, smiling ruefully and reddening.

'How so?' she asked, with a glance at him. 'I was merely stating a fact. Surely you 're not thinking of making love to me. So what does it matter whether I admire you or not? But evidently it 's a painful subject. Let us talk of something else. What have you been doing all these years?'

'Why,' he faltered, completely out of countenance, 'I have spent my time travelling and hunting, and, as you see, growing old. And you?'

'Carrying out your orders and keeping up appearances,' she answered serenely.

An angry retort rushed to his lips, but he repressed it, and raising his wife's hand kissed it.

'I am very grateful to you,' he murmured.

She was taken aback. Really he was admirable; his self-control never failed him.

'As you were so kind as to respect my wishes suppose we talk now without any bitterness?'

'Bitterness?' she queried with a little gesture of disdain. 'I don't feel any bitterness. To me, you are the merest stranger. I was merely trying to put a little life into a difficult conversation.'

Fascinated by her, in spite of her cynical attitude, conscious of a savage, irresistible impulse to master her, he continued to gaze at her.

Fully aware that she had hurt him, she pursued relentlessly:

'How old are you now? I always thought you were younger than you seem to be.'

He turned pale.

'I'm forty-five,' he replied. Then he added: 'I haven't asked you for news of the Princess de Raynes. Do you still see her?'

She threw him a venomous glance.

'Yes, continually. She is quite well, thank you.'

Both of them stung to the quick, they sat side by side, their hearts in a tumult.

'My dear Berthe,' he suddenly exclaimed, 'I have changed my mind. You are my wife and I insist on your returning to my protection this very day. It seems to me that you have gained both in beauty and character, and I propose to take you back. I am your husband and I claim my rights.'

Thunderstruck she gazed into his eyes, seeking to read his thoughts. But his face was impassive, inscrutable, resolute.

'I am very sorry,' she replied, 'but I have other engagements.'

He smiled.

'That is unfortunate. I shall avail myself of the powers the law allows me.'

They were approaching Marseilles. The train whistled and slowed down. The baroness rose and calmly rolled up her wraps.

Then she turned to her husband.

'My dear Raymond, do not try to take advantage of a *tête-à-tête* which I myself manœuvred. In deference to your wish, I was merely taking certain precautions to safeguard myself against you and the world in general . . . just in case . . . You're going to Nice, are you not?'

'I shall go wherever you go.'

'I think not. If you will only listen to me, you will be perfectly ready to leave me in peace. In a few minutes you will see the Prince and Princess de Raynes and the Count and Countess Henriot, who will be at the station to meet me. I wanted them to see you and me together so as to convince them that we two spent the night alone together in this compartment. Don't be alarmed. The two ladies will lose no time in spreading abroad this astonishing item of news. I told you just now that I had carried out your instructions and carefully observed the conventions. There was no question of anything else, was there? Well, in the interests of propriety I arranged this *tête-à-tête*. You particularly ordered me to avoid a scandal. Well, my dear Raymond, I have done so. . . . You see . . . I am afraid . . . I am afraid . . .'

She paused till the train drew up. Then, as a troop of her friends rushed to the carriage door and opened it, she completed her phrase:

'I am afraid I'm going to have a child.'

The princess held out her arms to embrace her, but the baroness drew her attention to her husband, who was dumb with amazement and vainly endeavouring to arrive at the truth.

'Don't you recognize Raymond? He is certainly very much changed. He offered to escort me, so that I shouldn't have to travel by myself. Sometimes we indulge in these little escapades. For we're very good friends, although we can't live together. But this is where we part. He has had enough of me already.'

She held out her hand, which he clasped mechanically. Then she jumped down on to the platform into the midst of her friends, who had come to meet her.

Too much agitated to utter a single word, or to take any action, the baron slammed the door. He could hear his wife's voice, her merry laughter, as it died away in the distance.

He never saw her again.

Was she lying? Was she speaking the truth? He never knew.

THE HORLA

8th May. What a perfect day! All the morning I lay stretched out on the grass in front of my house, under the towering plane-tree that spreads over the roof, giving protection and shade. I love this countryside, and love to live in this place, for here I am rooted fast by those deep and tender roots that bind a man to the soil where his forefathers lived and died, bind him to ways of thinking and eating, to customs and meat and drink, to the tones of the peasants' voices and turns of phrase, to the smell of the villages, the smell of the earth and of the air itself.

I love this house of mine where I have grown to manhood. From my windows I can see the Seine flowing by my garden, beyond the road, almost past my door—the broad River Seine, which goes from Rouen to Havre, laden with passing boats.

Away to the left lies the city of Rouen, blue-roofed beneath the throng of its pointed Gothic spires; above them all, slender but strong, rises the cathedral's iron shaft. They are innumerable, these spires—filled with bells that ring, under the azure of morning skies, sending forth their distant metallic humming, a brazen song blown by the breeze, stronger now and now fainter, as it rises and falls.

How lovely it was this morning!

Towards eleven, a long line of barges, drawn by a tug the size of a fly, groaning and straining and belching volleys of smoke, filed past my gates.

And after two English schooners, with red flags fluttering to the sky, came a noble Brazilian three-master, gleaming, spotlessly white from stem to stern. I saluted it; I don't know why the sight of this vessel gave me such pleasure.

12th May. For some days I have had a touch of fever; I feel unwell, or, rather, I feel depressed.

Whence come these mysterious influences, changing our happiness into gloom, our self-confidence into vague distress?

323

One would think that the air, the transparent air, was full of unknowable powers, whose mysterious presence affected us. I wake up gay as a bird, feeling as though I must sing. Why? I go for a walk downstream; and suddenly, after strolling a little way, I turn back feeling disheartened, as if some misfortune awaited me at home. Why? Is it some cold shiver, passing over me, that has shaken my nerves, overshadowed my soul? Is it the shape of the clouds, or the colour of the day, the ever-changing hue of things, that has entered my eyes to trouble my thoughts? Who can say? Everything about us, everything we look at but do not see, everything we brush against but do not know, everything we touch but do not feel, has, on ourselves, on our senses, and through them, on our thoughts, on our very heart, effects that are sudden, surprising, inexplicable.

16th May. I am ill, undoubtedly! And I was so well last month! I have a fever, a dreadful fever, or rather a feverish attack of nerves, that afflicts my mind quite as much as my body. I have this constant, horrible feeling of a danger threatening, this apprehension of impending misfortune or approaching death, this presentiment which means no doubt the inroads of some disease, unknown as yet, at work in my blood and my flesh.

18th May. I have been to see my doctor, for I could not sleep any longer. He found that I had a quickened pulse, dilated pupils, and jangling nerves, but no disquieting symptom. I am to have douches and take bromide of potassium.

25th May. No change whatever! My condition is indeed strange. As evening draws on an unaccountable restlessness comes over me, as if the night held some dreadful menace in store for me. I dine quickly, then try to read; but I do not understand the words; I can hardly tell letter from letter. Up and down my room I go, oppressed by a vague and overmastering dread—dread of sleep, dread even of my bed.

Towards two I go to my bedroom. No sooner inside than I turn the key twice in the lock and shoot the bolts. I am frightened . . . of what? . . . I who have never been frightened before. . . . I open my cupboards, look under my bed. I listen . . . listen . . . for what? Isn't it strange that a mere touch of something, a disturbed circulation, perhaps, some irritation of the network of the nerves, a slight congestion, a tiny interruption in the delicate and very imperfect working of the vital machine, can turn one of the bravest of men into a coward, one of the gayest into a victim of melancholia? Then I go to bed, and I wait for sleep as one might wait for the executioner. I wait in terror of its coming, with beating heart and trembling limbs; and my whole body shudders in the warmth of the blankets, up to the moment when I fall asleep of a sudden, as one would fall into a pit of stagnant water to drown.

I sleep—for some little time—two or three hours—then a dream—no, a nightmare, lays hold on me. I am quite aware that I am in bed and asleep—I feel it and know it—and I also feel that someone is drawing close to me, looking at me, feeling me, getting up on my bed, kneeling on my chest, taking my neck between his hands and squeezing . . . squeezing with all his strength . . . trying to strangle me.

And I struggle, bound down by that awful helplessness which paralyses us in dreams; I want to cry out—I cannot; I want to move—I cannot; with fearful efforts, gasping for breath, I try to turn over, to throw off this being who chokes and stifles me —I cannot!

Suddenly I wake, frantic, bathed in sweat. I light a candle. I am alone.

After this attack, which comes every night, I sleep peacefully until dawn.

2nd June. I am worse. What can be the matter with me? The bromide is useless, the douches are useless.

3rd June. An awful night. I am going away for a few days. No doubt a little holiday will set me right.

.   .   .   .   .   .

2nd July. Home again. I am quite myself now. And my little holiday has been delightful.

3rd July. Slept badly; clearly there is fever about, for my coachman is suffering from the same complaint as myself. Yesterday, as I came into the house, I noticed how unusually pale he looked.

'What's the matter with you, Jean?' I asked.

'It's like this, sir. I don't sleep now; me nights eat up me days. Ever since master left, it's been like an evil fate over me.'

The other servants are well; but *I* myself live in dread of a fresh attack.

4th July. A fresh attack, and no mistake! The old night-mares have come back. Last night I felt someone crouching on top of me, who, with his mouth to mine, was drinking my life through my lips. Yes, he was draining it out of my throat, as would a leech. Then he got off me, gorged, and *I* woke up, so battered and bruised and exhausted that I couldn't stir. If this goes on for many more days I shall certainly leave home again.

5th July. Have I lost my reason? What happened last night is so extraordinary that my head feels queer when I think of it!

As is my habit every evening now, I had locked my bedroom door; then, feeling thirsty, I drank half a glass of water, and I happened to notice that my water-bottle was full to the glass stopper.

I then went to bed, dropping off into one of my frightful dreams. After about two hours I was awakened by a seizure more frightful than any before.

Imagine a man who is being assassinated in his sleep, who awakes to find a knife in his lungs, and lies there covered with blood, with the death-rattle in his throat, unable to draw his breath, on the verge of death, understanding nothing at all—and there you have it.

When at last I recovered my senses, I was again thirsty; I lit a candle and went towards the table where my water-bottle stood. I lifted it, tipping it over my glass; nothing came out. It was empty, entirely empty! At first I was mystified; then, all at once, such a terrible feeling came over me that I had to sit down, or rather, I tumbled into a chair! Then up I jumped again to gaze about me! In a bewilderment of astonishment and fear I sat down once more, before the transparent water-bottle. I stared at it fixedly, trying to solve the riddle. My hands were trembling! Someone, then, had drunk this water. Who? I? I, myself, no doubt! It could only be myself! Well, then, I was a somnambulist; unknown to myself, I was living that strange double life which makes us wonder whether there are two creatures in us; or whether an alien creature, unknowable, invisible, quickens our captive limbs at times, when our mind is asleep, and they obey this other creature, just as they would, more faithfully than they would, obey ourselves.

Ah! who can understand my anguish? Who can understand how a man feels when, wide awake, and wholly reasonable, he stares in terror through the sides of a glass bottle, looking for a pint of water that has disappeared during his sleep! I stayed there until dawn, not daring to go back to bed.

6th July. I am going mad. My water-bottle was drained again last night, or rather, I drained it!

But did I do it? Did I? Who could it be? Who? Ah, God above! I am going mad! Who can save me!

10th July. I have just been making the most remarkable tests. Most certainly I am mad! And yet . . .

On 6th July, before going to bed, I set out on my table wine, milk, water, bread, and strawberries. Someone drank—I drank—all the water and a little milk. The wine was left untouched, also the strawberries.

On 7th July I tried the same test, with the same result.

On 8th July I tried without the water and milk. Nothing was touched.

And on 9th July I replaced the water and milk on my table by themselves, taking care to cover the bottles in white muslin, and to tie down the corks. Then I rubbed my lips, beard, and hands, with black lead, and went to bed.

The same inexorable sleep took possession of me, followed soon after by the horrible awakening. I hadn't stirred; the sheets themselves had no stain. I hastened to the table. The muslin covering the bottles remained spotless. I untied the strings, panting with fear. Every drop of water was drunk! Every drop of milk was drunk! Ah, God above!

I am leaving for Paris this morning.

.   .   .   .   .   .

30th July. I came home yesterday. All is well.

2nd August. Nothing new; beautiful weather. I spend my days watching the Seine flowing by.

4th August. Squabbles among my servants. They say that glasses are being broken in the cupboards at night. The butler accuses the cook, the cook accuses the washerwoman, and she accuses the other two. Who is the culprit? It would take a wise man to say!

6th August. This time I am not mad. I have seen! I have seen! . . . Doubts are no longer possible. . . . I have seen! . . . I am still cold to the finger-tips, quaking to the marrow of my bones. . . . I have seen!

At two o'clock, in bright sunlight, I was walking in my rose-garden . . . in the autumn rose-walk which is beginning to flower.

As I stopped to look at a *Géant des batailles* that bore three splendid blooms, I saw, I distinctly saw, quite close to me, the stem of one of these roses bend, as if some invisible hand had twisted it, and snap off, as if the hand had plucked it. Then the flower rose in the air, following the curve that an arm would make when carrying it to a mouth. And there it stayed, hanging in the translucent air, all by itself, motionless, a terrifying splash of red, three paces from my eyes.

Aghast, I darted out my hand to snatch it! My hand found nothing; it had vanished. I was seized with a violent fit of anger against myself, for it is not right that a serious-minded, reasonable man should have delusions like this.

But was it really a delusion? I turned round to look for the stem, and found it at once on the rose-tree, just freshly broken off, between the two remaining roses, still on their branch.

At that, I went indoors with my mind in a fearful state. For I am certain now, as certain as that night follows day, that living near to me is an invisible being, who feeds on water and milk, who can touch things, take them and move them about— governed therefore by physical laws, unperceived by our senses, and dwelling under my roof. . . .

7th August. A peaceful night. He drank the water in my bottle, but did not disturb my sleep.

I wonder if I am mad? While I was walking just now, in broad sunlight, along the river, doubts of my reason came to me —not vague doubts like those I have had so far; but doubts that were well defined, real. I have seen madmen; I have known some who remained quite intelligent, clear-headed, far-seeing even in all the things of life, save on one point only. And while they talked on any subject with clearness, penetration, and ease, suddenly their thought, striking on the reef of their madness, was rent in pieces there, scattered and foundered in that wild and terrible ocean, swept by the rushing waves and mists and squalls, that we call insanity.

Certainly I should believe I was mad, quite mad, if I was not conscious of it all, well aware of my mental state, if I was not perfectly clear-headed, when probing down into its causes. Probably, then, I am only subject to delusions, and retain my reason. Some unknown disturbance must have taken place in my brain. Is it not possible that one of the imperceptible keys of the instrument within my brain has refused its work? An accident will sometimes deprive a man of his memory for proper names, or verbs, or figures, or simply dates. And the fact that these divisions of our thought are localized in the brain is well established to-day. What cause for surprise, then, if the faculty that records within me the unreality of certain delusions should be dormant just now?

These were my thoughts as I strolled along the river-bank. The sunshine flooded the water, made earth a delight to behold, filled my heart with the love of life—love of the swallows, that rejoiced my eyes with their swiftness; of the sedges that charmed my ear with their rustlings.

Little by little, however, a strange uneasiness came creeping through me. Some power, as it seemed, some occult power was paralysing me, stopping me, restraining me from going farther, was calling me back. I had the uncomfortable feeling that I must return, such as oppresses you when a beloved invalid is left behind at home, and you are seized with the presentiment that a turn for the worse has come.

Back, therefore, I came in spite of myself, sure that I would find bad news at home—a letter or telegram. But there was nothing, and I was left feeling more uneasy and more surprised than if I had again been through some strange experience.

8th August. A frightful evening, last night. He no longer declares himself. But I feel him near me, eyeing me, pervading me, dominating me—and more to be feared, hiding so, than if he was making his continual unseen presence known by supernatural signs.

Yet I slept well.

9th August. Nothing; but I am afraid.

11th August. Still nothing; I cannot stay at home any longer with this fear lodged in my mind; I am going away.

12th August, 10 p.m. All day I have been waiting to leave the house; I couldn't. It was so simple, so easy, the voluntary act that I wished to accomplish—simply to go out, get into my carriage to drive to Rouen. I couldn't. Why?

14th August. I am done for! Someone is master of my mind and controls it! Someone commands my every act, movement, thought. I count for nothing, now, within myself; I am merely a terrified, slave-like witness to my actions. I want to go out. I cannot. He does not wish it; trembling and panic-stricken, I stay in the arm-chair where he keeps me. I want to get up, that I may believe I am still my own master. I cannot! I am riveted to my chair, and my chair cleaves so fast to the ground that no power could lift us.

Then, all at once, I must, simply must, go to the end of my garden to pick strawberries and eat them. And I go. I pick the strawberries and I eat them. Ah, God, God, God! Is there a God? If God there be, save me! Help me! Deliver me! Mercy! Pity! Grace! Save me! Oh, what agony! What torture! What terror!

17th August. Ah, what a night! What a night! And yet it seems to me that I really should be rejoicing. I read until one in the morning! Hermann Herestrauss, doctor of philosophy and theogony, has written a book on the history and manifestations of every invisible being that hovers around mankind or is dreamed of in their dreams. He describes their origin, their domain, their powers. But not one of them resembles my familiar. One would say that man, ever since he has been able to think, has had some nervous foreknowledge of a new being— more powerful than himself, his successor in this world, and that, feeling him near but unable to foresee the nature of this over-man, in his terror he has created imaginary occult beings, shifting phantoms which have been born of fear.

After reading till one in the morning I went to sit by my open window to refresh my forehead and my mind with the gentle air of night.

The air was warm and sweet. How I would have enjoyed that night in days gone by!

No moon. The stars flashed and sparkled in the black deeps of the sky. Who dwells in those worlds? What forms, what living creatures, what animals, what plants are yonder? They who think in these far-off worlds, what know they beyond our knowledge? What powers have they transcending our own? What things do they see that are hidden from us? And may not one of their kind, passing one day through space, come down to this earth of ours to conquer it, as the Normans once crossed the sea to conquer weaker races?

We are so weak; so defenceless, so ignorant, so small are we, on this whirling spot of slime mingled with a rain-drop!

I dozed off, dreaming in this fashion, in the cool night air.

After sleeping for about forty minutes I opened my eyes, awakened by some vague and strange emotion. At first I saw nothing; then, all at once, it seemed to me that a page of the book lying open on my table had turned over of itself. Not a breath of air had passed in through my window. I waited. After about four minutes I saw, I saw—yes, with my eyes I saw one more page rise, then close down on to the one before, as if a finger had turned it over. My arm-chair was empty, *seemed* empty; but I understood that he was there, seated in my chair, and that he was reading. With one wild bound, the bound of an infuriated beast about to disembowel its tamer, I dashed across the room to seize him, throttle him, kill him! . . . But my chair, before I reached it, tipped over as if someone had fled before me . . . my table rocked, my lamp fell and went out, and my windows shut to as if some thief, caught in the act, had darted out into the night, grasping the frames with both hands.

He had fled then; *he* had been frightened, frightened of me!

Well then . . . well then . . . to-morrow . . . or after . . . one day or another, I shall be able to seize him with my fingers and crush him. Are not dogs sometimes known to bite, to choke the life out of their masters?

18th August. I have been thinking all day. Ah yes! I shall obey him, follow his suggestions, do everything that he wills, make myself humble, a slave, a craven. He has the upper hand. But the hour will come. . . .

19th August. I know. . . . I know—all! I have just read this in the *Revue du Monde Scientifique*:

A curious item of news reaches us from Rio de Janeiro. An epidemic of madness, comparable to those waves of infectious insanity which attacked European peoples in the Middle Ages, is raging at the moment in the province of San Paulo. The frenzied inhabitants desert their houses, villages, and fields, saying that they are pursued, possessed, and controlled, like human cattle, by beings which are invisible though tangible, a kind of vampire which feeds on them during their sleep and also drinks water and milk without appearing to touch any other food.

Professor Don Pedro Henriquez, accompanied by several distinguished doctors, has left for the province of San Paulo, to study *in situ* the causes and symptoms of this extraordinary madness and to propose to the emperor the most fitting measures to restore the raving inhabitants to reason.

Aha, I remember, I remember the lovely Brazilian three-master that passed below my windows on her way up the Seine, last 8th of May! I thought her so beautiful, so white, so pleasant! The Being was on board, coming from the land where his race was born! And he saw me! He saw my white house too; and he leapt from the ship to the shore. Ah, God above!

And now I know, I foresee. Man's reign on earth is over.

HE has come, he that was feared in the innocent, trembling hearts of the early races. He who was exorcised by uneasy priests, whom sorcerers summoned on gloomy nights though invisible as yet to their sight, He whom the forebodings of earth's momentary masters clothed in the monstrous or pleasing shapes of gnomes, spirits, genii, fairies, and hobgoblins. After these first crude picturings of fearful minds, came men with greater insight, who foreshadowed him more clearly. Mesmer guessed at him; and, ten years since, doctors learned the precise nature of his power, before He himself had wielded it. They have toyed with this weapon of the coming Lord, the domination of a mysterious will-power over the enslaved human mind. They have called it magnetism, hypnotism, suggestion . . . and what not. I have seen them playing like thoughtless children with this horrible power! Woe upon us! Woe upon Man! He has come, the . . . the . . . what is his name? . . . the . . . it seems as though he were calling out his name to me . . . and I cannot hear . . . the . . . yes . . . he is calling it . . . I am listening! . . . I can't quite . . . again . . . Horla . . . I heard . . . the Horla . . . it is He . . . the Horla . . . he has come!

Ah, the vulture has devoured the dove, the wolf has devoured the lamb, and the lion the buffalo with his sharp-pointed horns; man has slain the lion with the arrow, the sword, and the gun; but the Horla will do unto Man what we have done unto the horse and the ox: his chattel, his servant, and his food, by the sole might of his will. Woe upon us!

.   .   .   .   .   .

19*th August.* I shall kill him. I have seen him! I sat down at my table yesterday evening, and I pretended to be writing with concentration. I knew, right well, that he would come roaming round me, close, close, so close that perhaps I could touch him, seize him? And then! Then . . . I should have the strength of a desperate man. I should have my hands, my knees, my chest, my head, my teeth, to strangle him, crush him, bite him, rend him.

I was watching for him, with every nerve in my body tingling.

I had lit my two lamps and the eight candles over my mantelpiece, as if all this light would help me to make him out.

Facing me was my bed, my old four-poster of oak; to the right, my fireplace; to the left, my door, carefully shut now, after standing open a long time, to attract him; behind me, a great, high wardrobe with a mirror that I used every day for shaving and dressing and always glanced into from habit, to see myself at full length, whenever I passed before it.

So I pretended to be writing, to mislead him, for he was on the watch; and, all of a sudden, I felt, I *knew* that he was reading over my shoulder, that he was there, touching my ear.

I jumped up, with hands outstretched, wheeling round so quickly that I nearly fell. Well? . . . my mirror was as bright as in broad daylight, and I could not see myself reflected. It was clear and bright and luminous to its very depth! My reflection did not appear there . . . yet I was standing right in front! I could see every inch of the clear tall mirror! Wild-eyed, I stared; and I hadn't the courage to advance one foot or make a single movement, knowing well as I did that he was there, but that he would escape me once more, the invisible-bodied one, who had swallowed up my reflection.

Imagine my fear! And then, behold! all at once I began to see myself in a mist, deep down in the mirror, in a mist as though through a sheet of water; and it seemed to me that the water was slowly gliding from left to right, leaving my reflection clearer with the passing of each second. It was like the end of an eclipse. The thing that shut me out did not seem to have clearly-marked outlines, but a kind of opaque transparence, thinning out by little degrees.

Then at last I was able to see myself perfectly, just as I do every day when I look in the glass.

So I had seen him! And the terror of it abides, making me shiver yet.

20th August. Kill him, but how? I cannot grasp hold of him. Poison? He would see me mixing it in the water; moreover, would our poisons have any effect on his imperceptible body? They would not, they would certainly not. What then? What then?

21st August. I have sent for a locksmith from Rouen, and have ordered iron shutters for my room, like those that certain private mansions in Paris have, before the lower story windows, for fear of burglars. He is also making me a door to match. I have got the name of a coward, but what do I care!

.   .   .   .   .   .

10th September. Rouen, Continental Hotel. It's done . . it's done . . . but is he dead? My mind is still in a whirl after seeing it all.

Yesterday, then, after the locksmith had fitted my iron shutters and door, I left everything open until midnight, although it was beginning to be cold.

All at once I felt that he was there; and was overjoyed, crazy with joy. I rose in leisurely fashion and sauntered up and down for a long while, to prevent his suspecting a thing; then I took off my boots and put on my slippers with a careless air; then I closed my iron shutters, and, strolling back to the door, shut the door also, turning the key twice. Returning then to the window I made it fast with a padlock and pocketed the key.

Suddenly, I realized that he was following me about excitedly; that he in his turn was afraid, that he was commanding me to open and let him out. I all but gave way; yet did not quite give way. Instead, I stood with my back to the door, opened a crack, just wide enough to let me slip through backwards; and as I am very tall, my head grazed the lintel. I was certain that he could not have escaped; and I shut him in, alone, alone. Oh, joy, I had him! Then downstairs I went at a run; in the drawing-room below my bedroom I took my two lamps and emptied the oil out over the carpet, over the furniture, and all about; then I set light to it, and escaped, after carefully locking the big front door with two turns of the key.

I went to hide myself at the bottom of my garden, in a clump of laurels. What a time it took! What a time it took! All was dark, silent, motionless; not a breath of air, not a star; mountainous clouds, that I could not see, but which weighed on my mind with a great and heavy weight.

I watched my house and waited. What a time it took! I was already beginning to think that the fire had gone out of itself, or that *He* had put it out, when one of the lower windows, yielding before the thrust of the fire, fell out with a crash. A flame, a great tongue of flame, yellow and red, long, soft, caressing, climbed up the white wall, licking upwards to the roof. A gleam shot out into the trees, into the branches, into the leaves; and a shiver too—a shiver of fear! The birds were waking; a dog began to howl; I thought day was dawning! Two other windows fell out the next moment, and I saw that the entire lower story of my dwelling was one raging furnace. But a cry, a dreadful cry, the piercing scream of a woman rang out into the night, and two garret windows flew open! I had forgotten my servants! I saw their terrified faces, their arms waving! . . .

Then, wild with horror, I set off at a run for the village, yelling: 'Help! Help! Fire! Fire!' I met people already on their way from the village, and turned back with them, to see.

But now the house was one vast, awe-inspiring bonfire, a monstrous bonfire that lit up the face of the earth; a bonfire in which human creatures were burning to death; and He, too, burned—He, my prisoner, the New Being, the new master, the Horla!

Suddenly the entire roof fell in, and a volcano of flames shot up sky-high.

Through every window opening into the furnace I could see the cauldron of fire; and I thought of him there, in that oven, dead. . . .

Dead? Perhaps? . . . His body? His body that was transparent to the light of day, could it be destroyed by the means that are deadly to our own?

And if he was not dead? . . . Time only, perhaps, can lay hands upon that Terrible, Invisible Being. Why this transparent body, this unknowable body—if he, too, must fear pain, wounds, sickness, and untimely death?

Untimely death? All human terror lies therein! First Man, then Horla. First comes he that may die on any day, in any hour, at any minute, through any accident; thereafter, he that shall only die when his day and his hour and his minute have come, because he has attained his life's bourne!

No, no, no, no . . . there is no room for doubt, no doubt at all! . . . He is not dead.

Well then . . . well then . . . the only thing left to do is to kill—myself.

Translated by Brian Rhys.